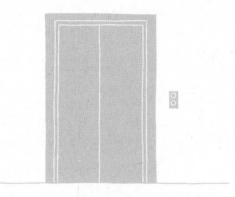

SEE
YOU
YESTERDAY

SEE
YOU

YESTERDAY

RACHEL LYNN SOLOMON

SIMON & SCHUSTER BFYR

NEW YORK   LONDON   TORONTO   SYDNEY   NEW DELHI

SIMON & SCHUSTER BFYR

An imprint of Simon & Schuster Children's Publishing Division
1230 Avenue of the Americas, New York, New York 10020

For information about special discounts for bulk purchases, please contact
Simon & Schuster Special Sales at 1-866-506-1949 or business@simonandschuster.com.
The Simon & Schuster Speakers Bureau can bring authors to your live event.
For more information or to book an event, contact the Simon & Schuster Speakers Bureau at
1-866-248-3049 or visit our website at www.simonspeakers.com.
Interior design by Laura Eckes
The text for this book was set in Adobe Garamond Pro.
Manufactured in the United States of America

2 4 6 8 10 9 7 5 3
Library of Congress Cataloging-in-Publication Data
Names: Solomon, Rachel Lynn, author.
Title: See you yesterday / Rachel Lynn Solomon.
Description: First edition. | New York : Simon & Schuster Books for Young Readers, [2022] |
Audience: Ages 14 up. | Audience: Grades 10-12. | Summary: After reliving the same day for
months, eighteen-year-old Barrett reluctantly teams up with her nemesis Miles to escape the
time loop, and soon finds herself falling for him, but what she does not know is what they will
mean to each other if they finally make it to tomorrow.
Identifiers: LCCN 2022002383 | ISBN 9781665901925 (hardcover)
ISBN 9781665901932 (paperback) | ISBN 9781665901949 (ebook)
Subjects: CYAC: Time—Fiction. | Interpersonal relations—Fiction. | Schools—Fiction. |
LCGFT: Romance fiction.
Classification: LCC PZ7.1.S6695 Se 2022 | DDC [Fic]—dc23
LC record available at https://lccn.loc.gov/2022002383

For Rachel Griffin and Tara Tsai—
I'd meet you at the bookstore café
again and again and again

If we belong to each other, we belong
anyplace, anywhere, anytime
—NENA

DAY ONE

/

Chapter 1

"THIS HAS TO BE A MISTAKE."

I pull the extra-long twin sheets up over my ears and mash my face into the pillow. It's too early for voices. Much too early for an accusation.

As my mind unfuzzes, the reality hits me: *there's someone in my room.*

When I fell asleep last night after testing the limits of my dorm's all-you-can-eat pasta bar, which involved a stealth mission to sneak some bowls upstairs that were forbidden from leaving the dining hall, I was alone. And questioning my life choices. All those lectures about campus safety, the little red canister of pepper spray my mom made me get, and now there is a stranger in my room. Before seven a.m. On the first day of classes.

"It's not a mistake," says another voice, a bit quieter than the first, I imagine out of respect for the blanket lump that is me. "We underestimated our capacity this year, and we had to make a few last-minute changes. Most freshmen are in triples."

"And you didn't think it would be helpful for me to know that before moving in?"

That voice, the first voice—it no longer sounds like a stranger. It's familiar. Posh. Entitled. Except . . . it can't possibly belong to her. It's a voice I thought I left back in high school, along with all the teachers who heaved sighs of relief when the principal handed me my diploma. *Thank god we're done with her,* my newspaper advisor probably said at a celebratory happy hour, clinking his champagne glass with my math teacher's. *I've never been more ready to retire.*

"Let's talk out in the hall," the second person says. A moment later, the door slams, sending something crashing to the carpet.

I roll over and crack one wary eye. The whiteboard I hung on Sunday, back when I was still dreaming about the notes and doodles my future roommate and I would scribble back and forth to each other, is on the floor. A designer duffel bag has claimed the other bed. I fight a shiver—half panic, half cold. The tree blocking the window promises a lack of both heat and natural light.

Olmsted Hall is a freshmen-only dorm and the oldest on campus, scheduled for demolition next summer. "You're so lucky," the ninth-floor RA, Paige, told me when I moved in. "You're in the last group of students to ever live here." That luck oozes, sometimes even literally, from the greige walls, wobbly bookshelves, and eerie communal shower with flickering light bulbs and suspicious puddles *everywhere*. Home sweet concrete prison.

I was the first one here, and when two, three, four days passed without an appearance from Christina Dearborn of Lincoln, Nebraska, the roommate I'd been assigned, I worried there'd been a mix-up and I'd been given a single. My mom and her college room-mate are still friends, and I've always hoped the same thing would happen for me. A single would be another stroke of bad luck after several years of misfortune, though a tiny part of me wondered if maybe it was for the best. Maybe that was what the RA had meant.

The door opens, and Paige reenters with the girl who made high school hell for me.

Several thousand freshmen, and I'm going to be sleeping five feet from my sworn nemesis. The school's so huge I assumed we'd never run into each other. It's not just bad luck—it has to be some kind of cosmic joke.

"Hi, roomie," I say, forcing a smile as I sit up in bed, shoving my Big Jewish Hair out of my face and hoping it's less chaotic than it tends to be in the mornings.

Lucie Lamont, former editor in chief of the Island High School *Navigator*, levels me with an icy glare. She's pretentious and petite and terrifying, and I fully believe she could kill a man with her bare hands. "Barrett Bloom." Then she collects herself, softening her glare, as though worried how much of that conversation I over-heard. "This is . . . definitely a surprise."

It's one of the nicer things people have said about me lately.

I should be wearing something other than owl-patterned pajama shorts and the overpriced University of Washington T-shirt I bought from the campus bookstore. Medieval chain mail, maybe. An orchestra should be playing something epic and foreboding.

"Aw, Luce, I've missed you, too. It's been, what, three months?"

With one hand she tightens her grip on her matching designer suitcase, and with the other she white-knuckles her purse. Her auburn ponytail is coming loose—I can't imagine the stress my appearance has caused her, poor thing. "Three months," she echoes. "And now we're here. Together."

"Well. I'll leave you two to get acquainted!" Paige chirps. "Or—reacquainted." With that, she gives us an exaggerated wave and escapes outside. *If there's anything you need, day or night, just come knock on my door!* she said the first night when she tricked us into playing icebreaker games by making us microwaved s'mores. College is a web of lies.

I hook a thumb toward the door. "So *she's* great. Amazing mediation skills." I hope it'll make Lucie laugh. It does not.

"This is unreal." She gazes around the room, seeming about as impressed with it as I was when I moved in. Her eyes linger on the stack of magazines I shoved onto the shelf above my laptop. It's possible I didn't need to bring all of them, but I wanted my favorite articles close by. For inspiration. "I was supposed to have a single in Lamphere Hall," she says. "They totally sprung this on me. I'm going to talk to the RD later and try to sort this out."

"You might have had better luck if you moved in this weekend, when everyone was supposed to."

"I was in St. Croix. There was a tropical storm, and we couldn't get a flight back." It's wild that Lucie Lamont, heir to her parents' media company, can get away with saying these things, and yet I was the pariah of the *Navigator*.

Also wild: the fact that for two years, she and I were something like friends.

She sets her purse down on her desk, nearly knocking over one of my pasta bowls. Spinach ravioli, from the look of it.

"There's an all-you-can-eat pasta bar." I get up to collect the bowls and stack them on my side of the room. "I thought they would cut me off after five bowls, but nope, when they say 'all you can eat,' they aren't messing around."

"It smells like an Olive Garden."

"I was going for a 'when you're here, you're family' vibe."

I take back what I said about killing a man with her bare hands. I'm pretty sure Lucie Lamont could do it with just her eyes.

"I swear, I'm usually not this messy," I continue. "It's only been me for the past few days, and all the freedom must have gone to my head. I thought I was rooming with a girl from Nebraska, but then she never showed up, so . . ."

We both go silent. Every time I fantasized about college, my roommate was someone who'd end up becoming a lifelong friend. We'd go on girls' trips and yoga retreats and give toasts at each other's weddings. I'd be shocked if Lucie Lamont went to my funeral.

She drops into her plastic desk chair and starts the breathing techniques she taught the *Nav* staff. Deep inhales, long exhales. "If this is really happening, the two of us as roommates," she says, "even if it's just until they move me somewhere else, then we'll need some ground rules."

Feeling frumpy next to Lucie and her couture tracksuit, I throw on the knitted gray cardigan hanging lopsided across my own chair. Unfortunately, I think it only ups my frump factor, but at least I'm no longer shivering. I've always felt *less* next to Lucie, like when we teamed up on an article about the misogyny of our middle school's dress code for the paper we were convinced was the epitome of hard-hitting journalism. *By Lucie Lamont*, read the byline, our teacher elevating Lucie's status above my own, and in tiny type: *with Barrett Bloom*. Thirteen-year-old Lucie had been outraged on my behalf. But whatever bond had once existed between us, it was gone by the end of ninth grade.

"Fine, I'll bring back guys to hook up with only every other night, and I'll put this sock on the door so you know the room is occupied." I reach over to the closet, which is just wider than an ironing board, and toss her a pair of knee socks that say RINGMASTER OF THE SHITSHOW. Well—just one sock. The ninth-floor dryer ate one yesterday, and I'm still in mourning. "And I'll only masturbate when I'm positive you're asleep."

Lucie just blinks a few times, which could be interpreted as lack of appreciation for my shitshow sock, a visceral fear of the *M* word, or horror that someone would want to hook up with me. Like she didn't hear about what happened after prom last year, or laugh about it in the newsroom with the rest of the *Nav*. "Do you ever think before you speak?"

"Honestly? Not often."

"I was thinking more along the lines of keeping the room clean. I'm allergic to dust. No pasta bowls or clothes or anything on the floor." With a sandaled foot, she points underneath my desk. "No overflowing trash bins."

I bite down hard on the inside of my cheek, and when I'm quiet a moment too long, Lucie lifts her thin eyebrows.

"Jesus, Barrett, I really don't think it's too much to ask."

"Sorry. I was thinking before I spoke. Was that not the right amount of thinking? Could you maybe set a timer for me next time?"

"I'm getting a migraine," she says. "And god help me for needing to acknowledge this, but I feel like it's common courtesy not to . . . you know. Indulge in that particular brand of self-love when someone else is in the room. Sleeping or not."

"I can be pretty quiet," I offer.

Lucie looks like she might combust. It's too easy, really. "I didn't realize this was so important to you."

"It's a very normal thing to need to navigate as roommates! I'm looking out for both of us."

"Hopefully by next week, we won't be roommates anymore." She moves to her suitcase and unzips a compartment to free her laptop, then uncoils the charger and bends down to search for an outlet. Sheepishly, I show her that the sole outlets are underneath my desk, and we discover there's no way for her to type at her desk without turning the charger into a tightrope. With a groan, she returns to her suitcase. "I can only imagine what your priorities would have been as editor in chief. We're lucky we dodged that one."

With that, she unpacks a familiar wooden nameplate and sets it on her desk. EDITOR IN CHIEF, it declares. Mocking me.

It was ridiculous to think I had a chance at editor when asking people if I could interview them sometimes felt like asking if I could give them an amateur root canal.

It doesn't matter, I tell myself. Later today, I'll interview for one of the freshman reporter positions on the *Washingtonian*. No one here will care about the *Nav* or the stories I wrote, and they won't care about Lucie's nameplate, either.

"Look. I'm also not entirely enthused about this," I say. "But maybe we could put everything behind us?" I don't want to carry this into college, even if it's followed me here. Maybe we'll never be the yoga-retreat type of friends, but we don't have to be enemies. We could simply coexist.

"Sure," Lucie says, and I brighten, believing her. "We can put your attempt to sabotage our school behind us. We'll braid our hair and host parties in our room and we'll laugh when we tell people you gleefully annihilated an entire sports team and ruined Blaine's scholarship chances."

Okay, she's exaggerating. Mostly. Her ex-boyfriend Blaine, one of Island's former star tennis players, ruined his own scholarship chances. All I did was point a finger.

Besides—I'm pretty sure the Blaines of the world won in the end anyway.

"I just have one more question," I say, shoving aside the memory before it can sink its claws in me. "Is it uncomfortable to sit down?"

She looks down at the chair, at her clothes, forehead creased in confusion. "What?"

Lucie Lamont may be a bitch, but unfortunately for her, so am I.

"With that stick up your ass. Is it uncomfortable to—"

I'm still cackling when she slams the door.

☾ ☾ ☾

College was supposed to be a fresh start.

It's what I've been looking forward to since the acceptance email showed up in my inbox, holding out hope that a true reinvention, the kind I'd never be able to pull off in high school, was just around the corner. And despite the roommate debacle, I'm determined to love it. New year, new Barrett, better choices.

After a quick shower, during which I narrowly avoid falling in a puddle I'm only half certain is water, I put on my favorite high-waisted jeans, my knitted cardigan, and a vintage Britney Spears tee that used to be my mom's. The jeans slide easily over my wide hips and don't pinch my stomach as much as usual—this has to be a sign from the universe that I've endured enough hardship for one day. I've never been small, and I'd cry if I had to get rid of these jeans, with their exposed-button fly and buttery softness. My dark ringlets, which grow out as opposed to down, are scrunched and sulfate-free-moussed. I tried fighting them with a straightener for years to no avail, and now I must work with my BJH instead of against it. Finally, I grab my oval wire-rimmed glasses, which I fell in love with because they made me look like I wasn't from this century, and sometimes living in another century was the most appealing thing I could imagine.

It was an understatement when I told Lucie the freedom had gone to my head. Every other hour, I've been hit with this feeling that's a mix of opportunity and terror. UW is only thirty minutes from home without traffic, and though I imagined myself here for years, I didn't think I'd feel this adrift once I moved in. Since Sunday, I've been shuffling from one welcome activity to another, avoiding anyone who went to Island, waiting for college to change my life.

But here's something to be optimistic about: it doesn't seem to matter if you eat alone in the dining hall, even as I remind myself that I'm New Barrett, who's going to find some friends to laugh with over all-you-can-eat pasta and the Olmsted Eggstravaganza even if it kills her.

After breakfast, I cross through the quad, with its quaint historic buildings and cherry trees that won't bloom until spring, slackliners and skateboarders already claiming their space. This has always been my favorite spot on campus, the perfect collegiate snapshot. Past the quad is Red Square, packed with food trucks and clubs and, in one corner, a group of swing dancers. Eight in the morning seems a little early for dancing, but I give them a *you do you* tilt of my head regardless.

Then I make a fatal mistake: eye contact with a girl tabling by herself in front of Odegaard Library.

"Hi!" she calls. "We're trying to raise awareness about the Mazama pocket gopher."

I stop. "The what?"

When she grins at me, it becomes clear I've walked right into her trap. She's tall, brown hair in a topknot tied with UW ribbons: purple and gold. "The Mazama pocket gopher. They're native to Pierce and Thurston Counties and only found in Washington State. More than ninety percent of their habitat has been destroyed by commercial development."

A flyer is thrust into my hands.

"He's adorable," I say, realizing the same image is printed on her T-shirt. "That face!"

"Doesn't he deserve to eat as much grass as his little heart desires?" She taps the paper. "This is Guillermo. He could fit in the palm of your hand. We're hosting a letter-writing campaign to local government officials this afternoon at three thirty, and we'd love to see you there."

I'm annoyed by what *we'd love to see you there* does to my camaraderie-deprived soul. "Oh—sorry," I say. "It's not that I don't care about, um, pocket gophers, but I can't make it." My interview with the *Washingtonian*'s editor in chief is at four o'clock, after my last class.

When I try to hand her back the flyer, she shakes her head. "Keep it. Do some research. They need our help."

So I tuck it into my back pocket, promising her I will.

The physics building is much farther away than it looked on the campus map I have pulled up on my phone and keep sneaking glances at, even though every third person I pass is doing the same thing. It wouldn't be as bad if I were excited about the class. I've been planning to switch out—registration was a nightmare and everything filled up so quickly, so I grabbed one of the first open classes I saw—but damn it, New Barrett is a rule follower, so here I am, trudging across campus to Physics 101. Monday-Wednesday-Friday, eight thirty a.m.

My T-shirt is pasted to my back and my perfect jeans' perfect buttons are digging into my stomach by the time I spot the building. Still, I force myself to remain hopeful. This probably isn't an omen. I don't think omens are usually this sweaty.

In my pocket, my phone buzzes just as I'm walking up the front steps.

Mom: How do I love thee? Joss and I are wishing you SO MUCH LUCK today!

The text is time-stamped forty-five minutes ago, which I attribute to the campus's sketchy service, and there's a picture attached:

my mom and her girlfriend, Jocelyn, in the matching plush robes I gave them for Hanukkah last year, toasting me with mugs of coffee.

My mom's water broke in her sophomore year British Poetry class, and as a result, I was named after Elizabeth Barrett Browning, most famous for *How do I love thee? Let me count the ways.* College is where the two best things in my mom's life happened: me and the business degree that enabled her to open the stationery store that's supported us for years. She's always told me how much I'm going to love college, and I've held tight to the hope that at least one of these forty thousand people is bound to find me charming instead of unpleasant, intriguing instead of off-putting.

"I'm just so excited for you, Barrett," my mom said when she helped me move in. I wanted to cling to her skirt and let her drag me back to the car, back to Mercer Island, back to the HOW DO I LOVE THEE? cross-stitch hanging in my bedroom. Because even though I'd been lonely in high school, at least that loneliness was familiar. The unknown is always scarier, and maybe that's why it was so easy to pretend I didn't care when the entire school decided I wasn't to be trusted, after the *Navigator* story that changed everything. "You'll see. These four or five years—but please don't get pregnant—are going to be the best of your life."

God, I really hope she's right.

Chapter 2

PHYSICS 101: WHERE EVERYTHING (AND EVERYONE) Has Potential, declares the PowerPoint. Beneath the text is an image of a duck saying "Quark!" I can appreciate a good pun, but two on one slide might be a cry for help.

The lecture hall is thick with the scent of hair products and coffee, everyone chattering away about their class schedules and the petitions they signed in Red Square. The professor is tinkering with a cluster of cables behind the podium. It's one of the larger auditoriums on campus and fits nearly three hundred students, though so far it's only a quarter full. Or three-quarters empty, but I'm trying not to be a pessimist this year.

I've never been a back-of-the-classroom person, despite how much some of my old teachers might have wished I'd been, so I climb the stairs and pause by an empty seat at the end of the fifth row, next to a tall, thin Asian guy glaring at his laptop.

"Hey," I say, still a little out of breath. "Are you saving this for anyone?"

"It's all yours," he says in a flat voice, without even looking up from his screen.

Yay, a friend.

I strip off my sweater and take out my computer, and I must make some amount of noise while doing this because the guy lets out a low hum of a sigh.

"Do you know the Wi-Fi password?" I ask.

Still no eye contact. Even the floppy collar of his plaid red flannel looks thoroughly annoyed by me. "On the board."

"Oh. Thanks."

Fortunately, I don't have any additional opportunities to bother him before the professor, a middle-aged Asian woman in a tangerine blazer with black hair cropped to her chin, switches on the podium mic. Eighty thirty on the dot. "Good morning," she says. "I'm Dr. Sumi Okamoto, and I'd like to welcome you to the spectacular world of physics."

I open a fresh Word doc and start typing. New Barrett, better Barrett, takes notes even for a class she's not sold on yet.

"I was nineteen when physics entered my life," she continues, her gaze flicking up and down the rows of the auditorium. "It was my last semester before I needed to declare a major, and I was stressed, to put it lightly. I'd never considered myself a science person. I started college entirely unsure of what I'd study, and my introductory class was life-changing. Something clicked for me in a way it hadn't in my other classes. There was poetry to physics, a beauty in learning to understand the world around me."

There's a clear sincerity in the way she speaks. The class is rapt, and I'm half compelled to stick it out.

"This course is going to be hard—"

Welp, never mind.

"—but that doesn't mean you shouldn't reach out if you need help," she says. "This may be an intro class, but I still expect you to take it seriously. I have tenure—I don't have to teach 101 classes. In fact, most people in my position wouldn't touch this class with a ten-foot pendulum." Laughter, I assume from the people who get the joke. "But I do, and I only teach it one quarter a year. Physics 101 is typically a survey course for non-science majors—well, not the way I teach it. Some of you are here because you're hoping to major in physics. Some of you are probably just here for a science credit. Whatever the reason, what I want you to take away from this class is the ability to keep asking questions. To wonder *why*. Sure, I'm not going to complain if this class ends up being some small part of your journey to, say, a PhD in physics." She allows herself a chuckle at that. "But I'll consider myself successful if I've gotten you to think about the *whys* of our universe more than you did prior to today.

"Moving on to some basic housekeeping: this university has a zero-tolerance policy for plagiarism. . . ."

"You're taking notes on this?" the guy next to me asks, freezing my hands on the keyboard. I stare down at what I've written. *Something about a pendulum. Questions: good. Course: hard. Plagiarism: bad.*

"Are you looking at my screen?" I hiss. "I'm trying to pay attention. You're the one who's been on Reddit this whole time. I think"—I crane my neck—"r/BreadStapledToTrees will be okay without you."

"So you were looking at *my* screen."

I slant my hand into the sliver of space between our seats. "It's impossible not to."

"Then I'm sure you know it's a very creative and uplifting subreddit."

Dr. Okamoto is heading up the stairs on the opposite side of the hall, passing out the course syllabus.

"I don't really need one," I say when my delightful neighbor hands one to me, though I take it anyway. "I'm switching out." Alas, he must know that despite the undeniable spark between us, our love may not be able to withstand the separation.

He actually laughs at this, a gruff under-his-breath sound. "All that note-taking, and you're switching out?"

"I took AP Physics last year, so." And got a two on the exam, which he doesn't need to know.

"Sorry, I didn't realize I was in the presence of a former AP Physics student." He taps the syllabus. "Then I'm sure you already know all about electromagnetism. And quantum phenomena."

This guy must have also gone to Lucie Lamont's School of the Outrageously Uptight and majored in Taking Everything Personally. I can't think of any other explanation for why he's so combative at 8:47 in the morning. In this economy? Who has the energy?

"You know, my brain's still waking up, so I'm going to have to take a rain check."

He looks unimpressed. His ears, I've noticed, stick out just a little. "My—Dr. Okamoto said she only teaches this class once a year. There's a waiting list. For physics majors."

"Which I imagine is what you are," I say.

"Let me guess: you're undecided."

I'm about to tell him that I have in fact decided, I just haven't declared it yet, but Dr. Okamoto is back at the podium and launching into today's lecture, which is all about what physics is and what physics isn't.

"I'm not the kind of professor who's satisfied with talking *at* my students for fifty minutes straight," she says. "Class participation is encouraged, even if you don't have the right answer. In fact, much of the time there may not even be a right answer, let alone *one* right answer." She gives us a Cheshire-cat grin. "And this is the moment when I pray to Newton, Galileo, and Einstein that more than two of you did the reading I emailed about last week. Let's start with the absolute basics. Who can tell me what physics is the study of?"

The reading she emailed about last week. Which I imagine is sitting in the school email inbox I haven't checked yet because there was a mix-up with another B. Bloom, and UW only assigned me a new username yesterday: *babloom*, which I believe is the sound one makes upon realizing they haven't done the assigned reading.

The guy next to me flings his arm into the air like he's a kindergartner desperate to use the bathroom. If I can't get into another class right away, I am definitely picking a different seat next time. "She's been taking really meticulous notes," he says. "I'd be curious to hear what she has to say."

And he's pointing at *me*.

What the fresh hell?

The professor throws him an odd look and then says, "All right. You—name, please?"

Shit. I consider giving a fake name, but the only thing that comes to mind is Namey McNameface. I'd kill at improv. "Uh. Barrett. Barrett Bloom."

"Hello, Barrett Bloom." She strides across the stage, leaving the mic on the podium. Her voice is strong enough to carry without it. "What is physics the study of? Assuming, of course, that you did the reading."

"Well . . ." That two in AP Physics is doing nothing for me. I adjust my glasses, as though seeing better will somehow illuminate the answer. "The study of physical objects?" Even as I say it, I know it's not right. We studied plenty of things last year that were intangible. "And also . . . nonphysical objects?"

Someone behind me muffles a laugh, but Dr. Okamoto holds up a hand. "Could you get more specific?"

"Truthfully, I'm not sure I can."

"That's why we're starting here. Miles, did you want to expand on that?"

The guy next to me scoots to the edge of his seat. Of course the professor already knows his name. I bet he got here early, brought her coffee and a muffin, told her how much he loved the assigned reading. "Physics is the study of matter and energy," he says smoothly, words slicked with confidence, "and how they relate to each other. It's used to understand how the universe behaves and predict how it might behave in the future."

"Perfect," Dr. Okamoto says, and I can practically feel the heat of how pleased Miles is with himself.

By the end of class, which Dr. Okamoto ends at 9:20 exactly, my neck aches from forcing myself to look straight ahead the whole time, never to my right.

Miles takes his time putting everything into his backpack. PHYSICS MATTERS, says one of the stickers on his laptop. There really is no shortage of puns about this branch of science.

"You didn't go to Island High School, did you?" I ask. It's possible I just don't remember him and he's carrying around the same grudge most of my classmates did.

"No. West Seattle." Ah. A city kid.

"I don't know what I did to offend you, aside from gently insinuating that I am not in love with physics, but there's a seventy percent chance my roommate is going to slip Nair into my shampoo later, so it's been a bit of a rough day. And what you did kind of made it worse."

His face scrunches in this strange way, dark eyes unblinking. "Yeah. Me too," he says quietly, folding a hand through a wave of dark hair. "The rough day, I mean. Not the Nair."

"I'm sure it was a real challenge," I say, "deciding which seat would best position you as the likeliest candidate for suck-up of the year."

"And yet you're the one who sat next to me."

"A mistake I won't make again." I grab my backpack and narrow my eyes at him, waiting for his façade to crack. I should be relieved—I've found the one other person who probably has more trouble making friends than I do. I'm no stranger to hostile, but this much, this early, and from someone I don't know? That's new. "Well. I want to say see you in class on Friday, but I'm on my way to see an advisor, so odds are this is the last time our paths will cross." I flutter my hand toward the classroom. "Have a great time understanding the universe."

ᴗ ᴗ ᴗ

Another thing college has an excess of: lines. In the dining hall, in the bathroom, in the freshman counseling center as all of us who messed up during registration wait to hear our fates. When I finally get to the front, I have to fill out a form and check my *babloom* email to see whether it's been approved.

My two-hour afternoon class is a freshman English requirement taught by a bored-looking but casually hot TA who spends half the time diagramming sentences. I get the feeling most professors aren't as lively as Dr. Okamoto, which makes me feel a little guilty about switching out but not guilty enough to stay.

What I've really been waiting for is my *Washingtonian* interview, since journalism classes filled up fast with upperclassmen and I may not have the chance to take any until later this year. The journalism building is just off the quad, near Olmsted Hall, which seems like a promising sign. On my way there, I watch a skateboarder ignoring the NO SKATEBOARDING signs in Red Square crash into the group of swing dancers, and in true conflict-averse Pacific Northwest fashion, all of them end up apologizing to one another.

I climb three flights of steep stairs and accumulate three times more sweat than I'd like before reaching the newsroom on the top floor. My phone tells me it's seventy-five degrees outside, unseasonably warm for late September in Seattle. I have to stop in the bathroom to make sure my makeup hasn't melted off my face.

The newsroom door is open and the place is already boiling, despite a few fans going. Inside are several pods of computers divided by newspaper section, with the fancier equipment in one corner for the videographers and the larger monitors for designers in the middle of the room. And then there are the walls, painted orange and scribbled over with Sharpie graffiti I learned the history of during the info session I went to yesterday. If I hadn't already committed myself to working for this paper, the walls would have done it. Every piece of writing is a quote attributed, without context, to someone who used to work for the *Washingtonian*, and at least a third of them are sexual. The newsroom rule is that if you say something someone else thinks is worthy, they yell out, "Put it on the wall!" It immediately became a dream of mine: to say something so witty that it got immortalized in Sharpie.

"Hi," I say awkwardly to no one in particular. "I'm here for an interview with Annabel Costa? The editor in chief?"

A girl with a blond pixie cut hovering over a designer's computer swivels her head toward me. "Barrett? I remember you from the info sesh! You were the one who asked all the questions."

I fight a grimace. "Sorry about that."

"Oh gosh, don't apologize! Asking questions is, like, sixty percent of being a reporter. You're already doing great."

She leads me into an office on one side of the room and tucks her long black dress underneath her as she sits down. The dress is simple, and she's wearing large tortoiseshell glasses, no makeup. And yet there's something about her that feels so much older than a junior or senior. More sophisticated, like she's had the time to figure out the true essence of Annabel Costa. There's a warmth to her that no one has shown me in a while—not anyone at Island, not Lucie, not physics stan Miles. It puts me at ease right away.

"You know the basics from yesterday, yeah?" Annabel says. "We used to be daily, but now we're Mondays and Wednesdays because of budget cuts. We usually bring on a half dozen new reporters every fall quarter, depending on what our staff looks like for each section." She leans back in her chair to see if the window behind her will open any further and sighs when it won't. "These interviews are always more fun when they're a little casual. Informal. I'm not going to sit here and ask you to tell me where you see yourself in five years. I have your résumé and the links to stories you did for"—she checks it—"the *Navigator*. Really impressive. You wrote . . . almost fifty articles in four years? For a monthly paper?" She lets out a low whistle.

"I didn't have many friends," I say, and her laugh is worth the drag of my own self-esteem.

"What initially drew you to journalism?" She wrinkles her nose, shoves her glasses higher. "Sorry, I guess that's one of those typical interview questions, but I swear, I really am curious!"

I smile back at her. Annabel and I could be coworkers—we could be *friends*, even.

"As we've already established, I'm extremely obnoxious. It's a natural fit." She laughs again, and I continue. "When I was little, my mom and I would geek out over celebrity profiles, the kind that would make you see someone in a completely different light."

Some of my favorites: a decade-old interview of Chris Evans in *GQ* that makes the reader question whether the writer had an intimate relationship with him. An oral history of *Legally Blonde*. And of course "Frank Sinatra Has a Cold" by Gay Talese, arguably the most impactful piece of pop-culture journalism. Sinatra refused to speak with him, but Talese followed him around for three months regardless, simply observing, talking to anyone close to Sinatra who'd allow it.

The result was a piece of narrative writing that rocked the journalism world—a vivid, personal story that read like fiction but wasn't.

"I love stories that take someone untouchable and make them *real*," I continue. "There's so much hidden beneath the surface most of us don't get to see on a regular basis."

None of this is a lie, but it's hiding an uncomfortable truth: I've never known how to talk to people in the way that comes easily to others. My whole life, I've been closer to my mom than to anyone else. In elementary school, I used that to avoid making other friends: *I have my mom; I don't need to hang out with other ten-year-olds!* Given she had me so young, my mom didn't fit in with the other parents, either.

Once I hit middle school, I realized that having my mom as my best friend didn't exactly make me cool, though it didn't feel that way when we stayed up late brainstorming borderline-inappropriate greeting cards she could absolutely never sell at her shop, or when we had themed movie marathons—Judy Greer Is Doing the Most Night, Modern Austen Weekend. I inherited both her taste in pop culture and her dry humor. By the time I thought I might want other people in my life, everyone had their solidly established friend groups, and it felt like I'd been left behind. Like I'd missed out on making those connections when I was younger, when everyone was supposed to.

And then I found journalism. In seventh grade, I was eating lunch alone in the library when a guy I didn't know approached my table. An eighth grader. "Hi!" he chirped. "Could I ask you a few questions?"

"I . . . don't think we know each other?" I said.

He laughed, the confident laugh of an upperclassman who didn't eat lunch in the library. "I know. It's for the school paper."

The guy's article was a fluff piece about the remodeled library that included some talking heads, with me saying "I love eating lunch in here!" along with a photo mid-blink. When it was time to sign up for classes for the next semester, I picked newspaper, and what began as something of a social experiment grew into a deeper love for storytelling.

Seeming satisfied with my answer, Annabel cycles through a few basic interview questions before getting more specific. "We have openings on every section—news, features, arts, sports," she says. "Would you have a preference?"

"I did a handful of news and features—well, as much 'news' as you can get in high school, which was usually a new pizza topping on the cafeteria menu," I say. "Honestly, I'd report on the school sewer system if you wanted me on staff."

"It's a very in-demand beat." On her computer, she gestures to something I can't see. "What I'm really curious about is this article you did a couple years ago on the tennis team."

"Are you sure? Because I think 'Down the Drain: Secrets of the Sewer System' could be very hard-hitting journalism. I'm ready to run with it."

Annabel's smile falters. Whatever amount of charm I have, it's wearing off. "There's a note here that says comments have been disabled," she continues, "which doesn't seem to be the case with other articles."

I force myself to take a few deep breaths. It's not that I'm ashamed of the story itself—it's everything that happened afterward that I can't allow my mind to linger on. And I won't. Not here. "I found out that a bunch of tennis players had cheated on a test," I say, working to keep my voice level, choosing my words carefully. "There was this one trig midterm that was impossible—almost no one did better than a B-minus. But all the tennis players in my class managed to get As, and when I started poking around, I realized that was the case in every one of that teacher's classes."

Mercer Island: a wealthy Seattle suburb where the public schools feel like private schools. Because of our moody weather, you pretty much had to belong to a club to play tennis, and those clubs were expensive. The tennis players owned Island High, with their shiny racquets and polo shirts and district championship banners. When they won state for the first time in the spring of my freshman year, the school canceled classes for half the day and threw them a special assembly.

Ms. Murphy had a terrible poker face, and when I confronted her, she immediately confessed. The most ridiculous thing was that I actually felt *proud* when I broke the story. I imagined myself winning student-journalism awards, maybe even scholarships—for about five minutes. The evidence was so damning that Island was disqualified and a dozen players wound up in summer school. Blaine, Lucie's boyfriend at the time, was one of them, and she blamed me for their subsequent breakup. Stopped talking to me, except when necessary. Made sure her wealthy, powerful friends did the same.

Just like that, I turned the entire school against me.

"Oh, I heard about this," Annabel says. "I went to Bellevue, but everyone was talking about it."

It has to be some kind of accomplishment that my notoriety spread to schools I didn't even go to.

"The aftermath was a little rough, as you can imagine." A shaky breath, and then I can keep going. If I make it to the end of the week with all the buttons on these jeans intact, it will be proof there is a god. "But I think it helped me become a better journalist."

"How so?"

"For one, I'm not afraid to make enemies."

Annabel frowns. "We may be a student paper, but this is a professional environment," she says. "We don't want anyone using our name to tarnish our reputation."

"I'm not phrasing that right," I say, anxious to get this interview back on track. "What I mean is—I don't have a problem ruffling some feathers for the sake of a story. If you need anyone to get in there and ask the questions no one's asking, even if it means acting like a complete asshole, I'm your girl." I force a laugh, trying to sound self-deprecating. "I've had plenty of experience with people hating me. Take my roommate, for example—"

"Your roommate already hates you?"

"No, no," I rush to say. *Rein it in.* "Well—yes, but only because we went to the same high school. It's . . . hard to explain."

And somehow I've made it worse.

"Ah." Annabel's gaze drifts toward a stack of paper on her desk. Other students' résumés. *Shit.* I'm losing her. Telling someone you're capable of acting like a complete asshole: a great interview strategy.

Surely my high school reputation can't cling to me forever. I spent so many nights convincing myself of that while I dug through *Vanity Fair* archives, so many days walking the halls with metaphorical armor. Logically, I knew not everyone cared about the tennis team, but *god*, it felt that way. I had to act like I didn't give a shit—not when kids mimed smacking tennis balls in my direction, not when they paused at my desk to assure me they weren't cheating when they handed in a test. Not when a history teacher assigned me a report on Benedict Arnold and my classmates muttered "traitor" under their breath when I got up to present.

Because the alternative, letting them break me again and again, was just . . . so much worse.

For months I wondered whether I'd done the right thing, but I always came back to the same place: this was a preview of what I'd be dealing with as a real journalist. My skin just had to get tougher.

Despite where it led me, my love for journalism has never wavered, and I've remained one of a dwindling number of print subscribers to the *New York Times* and *Entertainment Weekly*. A job on this paper would mean New Barrett really is an upgrade from the previous model. That journalism is the right place for me.

"This has been really enlightening, Barrett," Annabel says after a couple more questions, but I can tell her heart's not in it. She gets to her feet and extends a hand across her desk. "Like I said, we only have a few open staff positions, and it might be competitive, so . . . we'll let you know."

Game, set, and match.

Chapter 3

WAITING IN YET ANOTHER LINE IN THE DINING hall sounds about as appealing as the acrobatic act that is shaving my legs in Olmsted's microscopic shower. Instead I take a long, long walk through campus, the almost-fall foliage and the century-old brick buildings contrasting with the newer, energy-efficient ones with their sharp angles and glass walls.

It always felt magical when my mom took me here as a kid, pointing out her favorite spots, pausing by the building she was in when she went into labor. The relationship between my mom and dad didn't last much longer than the pregnancy, and he wasn't interested in becoming a father. But my mom is all I've ever needed. It was tough, finishing her degree with a new baby, but with some help from her parents, she did it, and I've always admired her for it. "This school is in your DNA," she'd tell me. Part of me thought it was cheesy, but I believed her. We had a connection, the university and I.

Now all I feel is how astoundingly easy it is to blend in with everyone else. The *Washingtonian* was the one thing I was certain about, and I screwed it up. Because somehow, even when I knew it was going off the rails, I couldn't stop talking.

My mom calls while I'm mope-walking, but I send it to voice-mail. Then she texts me, and I feel guilty for not answering.

Mom: If you miss your dear old mom yet, what say you about Thai takeout tonight? I'm dying to hear about your first day.

Mom: Fine, it's me. I'm the one who misses you.

The first thing I want to do is tell her what happened, but she doesn't know the full extent of what high school was like for me. She's never overly mommed me, and I didn't want Island's post-tennis witch hunt to change that. If she swept in and tried to solve my problems, it might wreck the balance between us.

Barrett: Drowning in homework. Day was good. How about this weekend?

It's dusk when I get back to my dorm. I'm not expecting the sheer delight that overcomes me when I unlock the door and find Lucie inside our room, an array of makeup and clothes spread across her bed and both our desks, despite the cleanliness lecture she gave me earlier. An extension cord connects her curling iron to the outlets beneath my desk, and she's blasting something I don't recognize.

Lucie Lamont can be a mess too. I'm going to give her such shit for this.

She rims one eye with liquid liner. "Don't worry," she says to the mirror attached to her sliver of closet. "I'll be out of here soon, and then you can perform whatever ritualistic sacrifices you have planned."

"It's actually really helpful if I get a lock of your hair first." I shut the door, and we awkwardly move around each other before I flop onto my bed.

"Rough day?"

"You could say that," I mutter into my pillow. "We don't have to talk just because we're in the same room."

"If that's what you want." Her good mood is both unexpected and a little alarming.

"Did you talk to the RD? Are our days together numbered?"

"Even better," she says. "I'm going to rush a sorority."

"So you couldn't get a single."

Her cheery tone falters. "I'd been thinking about rushing anyway. I'm a legacy—my mom is a Gamma Tau. And . . . I couldn't get a single."

I roll over so I'm not crushing my phone. I pull it out of my pocket, but no one's texting me. No one's calling me.

"Anyway," Lucie says, winding a section of red hair around her curling iron, "rush is this week, and I'm meeting up with some girls to go to a party on Greek Row. But I think there's a movie playing in the quad tonight, if you're still looking for something to do. *Groundhog Day*, I think?"

"Assuming I don't already have a wild Wednesday night planned?"

"We both know your idea of fun involves watching *Veronica Mars* with your mother."

My mom shared all her favorite TV shows with me, and during our brief fragment of friendship, Lucie even came over to watch with us. We'd only just bridged the gap between school acquaintances and rest-of-the-time friends. Her bringing it up now makes me wonder if she remembers too.

"Don't drag *Veronica Mars*. It's a mid-2000s classic." I gesture to Lucie's oversize bell-sleeved shirt, which she's paired with expensive-looking black leggings that might be made of leather. "It's a themed party, yeah? Dress like your favorite founding father? Or the least-racist founding father?"

"I'm pretty sure all of them were racist. And the theme is go fuck yourself," she says sweetly, but she does roll up her sleeves and untuck the shirt to knot it at her navel.

"I might. It's a wild Wednesday night, after all."

It might be wishful thinking on my part, but I think she muffles a laugh.

There's this moment where I'm almost *disappointed* that she's going to be rushing, though I know her minute of decency was sparked only by the knowledge that she won't be living with me. For a second, I even want to ask if Lucie interviewed for the *Washingtonian* too, but I'm afraid to learn she won a coveted spot.

It's also possible that the day has simply been too much, and my emotions are manifesting in strange ways. That sounds far more realistic.

"The party's at Zeta Kappa," she's saying. "It's that big frat on Fiftieth Street, the one with the massive husky statues outside?" The husky is UW's mascot, and they parade around a puppy named Dubs at sporting events. It's the kind of thing that could inspire me to attend a sporting event.

I've driven by that frat plenty of times—it's the gaudiest one. "Why are you telling me?"

"I . . . don't know." Lucie unplugs her curling iron. Her hair is so pin-straight, it's already struggling to hold a wave. "We're roommates. For now, at least. If one of us is going off campus at night, it just makes sense."

"Okay." I root around in my bag for my pepper spray. "Do you want to take this?"

She unzips a metallic clutch and holds up her own canister. "Already covered." After tidying up the room, she assesses herself in the mirror again, fluffing her hair in a final attempt to give it volume. "Well. Night."

I grunt at her in response, and it's only once she leaves that I get the idea—a way to salvage if not my entire college experience, then at the very least this disaster first day.

☾ ☾ ☾

It's a good thing I didn't lend Lucie my pepper spray, because I have one hand on it as I trek north through campus. Do I know how to use it if someone leaps out of the bushes and demands all seven dollars in my wallet? No. Do I trust my brain to adequately react to the situation and hit the red button instead of screaming, running away, and inevitably tripping over something? Also no.

The walk is uphill, and a minute in, I'm already panting. College is either going to kill me or turn me into a division-one power walker. I will carry UW to our first championship. Shoe companies everywhere will beg to sponsor me. *How did you do it?* they'll want to know. *Perseverance,* I'll say. *Perseverance, and grit, and the right pair of sneakers.*

"Barrett?" calls a male voice.

I whirl around to spot a shadowy figure approaching. I don't know where he came from or who he is or how he knows my name, but the guy has his hands in front of his face and my finger is on the trigger thingy and I squeeze my eyes shut and I probably should have read the instructions and—

"Wait—I'm not—"

I'm so startled I drop the can of pepper spray. "Oh my god oh my god oh my god. I'm so sorry."

"You almost pepper-sprayed me."

"I'm sorry," I repeat, my hands still shaking, and then he comes into view and maybe I'm not actually that sorry. Miles, Mr. PHYSICS MATTERS. Who better to run into on a darkened path at . . . well, it's only a quarter past nine, but still. The only ideal time to run into someone who publicly humiliated you is never o'clock.

"Campus can be dangerous at night," he says. "You shouldn't be walking alone."

He's changed into a plain navy T-shirt and his dark hair is mussed, like he's been scraping his hands through it. The way his ears stick out isn't so dramatic that it was the first thing I noticed about him, but it's enough to make me wonder whether bullies made life hell for him at some point. And while he's tall, much taller than my five-three frame, he doesn't carry it in an imposing way. Maybe it's the way the streetlight catches the angles of his face, but there's a weariness to him I didn't notice in class. A resignation.

"Maybe strange guys shouldn't yell out my name and scare me half to death?"

"Fair point. I'm sorry." And he does look a little sorry as he rakes a hand through his hair, confirming my theory: Miles, whoever he is, is a fiddler.

"And besides. I have this." I retrieve my trusty red canister and hold it up. I swear I'm going to end up spraying myself in the face.

"Please don't wave that thing around," he says, and he has a point there, so I drop it into my bag. "Where are you heading?"

"A party. You?"

"Meeting a friend."

It's gotten chilly, and I pull my sweater tighter. The drama building is on our right, the business school on our left. If we're heading off campus on the same path, then we're kind of forced to walk together.

"So, did you switch out of physics?" he asks just when the silence is moments from becoming unbearable. He's fiddling again, this time with the smart watch on his wrist.

"Not yet. I had to fill out a form, and now I guess I pray to the gods of people who don't do the assigned reading that it's approved."

"Ah. Those gods. I think they're usually pretty busy preventing those people from being called on in class, but hopefully they'll find the time to help you."

His sense of humor catches me off guard. "Speaking of being called on in class," I say, "you aren't going to apologize for what happened in physics today?"

"Refresh my memory."

I stop walking. "Seriously? You raised your hand and told the professor you wanted to hear what I had to say about the study of physics. On the *first day*. And for some reason, the professor listened to you!"

Miles blinks, like maybe I really did need to refresh his memory, but come on—it happened only hours ago. Something that may be regret passes over his face, his brows scrunching, and he relents. "You're right. That was shitty of me, and I'm sorry. It's been . . . a weird week."

Maybe it's the shock of a man admitting he did something wrong, but I might actually forgive him. I'd probably have found some other way of humiliating myself if he hadn't sped the process along.

Though he doesn't elaborate on his weird week, I let out a resigned breath. Fine, he can walk with me. No, not *with* me—next to me.

I check the map on my phone as we hit the first intersection at the campus entrance, the one with the giant bronze *W*. We cross the street together, though I have to hoof it to keep up with his longer strides. I will not lose my power-walking title.

"Where does your friend live?" I ask.

Another scratch at his wrist. "Couple blocks away."

And yet he doesn't veer from my path, even as we reach the house with the husky statues in front.

I stop.

He stops.

We both turn to go up the walk.

"I thought you said you were meeting a friend," I say.

"I am. At a party."

As melodramatically as I can, I thrust out my arms, gesturing for him to go in front of me, and after a moment's hesitation, he does. Of course we wound up at the same party. Of course the universe would find this hilarious.

"You two together?" the guy at the door asks as Miles approaches, craning his neck to get a look at me. I wonder if bouncer is a job for someone very high or very low in the frat hierarchy. "We're trying to keep things balanced—we don't want more guys than girls. I can't let you in unless you're with her."

Miles gives me a pleading look, and I don't know what he's doing here, if one of these frat bros is his friend or if he just wants to get smashed after a "weird week." I also don't want to get into this bullshit binary gender ratio.

"He's with me." The guy steps back, allowing us to pass. "You owe me," I hiss at Miles as we make our way inside.

"I'll be your physics tutor," he says with this little quirk of a smile. A parenthesis sliced in half.

And with that, he blessedly disappears into the crowd.

In my imagination, Zeta Kappa was a flashing-black-light mess, people making out against the wall, alcohol spraying everywhere. In reality, it's a charming old house from the outside that's no one's given enough love inside. None of the furniture matches, and most of it is falling apart. People are drinking and dancing and playing beer pong in small groups. There are people in UW jerseys and people in dresses and people in just jeans and T-shirts, and the hall is lined with frat photos from throughout the years. Nearly as many white guys as the RNC.

My mission: a normal college experience. That means I have to talk to someone. I will make polite conversation, I will make them laugh, and afterward we will follow each other on Instagram. I've been on campus for only four days, and already I can see this year stretched out in front of me, a facsimile of last year and the year before that and so on. I've waited too long for this year not to be different.

I make my way into the kitchen and let a guy fill a cup of beer for me from a keg. I can be a normal college student blowing off steam at a party. I can talk to *one* person like the well-adjusted human I've long suspected I am not.

Except I don't know anyone, and this may be a startling revelation, but I didn't go to very many parties in high school. In fact, I went to one, after prom. I should have known better—should have known that Cole Walker, who kissed me sweetly on the dance floor and beneath the sheets in a hotel room afterward, who let me think maybe I wasn't such a nightmare after all, had done it as a joke. I deflowered Barrett Bloom, he wrote in a group text that wound its ugly way through school, along with a string of flower emojis. #debloomed, one of his horrible friends texted back.

When I opened my locker the Monday after the dance, roses and tulips and daisies spilled out. I'd always liked my very Jewish last name, but for the last month of school, it gave me a new reputation, one that cracked me open and threatened to let out every emotion I'd locked away for years.

Island had nearly two thousand kids, more than a dozen with the last name Walker. And my prom date turned out to be the brother of Blaine Walker, who'd lost his college scholarship after my article undid the tennis team's win.

Pushing all that away before my lungs get too tight, I glue my back to the wall and pretend I know the song everyone is belting the lyrics to, idly wishing my mom's taste in music were more current. And then I do the Lonely Girl Party Trick: I pull out my phone and alternate between sipping my beer and scrolling my news apps— *New York Times*, CNN, the BBC. And, begrudgingly, Elsewhere. Because yes, it's a news site run by the people who created Lucie, but they have some damn fine journalists on staff, with long-form reporting that's won multiple awards, including an oral history of *The O.C.* that both my mom and I devoured last year.

"Hey."

I glance up at the guy leaning against the wall opposite me, blond hair curling past his ears. He's in a purple Zeta Kappa shirt.

"Hi. This your place?"

"It is indeed," he says. "Great, right?"

I lift my cup of warm beer. "Compliments to your sommelier."

When he laughs, his eyes crinkle at the corners. "You're funny. I'm Kyle."

"Barrett."

It's not too common a first name, so the way this plays across his face, his eyebrows creasing together for a moment, isn't entirely unusual. "Like . . . ferret?"

"If it helps you remember, sure." I sound too combative. I'm not auditioning to be the moody new girl with a dark past on a CW show. I'm trying to get someone to like me. So I switch gears, pretending he's a deeply interesting person I'm interviewing for an *Entertainment Weekly* cover story. "What originally drew you to the Zeta Kappa fraternity?"

"All the men in my family went here, so it was pretty much a given."

"Why break with tradition, right?"

"Exactly." Another grin. "I like a thick girl," he says in a low voice, and I abandon any hope of this becoming a friendship. "That's, like, all woke and everything to say these days, right? Or are you guys reclaiming the word *fat*? I might have read something about that online."

He phrases it like this is a completely normal conversation to have. *You guys.* Like I'm a representative for the entire group and we've just had our annual Fat Girl Convention, during which we've discussed our preferred terminology.

"I have to vomit," I announce, and he shrinks back against the wall.

The house has gotten more crowded, hotter, too many sweaty bodies pressed up against one another. I have no idea where Miles disappeared to or what to do next.

I squeeze through the hall, trying my best to appear like I belong—and nearly choke on the rest of my terrible beer when I spot Lucie playing flip cup in the game room. She's with a big group, and while I can only see half her face, I'm positive she's having a blast, given how raucous the room is, full of cheers and laughter and hugging and dancing. They make it look so fucking easy, like it's natural to enter a house as strangers and have new best friends within the hour.

Someone behind me shoves inside, and when Lucie's head turns toward the door, I escape as quickly as I can.

I wind up in the backyard, where a line of Tiki torches lights the path, because it's not a college party without a little cultural appropriation. There are people playing volleyball and people grilling burgers, and everyone just looks so *right* in this setting that my chest aches. I usually don't allow it to, but tonight I don't have the energy to fight it.

It's a quarter past ten, the moon a silver shard in the sky.

Logically, I know this isn't my scene. I thought that scene would be the newsroom, but maybe the sad truth of my life is that I don't fit anywhere, which only becomes brilliantly, painfully clear on those rare occasions I'm trying to force it. I held out this hope that college would be different, but I'm not sure how to make that happen when the past is determined to follow me.

Although since I heard about this party from Lucie, maybe I'm the one following it.

"Watch out!" someone yells as a volleyball hurtles my way, along with a shirtless guy chasing it.

I back up, trying my hardest not to get squashed by either of them, and stumble into something long and tall and warm.

A Tiki torch.

It breaks my fall but only slightly, and I land with a grunt, my Fat Girl Convention–approved butt cushioning my fall. My stomach is coated with beer, my cup a few feet away. At least I land in the grass—while the torch sways ominously back and forth.

No no no no no.

I scramble to my feet, but I'm too late. It seems to happen both in slow motion and all at once: the torch tips over, liquid gold slicing through the darkness as a breeze lifts billows of white smoke into the air. A rhododendron bush catches fire, and then the ivy twisting up the side of the house, leaves turning black as the flames climb higher, higher . . .

For a moment, all I can do is stare.

I just set a frat on fire.

Chapter 4

"OUT OF THE HOUSE!" SOMEONE SHOUTS. PEOPLE stream into the street, a few racing to the backyard to see what's going on while most keep their distance. There's Kyle, his arm around a girl probably less unpleasant than I was. I don't see Lucie. I don't see Miles.

A smoke alarm is going off, its shriek drawing partiers out of neighboring houses. Everyone is yelling and one girl is crying that she can't find her sister. The flames advance up the side of Zeta Kappa, turning the air to smoke. It could be five seconds or five minutes before my mind starts working again, and I push to my feet just as a couple of bright young minds start dousing the fire with their drinks.

"Alcohol makes it worse!" I yell, torn between trying to help, though I have zero idea how, and disappearing into the night. The crowd is small, the fire flickering off glasses lenses and phone screens.

My heart slams against my rib cage as I search a nearby cooler for bottled water. This can't be real. I can't have set a building on fire at a party I wasn't invited to, with god knows how many people still inside.

In the distance, a fire engine howls.

"How the hell did this happen?" asks a tall, built guy in a business-school shirt, elbowing through the knot of onlookers.

"It was her." A girl points right at me just as my hand closes around a bottle of Dasani. "She knocked over the torch."

I withdraw the water, holding it to my chest like a shield. "I didn't—I'm sorry—it was an accident—"

The crowd tightens, as though making a collective decision to prevent me from escaping. I spot Miles a dozen feet away, near the border between this property and the next. For some reason, he doesn't look nearly as concerned as the rest of the group. He's calmly sipping something from a red cup, just . . . observing.

I'll add it to the list of things about Miles that don't make sense and that I don't care enough about to investigate. Especially not right now.

"Who the fuck is this?" the first guy says, jabbing a thumb toward me. "Does anyone know this chick? Because I've never seen her before in my life."

A wave of murmurs rolls through the crowd. No one knows me. It shouldn't sting, and yet it does, this reminder that I am an outsider. An outsider who forced her way in and is in the process of destroying something so many of these people loved.

"Barrett?" Lucie pushes to the front of the crowd. Any amount of curl her hair had is gone, and it hangs limply to her shoulders. "What the fuck? You couldn't have found some other party to crash?"

The relief that she's okay is immediately overpowered by a fierce sense of betrayal. Lucie's the one person who can make this night worse—because up until a few seconds ago, I was anonymous.

"I wasn't crashing," I say, rage sharpening my words. Each one, I point right at her. "I was just—"

"You know her?" the first guy says. The frat president, maybe.

I catch Lucie's gaze, hoping she sees the panic in my eyes. Hoping she cares, even the tiniest amount. *Please,* I try to communicate to her. *Don't say anything.*

"Barrett Bloom," she says smoothly, clearly loving that she's throwing me to the wolves. "We went to high school together. Unfortunately."

Apparently, that moment in our room meant nothing.

"The cops are out front," another guy says. "They want to talk to any witnesses."

No. This *cannot* be happening, my first day of college literally going up in flames.

I don't think. I just run.

ʊʊʊ

Junior year of high school, I ran a sixteen-minute mile. When I crossed the finish line, my legs burning and my throat dry, the gym teacher, who was also the tennis coach, brought up some statistics on his phone.

"Congratulations," he said, shoving his screen in my face. "You ran that about as fast as the average seventy-year-old."

There's something to be said for adrenaline, though. Because tonight I'm pretty sure I could leave those septuagenarians in the dust. I speed through Greek Row, past other houses celebrating first days and new friends and the seductive thrill of independence. I don't know where I'm going as my feet bash the pavement, only that I have to get as far from Zeta Kappa as possible.

I push myself uphill along University Way, the street bordering UW that everyone calls "the Ave." It always held this magic for me as a kid when my mom and I visited, all these cheap restaurants and cute shops and cafés filled with college students studying, looking impossibly mature and sophisticated. Tonight, there's none of that.

It was an accident. I know I'm not at fault, and I think—god, I *hope*—everyone had enough time to get out of the house. If I'd stayed, the police would have questioned me, and hopefully they'd have believed that it was an accident. There would be no proof I'd done anything criminal. But all those accusatory glares, the way the whole crowd turned on me . . .

Well, it felt like I was back in high school.

Eventually my legs give out. I bend over and clutch my knees, panting. I'm still death-gripping that bottle of water, and I drain half of it in a single gulp. My thighs are burning and the denim is rubbing against my skin in all the worst places. In related news, these are no longer my favorite jeans. No one's chasing after me, at least, but I'm pretty sure I'm lost. My phone is at 3-percent battery, and it dies just as I'm opening Google Maps.

I feel like a fucking fugitive. This is absurd. Beyond absurd. I have no idea how this day went from an uncomfortable roommate situation to an actual *house on fire*. Disaster has always found me, but this is next-level. A disaster that's graduated from Harvard and joined Mensa and won a Nobel Prize.

I force myself to take deep lungfuls of night air, work to soothe my racing heart. I can't give in to panic. Not yet.

I track the numbers on the houses and street signs, decide I need to head south, and after a dozen more blocks . . . *there*. There's the edge of campus, and there's the big bronze *W* that stands for *What Did You Just Do?* and *Who Are You Trying to Fool?* and *Why Did You Think College Would Be Any Different?*

I don't know, I don't know, I don't know.

By the time I swipe my student ID card at Olmsted, I'm beyond panic and well into misery. I slump against the wall of the elevator, catching my reflection, and I look about as wrecked as I feel. Mascara streaked down my cheeks, glasses smudged, face a shade lighter than a Solo cup. Hair a mess of snarls that won't be fun to untangle tomorrow, but at least tomorrow will mean today is over.

I jam my key in the lock, and sure, the small amount of beer I had combined with my invigorating nighttime jog have made things a bit blurry around the edges. But the door to room 908 won't budge. I heave all my weight on it, turn the key as hard as I can.

She dead-bolted it. *Fuck.* She either raced home before I could or I was out much longer than I thought.

"Lucie!" I whisper-shout, banging on the door. I imagine the new Olmsted won't have dead bolts, which Paige told me were installed during protests in the 1960s to keep students safe. "Lucie—come on. Open up."

No response.

"Lucie. Please." I'd laugh if I weren't about to cry. I'm so close to hysteria I'd do both if I had the energy.

Instead, after a few more minutes of unsuccessful knocking, I

45

drag myself to the common room on the opposite end of the floor, which contains two battered couches, a TV, and a heap of questionable blankets. There's just no chance someone hasn't had sex in here.

I choose the less battered but still threadbare couch, which squeals when I sink onto it, as though even the furniture is protesting Barrett Bloom. Surely, none of this would have happened if I'd roomed with Christina Dearborn of Lincoln, Nebraska, the way I was supposed to. Or maybe they should have ripped this building apart over the summer instead of making all of us suffer like this.

One thing this room has going for it: a universal charging station. My brain won't calm down, so I plug in my phone, clean my glasses with the edge of my T-shirt, and start doom-scrolling. The good news is that every outlet reporting the fire indicates there were no injuries, just the loss of some Zeta Kappa heirlooms. That loosens some of the tension in my twisted-up body. The bad news is that I've been tagged. In a not-insignificant number of pictures. A few were snapped while the fire was still raging, me at my most unflattering angles. Others were grabbed from my own Instagram, which I instantly make private but it's too late. The photos are paired with words like *BANNED FOR LIFE* and *FIRESTARTER* and *WE'LL FIND YOU, BARRETT BLOOM*. And those are the nice ones.

My hands shake, a knot forming in my throat. All of it takes me back to high school, back to that wreck of a week after prom. *#debloomed* all over my Instagram, along with my freshman yearbook photo. A persistent, bitter ache in my stomach that followed me to graduation. One of Cole's posts explained how after Blaine lost his scholarship, their parents took away his car and he spent a year at community college, struggling to get back on his feet. By the time he applied to transfer, he was so out of practice that he couldn't get onto a tennis team anywhere, not even at the division-three school he wound up at. I'd ruined his brother's life, Cole wrote. So, apparently, it was only fitting that he ruin mine.

Every time I reported one of those posts for harassment, Instagram told me it didn't "violate our community guidelines." If I scroll down, they're still there, this digital record of exactly what people in high school thought about me. I have to stop myself before I scroll too far or I'll never be able to fall asleep, my too-tight lungs and too-shallow breaths keeping me awake the way they did most of May and June, some of July, and only a little of August. I thought I was getting better. Putting all this behind me.

The way Lucie and the rest of my Island peers treated me after the article—that, I could get over. I could stand by my investigation and know I'd done the right thing. But the flowers in my locker and the posts and the hashtag felt different. I hadn't known my heart was capable of breaking in that specific way, and that's why it's crucial no one ever sees those jagged pieces.

Over the past few months, I've practiced tucking it all away in the darkest corner of my mind, where it belongs. Today was supposed to be a fresh start, and yet here I am, in the middle of another mess. I've never stopped to consider the possibility that college could actually be *worse* than high school.

My phone hits the floor with a soft thud as I bury my head in a floppy gray pillow.

I am the same disaster of a person I've always been, no matter how much I wish I could leave her in my past.

DAY TWO

‖

Chapter 5

"THIS HAS TO BE A MISTAKE."

God, I hope so.

I roll over, anticipating sore limbs and the rough scrape of the couch against my face. I remember unpacking a Costco-size bottle of Tylenol, but I'm not sure where I put it. If Lucie hasn't unlocked the door, I might have to get the RA. And then I'll face my Thursday classes, receive a "thanks but no thanks" rejection from the *Washingtonian*. Contend with my social-media notoriety.

On second thought, I could camp out here.

Except . . . something isn't right. The surface beneath me, while not exactly comfortable, is much softer than the couch I fell asleep on in the common room.

Where I am currently, decidedly not.

"It's not a mistake. We underestimated our capacity this year, and we had to make a few last-minute changes. Most freshmen are in triples."

"And you didn't think it would be helpful for me to know that before moving in?"

I throw back the sheets—my sheets. My bed. My dorm room. I fumble on the desk next to the bed for my glasses and shove them on crookedly. "What the hell is going on?"

They whirl to look at me, Lucie Lamont and Paige the RA.

"I'm so sorry," Paige says. "I hope we didn't wake you. I was just about to tell Lucie that we should talk out in the hall."

Lucie, who's standing there in the tracksuit she wore yesterday, a hand on her suitcase, her duffel on the other unmade bed. "Apparently," she says, her icy glare sending a shiver through me that has nothing to do with her, "we're roommates."

I'm too shocked to formulate a response. When they head out into the hall and Lucie slams the door, the whiteboard shudders before dropping to the floor. Again.

What the actual . . .

I blink blink blink and assess the room, not believing my eyes or my brain. There are the pasta bowls from the day before yesterday, the ones I wasn't supposed to take from the dining hall, illuminated by the smallest sliver of light the window lets in. The shelf stuffed with issues of *Vanity Fair* and *Rolling Stone*. Could I have sleep-walked back into my room? Except—I'm in my UW T-shirt, not the Britney tee and perfect-imperfect jeans I wore yesterday, and it doesn't smell like ashes and crushed dreams. When I grab my phone and pull up Instagram, there's nothing. No posts, no tags, no warrants for my arrest.

And the date, staring back at me like a breaking-news alert: September 21, 7:02 a.m.

Yesterday.

A thread of unease works its way up my spine as I swipe through my trifecta of news apps, looking for signs of . . . what? A species of aliens that landed in the middle of the night and erased Lucie's memory but not mine? A widespread news hack or Android glitch? Whatever it is I'm hoping to see, I don't find it.

Maybe I'm still sleeping—that's the only thing that makes any amount of sense. The other possibilities are almost too frightening to consider. Maybe I drank more than I thought, or maybe—oh god—someone spiked my drink. Or I slipped and fell when I was running, hit my head, and now I'm suspended in some kind of not-life, not-death scenario. I feel like that's a thing.

Okay. Let me approach this logically. Mentally retrace my steps. I remember coming back to the dorm and Lucie dead-bolting the door. I remember sinking onto that shabby couch. I remember the abject misery that weighed me down as I fell asleep.

The door opens, and there's Lucie and her September 21 scowl.

"I don't understand how this is happening," I say, pinching my wrists, trying to feel around my head for bumps or bruises. This right now feels real, which makes me wonder if yesterday was the dream. But it was so vivid, too vivid, and I've never been able to recall a dream in that great detail.

Maybe I'm simply losing my mind.

"That makes two of us." Lucie's gripping her suitcase, her ponytail looking as indignant as it did yesterday.

Paige grins, but now I can see the clear signs of *too awkward, must escape.* "Well. I'll leave you two to get acquainted! Or—reacquainted."

When she leaves, I just stare. At the door. At the fallen white-board. At my pasta bowls.

"You're not blinking," Lucie says, taking tentative steps toward her bed. "And what are you doing to your head?"

I drop my hands. "Nothing. I'm fine."

"I'm as upset as you are," she says. "I was supposed to have a single in Lamphere Hall. They totally sprung this on me. I'm going to talk to the RD later and try to sort this out."

"But you were in St. Croix," I say quietly. "There was a tropical storm."

One of her eyebrows arches. "Creeping on my social media?"

"No, I . . ." *You told me yesterday?* "Yeah. I like to keep tabs on all my favorite Island people."

She sets her purse down on her desk, nearly knocking over one of the bowls. From two days ago. When she looks at me, demand-ing an explanation I already gave her, I stammer out, "All-you-can-eat pasta bar. I, uh, partied a little too hard with it."

"It smells like an—"

"Olive Garden?" I say. I might be trembling. My heart has never worked this hard, not even when I ran that sixteen-minute mile.

Lucie softens only the slightest bit. "I love endless salad and breadsticks as much as the next person, but this is ridiculous. If we're really going to be rooming together, even if it's just until they move me somewhere else, then we'll need some ground rules."

"Ground rules. Right." And this was the moment I made a dirty joke she didn't appreciate. I'm half tempted to make it again, but now all I want is to pacify her. To finish this conversation so I can get some time alone and figure out why the hell the last twenty-four hours seem to have been erased when they're still so clearly imprinted in my memory. "I'll clean everything up. I'm sorry."

My acquiescence seems to stun her. Like she wanted a fight. She did yesterday, after all. "Oh—okay, then. Good."

Before she can unzip her suitcase and discover the sole outlets beneath my desk, I get out of bed and grab my shower caddy.

"I'm going to shower," I say, and then I stumble down the hall.

ひ ひ ひ

I don't find answers in the grout or grime. I'm not sure how much time I spend shampooing, conditioning, scrubbing every pore on my body, but when I get back to the room, Lucie's gone.

With my hair in a towel, I pull my laptop onto my bed and prop myself against the wall. There has to be a rational explanation for what's going on. I'm a journalist—I can figure this out.

I try a few searches: *woke up on the same day, no one remembers yesterday, day repeating itself.* Most of what comes up is pure fiction, movies and TV shows about time travel. Hypotheticals. A BuzzFeed listicle: "Seventeen Things to Do If You're Stuck in a Time Loop."

Time loop.

I choke on a laugh—the theory is that absurd. And yet a panicky lump settles into my throat as I scroll past a Reddit thread with the title *Might be trapped in a time loop?*

I shut my laptop.

No. It's not possible. I am not in a fucking time loop.

All of this happening around me—it can't be real. Maybe there was a gas leak in the building—surely some chemical can cause ultra-vivid dreams. Or maybe I'm in a coma, my brain working hard to get me back online. I could be disconnected from my real body, reliving this day inside the surreal-but-safe boundaries of my own head.

It's absolutely batshit, but it's the only thing that makes any amount of sense. I'll just . . . let the dream play out.

When I open my closet, something stops me from reaching for the Britney Spears shirt I wore yesterday. If I keep doing the same things, I'm going to freak myself out even more. So I go for a long skirt and floral tee. Tassel earrings. Then, instead of waiting in line in the dining hall for the Olmsted Eggstravaganza, I buy a breakfast burrito from a food truck in Red Square.

In between bites, I call my mom.

"Hey," she says, picking up after the first ring. "I was just about to text you."

"Is everything okay?" I try to keep my voice from sounding frantic, but my words have a breathy edge to them. If there's anyone who can reassure me, it's my mom. She's always been able to handle a scraped knee or a bruised ego with ease—with the exception of what I didn't tell her about prom.

Granted, if this is a dream version of my mom, she won't know anything I don't know.

"Hi, Barrett!" Jocelyn calls in the background. "We miss you!"

"Miss you too," I say, a chill running up my spine.

I imagine yesterday's Mollie Bloom, not this fragment created by my subconscious, getting ready for work at Ink & Paper, the shop she runs in downtown Mercer Island, which features the work of local artists as well as cards and crafts and other tchotchkes from around the Pacific Northwest. She was probably listening to a pop-culture podcast with Jocelyn as she swapped her robe for jeans and a graphic tee. It soothes me, thinking of her spreading cream cheese onto a bagel and swearing to me that one day I will experience the pure joy of a New York City bagel, and then and only then will I understand my Jewish roots.

"Why wouldn't everything be okay?" she says, and some part of me deflates. She sounds normal—like someone who hasn't woken up on September 21 for the second time in a row. *No,* I tell myself. *You're dreaming, remember?* "Is this your first-day nerves talking?"

"Probably." I dart out of the way to avoid a pair of swing dancers spiraling across the square. "I guess I just . . . wanted to hear your voice. That's corny, isn't it?"

"It absolutely is, but I still like you. Let me know how it all goes today?"

"Yes. Of course."

As I hang up, I stumble into a girl waving a stack of flyers. "Hi! We're trying to raise awareness about the Mazama pocket gopher—"

Odd that my halluci-dream would bring her back. "Sorry, I can't. But good luck!"

I take my time walking through campus, ensuring I won't be sweaty when I arrive at the physics building. Even though none of this is real, some part of me is certain physics is where I'm supposed to be. There's no one in the front row, and though I imagine that sitting in the front row of a several-hundred-person lecture hall carries some kind of nerd stigma, I grab a seat. The professor said this was a serious class, so here I am, taking it seriously.

Physics 101: Where Everyone and Everything Has Potential.

Every detail, perfectly re-created.

I nearly gasp when the realization hits me: maybe my subconscious is giving me a chance to fix what I did yesterday. Maybe once I do that, I'll wake up in a hospital bed, my mom telling me that it was lucky I got out of Olmsted before the whole thing collapsed.

Yes. That has to be it.

Except when Miles walks in, wearing the same red flannel he wore yesterday, his hair damp from a shower, he scans the room before his gaze lands on me, his mouth kicking up into the smallest of smiles. Almost as though—and I realize it's ludicrous even as I think it—as though he was looking for me, and he didn't expect me to be in the first row.

Despite the couple hundred other empty seats, Miles heads right for me, and my stomach prepares for battle with the breakfast burrito.

"Is this seat taken?" he asks, fiddling with the frayed strap of his backpack.

"The whole row, actually." I do my best to act normal, a calm and collected Barrett who will not let this guy get me in trouble with the professor, even in a dream. "I've got a lot of friends. Popularity is a burden."

His jaw twitches. "Okay" is all he says before taking a seat in the row right behind me.

Dr. Okamoto repeats her introduction, and this time I don't take notes. Especially now that Miles has a clear view of my laptop.

I'm paranoid about what my subconscious's version of him can see, so I shift in my seat to shield it from him.

"Government secrets?" he asks in a whisper when Dr. Okamoto's PowerPoint freezes up for half a minute, the same way it did yesterday.

"So many," I whisper back. Not provoking Miles, even though he's the one who provoked me first: that's one way I'll do this right.

Then the slide unfreezes, and Miles doesn't say anything for the rest of class.

Good. I have bigger things to worry about.

Chapter 6

EVEN THOUGH I'VE CONVINCED MYSELF TODAY IS an elaborate hallucination-slash-dream-slash-out-of-body-experience, that doesn't make it any less eerie. I feel full of contradictions: my mind is hazy, while in front of me, too many details are painted in the brightest colors, exactly as they were yesterday. The gopher girl. The clubs and food trucks. The swing dancers in Red Square.

Still, I'm set on proving to my subconscious, or whatever part of me is in charge here, that I can get this right. I don't go to the counseling center to try to swap physics for something else, and I even raise my hand in my English class.

"Comma splice," I say, and the TA, a spectacularly eyelashed grad student named Grant, snaps out of his sleep- and/or weed-induced haze and offers me a half smile.

"Perfect," he says from his chair across the circle. That was how he instructed the twenty of us to sit—no desks. *I am a cool TA,* this said. "Barrett, right?"

The way he says my name isn't the way teachers back at Island said it: *Oh. Barrett*, accompanied by a forced smile, a pinch of their foreheads. So, just for fun, I raise my hand a few minutes later and answer another question.

But by the time I'm pounding up the steps of the journalism building after having watched that skateboarder plow into the group of swing dancers once more, the déjà vu is so intense that the haziness has given way to a full-on headache, a slight but insistent stabbing right between my eyebrows.

"I remember you from the info sesh," editor in chief Annabel Costa says when I introduce myself. "You were the one who asked all the questions."

"It's at least sixty percent of being a reporter, right?"

A flash of *something* crosses her face. "Exactly what I was going to say. Let's talk in my office."

And there we are, corralled by the Sharpied orange walls, Annabel looking just as comfortable as she did yesterday as she tucks her black dress underneath her. It's unsettling, being this close to her, anticipating every move she makes. I find I even remember when she gets fed up with her long blond bangs and fishes inside the desk drawer for a bobby pin.

"You know the basics from yesterday, yeah?" she says, hooking the bobby pin into her hair.

"From . . . yesterday?" I repeat, wondering if she's talking about the real yesterday, the one none of these dream beings remember.

"The info session? We just talked about it five seconds ago?"

"Right. Of course," I say. "Reporters are assigned to different sections—news, sports, features, arts. And the paper comes out Mondays and Wednesdays."

Annabel nods. "Budget cuts have been rough. But we're still kicking, and I think the quality of our reporting is the best it's ever been. We were named the best non-daily college newspaper by the Society of Professional Journalists two years ago." Her mouth pulls into a frown. "Are you okay?"

It is at this moment I realize I've been inexplicably tapping my foot against the leg of the chair. Loudly.

Be fucking normal, I tell myself, repeating it in my head like a mantra. Maybe that's what I'm supposed to do here: no jokes, no outlandishness, just a Barrett Bloom who lives and dies by the pen.

"Sorry. A little nervous," I admit. It's not something I'd typically say, and it makes Annabel soften. Suddenly, it feels perfectly valid that my mind re-created this scenario so I could ace my interview. I'll wake up, march back to the journalism building, and charm Annabel into giving me another chance. That has to be it.

"No need," she says. "These are always more fun when they're a little informal. Casual. I'm not going to sit here and ask you to tell me where you see yourself in five years. I have your résumé and the links to stories you did for"—she peeks at her screen—"the *Navigator.* You wrote . . . almost fifty articles in four years? For a monthly paper? *Wow.*" A low whistle.

Yesterday I told her it was because I didn't have many friends. I'll go for a different angle this time. No self-deprecation.

"Journalism is my life." I pour as much earnestness into it as possible, and yet it comes out sounding robotic. "I'm always seeking the truth, you know? I love writing profiles and learning about people I might not otherwise . . . um, learn about. I like . . . hearing what people have to say. That's the beauty of it."

If you gave a pocket gopher a typewriter and asked how it feels about journalism, surely it would come up with something better than this.

"The beauty of . . . ?"

"Journalism," I say, and promptly want to fling myself into the sun.

The pressure between my eyes grows more brutal. About 30 percent of me is here in the newsroom with Annabel while the rest of me puzzles out an impossible equation. I have a great memory, but there's no way I could re-create everything to this degree. I'm not giving my brain enough credit for that.

There's something unsettling building in my stomach, a strange sense that none of this is made-up at all.

Annabel's smile falters, and though the impetus is different, the reaction is the same. Recognizable. "Right. Well, we don't want you to overwork yourself. Most of our new reporters start out with one story every couple weeks or so."

She cycles through the same questions as yesterday: what drew me to journalism, my favorite topics to write about, what I'm hoping to get out of working on the *Washingtonian*. And every time, I can barely string a sentence together, like I'm speaking around shards of glass.

"I'm really curious about this article you did a couple years ago on the tennis team," she says eventually, gesturing to her computer screen. "There's a note here that says comments have been disabled, which doesn't seem to be the case with other articles."

"Cheating scandal." I try to keep my voice as level as possible. "It was devastating, really—it was their best season in ages. But I had to follow the truth." Surely if I keep mentioning "the truth," one of these times I'll attach some significant meaning to it.

I should tell her about my favorite piece for the *Nav*, the one I wrote about the custodian who moonlighted as an extra in just about every famously shot-in-Seattle film you could name. But now my head is pounding, and I have to gnash my teeth together against the pain. I whip off my glasses and press the heel of my hand into my forehead.

"Are you sure you're okay?" Annabel says, and no. No, I am not.

"I'm sorry—" I break off as another flash of pain rips through my skull. "Will you just—excuse me for a second?"

And once I get into the hall, I race all the way back to my dorm.

☾ ☾ ☾

I am following my truth—read: lying facedown on my bed, head beginning to fuse with pillow—when Lucie enters the room, her phone pressed to her ear.

". . . and I really think if you just—hello? Did I lose you?" With a sigh, she hangs up, cursing under her breath.

"It's kind of a reception dead zone in here," I say, mostly into my pillow. The headache has faded just a little, but it's still there.

This startles her. "Barrett? Sorry, I didn't see you." She swipes at something on her phone and holds it back up to her ear. Groans. "One more reason to get out of Shithole Hall."

"It's not that bad," I say, rolling over so I can gesture to a swirl of a water stain on the ceiling. "Do you see that? Not many people know this, but that's not a water stain at all. It was actually part of the original design for this building. The architects thought it would give it a more lived-in feel."

At that, she cracks a smile. A small one. Right: this is Sunshine Lucie, Lucie who's rushing a sorority and leaving me to rot in Olmsted all by my lonesome. My little cave o' chaos that's broken my brain.

Because ever since I got back to the dorm and collapsed onto my bed, one thought has been running through my head and one thought only:

This is real.

Somehow, I know this in my bones.

I don't know how or why, only a strong flare of certainty that's becoming impossible to ignore. This world has too many details, too much color, too much *feeling*. Add in the simple fact that this has never felt like a dream, despite what I forced myself to believe a few hours ago when it was all too much.

Maybe I really am losing my grip on reality, or maybe the entire campus is playing a prank on me, but I'm altogether too drained to make sense of it right now.

Lucie points to where I haphazardly tossed my backpack on my desk chair. "Rough day?"

I let out a grumble-sigh in response. "What about you?" I ask, trying to draw out this peace between us. I wasn't as obnoxious to her this morning—it tracks for Lucie to be less combative too.

"Oh, it was fine." She says it dismissively, like it's not on-brand for Lucie Lamont to have anything less than a good day. She's dressed for one: black mock-neck sweater, short denim skirt, sleek auburn hair pinned back on one side. "I'm actually going to rush a sorority, so . . ."

"So our days are numbered."

"Yep." Lucie searches her sweater for wrinkles, flicking aside a speck of lint. A silence elapses between us, one that makes it too easy for me to stumble into a memory.

As freshmen, we stayed late at school to copyedit the paper, which meant a crash course in the *AP Stylebook*. No one else had wanted the job, and we spent hours quizzing each other on obscure grammar and punctuation rules. "Our school's paper, comma, the *Navigator*, comma," I'd say, "because we only have one school paper. So you can get rid of what's inside the commas and the sentence still makes sense."

"My friend no comma Barrett no comma, because I have more than one friend," Lucie said.

My friend, comma, Lucie, comma, I thought, but didn't say. For the rest of the week we said "comma" when we spoke to each other. I'd never had an inside joke with anyone but my mom.

In some alternate timeline, maybe Lucie Lamont and I could have remained friends.

"This is strange," she says now. "I'm not used to seeing you this . . ."

"Pathetic?"

"I was going to go with sad, but sure."

In spite of everything, I let out a laugh as I roll to my side, readjusting my skirt and reaching for the glasses I abandoned on my desk. "I guess college isn't . . . quite what I imagined, so far."

And that's the truth, isn't it? Sure, it's only the beginning of the quarter, and it's not that I thought people would be clamoring to befriend me, but I didn't think it would feel like *this*. Somewhere between the tennis exposé and now, I lost the ability to connect with other people. My confidence plummeted, and the only thing to do has been pretend I've always had plenty of it. If I am Too Much, at least I can say I have an excess of *something*.

"I might regret this," Lucie says as she drops to her knees, fumbling with a power strip to plug in her curling iron, "but I'm going to a party at Zeta Kappa tonight. That big frat on Fiftieth, the one with the massive husky statues outside? You could come. If you want."

I just blink at her. I had planned to lock myself in this concrete box for the rest of the night. If today is really happening, it only makes sense that I should, you know, not set a building on fire my second time around. Maybe that's the reason I'm here: I'm supposed to save Zeta Kappa, though even in my head, it sounds like a bit of a stretch.

The last thing I expected was for Lucie to invite me.

"I don't know if I can."

Lucie lifts a single eyebrow, and I'm so jealous she has this mastered. My whole life, I've wanted to be able to do that. "Wild Wednesday-night plans?"

"Not exactly, but . . ."

Lucie turns to her half of the closet, searching for what I know is an oversize white shirt. "We're in *college*," she says. "This is what we're supposed to do, Barrett. No parents. No curfew. It's *freedom*."

"Sounds fake."

I can't count the number of times I wished for this kind of invitation in high school. First when Lucie stopped talking to me, stopped responding to my texts. I'd see her with her friends at lunch and wish I knew what they were laughing about—except when their gazes flicked over to me, and I knew exactly what they were laughing about. Or when Lucie as editor in chief assigned me the articles no one else wanted to write, and I did the best I could with them anyway.

I spent so much time telling myself I was fine with the way things were. Fine with the occasional shove I'd get in the hallway, so deep in a sea of students that I could almost convince myself I'd imagined it. Fine with the single red roses that showed up on my desk in homeroom every day after prom. Pretending I didn't feel physically ill with each new post with that hashtag. Our administrators were monsters, really, for scheduling prom a whole month before graduation.

And here is an opportunity to become someone else, to *belong*, and I'm turning it down.

"Weren't you just saying college isn't what you imagined so far?" Lucie looks like she doesn't quite believe she's putting in this much effort for someone she's spent so much energy disliking. "I mean, I'm not going to beg you. It's up to you. You can be someone new in college, or you can be . . ." Her eyes scan me, head to toe. But she doesn't finish the sentence.

You can be . . . nothing. A blank.

Just like that, she's got me.

"Should I change into something else?" I ask, and though I'm gesturing to my outfit, I wonder if I might really be asking a different question entirely.

By nine, Lucie's dressed in the same thing she wore yesterday, and I've swapped my T-shirt for a fresh once since I sweated through it during my *Washingtonian* interview, something Lucie doesn't need to know. I can almost forget the gnawing sense of déjà vu as we walk north through campus. I've got to say, it's better than going alone.

This version of the party will be different. I'll be pleasant and palatable, and I'll pay attention to those Tiki torches, and—no. I won't even go outside. And I'll be with Lucie, who with her uncanny ability to instantly belong is the best kind of social armor I can imagine.

Except for some occasional small talk, we walk in relative silence. Proof that we're not friends, that this is just a last hurrah as roommates before she's absorbed into the Greek system. I feel too tall walking next to her, Lucie's tiny heeled boots clacking against the sidewalk.

We're not even halfway there when she stops suddenly. "What's that?" she says.

"What?"

She clamps a hand around my arm, her grip tighter than I'd expect it to be. "Something in the bushes," she says, pointing to a row of shrubbery, and I hear it too. A rustling. The sound of someone breathing.

Slowly, I reach for the canister of pepper spray in my purse. Then, before I can process what's happening, the leaves part and my heart slams against my ribs and Lucie's shriek pierces the night.

This time, I smash my finger down on the trigger.

And this time, it sends a sharp burst of orange right into Miles's face.

Chapter 7

MILES FLINGS HIS HANDS TOWARD HIS FACE, squeezing his eyes shut and letting out a low moan.

"Oh my god oh my god oh my god!" I stuff the can back into my bag. "I'm so sorry!"

Next to me, Lucie is ghost pale, frozen in place.

"You sure you didn't do that on purpose?" Miles bends over, dropping his hands to his knees. This puts him right in the path of a streetlamp, which illuminates the orange-red spray around his eyes and across the bridge of his nose. "*Jesus*, that stings."

"On purpose?" In this version of September 21, Miles and I barely interacted. And we were nothing but cordial to each other. "Why would I—I hardly know you." Instantly, I amend the statement. "I *don't* know you."

"Well, then." A grimace twists his words. He hasn't opened his eyes yet. "I'm Miles. I'd say it's nice to meet you, but . . ."

Lucie holds up her phone with a shaky hand. "Should we call 911?" she asks, blue eyes wide and worried.

"No—don't," Miles says, right before he groans again, swearing under his breath.

"I'm so, so sorry." I repeat it approximately a hundred more times for good measure. "It's dark, and you surprised us, and my mom had me carry around this pepper spray. . . . I just didn't think I'd be using it so soon."

A thin scrape of an exhale. "Mmm."

"We have to get you to a hospital. Or to, I don't know, poison control or something?" I slip my phone from my skirt pocket. "What should you do if you get pepper-sprayed?" I ask it.

"Sorry, I didn't understand that," the warm robotic voice answers. And they say one day technology will replace us all.

Lucie looks a split second from either fainting or sprinting as far away from us as possible.

"You go to the party," I tell her. "I'll help him."

"You sure?" she asks. Upon my nod, she reties her shirt's knot at the navel and takes off, all too eager to disappear into the night.

And then it's just Miles and me, and a couple groups of students on the opposite side of the street too wrapped up in their own worlds to notice.

I try to remember that breathing technique Lucie taught us at Island. Box breathing, she said it was called. Eyes closed, deep breath in through the nose, hold for four seconds, exhale . . . or something. Whatever it was, it's not working for me right now.

"Does it hurt?" I ask.

Finally, Miles opens his eyes. The whites of them have turned a painful pink. "What do you think?" He blinks a few times. Squints.

"I'll be fine in an hour or so. You can go to that party with your friend, if you want."

"What, have you been pepper-sprayed before?"

"I—not exactly."

"It seems like something one would remember."

A pause, and then: "Fine." He nods toward my phone. "What are we supposed to do?"

"It says you're not supposed to rub your eyes, for one. 'Wash your face with running water and non-abrasive soap for at least fifteen minutes,'" I read from Google. "I guess milk can also help with the irritation, or, um, diluted baby shampoo?"

"Perfect, I've got a whole case of that back in my dorm. For all the infants living on my floor."

I fight rolling my eyes. He's just gone through a traumatic experience. He's more than earned the right to be sarcastic.

I scroll through a few more pieces of advice before typing in *Can you go to jail for pepper-spraying someone?* Not that I'm worried. It's just good to know these things.

"Let's go back to the dorms," I say. "We can grab some milk from the dining hall."

"I'm in Olmsted. Down that hill."

"Oh. Me too. Guess I haven't seen you there." Then again, we did only just move in. "Can you walk okay?"

"Well, I can't see."

"Right. Right." A shaky breath. I don't need to have one whole panic about touching a human male, even if he's the only one I've touched since Cole Walker on prom night. I definitely didn't think the next time I touched a guy, it would be because his eyes were burning so badly, he couldn't walk. "If you put your arm around my shoulders, then I can put mine around your waist? Is that . . . okay?"

I'm shorter than he is, but my frame is what some might call sturdy and certain members of Zeta Kappa would call thick, so I imagine I can easily support his weight.

"I don't see another option."

I decide to interpret that as a *Yes, Barrett, please valiantly carry me to safety; I am but a helpless man.* And then I realize I haven't actually told him my name yet.

"I'm Barrett, by the way," I say as I slide my arm around his back, a couple inches above his belt. It's a chilly night, but his skin is warm through his T-shirt. Navy, same as yesterday. If the situation were reversed, I'd probably have already soaked my shirt with sweat. "And I really am so, so sorry."

Miles drapes his arm over my shoulders, though I can tell he's not putting as much weight on me as he could. I'm not sure whether that means he doesn't trust me to support him or he doesn't want to hurt me, or maybe something else entirely. "You've mentioned that once or twice." He shifts against me. And then, after a moment: "Thanks."

Together we hobble down the hill, our hips knocking together with every step. If I'm not muttering "sorry" between huffs of breath, then he is.

"Partied himself out already, poor thing," I tell a group of passersby, all dressed up for what looks to be an eighties-themed party. Sweatbands and knee socks and neon. "And before nine thirty!"

"Kicking me when I'm down, huh?" Miles says, but I might

hear a half laugh somewhere in there. In between the distaste and humiliation.

And then, an awareness so startling that I nearly drop him: his scent, something fresh and woodsy with just a hint of citrus. I'm not sure what I expected—eau de physics? Does being infuriating have a smell?—but it's not *this*.

By the time we arrive at Olmsted, I'm starting to think my sturdiness was not, in fact, doing me any favors. I'm going to be sore tomorrow, I just know it.

Tomorrow.

Please, god, let me have tomorrow. Let it be normal.

I push it away. Focus on helping Miles, righting this wrong, doing this One Good Deed. Based on everything I've learned from pop culture, that's what unsticks people when their timelines hit a snag, right? I can't linger on that thought for too long without hitting a mental panic button and spiraling into the depths of whatthefuckville, but if that's what's happening here, I will good-deed the shit out of this.

After depositing Miles on a couch in the lobby, I rush into the dining hall and buy three bottles of milk, a bottle of water, and a salted chocolate-chip cookie as big as my face as an *I'm sorry I sprayed you with a toxic substance* gift. Then we shuffle into an elevator, Miles cracking one eye to hit the button for the seventh floor.

"Do you need help?" I ask before he goes into the communal bathroom. For his sake, I hope it contains far fewer opportunities for fungal infection than the one on the ninth floor.

He lifts his eyebrows at me, made all the more menacing by the puffy redness around his eyes. "I think I can manage."

While I wait, I lean against the wall next to a bulletin board that says JUST KEEP SWIMMING—AND STUDYING! It's adorned with *Finding Nemo* cutouts and study tips. Every floor has a different theme, and on the ninth, Paige went all out with candy. On my door, my name was bubble-lettered onto a green Sour Patch Kid. I wonder if she spent time making one for Lucie today. Being an RA seems to involve a very specific skill set: mediating roommate disputes and making construction-paper art.

Ten minutes later, I'm well acquainted with what have turned out to be the most obvious study tips on the planet—*#5: Study with friends!*—when Miles reemerges, the skin around his eyes less angry. Some of his dark hair is damp, mussed, I assume from all the washing, and when he combs a hand through it, he only succeeds in making it messier.

"Better?"

"It was touch and go for a while, but I think I'll survive. At least the burning is at a more manageable level." Then he looks like he wants to say something else, his eyebrows pinching together for a moment. "Thank you," he finally says, more warmth in his voice now. "I hope I wasn't too much of a dick. I know it was an accident."

I wave this off. "Let's chalk it up to first days and new experiences."

"I can do that." He holds up the bag from the dining hall. "And I love cookies too large to conceivably eat in one sitting unless you're feeling especially ambitious. Which I'm not sure I am tonight. Do you . . . want some?" There's an odd expression on his face, like he got trapped halfway to a smile.

"I don't want to take your apology cookie," I say, trying for a smile of my own.

We both go silent. My smile has probably turned goofy, or, worse, disingenuous, and Miles is making sustained eye contact with the carpet. But I don't know how to friend, and if this is an opening, I've surely wasted it.

Still, today has to be an improvement over yesterday. I didn't publicly humiliate myself or insult anyone or burn down a frat. All I did was pepper-spray Miles, but he's going to be okay. No lasting damage.

"Well. I'm up there." I point my thumbs toward the ceiling. "Any time you need someone to endanger your life and then heroically attempt to save it, you know where to find me."

"You're not going to go back to the party?"

I shake my head. "Nah. I think the partying mood has officially passed."

"Right." Another silence as he glances down the hall, in the direction I assume his room is in. I wonder what Disney characters are on the door. "See you later, Barrett. If you decide to stay in physics."

It's only when I'm back in my room, white-knuckling my remaining shreds of sanity and focusing all my energy on box-breathing my way into September 22, that something hits me.

I never told him I was planning to switch out.

DAY THREE

|||

Chapter 8

"THIS HAS TO BE A—"

"No no no no no." I let out the groan to end all groans as I fight with my sheets, kicking until my legs are free.

There's Lucie in her tracksuit, Paige in a sweatshirt I'm only just now noticing is patterned with tiny lollipops. Both staring at me. Lucie's jaw is slack, and Paige's eyes are wide with concern. This must be so far outside the realm of what she thought she'd be doing as an RA. And on her ~~third second~~ first day, too.

"Is everything okay?" Paige asks, and given the way she rubs at the back of her neck, digging her hand into her short dark hair, I get the impression she's only prepared to deal with one answer.

"Fine!" I squeak, snatching up my cardigan and shower caddy, stumbling forward so suddenly that they have to jump out of the way, Lucie flattening herself against what would have been her bed. I barrel past them and out into the hall. I couldn't breathe in there. Those rooms weren't made to hold three people, even if Paige ~~was~~ is about to tell Lucie that she's lucky she's not in a triple.

"There was always something a little off about her," I hear Lucie say.

It shouldn't hurt, and yet I thought we had a connection last night. Thought we'd made progress. Of course Lucie doesn't remember any of that. She doesn't know about the empty pasta bowls on the floor or the outlets she'll have to stretch an extension cord across the room to use. She doesn't know that she plans to rush a sorority to get away from Olmsted and/or me.

Holy fucking hell, this *cannot* be happening.

Again.

A visceral panic twists in my stomach. I'm no longer just a resident of whatthefuckville—I'm the mayor, president, supreme ruler.

The other residents of the ninth floor dart out of my way, give me strange looks, muffle their laughter. I'm still in pajama shorts, my arm through one sleeve of the cardigan, the rest of it trailing behind me. And I must not have put the shampoo cap on all the way because I'm squeezing it too hard and it's definitely leaking all over my hand, dripping down my fingers and onto the carpet.

Some part of me wants to laugh at this ridiculous image. A very small part.

The rest of me wants to cry.

Once I'm safely locked inside a stall—in a real plot twist, this bathroom has become my safe space—I swipe through my phone, checking all the things I checked yesterday, at least before the shoddy service kills my 5G. I even (finally) check my student email, babloom@u.washington.edu, and there's Dr. Okamoto's assigned reading waiting for me, chapters 1 and 2 in a textbook I haven't bought yet.

Still Wednesday. Still September 21. Still a chaotic, inexplicable nightmare.

With trembling fingers, I navigate back to that Reddit thread I found ~~yesterday~~ today, in the r/Glitch_in_the_Matrix subreddit. I left my glasses in my room and have to squint.

The post is a few years old, the author talking about a five-minute stretch of time where he was convinced he was trapped in a time loop. He was at a café when he saw a truck with the vanity license plate CHWBCCA drive by a total of six times, followed by the same guy pushing a double stroller with twin toddlers inside. Every five minutes, this seemed to repeat, until he was so spooked, he left the café.

In the comments, people ask the OP for more details, though most of his responses appear to have been deleted, and some comments even report similar experiences.

Then comes more frantic googling. *How did I get into a time loop? How do I get out of a time loop?*

A time loop. It defies every bit of logic that's governed my eighteen years on this earth, and yet it's suddenly the only thing that makes sense. That's what this is, and now I'm nearly certain of it.

I've never been very religious, but I can't not think about religion when I'm questioning the laws of the universe. My mom and I go to synagogue once or twice a year, and Hanukkah's always been a competition to see who can find a gift that makes the other person laugh the most. That's how I wound up with my RINGMASTER OF THE SHITSHOW socks a few years ago and loved them so much I bought a matching pair for my mom. Another reason I'm hoping its mate shows up. I've never been spiritual, either—I don't believe in karma or magical thinking, and I have no clue what happens to us when we die.

But if I lived yesterday twice, while Lucie and Paige and everyone else on the ninth floor seemingly did not, then maybe this is a sign from the universe. Whoever or whatever is out there must have decided my first and second September 21s were so much of a disaster that they merited another try.

I may be an utter mess of a human, but I don't think I'm a bad person. Not entirely.

If what's happening is any indication, the universe, apparently, thinks otherwise.

Everything I did ~~two days ago~~ yesterday before—I'll do the opposite. I'll keep my mouth shut. I won't annoy Miles and I won't rant about tennis and I sure as hell won't go to that party. I can be a dull and muted version of myself, and then I'll wake up on September 22 with a job on the *Washingtonian* and a passion for elementary physics. Lucie and I will tolerate each other. The Zeta Kappas will never have heard of me. If this is some wrinkle in the fabric of reality, maybe all I have to do is iron it out.

At the very least, a tangible mission will help keep me from further unraveling.

I emerge from the stall and approach the long line of sinks. In movies, people are always splashing cool water on their faces when they're stressed. I have never before done this in real life, but right now, I'm desperate. Sure, maybe it doesn't instantly right my world, but it doesn't feel terrible. I do it again, sputtering when I splash water up my nose.

"You okay, sweetie?" The girl at the sink next to me meets my gaze in the mirror. "You have a little something . . ." She taps the side of her head.

I claw a hand through my hair. Shampoo? Mystery goo that leaked from the ceiling overnight? We may never know. "I'm fine." I resist asking if she, too, is stuck in time. "Thanks," I add. *Not on the edge of a nervous breakdown. Not questioning my sanity and everything I thought I knew about how the world is supposed to work.*

I leave the bathroom without showering, not bothering to bring my caddy with me.

Today my aesthetic is solidly idgaf, since evidently the universe is unbothered by my fashion choices. I put on an old sweatshirt of my mom's and a pair of threadbare leggings from the back of the flimsy storage tower I hung in the closet, the ones with the tiny hole in the crotch that are only meant for lounging. I don't even attempt a hairstyle, allowing my curls to be the wild mess they were always destined to be. No point in impressing anyone if they won't remember it tomorrow.

Mom: How do I love thee? Joss and I are wishing you SO MUCH LUCK today!

Once again, my phone buzzes at eight fifteen for a text sent at seven thirty. My mom's words only make my heart ache.

I have half a mind to skip physics entirely, but I can't bring myself to go through with it. Even when school was bad, I never skipped a class.

I just don't know what my other options are. This feels like something I should be able to share with some trusted confidant, but the only person who fits that description is back in Mercer Island. I don't want to be the person who can't handle ~~three~~ two one day of college and needs to run home to her mother. We may be close, but that doesn't mean I have any idea how she'd react to this. Or whether she'd believe me.

ʊ ʊ ʊ

Quark! says the PowerPoint duck. I take the front row again, if only because I'm hoping it acts as some kind of people repellent. All around me, September 21 is proceeding exactly as it did yesterday and the day before. I'm the only variable.

I stare at the slide, willing it to give me some answers. Physics is all about making sense of the universe. Maybe this is the universe's way of telling me to get the hell out of this class I never belonged in. Sure, it's a leap, but I'm no longer safely swaddled in reality. If the problem doesn't make sense, maybe the solution won't, either.

"You know," someone says from behind me, "people who sit in the front row are usually planning to actually take the class."

I nearly jump out of my seat. "Jesus Christ," I mutter as I turn my head, but of course it's Miles. I didn't even see him come in.

His words are slow to register, but when they do, they hit me with the force of a truck with a CHWBCCA license plate. *If you decide to stay in physics,* he said yesterday. He can't possibly know I'm trying to switch out of this class. If this is some kind of X-Men shit, and I'm stuck in time and Miles can read minds, I'm going to be deeply pissed.

"I'm taking this class," I say slowly. Carefully. If he remembers . . .

"Then why is the schedule-changes page up on your laptop?"

Oh. It is. So maybe he's just as clueless about yesterday as everyone else.

"Fine." I tilt my laptop away from him. "Yes, I'm thinking of switching out. Physics . . . just isn't for me."

"I see," he says, and it's impressive, the amount of condescension he slips into those two words. "Not everyone can handle it, I guess."

"Oh, I can handle it." I turn, pinning him with a glare. "I simply choose to expend my energies elsewhere."

And even though I know there won't be any evidence of what happened last night, I scrutinize his face as sneakily as possible, which, as it turns out, is not very possible at all. But nope: there's no puffiness, no redness. No indication that a potential time traveler pepper-sprayed him yesterday.

There's a faint scar beneath one eye, so barely there it could almost be the crease of his skin against a pillow overnight.

"Is there something on my face?" he asks, and it's only then that I realize I've essentially been gawking at him.

I shake my head. "No. Sorry."

When class starts, I feel a little like an asshole in the front row, given I'm not listening to anything the professor is saying, but then I remind myself this is my third time through. On day one, I paid attention.

After Dr. Okamoto discusses the syllabus, she asks if anyone has any questions. There's a shuffle behind me as Miles's hand flies up—because of course.

"Dr. Okamoto? This isn't a question, exactly, but I'm curious what you might say to someone trying to switch out of this class. How you might convince them to stay."

An odd smile crosses her face. "Are you planning to switch out, Miles?" There she is, already knowing his name. I should have asked him about that last night.

He lets out a soft laugh. "No," he says, "but she is."

What. The fuck.

Even with my back to him, I can tell he's pointing at me, gesturing at me—whatever he's doing, he's incriminated me. The lecture hall goes silent, and my face burns with the heat of several hundred strangers' stares.

I should have known I'd regret sitting in the front row.

To my shock, Dr. Okamoto seems to take Miles's question seriously. She steps away from the podium, leaving her clicker behind. She pauses a few feet in front of me, her dark eyes filled with an intensity I'm not sure I've seen on a teacher's face before.

"What's your name?" she asks calmly.

"Barrett."

"Are you a freshman, Barrett?"

I nod. If she starts quizzing me about the reading, I'll make a run for it. Two extra days, and I haven't done the reading, because nothing could feel more insignificant than those few chapters right now.

"Tell me. Do you already know what you want to study?"

"Journalism," I say, unsure if her question is rhetorical.

"I see. If you'd like to leave my class because you're not interested in physics, or because you think it'll be too difficult, by all means, go ahead. And that goes for all of you." She keeps pacing the front of the room. "Maybe I can't convince you to love physics," she continues. "Maybe you've already convinced yourself you're not a STEM person, or that you're right-brained. And to that I say, bullshit."

A couple scattered laughs as the shock of *oh my god, the teacher just swore* makes its way around the room.

"Anyone can learn this. Sure, it might be hard. It *will* be hard. But telling yourself it's not for you is the quickest way to fail. You seal your fate if you begin something, *anything*, with that mindset. Most of you are freshmen, and for many of you, this is your first real taste of independence. To me, college is about new perspectives, seeking out the things that make us uncomfortable and test us and reveal who we really are. It's a privilege, this job—one I've never taken for granted. It's a privilege to have all of you in these seats, telling me you're up for the challenge."

I'm no longer sure whether I'm terrified of her. When Dr. Okamoto speaks like this, I believe her. And that means I might have to believe in physics, too.

When she dismisses us, I pack up as quickly as I can, waiting just outside the door until I spot the red blur of Miles's shirt.

And then I round on him. "What the fuck was that?" I hiss, falling in step next to him. "In what world is it okay to do that to a total stranger? I don't know what the hell kind of superiority complex you have, but that was completely uncalled for."

Miles blinks at me, looking almost a little dazed. He hitches his backpack higher on his shoulders, slowing his steps. "I'm sorry?"

"Is that a question?"

"No—it's not. I'm sorry." His fingers dig deeper into his backpack straps. "Period. Exclamation point, even!"

Students rush past us, hurrying out of the building and to their next classes.

"Somehow, I get the feeling you're not an exclamation-point kind of person."

"Depends on what I'm exclaiming over," he says with a sliver of a smirk.

This boy is impossible. If he were anyone else, the sentence might sound flirtatious, but I'm positive there's nothing further from the truth.

"You ratted me out to the professor in there, and then the way you—" I have to hold my tongue, reminding myself I can't get upset for things he did yesterday or the day before.

The day before—when we ran into each other on the way to the Zeta Kappa party and it took a moment for him to remember what he'd said in class.

Just like what happened now.

"The way I what?"

I shake my head. "Nothing. This is the first time we've met, right? Why would there be anything else?"

I expect this to confuse him. In a normal world, I imagine it's not the kind of thing you can say to someone without getting at least a raised eyebrow.

Instead, he looks almost . . . stricken. Eyebrows pulled together, a strange kind of uncertainty in his eyes. The light pouring in from the bank of windows catches his scar, and I hope he doesn't think I'm staring at it.

"You're right, that was uncalled for," he says. "I was an asshole. I'm sorry."

Now it's my turn to be taken aback by the apology. "Oh . . . okay? I get that you're a teacher's pet—I mean, the professor knows your name? On the first day of class?"

The smallest quirk of his mouth. A nano-quirk. Every one of his expressions is a study in subtlety. "Dr. Okamoto is my mother."

Oh.

"I had no idea."

"It's not something I plan to advertise."

The corridor has cleared out now. Miles leans against the wall, next to a sepia portrait of the first head of the physics department. An old man with a wiry mustache.

There's something so disarmingly casual about Miles's stance, I can't put my finger on it. He even seems to soften, shoulders becoming more relaxed, posture less stiff. Maybe because he's all sharp edges at first, it's impossible not to notice the way he retracts those claws.

He toes a dimple in the floor with one forest-green Adidas. "Do you think we could maybe meet up later? Somewhere quieter." When I open my mouth to protest, he holds up a hand. "I just want to talk. And not about physics."

ʊʊʊ

The Dawg House is UW's student-union building, twin bronze husky statues guarding its entrance. A massive purple-and-white banner draped across the front declares WELCOME, STUDENTS! Clubs are tabling on the lawn, and inside, there are a number of restaurants, cafés, and student-activity offices. There's even a bowling alley in the basement, which I believe is legally required to be mentioned on campus tours.

I pull out my phone to text Miles, realizing too late that we didn't exchange numbers. We agreed to meet at two thirty—apologies to the hot TA in my English class—and it's two forty-five when I finally find him, sitting in a booth near a burger place, a basket of mozzarella sticks in front of him.

I give him a small wave as I take a seat across from him, dropping my bag next to me. For the past few hours, I've been holed up in a lounge on the Dawg House's top floor, quietly panicking, trying to plan out my next steps. If Miles were less of an annoyance and more of a dreamboat, maybe I'd regret my hair-and-outfit situation, but I can't quite bring myself to care about that right now.

"Have you had the mozzarella sticks here?" he asks. "They're incredible."

"I'm good." I let out a shaky breath that does nothing to alleviate my anxiety. "So. Do you want to explain to me what the hell is going on and why you wanted to meet? Because I'm guessing it's not to make sure I experienced the joy of student-union-building fried food."

"You tell me," he says calmly, dipping a mozzarella stick in marinara sauce. "What, exactly, the hell is going on with you?"

He can't really be asking what I think he's asking. There's no way.

"Nothing," I say. "I'm just peachy. I might even dress up like Kermit the Frog later and run around campus singing 'Walking on Sunshine' and throwing glitter at people, haven't decided yet."

Ever so slightly, a muscle in his jaw twitches. "So you're having a good first day, then?"

I heave a sigh, dragging a hand through my hair. "Fine, Miles. It's been a shitty day so far. Happy? You're part of the reason for that, but ultimately, I think I can only blame myself."

"Can you elaborate on that?"

"If you asked me here just to interrogate me, then I should really get started on that Kermit thing—"

"No," he says quickly. "I'm sorry. I just . . . really want to hear about your day. Your first day."

The emphasis he places on *first* is subtle, but I catch it.

I swallow hard, examining the odd but annoyingly compelling person across from me. When our eyes meet, he doesn't blink, just holds my gaze with a steady intensity. All the hints are there. The way he's acted unfazed by my strange statements. *If you decide to stay in physics.* The fact that he's sitting here right now.

He's done nothing to indicate I can trust him, except maybe asking these questions. If he's messing with me, he's doing a hell of a job.

"I woke up at six fifty to the sound of my roommate begging our RA for a room change," I start, almost wishing I'd taken a mozzarella stick to keep my hands busy. "I went to the ninth-floor bathroom but didn't shower. Went to physics, during which you kindly informed your professor-mom I was planning to switch out. Then you asked me to meet you here and tried to force your mozzarella sticks on me."

"And before that?"

"Before I met you here, or . . ."

He leans back in the booth, bending an elbow and propping one hand behind his head. "Dealer's choice."

It's ridiculous, how close I am to telling him, this near stranger—and yet the thrill of it is a decadent, addictive thing. I can't shake the feeling that he already knows what's going on and he's trying to get me to admit it first. Worst-case scenario, he laughs me out of the Dawg House and I spend the next four years avoiding him. Best case . . .

"On my first day . . ." I lower my voice, worried people will overhear us. Pushing each word past my lips feels like spilling a secret I've been sworn never to tell. And god, I can't keep it inside anymore. If there's the smallest chance I'm not the only one with a glitchy timeline, I have to go for it. "I fell asleep in the common room on my floor, and I woke up back in my room. On September twenty-first."

As soon as I've said it, I start questioning myself. He's going to think I'm losing my mind. I watch his face carefully, but there's no indication he finds this even remotely unusual.

"That's it?" he asks. "Just those two times?"

Just those two times, as though repeating a day once is completely normal.

"Today's my third time. Hence my outfit choice." I cross my legs, aware of the unfortunately placed hole in these leggings.

Something odd starts happening to his face then. He wrenches his mouth to one side, as though he's trying not to react, before he gives up, allowing the muscles in his face to take control. Somehow, I get the feeling Miles is often waging war against them. It's a slow surrender, his lips curving into what might be the sunniest smile I've seen from him so far.

"I thought I was the only one," he says. "I've been stuck here for months."

Chapter 9

I STARE AT HIM, THE WORDS SLOW TO SINK IN.

I've been stuck here for months.

"Sixty-one days, to be exact," Miles is saying. "I haven't found an ideal way of keeping track yet. I figure I'll lose count at some point, but"—he taps his head—"this old thing is proving to be even more remarkable than I thought. I've always had a photographic memory, which has really come in handy while I've been trapped in this . . . anomaly."

Anomaly. The word isn't nearly complex enough for the reality.

"You're repeating this day too." I'm too stunned to linger on the brag about his photographic memory. "It's not—it's not just me."

The relief feels like a sun break after weeks of Seattle gloom. A gulp of water after running a sixteen-minute mile. Because if Miles is here too—even if I like him about as much as the student body of Island High School liked me—then maybe that means there's hope.

Maybe I'm not alone in this.

"I had a hunch yesterday," he continues, "when you were already in class before I got there. But I didn't want to leap to a conclusion before I was certain." How very scientific-method of him. "This is—this is incredible." At that, his eyes light up, and for the very first time, he looks genuinely excited, gesturing wildly with his hands. "You know what this means? Parallel universes, split timelines, relativity—there are endless explanations. Endless possibilities."

"Incredible," I repeat, voice flat, as my head keeps spinning. "Probably not the word I'd use."

"Watch out for the ketchup," he says.

"What?" Over his shoulder, one of the café employees narrowly avoids slipping on a reddish puddle on the floor. "You could have at least wiped that up for her," I mutter.

He levels me with a matter-of-fact glare. "I have. About thirty times."

A chill skates down my spine. "Maybe—maybe you saw that before you sat down. How do I know this isn't some huge prank?"

Part of me doesn't want to believe him just yet. The relief has morphed, or it's clinging to the residual fear. The rational part of my brain can't accept it, even though I've been living it for the past ~~one two~~ three days.

"You want me to prove it? That's fair. It's what any good scientist would do, repeating the results of an experiment. Making sure they can replicate it." He nods toward his left. "Do you see that girl throwing away her trash? She's going to drop her empty cup and let out a sigh like the world has committed some terrible crime against her, before kneeling to pick it up."

We watch as precisely this happens.

I lift my eyebrows at him, unimpressed. "Is that the best you can do? Anyone could have guessed she was carrying too much."

"You're a tough audience. Okay. That guy over there, next to the soda fountain?" He glances down at his smart watch. Taps it. "It's going to explode all over him in about ten seconds."

And it does, thoroughly soaking him with brown-orange liquid. A couple of café employees rush over with napkins.

"No," I tell him, despite all the evidence to the contrary that's piling up. "*No.* This isn't happening. This *cannot* be happening. I'm going to wake up tomorrow, and it'll be Thursday, and everything will be fine."

"You're probably right," he says, settling back into the booth, amusement still flickering in his eyes. "I must be a figment of your imagination."

"Even my imagination wouldn't be that cruel."

"You really should try one of these." He keeps dunking mozzarella sticks in marinara, oblivious to my panic. "They're crisp but not burnt, and the cheese is so perfectly gooey, it melts in your mouth. I keep trying to pace myself, but I think I've eaten them at least every other day since I've been—"

"I don't want a fucking mozzarella stick!" I say, and it's only when heads whip in our direction that I realize I've nearly shouted it. I'm breathing hard, my chest rising and falling with the effort of trying to convince Miles . . . what, exactly? That we're not the only two people on campus trapped on September 21? That the strings holding my reality together haven't been completely and irrevocably severed?

Miles pushes away the basket, the force of it causing a river of marinara to spill down the side of the compostable sauce cup. "Okay," he says, more seriously now, aware he needs to keep me from losing my shit in the middle of the Dawg House. His eyes meet mine, dark and resolute, and maybe I was wrong. Maybe there's a trace of panic in there too. "Okay. Let's back up and try this again. I get it—I was angry at first too."

"And now you've, what? Accepted it? Because you're acting pretty goddamn nonchalant."

"I've cycled through just about every other emotion, Barrett. I'm not sure what else is left."

I try to ignore the eeriness that hangs on his words. There's something hollow in his voice, a weariness that could only come with having been stuck here a very long time. My three days, multiplied by twenty.

The third and final class on my schedule to bring my credit count up to fifteen, an intro psych course, meets Tuesdays and Thursdays. It must be a sign I'm losing it that it crosses my mind at this moment. I don't have an attachment to the class aside from the fact that it sounded interesting, but now there's a real possibility I may not even get to take it.

"You lied," I say. "You said we weren't going to talk about physics. I feel betrayed."

As though sensing I'm on the brink of emotional collapse, Miles slides the basket across the table toward me. Reluctantly, I take a mozzarella stick, drag it through the marinara . . . and, ugh, he was right. They're heavenly. The cheesy, saucy goodness drops me from an eleven to a ten-point-five.

"What did you do?" I say between bites.

"Do?"

"You're the one with a raging hard-on for physics. You just said you've been here longer than I have. So what'd you do, upset the ghost of Albert Einstein? Piss on Isaac Newton's grave?" I trail off, out of recognizable physicists. It's possible Dr. Okamoto's class would be really good for me.

He's just staring at me, mouth slightly open. "I'm not even sure where to start," he says. "The notion that ghosts are real? That you think I'm capable of understanding the intricacies of time travel, something that has eluded scientists for hundreds of years? That I just happened to be in Westminster Abbey, somewhere I've always dreamed of going, and would desecrate the burial place of Sir Isaac Newton like that?" He chokes out something that might, in some alien languages, be considered a laugh. "Or the completely inappropriate sexualization of a branch of science that has been at the forefront of—of *everything* for hundreds of years."

"I bet you're fun at parties."

"You tell me, seeing as we've attended the same one."

I fist a hand in my curls. "I can't even have a normal conversation with you! At least not one that doesn't make me want to pepper-spray my own face. How are we supposed to figure out what's going on?" I pause. "Oh my god. When I asked if you'd been pepper-sprayed before and you were weird about it. Was that—did I pepper-spray you? When you were reliving this day before I got stuck?"

As if on instinct, he reaches a hand toward his eyes, his thumb grazing his scar. "You did. Four times."

"Ahhhh. I'm sorry," I say, ignoring how thoroughly bizarre it feels to be apologizing for something another Barrett did. "Wait. You and I haven't had this conversation before, have we?"

"No. This is the first time I've found out anyone was stuck with me. I had an inkling yesterday that something was off. You did something different—you sat in the first row, and you got there before I did. That had never happened before."

I shake my head, as though that'll somehow make all these absurd pieces fit together. "I'm not sure I understand some of the finer details. How is it possible that I experienced three days during the same time that you experienced sixty?"

Miles leans forward, one side of his mouth attempting a smile. I wonder how many smiles this boy has to fight on a daily basis. "Are you familiar with the concept of relativity?" He says it as simply as if he's asking whether I'm familiar with the concept of toast. I give him my guiltiest grimace. "Let's say you're somewhere out there, traveling in a spaceship at a fairly brisk speed."

"A typical Saturday for me."

"You pass a friend in an identical spaceship going much slower. Your friend's watch would be operating slower than yours," he says. "In the simplest of terms, that's special relativity. General relativity posits that massive objects warp both time and space around them, and that warping is gravity. Again, in the simplest of terms. And because it can bend both space and time—space-time, an integral piece of Einstein's theory—you could be on top of Mount Everest with a watch moving faster than someone standing at the bottom.

"The first time I went through September twenty-first, you and I barely interacted," he continues. "You sat next to me in physics and asked for the Wi-Fi password that was very clearly written on the board." I fight rolling my eyes at this. "But that was it. I didn't know about the fire at the frat until I heard people talking about it in the dorm that night, and it took me a few more repeats to connect it to you."

"You mean you weren't originally invited to the party?" I splay my hands on the table between us and school my face into a serious expression. "Does the president of Zeta Kappa know about this? No—maybe we should take it up with the president of the university? I want to make sure this doesn't happen again."

Shocker: Miles is unamused. "You know, you'd probably grasp this quicker if you stopped making jokes about it."

"My first day wasn't the same as yours, then," I say. "On mine, you called me out in front of the whole class. And we wound up walking to the party together when you were creeping in the bushes."

"I was not *creeping*. It's a shortcut through campus." He squints, as if trying to pull something from his memory. "That must have been . . . day fifty-nine for me. What I think is happening is that when I got stuck, my time started operating at a higher frequency than yours. That means I was experiencing more days in the same period of time that you—and everyone else—were experiencing far fewer."

"Okay . . ." I have never felt less intelligent than I do in this moment. Stalling for time, pretending I'm taking in everything he said, I hook a finger around one arm of my glasses and spin them around a few times. "So when I told you I took AP Physics, I kind of got a two on the test. I'm still not sure I understand how we had two completely different Wednesdays before getting stuck."

I expect him to grow frustrated with me, but instead he reaches for a mozzarella stick, ripping it in half, and placing the two ends next to each other. "Picture it like this. For eighteen years, our timelines have, to the best of our knowledge, moved along at the same speed. Until my first Wednesday." At that, he splits one of the halves into two. "This is the version of you I met on that day, while this other version of you—that is to say, the version sitting next to me right now—was moving so slowly that it took her a while to catch up to that day." He keeps tearing off hunks of mozzarella, representing all these Barretts I've been and never will be. "When your time caught up to mine, I had already experienced fifty-eight versions of that day."

Oh god. This is too much. "And what if one of us suddenly starts moving at a regular speed again?"

"Then we'd need more mozzarella sticks." He gestures to the not-Barrett Barrett sticks. "We can assume that everyone who isn't stuck—like all these versions of you before you did get stuck—is moving at a much slower frequency than either of us. Now that we've caught up to each other, I think it's safe to say our time is moving at a similar rate."

"So there are all these different versions of me out there, continuing on their own timelines after their version of September twenty-first?"

"If you believe in parallel universes, then yes. Potentially," he says, "but again, this is just a theory. I can't answer that with any amount of certainty."

"That would be a first." Still, I'm grateful for the explanation.

I'm light-headed and untethered and a little queasy, but grateful nonetheless.

"I've been trying to figure out why you've acted differently over the past few days," Miles says. "Usually, you keep to yourself. Unless . . ."

"Unless what?"

He turns sheepish. "Unless we interact."

"So you're the one who dragged me into this," I say, the gratitude vanishing. "Your timeline got all screwy, and you passed it along to me."

"That's—that's not how this works." Miles huffs out a breath, pinching the bridge of his nose. Like he's offended on behalf of physics.

"You just admitted you don't know how it works!"

"Not *entirely* how it works," he corrects in this pompous voice that makes me want to dunk his face into the dish of marinara. "Time isn't the common cold. I didn't sneeze on you and create a parallel universe."

"But if your timeline was fucked, and then you interacted with me and made me do something different . . . could that have messed with space-time, or whatever?"

His expression shifts, like he knows I've made a good point but would sooner switch his major to fingerpainting than admit it. "I suppose that's not impossible," he relents.

"Take that, AP Physics." I hold up a victorious fist. Then something dawns on me. "The friend you were looking for at the party. That was me." He nods. "And that's why you sat behind me." I steal another mozzarella stick. "You act all spacey sometimes. Like on my first day. You called me out in class, and then you forgot about it."

"When you're stuck here for sixty-one days, things get a little . . . blurred together." But he frowns, his eyebrows pulling together again, and I get the feeling there's something he wants to say but isn't going to.

"Neither of us is alone now, I guess," I say. "That's something."

Before Miles can assure me that yes, of course he's thrilled to be stuck with me, his phone rings.

"Do you have to get that?"

Without looking at it, he rejects the call and flips his phone facedown on the table.

Guess he already knows what they have to say.

While Miles stares down at his hands, I make a play for the last mozzarella stick. He doesn't seem to care that I'm taking it. That kind of thing probably feels insignificant to him at this point. "So we're the only two people—that we know of—trapped on September twenty-first," I say. "And yet we barely know each other, Miles Okamoto."

"Kasher-Okamoto," he says, blinking as if to refocus on me. As if he's been lost in thought, and this is only now bringing him back to earth, back to this booth. "My dad is Nathan Kasher. He teaches Jewish history, and he's always saying he's heartbroken I picked my mom's field instead of his. It's an ongoing joke between my parents—a friendly competition that my mom is winning." He holds up a hand, puts down two fingers. "There. Now you know at least three things about me."

"Jewish history." I feel like a complete idiot for not even knowing that was something we had at UW. "Are you Jewish?"

"My dad is. I was raised Jewish, so you can try to tell me I'm only half, or that I'm not *really* Jewish, since it's matrilineal, but—"

"I wasn't going to."

"Oh."

"Have people done that?"

"My whole life," he says quietly, and I'm surprised by the way this tugs at my heart.

"So you're Jewish, then," I say, and at the simple fact of the statement, he relaxes. Nods. "I am too. There's probably a joke somewhere in here about both of us being Chosen." This earns me only a soft *ha*.

On the one hand, it's a relief not to be alone in this. On the other hand . . . it's Miles. I can't recall ever having been this infuriated by someone in the course of a single conversation. He's seemingly immune to humor, so rigid his spine is probably made of Kevlar. I'd have gladly taken Annabel or Gopher Girl or Grant of the Spectacular Eyelashes. Even Lucie and I would have made a better team. It's just my luck that the guy I'm trapped with turns out to be an impossible human to get along with.

"We should at least trade numbers," he says. "In case we get separated."

"I guess there's no point putting it in my phone," I say.

"Probably best if we memorize them."

"Right." I tug on the strings of my sweatshirt, thinking. "Maybe this isn't based in real science. I've seen this plot in movies before. Maybe someone or some*thing* out there decided we didn't do today right the first time through. We weren't ready to move on to the next day without accomplishing . . . something. And now we're supposed to do good deeds, or selfless acts, or find true love, and that's what'll get us back to normal."

"Who are you going to find true love with in a single day?"

I bat my lashes at him in the most exaggerated way I can. "Looks like I've got just one option, buttercup."

At this, Miles does something I was not at all expecting.

He *blushes*.

And not just the tips of his ears—his *whole ears*, and the way they're sticking out makes it impossible not to notice. A muscle in his jaw pulses, only this time I am certain he's not fighting back a smile. Miles Kasher-Okamoto, ladies and gentlemen, allowing himself to experience an emotion.

Then he clears his throat, soldiering on. "I've been going to the library on most days, reading as much as I can about time-travel theories, relativity, quantum mechanics. We could probably make a lot of progress if we work together."

I gape at him. The idea of spending hours upon hours in the library with Miles, poring over books that make no sense to me . . . I'd rather eat Cheerios off the floor of the communal bathroom. "You're repeating the day over and over, and you're spending it *in the library*?"

At that, Miles finally snaps. "I don't know what the fuck else to do!" he says as he springs to his feet, and now it's his turn to be shocked by the volume of his voice. Except he doesn't collect himself, he just takes these sharp, jagged inhales, his cheeks pink. He's been calm up until now, but evidently, I've pushed him too far.

"You're the one who seems intent on challenging everything I say, despite having no scientific background whatsoever."

"I'm just as clueless as you are." I get to my feet, trying my best to keep my voice level. "And I'm sure it's really hard to admit that you're clueless, but it's the fucking truth. Neither of us knows shit about time travel because up until three days ago for me and sixty-one for you, neither of us knew it actually existed."

"So you're going to go out there and find your soul mate?"

"Maybe!" I hoist myself onto the booth, the vinyl springy beneath my feet. I throw my arms wide, beckoning to the dining area around us. "Hey! If anyone here thinks they might be my one true love, I'm in Olmsted 908."

A few people give us strange looks, while most go back to their food. It's a rush, yelling like this without consequences. "Anyone?" I say.

"*Stop,*" Miles says, jaw clenched. "This isn't accomplishing anything."

I glare down at him. "Why? No one's going to remember this tomorrow." I turn back to the Dawg House. "I'm pretty low-maintenance. No fancy dates or anything, but I *will* get upset if you ever forget our anniversary." I spin around, assessing the clusters of tables. A couple people have their phones out, but most aren't paying attention to me anymore. "No takers? Really? It's okay, I can be shy too."

Miles drops back into the booth primly, posture straight, not meeting my eyes. "When you're ready to take this seriously," he says, "you know where to find me."

"Enjoy the library," I snap back, landing on the booth with a resounding thump. We're sure as shit not finding any answers in a half-century-old textbook.

He thought I was an ally. A confidant. A partner in crime.

He couldn't have known that Barrett Bloom has always worked alone.

Chapter 10

I DON'T WANT IT TO SEEM LIKE I WENT RUNNING home to my mom when things got hard, but here I am. In Mercer Island. With my mom.

"Already homesick?" she says when I show up at Ink & Paper. Then she frowns, stepping out from behind the cash register so she can get a better look at me. "Barrett. My darling of darlings. Treasure of treasures. Please don't tell me this is what you wore on your first day of school?"

After waiting for the bus in the rain, I can only imagine what I look like. The waistband of my leggings has migrated down to my hips, so I reach down and yank them up. I think the hole in the crotch is getting bigger. It'll be a small miracle if I make it through the rest of the day without flashing anyone my underwear patterned with dancing doughnuts.

The rest of the day. Nope, can't think that far ahead. Because on the other side of *the rest of the day* is a fucking black hole.

"Absolutely not," I tell her, and it isn't technically a lie. "I changed after my last class." I pass a display of velvet-covered bullet journals we arranged over the summer. "Does a daughter need a reason to visit her beloved mother?"

She ropes me in for a hug, and I inhale the scent of the organic rose body butter she uses every day. "Is it pathetic to say that I miss you?" she says. "The house just isn't the same without your wisecracks."

When I try to laugh, the sound gets lodged in my throat. "See, I'm just looking out for you."

My mom releases me and rummages for something behind the counter. As expected, she's in jeans and a graphic tee with a pencil sketch of the Seattle skyline. We have the same shape, curves in places I used to think were supposed to be straight lines until I realized that was bullshit. I've always wanted to be as fearless about my body as she is, and even if I'm halfway there on most days, she's carried hers with confidence for longer than I have, and sometimes I wonder if I'll ever get there.

The major difference is our hair. Hers is dark blond and cut short, while I have my dad's side of the family to thank for my tight ringlets.

"Now that you're here . . . look what showed up yesterday." When she holds up a package of greeting cards, I don't even bother fighting back a squeal.

I know exactly what they are, only because we've been talking for the past few months about the new Seattle company that made them, using only found materials and two gorgeous vintage letter-presses we toured over the summer.

"They're even more perfect in person," I say, reaching out to stroke one. GREETINGS FROM THE PACIFIC NORTHWEST, the card says, in a perfect blue font swirled with raindrops that dip when I run my thumb along them. "I'll take twenty."

My mom tidies up the shop, getting ready to close for the evening, while I hop onto the counter after she insists she doesn't need my help. It's not quite as seamless a hop as it was when I was younger, sitting up here and sorting inventory for her.

The shop has been a downtown Mercer Island staple for the past nine years, almost as long as the Blooms. My mom grew up in Seattle and lived with her parents until she graduated college with a business degree, then moved the two of us into a microscopic studio apartment. Mercer Island had been touted as this idyllic Pacific Northwest suburb, the perfect place to raise a family. Plus, there was more space than she had in the city. She found the storefront and an apartment to rent in a single weekend, which she said felt like fate, and her sharp eye and incredible taste made Ink & Paper an almost-instant success.

But Mercer Island was also a place where the line between haves and have-nots was especially stark. By the time we moved into a house, my classmates were remodeling and upgrading and excavating their backyards to add swimming pools.

My mom switches off the lights and locks the doors, and I follow her out to the car. "How do twice-baked potatoes sound?"

"Like cheesy, carby perfection."

A pause, and then: "You okay if Jocelyn comes over for dinner tonight too?"

"Why wouldn't I be? She practically lives there anyway."

"True. But even so . . . it's quieter without you there. I didn't may or may not be wrong with me and/or the universe. We busy ourselves in the kitchen, grating cheddar and scooping the innards out of potatoes until Jocelyn shows up.

And it's only when I hear her voice that I remember.

Jocelyn is planning to propose to my mom tomorrow night.

In all the chaos of the past ~~three~~ days, I completely forgot. A few weeks ago, she volunteered to take me shopping for some last-minute dorm essentials. After we filled the trunk of her Kia Soul with notepads and staplers and silverware, we stopped for tacos and she showed me her grandmother's ring, a shimmering emerald. Jocelyn is a lawyer, and I'd never heard her voice shake as much as it did when she talked to me about the proposal. She wasn't asking for my permission—nothing as archaic as that—but she wanted to take my temperature on it first. "My temperature is off the charts," I told her emphatically. "I have a fever, and the only prescription is you proposing to Mollie Bloom."

"Mollie?" Jocelyn calls from the hall, deep-red lips curving into a grin when she spots me. "Double Bloom! I thought we wouldn't see you until Thanksgiving."

My stomach lurches. I want to be happy to see her, this shred of familiar normalcy that I've missed over the past few days. I want that feeling from the drive home: sun on my face and a sense that everything might be okay.

When, in reality, I am stuck in the day right before what might be one of the happiest moments of my mom's life.

"Wishful thinking?" I ask, clinging to the hope that sleeping here, or perhaps not sleeping at all, will jump-start my timeline.

After she kisses my mom hello, Jocelyn lassos me for a hug.

expect that." Her expression changes. Turning wistful, maybe. "I thought I was prepared to be an empty nester, which still sounds like something I'm nowhere near old enough to be. I know it's only the first week, and it'll get easier—for both of us."

"It will," I say, hoping I sound more reassuring than I feel.

Now that I'm off campus, I can breathe a bit easier. The air out here is less stifling, almost letting me believe it's no longer September 21.

Maybe that's it—the university is cursed, and if I fall asleep here, I'll wake up where I'm supposed to be.

Unless . . . I can't wake up on Wednesday if I simply don't go to sleep.

I can't believe I didn't think of it sooner.

"So. Are you going to tell me what happened?" my mom asks as we pull into the garage.

"Who said something happened?"

"Barrett, I know you. Your tone is weird. And you're wearing mopey clothes, even if I have been wondering where that sweatshirt went."

"It's so soft and perfectly worn."

"Exactly. That's why it's my favorite."

"I really am fine," I tell her, pushing the words past my teeth. It's an effort, but I manage it. "It's just been . . . an adjustment."

Her dark eyes search my face for a long moment, as though trying to find evidence of something being wrong in the faint freckles across my cheeks or the bend of my chin. Then her phone lights up in the cup holder. "That'll be Jocelyn. She just got off work."

Fortunately, cooking is enough to distract my mom from wh

"Never." She hangs her coat on the back of a kitchen chair and runs a hand through her long dark hair.

Over the years, my mom has dated both men and women, and as far as I know, Jocelyn's her longest relationship. They met two years ago at her shop, when Jocelyn Thierry, a willowy brunette with a penchant for bright lipstick who terrified most of the other lawyers at her firm, lamented the difficulty of finding wedding cards for queer couples, and my mom proudly pointed her toward Ink & Paper's inclusive selection. She came back every weekend searching for a different kind of card, until she ran out of people to mail them to and bought one to send to my mom, asking her out.

The framed card hangs in our living room: a tiny hedgehog holding a bouquet of roses with Jocelyn's neat cursive inside.

It must be a side effect of growing up in a stationery shop that I'm so eager to see the cards flood in for my mom and Jocelyn. Aside from me, she's been the steadiest person in my mom's life. Even though we had help from my mom's parents, they weren't wealthy. She built her store from the ground up, rarely taking a day off, and she hadn't left the West Coast before she met Jocelyn. She'd been wholly focused on the store and on me, anxious to give herself permission to even get out of King County. Jocelyn's adventurous streak and love for travel have made my mom lighter, more fully *herself,* someone capable of taking vacations and hiring another employee to watch the shop while she's gone. She's never been happier than when she's with Joss—except for when she's with me, but it's a different kind of happiness. And especially now that I'm in college, I hate the idea of her spending nights and weekends with only Netflix for company.

Whether their timelines are slowed down like Miles said or they're simply suspended in space somewhere—I have to get out. For all of us.

Jocelyn leans against the opposite counter, munching on a handful of cheddar cheese. Her blunt bangs skim the tops of her eyebrows, a look I'd never be able to pull off. "So, did your elusive roommate finally make an appearance?"

"Unfortunately." I line up the potatoes on a baking sheet. "Do you remember Lucie Lamont?"

"Editor in chief of the *Navigator*? Lucifer in tiny human form?" Jocelyn exaggerates a shudder. Lucie and I were already past-tense when she and my mom started dating. Then realization settles on her face. "No. She's your roommate?"

My mom looks up from the potatoes. "You didn't mention that."

Because it's been three days and the shock's worn off. "Yeah, uh, it was definitely a surprise at first. They had to do some last-minute reorganizing. But I think she's joining a sorority. So either I'll be roommateless again or I'll get someone new."

"My college roommate and I talk every weekend," Jocelyn says. "Carrie—you met her when she came to visit last year. I still remember when we flooded our sorority's second floor in the winter and it froze, because Minnesota. We turned it into an ice-skating rink, which was pretty epic until the floor caved in. Law school was a little more serious. But undergrad was a wild time. *God.* College. They really are the best four years of your life." She turns a smile on my mom. "*Except* for the year I met Mollie Bloom. And every day I've been fortunate enough to spend with her since then."

My mom opens the oven and slides the potatoes in. "I'm sure college was great for everyone who wasn't raising a screeching, vomiting infant," she says.

"I thought you always said I was a good baby."

"Sure, but you were still a baby."

"You must be confusing me with someone else. I'm pretty sure I was one of those babies who never pooped or spit up."

"Just keep believing that."

"Let us know who you end up with," Jocelyn says. "So we can plan to intimidate them into submission, if necessary."

My mom grabs a spatula, flicking blond hair out of her face as she brandishes it like a weapon. "We show no mercy. Not to anyone who double-crosses the Blooms."

Jocelyn follows suit, swiping up a wooden ladle and thwacking her palm with it. "No mercy. Not from the kitchen utensil gang," she says in this darkly evil voice that makes my mom break character, dissolving into laughter.

Please, I send out into the universe. *Please let me find out what happens. Please let Lucie rush a sorority. Please let me have September 22.*

☾☾☾

I used to take a lot of pride in my room. Oh, it's a complete mess, a hazard zone, but there's a hominess that I'm not sure I'd be able to replicate in a dorm. Far too many throw pillows, *Nav* articles pinned to the bulletin board, an arc of greeting cards clipped to a clothesline.

I am a stationery hoarder: I save them because I can't bear to part with them. Stickers and washi tape and cards and notebooks. I own at least a dozen floral journals, all of them blank. It's a side effect of my mother owning a stationery shop, but they're also very, very cute.

Then there's the HOW DO I LOVE THEE? cross-stich, the one my mom made when I was a baby, hanging above my bed. It's imperfect, stray threads scattered throughout, but I've always loved it. And yet tonight there's something about it that makes my heart ache.

For the past few months it's been painful, keeping prom from her. It was easy to say yes when Cole asked me. He'd sat beside me in AP US Government all year, and he seemed smart and kind and generally well liked. Then it was easy to say yes to the hotel room he reserved for us, and yes again when he asked if I was sure, after I told him I'd never done this before. Someone wanted me, and maybe it wasn't the way I'd imagined being wanted, but it was *happening.* Three years as an outcast, and the sudden attention was almost overwhelming.

Then came the flowers in my locker. The hashtag. The too-late revelation that Cole's brother had been on the tennis team. How stupid and powerless and *small* I felt when after four days of roses and tulips, I went to see the principal. "You're upset because someone put flowers in your locker?" he said with a laugh. "I know a lot of young ladies who'd love to be in your position."

Over the summer, I told my mom I'd had sex, but not what happened afterward. She said I could tell her everything or I could tell her nothing—whatever I was comfortable with.

And for maybe the first time in my life, I told her nothing.

Someone knocks on my door.

"I'm having emotions, seeing you in here like this," my mom says when she pushes it open. There's a wistful thread in her voice I can't remember hearing even when she dropped me off at UW.

"That screeching, vomiting baby is all grown up?"

She joins me on the bed, tucking a wayward curl behind my ear. As always, it doesn't obey. "Something like that."

I bring my legs up onto the bed, wincing when the crotch seam of my leggings rips a bit more. "Mom. If something were going on with me, you'd want to know, right?"

"I knew it!" she says. "I knew there was a reason you seemed off." Then her mouth falls open. "Barrett Lorraine Bloom, do not tell me you're pregnant."

I lay a hand on my stomach and flash her my biggest grin. "It's twins."

"You are going to send me to an early death."

"I am the light of your life!"

"Unfortunately."

"I'm not pregnant." A few deep breaths as I weigh what to say next. As disastrously as it ended, talking to Miles helped. Telling my mom would feel even better. In the sliver of a chance she believes me, maybe she'd know what to do. "I'm . . . a time traveler."

I haven't figured out the right words yet. Miles called it an anomaly, but *time anomaly* doesn't have the same ring to it. I can't help wondering what he's doing this evening, how many books he's buried his face in. If he's made any breakthroughs without me.

"Oh, that's it? We can deal with that," she says, matter of fact. "Where are you traveling from? Did you come from the future to tell us we're in grave danger? A meteor is about to hit Earth? No, wait, I don't want to know."

"Mom, I'm being serious."

"So am I. I really don't want to know."

I could riff off her joke, a rhythm the two of us know well. And yet the truth comes tumbling out, desperate for her to hear it. "I—I've kind of lived this day before. Well, not this *exact* day—I haven't seen you today yet. But, okay, so I had this really terrible first day. First *first* day." I run through what happened, ending with Zeta Kappa, aware I sound like I'm explaining the plot of a movie and not something I actually experienced. "And I may have . . . set a frat house on fire."

My mom springs to her feet, no longer playing along. "You *what?*"

I hold up my hands, urging her to sit back down. "No, no. It didn't actually happen. Or it did, but in another timeline? I'm not exactly clear on how all of it works. Because when I woke up back in my room, it was September twenty-first again. And then it happened this morning too."

Eighteen years, and I've finally found a way to render Mollie Bloom speechless. Some part of me thought that instinctually, as a result of us sharing a body for nine months and then the same small space for nearly two decades, she'd know this is real.

Instead, after a few silent, agonizing seconds, recognition crosses her face and she lets out a laugh. "Is this for your psych class? Some kind of experiment?"

I don't have psych until tomorrow, I want to say.

Instead I give in, forcing a smile onto my face while a strange, lonely sadness grips me. "You got me. Psych experiment."

"Well, you know you're welcome here anytime," my mom says. "Even if you're going to try to break my brain."

"Right. Thank you." I drag my fingertips along the paisley bed-spread, trying to sound casual, as though I am not at all concerned about getting my timeline moving at the right frequency again. "Is it okay if I sleep here tonight?"

"On one condition."

"Hmm?"

She pats my knee. "I say this with all the kindness in the world: you have to throw away those leggings."

DAY FOUR

||||

Chapter 11

WHEN I WAKE UP BACK IN OLMSTED WITH LUCIE and Paige and my illicit pasta bowls, I have to fight the urge to hurl one of them against the wall.

After my mom and Jocelyn went to bed, I crept downstairs to the fridge and plucked out a few cans of the oat-milk lattes my mom's obsessed with. I downed them all, then alternated between peeing, reading a profile of an ex-con who opened a gluten-free bakery, and wondering what was happening back at UW without me. If Zeta Kappa was still standing. If Miles went to the party alone.

Every time I felt myself getting drowsy, I'd pinch my arm or splash my face with cold water or turn up the music in my headphones. I made it to at least two in the morning, but I must have nodded off at some point after that. Because here I am, no closer to a solution.

If I can't make it to September 22—or the part of September 22 on the other side of those early morning hours—then Jocelyn won't propose to my mom. The thought fills me with a raw determination, sparking through my veins and turning me electric.

What I tried last night may not have worked, but I tried *something*. And today I'll try something else.

I keep my eyes squeezed shut, my breaths even, while Lucie complains to Paige about me. Once they're gone, I set my plan in motion: I am going to be the best fucking person this campus has ever seen. Proving to Miles that we can't library our way out of this will be an added bonus.

I give my phone's AI another chance. "How do I become a good person?"

"I found something that might help. Here is a list of Nobel Peace Prize winners—"

Exiting out of the search, I type *how to be a good person* into Google, because that seems like a solid, if not extremely obvious, way to start. The first result is a simple fifteen-step plan with gems like *compliment yourself every day* and *find a role model* and *listen*. I need something instant. Something I can accomplish in a single day.

I head down the hall and knock on Paige's door. *Meet your sweet new RA,* says the poster next to her room, designed to look like a gumball machine. Inside construction-paper gumballs are fun facts about her. *I'm from Milwaukee! I'm an art history / Italian language double major. I'm allergic to celery!*

"Oh—hi," she says when she opens it, chewing quickly and then swallowing. I've interrupted her breakfast. "Barrett?"

Point for Paige. I flash her a smile. "I was wondering if I could get your help. I was thinking about collecting some clothing donations for a local shelter?"

Paige is quiet for a moment. "On your own? You know, there

are a lot of service-focused clubs you can get involved with. I know there's one that meets in the third-floor lounge every Thursday."

"I was sort of hoping to do something today."

"On the first day of classes?"

"Light schedule."

"Hmm." Paige goes silent again, twisting a hand through her short dark hair, as though weighing the kindest way to express her disapproval. "I'm not sure if that's the best course of action this early in the quarter. Everyone just moved in, and people probably aren't thinking about what they want to give away. Plus"—she gestures to a formidable book tower on her desk—"a lot of them are going to be distracted by classes."

My shoulders slump. She has a point.

That new resolve fizzles just slightly.

"But as far as other service activities," she continues, "I donate blood every other quarter down at UWMC."

"That's perfect!" My mom does it regularly, and I've always considered her a Good Person. I don't love needles, but as long as I don't look, I should be okay. "Thank you so much!"

And if there isn't a spring in my step as I make my way out of Candy Land.

It's a ten-minute bus ride to the medical center on the other side of campus, near the freeway. Miles is probably in physics, wondering where I am. Surely, he'd discard my plan for not being scientific enough.

Some of my pep fades as I'm filling out paperwork, a hollow pang settling in my stomach. It might have been wise to eat something first.

"Barrett?" a man in magenta scrubs calls, and it's too late. Good person now, food later. I follow him into a curtained-off room, taking a seat beneath a painting of sailboats. "Just a little poke."

A little poke. That's not very bad at all—it even sounds gentle.

Except then he uncaps a vial and *ohhhhh no*, I make the fatal mistake of looking at the needle.

My vision narrows to a pinprick, and the world goes dark.

ᘐᘐᘐ

"Is it Thursday?" I ask when my eyes flutter open, reaching for my glasses before realizing they're still on my face. I'm sprawled on an exam table in a different room, my head fuzzy and limbs still tingling.

Miles Kasher-Okamoto is in the seat across from me, long legs crossed at the ankles, holding out a glazed doughnut and looking as smug as ever. "Not going to work," he says. He's in his usual plaid flannel, and there's a dusting of powdered sugar across the left pocket.

Maybe I should have remained unconscious. "Did you follow me here?"

"I saw you leave the dorm when I was on my way to physics and wondered where you were going." He pauses, considering this. "So, yes. I guess I did. You fainted, by the way."

"Charming." Only because my blood sugar needs it and *not* because I'm grateful he brought me one, I snatch the doughnut and stuff it into my mouth.

"It was a valiant attempt." Miles notices the powdered sugar on his pocket and brushes it off with a casual sweep of his fingers. "Unfortunately, it was also a futile one."

"Maybe this time," I say, "but I'm going to figure this out." Part of me wonders, though—if I manage to escape on my own, what happens to him? Do I start the next day with a different version of him? Or what if he finds something in one of his books and leaves *me* behind? It's hurting my brain too much, so I take another bite of doughnut, hating how good it is. "This is just a minor setback."

His mouth curls into a smirk that'll haunt my nightmares, assuming I'm lucky enough to have any tonight. "I suppose I could use a bit of entertainment."

DAY FIVE

||||

Chapter 12

"SAVE THE GOPHERS!" I SHOUT, WAVING A SIGN emblazoned with those words in bright purple. "Their home is disappearing, and we're running out of time to stop it!"

If I'm being given a do-over, maybe I'm meant to fix something I did wrong on my first day. And, after racking my brain, I realized I'd blown off Gopher Girl not once but three times.

Would teaming up with Miles be the most logical thing here? Yes.

But a tiny part of me doesn't trust him just yet. I can't help thinking that the last time I was alone with a boy, it led to the worst days of my life. I've gotten used to being alone, even if I've wanted college to change all that.

Yesterday, I successfully donated blood later in the afternoon, but the good deed didn't kick-start my timeline. That's fine. It's also fine that I chugged two bottles of 5-Hour Energy last night, to no avail. I have plenty more ideas. I am optimism and determination and grit! I am Saving the Gophers!

"Did you know that the Mazama pocket gopher is crucial to

maintaining biodiversity?" I ask two people walking through Red Square. They quicken their pace and avert their eyes. "Each gopher can turn over several tons of soil per year. It's a crime that not enough people are paying attention!"

"You're doing amazing, Barrett," says Kendall, my esteemed gopher guide. It feels great to be good at something, even if I'm only good at it because I asked Kendall about a hundred questions this morning.

A few yards away, there's a flash of red flannel near an abstract sculpture. "Miles," I call out, dropping my sign. "I can see you over there."

He emerges from behind the sculpture and holds up his hands. Guilty. *He's still here.* I can't deny that it's a relief he hasn't escaped and left me behind.

"Do you really have to watch?" I ask as he makes his way to our table. He must be taking a break from his very important library research. "You're making me nervous."

"What, you think you won't successfully save the gophers otherwise? Therefore causing you to remain stuck in September twenty-first forever?" There's a slight tug at the corner of his mouth, but I think it would take an electromagnetic force to get him to smile.

"Maybe! I don't know the rules." I keep my voice low so Kendall doesn't overhear us.

"Cute shirt, by the way." He gestures to the Guillermo the Gopher tee I'm wearing, which matches Kendall's. "They're kind of like groundhogs, right?"

"That's actually a common misconception. They're much smaller, and they spend much less time aboveground." I pick my sign back up and hoist it high. "Equality for all creatures!"

Miles places a hand on the cheap card table that's been our base of operations. "Who's in charge here?"

"That would be me," Kendall says from the other side of the table, where she's been tidying a stack of flyers. Miles isn't short, but she has a good three inches on him, her brunette topknot giving her even more height. She reaches for a flyer. "Are you interested in joining us? We're staging a protest in Olympia next week."

"I prefer to let my bank account do the talking." He slides his phone from his pocket. "Do you guys have Venmo?"

I level him with a deadly glare. "You're not serious."

"You've convinced me. Especially this one right here," Miles says with a nod toward me. He may not have mastered smiling, but he has a hell of a smirk.

Kendall points to a URL on the flyer. "You can donate through our website. Every little bit helps."

"Then this ought to make a sizable dent." He swipes through his phone before tilting it toward me, and I watch as he hits submit.

On a ten-thousand-dollar donation.

"That's a very generous donation, *sir*," I say through gritted teeth.

Kendall stares down at the alert on her own phone, eyes going wide as she presses a hand to her chest. "That's—oh my god. Oh my *god*."

"Excuse us." I grab Miles's sleeve, hauling him away from our table and back over to the sculpture where he was spying on me. "What do you think you're doing?" I hiss. "You're ruining my good deed!"

"Look, some of us fight with our words, and some of us with

our time, but we all know that our wallets speak the loudest." He gives me a very serious look, every facial muscle schooled into submission. It must hurt, resisting emotion like that.

"I didn't realize you were so passionate about nearly endangered rodents." I release my grip on his shirt, hoping he can feel every bit of resentment in my eyes. "You're unhinged."

"Maybe." He props an elbow against the sculpture, perfectly calm and frustratingly self-assured. It takes all my willpower not to knock his elbow off. With his lashes at half-mast, he looks properly evil as he leans close, his breath warm against my ear. "Still not going to work," he whispers.

DAY SIX

丬卄丨

Chapter 13

"THIS HAS TO BE A MISTAKE."

"Yeah, no fucking shit," I mumble.

Lucie and Paige turn to gape at me, and with a defeated groan, I fling the covers back over my head.

DAY EIGHT

𝗛𝗛𝗛 𝗜𝗜𝗜

Chapter 14

"HAPPY SEPTEMBER TWENTY-FIRST," MILES SAYS
in his cheeriest voice when I walk into physics, his eyes bright
and thoroughly judgy. He's not exactly smiling, but then again,
I'm not sure I've seen a real smile from him yet. Miles treats smiles
the way I do stickers and stationery—reluctant to part with them,
as though they are precious things he has a finite number of.

"I despise you." I take the seat in front of him, out of habit more
than anything else. He's back in that middle row from my first
day—which wasn't his first day, according to his mozzarella-stick
simulation. Again, I wonder about everything he's done over the
past two months. I've been stuck for a week and I've already been
stretched to the point of nearly snapping. I can only begin to imagine how frustrated he's felt.

How lonely it's been.

And how as soon as I found out he was trapped, my first instinct
was to push him away.

While I attempt some halfhearted notes to pass the time, I'm intensely aware of Miles behind me. I'd kill to read minds instead of travel through time. All my bravado, all my insistence I could figure this out on my own, and now he knows I've failed. Worse, it's time for me to start groveling.

STOP STARING AT MY SCREEN, I type in a Word doc in forty-eight-point font, just to see if he's watching me. When I hear a muffled snort, I add a few exclamation points.

A squeak as he leans forward in his seat. "How'd it all go?" he whispers over my shoulder. "Because I'm guessing if you're back in class, you wanted to talk to me. Does this mean you're finally ready to do things my way?"

Or maybe I don't have to grovel at all.

AGAIN, I DESPISE YOU.

BUT YES.

Unfortunately, that's exactly why I'm here. Yesterday, after Lucie did her typical *woe is me for being forced to room with the monster that is Barrett Bloom* routine, which is really wearing on the fragments of self-esteem I escaped high school with, I gave myself a day to wallow. One full day, during which I ignored Lucie, ordered two Neapolitan pizzas and a dozen artisan cupcakes, and watched a season of *Felicity*—which my mom always says never properly prepared her for college—and tried to convince myself this wouldn't break me. Not until I'd exhausted all my resources, tried every wild idea.

Emphasis on the *exhausted.* That was the truth of how I was feeling as Miles's words from ~~however the hell many~~ five days before pulsed in my ears. *When you're ready to take this seriously, you know where to find me.* A full week of trying to get to Thursday, to

Jocelyn's proposal, and I'm no closer to knowing what's going on.

And this means I need help.

Although I can't see him, I'm positive he's smirking right now, a fantastically infuriating victory smirk.

"Meet me in the physics library after class." Miles's voice holds a quiet confidence. A secret between the two of us, and maybe the universe, too.

FINE. LET'S RESEARCH THE SHIT OUT OF THIS.

ᘖᘖᘖ

Later that morning, I learn that UW has not one but three science libraries, and the one devoted to physics is the least loved of the bunch.

Most of the school's libraries are either modern state-of-the-art structures or old brick buildings, gorgeous and perfectly preserved. But this one just looks . . . sad. Like the seventh kid in a family, cursed to wear hand-me-downs for the rest of their life. It's in the basement of the physics building, brown-carpeted and dimly lit, probably to hide the fact that this place hasn't been deep-cleaned since UW's first graduating class. But, maybe most importantly: it's empty.

"This is where you've been for the past sixty-five days?" I follow him through a maze of dusty shelves, fighting a sneeze.

"Sixty-six." He slides his backpack onto what I assume is his usual table, given how he picks a seat without even glancing at it. Or, who knows, maybe he mixes it up, chooses a different table each time. Miles seems like the kind of guy who lives on the edge. "And for the most part, yes."

"God, you could probably have your PhD by now."

"Please," he says with a scoff. "I'd need two years of advanced coursework and at least that many years spent on a dissertation to get to that point. The idea that I'm even close is laughable."

"But you want to," I say.

A shrug. "Maybe." Then he clears his throat and turns to a chalkboard—a chalkboard, not a whiteboard—positioned behind the table. It's not a brush-off, not quite. With a bachelor's degree in physics, I assume he could get plenty of jobs . . . physicsing. It would probably be helpful if I had any sense of what a professional physicist does.

Miles picks up a jagged piece of chalk. "We both have heavy research backgrounds. You're the journalist. I'm the scientist. We should be able to figure this out."

"Right." A journalist who can't even get onto her college paper. Lately, all those magazines in my room have been mocking me. Surely, Jia Tolentino and Peggy Orenstein and Nora Ephron would have had no trouble making it onto the *Washingtonian*.

He either ignores the flatness in my tone or doesn't notice. "Can you give me an abstract of what you've done during each anomaly, as best as you can remember?"

"An abstract?"

"A summary. A synopsis. A run-through."

"I know what it means. I'm just not sure I've ever heard someone use the word in that context in casual conversation." I drum my fingertips on the table, aware I'm about to rile him even more but diving in anyway. "If we're going to do this, we need a better word than *anomaly*."

Miles clutches the chalk tighter. "I'm open to suggestions," he says, "as long as we can get off this tangent sometime today."

"What about just *loops*? Simpler."

"I can live with that."

I explain to him everything I've done so far, and he writes it all down in neat but cramped letters. I get a flash of a future Miles as a physics professor: a crooked tie, a shirt rolled to his elbows, so excited about physics that he forgets to dot his *i*'s and cross his *t*'s.

When I finish, he draws a line down the board and, lightning fast, scribbles down his loops. *All* of his loops, from the look of it, and I just watch, trying to keep my jaw from dropping. He wasn't lying about his stellar memory. There are several dozen that say *library*, a handful of *PHYS 101*, and some that are abbreviated in ways I imagine make sense only to him, like *LHC attempt* and one that's simply *M*.

"Is LHC a drug?" I ask.

"Large Hadron Collider," he says. "In Geneva. I tried to stay awake on the flight, but I must have fallen asleep somewhere across the Atlantic, because I woke up back in Olmsted."

"You have to re-create this every day," I say, some amount of awe in my voice, despite the evidence that he's spent most of those days in the library.

Another shrug. He takes a few steps back, assessing the two columns. "I've been lazy some days." I have to hold back a snort. *Lazy* is not a word I can imagine someone ever associating with Miles Kasher-Okamoto. It wouldn't just be an insult—it's laughable. "And I created a mnemonic to help remember everything. I suggest you do the same."

"What, like ROY G. BIV?"

"Less rudimentary, but yes."

"I'll try to come up with one worthy of your advanced intelligence," I say sweetly. I nod toward the chalkboard. "Learning to drive stick really didn't work? I'm shocked." But something is weighing on me, and I'm not sure I can commit to all this musty library research without an answer. "Before we get too deep in this . . . I know that you've apologized, and I'm over it—really. But I have to know. Why were you such a jackass to me in class?"

This seems to catch him off guard. He presses his lips together and turns the chalk over and over in his hand, as though the answer is written on it in the tiniest font. "That was uncalled for. I know. I think part of me was . . . I don't know, testing the limits of what I could get away with."

"Because you could be as cruel as you wanted, and I wouldn't remember it the next day?" *Until I did,* I imagine we're both thinking.

"Not quite," he says. "I guess I was just frustrated with everything, and I may have taken it out on you because you happened to be sitting next to me. It was immature—I see that now. I really am sorry, Barrett."

And maybe this will come back to bite me later, but I believe him. I believe that he's sorry and, after all my failed attempts and determination to stay positive, I can't blame him for wanting to test the limits.

"Thanks." I can't describe the feeling of imagining another version of myself out there, doing something this version of me ~~has?~~ ~~had?~~ has no control over. It feels like a violation, almost. "How do we even know these are our real selves right now?"

A wry smile. "We don't." *Cool. Cool. Love that uncertainty.* "In a way, all of them are our real selves. That is, assuming those other versions of us are still out there, living their lives. We of course have no way of knowing."

Naturally. I gesture back at the chalkboard. "What does the dot mean?" He's added one to a big chunk of his earlier loops and scattered throughout.

"Oh. Those are the days Zeta Kappa goes up in flames."

I gape at him. "You're telling me that in every version of this day before I got stuck, I set fire to that frat?"

"Not every day," he says, and some of the tension leaves my shoulders. With his chalk, he points to loop 27. "There was one day you, uh, accidentally set yourself on fire."

"It's a wonder I don't have guys lining up to date me."

"Your stop, drop, and roll was really . . . athletic, though. And another day, you—" His piece of chalk falls to the floor, and he hurries to pick it back up, not meeting my eyes. I'm not sure a single living human is more awkward than Miles Kasher-Okamoto. That has to be a scientific achievement all its own. "You took control of the barbecue and made everyone hot dogs. But generally, unless I intervened . . . yes. You burned down Zeta Kappa."

"Brilliant. I'm a fucking pyro." I inhale deeply to ward off another sneeze and perhaps also a panic attack. "Somehow I get the feeling the universe isn't doing this because it wants me to save a frat."

"At first I thought that was what I was supposed to do. Stop the fire from happening. Once I found out about it, I kept trying to prevent it—and I almost never could. The couple times I did succeed, I still woke up on September twenty-first. Because, see, that's the trouble," Miles says. "Personifying the universe. We don't know if this is something that someone is actively controlling, if there's some puppet master out there pulling the strings, or . . ."

"Or if it's something that can be explained with science."

A slow, sly almost-grin. "Exactly. And that's what I've been trying to figure out. I've found some articles over the years where people claim they've been stuck in a time loop, and if you dive deep enough online, there are plenty of message boards and conspiracy theories."

"I've seen a bunch of those too," I say.

"But I can't shake the feeling that if we're going to find something, it's going to be in here. I'm trying to learn as much about relativity as possible, just to see if I can come up with additional theories. And then there's the question of quantum mechanics, which, admittedly, I'm not as familiar with yet as I ought to be."

"I'm just going to put this out there," I say, because a tension headache is already building behind one eye, "but what if the solution really is *Groundhog Day*–ing it, and we're stuck here until we become better people? It's possible I was rushing through my attempts over the past week. If we tackled it together, I'm sure we could come up with something better."

I mean for this to be a perfectly logical idea, but Miles flicks his chalk onto the table and grips the top of the chair next to me. "No."

"Isn't that just as valid as any of your theories?"

He barks out a sound, a sharp *ha* that's never sounded further from a laugh. "My theories are grounded in the fundamental laws of nature."

So working together is to be torture, then.

"We're already experiencing something that goes against everything we thought we knew about the 'rules,'" I say, hoping my use of air quotes annoys him as much as his unchecked arrogance annoys me. "Maybe a witch waved a fucking magic wand and cursed us. Because that sounds just about as likely as *science* forcing us to repeat the same day over and over."

"I thought you were here because you wanted to do things my way."

"Oh, I'm sorry. I didn't realize I was just your research assistant."

His hands tense, his eyes flashing with a thousand megawatts of electricity. "Well, I'm the one with more experience. Maybe you should be."

"Classic. A man eager to steamroll a woman and make her work for him." In one swift motion, I push out my chair and get to my feet, hating the feeling of him towering over me. I can send all that electrical energy right back to him. "That's what your scientists were so good at, right? I know all about Rosalind Franklin."

"What are you—" Miles tries between sharp breaths, as though arguing with me is diminishing his lung capacity. "What does that have to do with—"

"Anything I can help you with?"

A librarian is standing on the opposite side of our table, probably drawn by the sound of our raised voices. She's a middle-aged white woman with graying brown hair in a cute wavy bob and an oversize houndstooth sweater I would absolutely wear.

My heart is racing, and I savor the chance to get a proper inhale. "We're fine. Thank you."

"You just holler if you need anything," she says, giving us a warm smile before retreating into the stacks.

"Happens every day," Miles says when she's gone. "She's actually been quite helpful, but now that I know my way around the library, I always feel bad telling her I don't need anything."

I grunt in response, slumping into my chair and refusing to make eye contact. Maybe I really did die and this is my hell: trapped in a library, forced to research quantum mechanics for all of eternity. I'd much rather have all my body hair plucked out strand by strand, thanks.

A soft creaking as Miles sits down next to me. "Can we at least *try* it my way?" I can tell it's taking all he has to keep his voice level.

"Fine," I say, considering I don't have any other options. "But I'm not your fucking assistant."

"Noted. And—I'm sorry. Again. For being on edge . . . again." He plucks a notebook from his backpack and opens it up, I'm guessing because the chalkboard's run out of space. "With time travel, time loops, anomalies, whatever you want to call them—it's all about finding patterns. What I want to know," he continues as he writes this next question in bold ballpoint-pen lettering, "is why us? Out of all the people on campus, assuming this doesn't go beyond UW, why Barrett Bloom and Miles Kasher-Okamoto? Aside from the fact that we're both in Physics 101 and live in Olmsted, but that could apply to a thousand different people. I keep coming back to thinking we might have done something the day before we got stuck that triggered it."

"Like, what, we both tripped and fell into a swirling vortex of doom? I feel like I'd remember that."

"Swirling vortex of doom," he repeats, another one of those half smiles playing on his lips, and against all my natural instincts to loathe him, it makes me soften a little bit. I keep waiting for him to go all out with one of his smiles, but I'm not sure I'd be able to withstand its power. "Sounds like a heavy metal band." Then he refocuses, that ghost of a smile gone. "What were you doing the day before you got stuck? September twentieth?"

I've been so focused on Wednesday that Tuesday feels like a life-time ago. "I woke up. Obviously. I had cereal for breakfast, I think? I went to an info session for the *Washingtonian*, went to a freshman orientation. Walked around campus, pretending I knew exactly where I was going because I'd been there dozens of times with my mom, even though I definitely didn't."

Watched everyone taking selfies with their friends in the quad. Signing up for clubs. Eating dinner together. And thought, *My life is about to change. This is the place it happens.*

"I did some laundry, because I planned poorly and didn't end up doing enough of it before I moved in. Lost a sock, because that's what I get for trying to have clean clothes, apparently." RIP, SHITSHOW sock. "The Olmsted dining hall was serving all-you-can-eat pasta, so I did some damage there, and then I managed to sneak into the elevator with a few bowls I wasn't supposed to take upstairs. And then, well, my roommate hadn't moved in yet, so I took advantage of the alone time and did some . . . solo self-care."

"Took advantage of the—" Miles's pen stutters in his notebook, a little squiggle that looks like a spike on an EKG. A blush spreads across his cheeks, the tips of his ears. "*Oh.* I'm, ah, not going to write that one down."

My brain-to-mouth filter has not properly functioned for years. It's possible I've never had one.

"I highly doubt my orgasms were so momentous that they literally stopped time." I really had to go ahead and make it plural. Surely, I'm about to make a scientific discovery of my own: whether it's possible to die from embarrassment.

"If that were the case," Miles says, still staring down at the paper, "then I'm shocked more of us aren't shuttled through time on a regular basis."

Is he . . . making a joke? I've only had a few glimpses of the Miles who isn't this buttoned-up academic, this person with empathy and a sense of humor. In another universe, because I've halfway lost hope in this one, maybe Miles is even capable of *fun*.

"Anyway," I continue, eager to move past this topic, my face painfully slow to cool down, "nothing I did was life-altering. Or timeline-altering. Clearly."

Miles tugs on the collar of his shirt, his cheeks returning to their normal shade. The tips of his ears, however, still glow red. "Mine wasn't very noteworthy either," he says, and proceeds to recount his day in excessive detail, from the type of toast and jam he had (multigrain and raspberry) to a play-by-play of the floor meeting his RA held.

"We weren't even in the same buildings for very long," I say. "Or at the same time. It wasn't like some chunk of metaphysical space junk fell on top of us, unless that's what you want to call whatever's on the floors of the Olmsted bathrooms." There was a reason I'd ranked it dead last on my residence-hall application.

"And no swirling vortex of doom," he agrees. "Which doesn't

mean my theory is wrong, necessarily. It just makes this a little more challenging."

After more discussion, we find we have one thing in common: both of us wake up at 6:50 every morning, meaning the day doesn't reset at midnight, and we've never been able to successfully stay awake to outrun the loop. When I passed out at the hospital, that didn't restart the loop either.

"In terms of rules, at least we have that," I say.

"But we also don't know if the rules are always changing, or if they're fixed," he counters. "Since you weren't stuck from the beginning, it makes me think they're not entirely fixed."

For all my hostility, I should probably give Miles a marginal amount of credit here. Would I prefer to be stuck in a time loop with an early-2000s Milo Ventimiglia? One hundred percent. But maybe being here with a budding physicist has its benefits. What was it that Miles said about it on my first first day? Something about how the universe acts, and predicting how it might act in the future. If there's an explanation for what's happening to us, physics might lead us to a solution.

"I'm sorry I don't have the answers," Miles says, maybe interpreting my silence as frustration. "I wish I did. I'm trying." Then he corrects himself: "*We're* trying."

Of course, that raises another question. "I'm still not sure why you want to help me, aside from the fact that we're in this together. I've pepper-sprayed you *multiple times*, Miles. The librarian had to come check on us. It's pretty clear we get on each other's nerves."

At that, his face relaxes into a new kind of expression, one that restores some of my hope in the universe that trapped us here together. "Because somehow, against all my better judgment . . . I like you."

The words stun me, settling against my chest with an unexpected warmth, stealing any comeback I was about to make. *I like you.* He says it in a way that's so straightforward. Uncomplicated. So few people say what they really mean, and even if I never doubted the way my fellow Islanders felt about me, plenty of times I've had to nudge my interview subjects for clear answers.

As much as I wish this weren't true, and I'd never admit this to Miles, I can't remember the last time someone said something that nice to me. There's a loveliness in those three words, the simple fact of someone liking your company.

Of course, he has to follow it up by saying, "Not in *that* way." He tilts his face away as it reddens again, and I'm going to guess that he hasn't had much experience with people in *that way.* Then again, neither have I. "Just that I don't find you completely miserable to be around. Only sixty percent or so."

I roll my eyes. "Thanks for the clarification. I wasn't thinking that, but I'm glad you set the record straight."

He motions for me to follow him into the stacks, and after a few minutes of browsing, he passes me a book, that strange moment forgotten. Except in my mind, where it remains pressed against all the softest corners.

"This one might be promising," he says. "It's popular science, so it's a bit more readable."

The cover reads *Black Holes and Baby Universes*, by Stephen Hawking.

"Aw, baby universes," I say, regarding the book like it's a puppy. "So you want me to just . . . start? Now?"

"No time like the present," he says with another one of those infuriating non-smiles, and so I crack the book and begin reading.

DAY ELEVEN

꧇꧇꧇꧇꧇

Chapter 15

WE'VE BEEN IN THE LIBRARY FOR THREE DAYS. MY brain is soup, a simmering mess of neurons stumbling their way around dimly lit pathways.

I drop my head to the table with a soft thunk, glancing sideways at Miles through crooked glasses. He's stiff as always, perched on the edge of his chair, head bent at a ninety-degree angle, eyes flicking across pages at twice my usual speed. I'm not sure it would be physically possible for Miles to slouch or even sit cross-legged. I don't think his body would allow him to. Meanwhile, I've draped myself over two chairs, legs propped on the second one, one of my shoes lost somewhere in between the FARADAY, MICHAEL and OPPENHEIMER, J. ROBERT shelves.

Miles reminds me of the kind of comic-book scientist who gets too absorbed in their work, then falls into a vat of acid or gets bitten by a genetically modified creature and becomes a supervillain. When I told him this either a few minutes or a few hours ago, he wanted to know what his powers would be, and I informed him that he'd be able to successfully complete boring tasks at an alarming rate.

"I want a better superpower."

"Nope," I said. "You don't get to choose."

Now I turn the page in a yellowed textbook that has seen better days. "It's hopeless." I haven't processed anything for at least the past fifty pages. Stephen Hawking's pop science? Parts of it were interesting, even if the baby universes were not quite as adorable as I'd hoped. This book, the collected lectures of some physicist I've never heard of? Impenetrable. "What are words? I don't know what we're even looking for anymore."

"A way out," he says, but as he swipes a hand through his disheveled hair, I can tell he's fading too. The slightest amount, but it's there. The scar beneath his left eye—now that I've spent so many hours sitting next to him, I know it's shaped like a crescent moon.

"Your mom is a physics professor," I say. "Maybe we should talk to her?"

"I've done it." Miles points to the chalkboard, where he's insisted on drawing up his loops every day.

"Because I'm supposed to know what all your little symbols mean."

A sigh, which is the primary way Miles and I interact. I can categorize almost all his sighs at this point: there's the *that was a weird joke but okay* sigh, the *your mere presence exhausts me* sigh, the *frustrated but just going to ignore you* sigh. This one is a *the answer is obvious* sigh.

"My mother is a scientist," he says. "A natural skeptic. The few times I've told her, she didn't believe me."

"Did you try what you did with me, anticipating what's going to happen around you?"

"I'm not sure how she'd react." He flicks the cap of his pen, back and forth and back and forth. Maybe he's always fiddling with something because his posture is otherwise so stiff, so rigid. His body is crying out for freedom, but he only allows it in the tiniest of doses. "There are some scientists who *want* to believe the extraordinary is possible. Some who dedicate their lives to it, even, for better or for worse. But others . . . they're motivated by constant questioning. It's not that they want to disprove every theory they come across—it's that they're going to need a hell of a lot of evidence to back anything up."

"And I'm guessing Dr. Okamoto is the second type."

He points a finger at me. "Yep."

His phone lights up next to him, and without glancing up from his book, he switches it off. This has happened every day, and he never picks it up.

"You can answer it," I say, checking the time. 3:26. But he doesn't.

I don't think I've stretched my legs in four hours. I push the book of lectures with too much force, sending it careening toward a stack at the edge of our table. A few books topple over, landing on the carpet in a series of muted thumps. Just like that, Gladys is by our table, eyes wide with worry.

"Sorry, sorry," I whisper, scrambling out of my chair to pick up the books. I have to admit, she's nice company, even if we have to reintroduce ourselves to her every day.

"Just making sure you two are okay," she says sweetly. "Some of those books are heavier than they look."

I frown at the stack I've just tidied. I'm not actually sure which book I was in the middle of—that's how far gone I am.

We can't approach this logically. We can't use logic to solve something illogical, and Miles eats logic for breakfast with a side of whole-grain critical thinking.

I gesture to his book. *A Short History of Nearly Everything*, because sure. Why wouldn't that be what it's called? "Have you learned it all yet? Nearly everything?"

"Almost," he murmurs.

"I'm going to make a deal with you," I say to research-trance Miles. He sticks an index finger in the book, bestowing upon me the honor of eye contact. "It's not that I don't find all of this enthralling, but I can't do this every day. And not just because we're eventually going to be so deficient in vitamin D that the sun will melt our skin off our faces the moment we step outside again."

"What's the deal?"

"We try this half your way, through research. And half my way."

His brows push together in a dubious furrow. "If you make me wave around one of those gopher signs—"

I hold up a hand, not in the mood for any of his whole-grain Miles logic. "My way means accepting this might be magic, and not science. I've seen this kind of thing play out before. In fiction. I may not have a photographic memory, but there's a lot of pop-culture knowledge stored up in here." I tap my head the way he did ???? a few days ago. "And it means no wisecracks about my methods. I respect your way of doing things, and you respect mine. You're the scientist. You should want to test multiple theories."

I expect him to protest, to tell me no way is he putting any stock in something he can't find in a textbook that smells like sadness. Instead, he nods.

"Okay," he says. Miles Kasher-Okamoto, agreeing with me just like that. "We'll try it."

His dark eyes are heavy on mine. Weary. When I look at him, I don't only see the reserved, stoic boy from day one. I see someone who's just as lost as I am, someone who was maybe lost before his timeline ever veered off course. Sixty-nine days, and he's spent nearly all of them in the library, and there's something about that that makes me incredibly sad, all of a sudden.

Because yes, this is frustrating as all hell, but it's also something else: an opportunity.

One that I don't think Miles, with his rationed smiles and his loops painstakingly documented on that chalkboard, has taken advantage of.

"I need a break," I say, wrenching my gaze from his, aware I've been staring a few moments too long. Trying to make sense of him. "Stretch my legs, reset my brain. Could we meet back up later? I'll text you." The three numbers I now know by heart: my mom's, the landline we haven't had since I was eight, and Miles Kasher-Okamoto's.

He sighs again, a new type of sigh I haven't been able to categorize yet. I hope it isn't resignation. "Yeah. Of course." Halfheartedly, he drags a highlighter through a sentence in his book. The first time he did this, I gasped, imagining the kind of fine he'd have to pay—before realizing the mark would be erased tomorrow. "I'll see you."

Just when I think we might be making progress, he shuts back down. All right, then.

As I make my way across campus, there's none of that first-day excitement anymore. I know that outside the engineering building, there's a poster for UW's bird-watching club that missed the recycling bin that no one's going to pick up. I know that guy who's not supposed to be skateboarding in Red Square is going to collide with those swing dancers and eat brick in about three seconds.

"Look out!" I tell the skateboarder, if only because I can't help myself.

When he glances my way, he loses focus—and barrels into a booth of student-government candidates instead. They let out a shriek as he knocks over their table, sending their papers flying.

"Sorry, I was—" the skateboarder says as he examines a scraped knee, but when he turns to point at me, I'm already tearing out of the square.

Jesus, I'm incapable of doing a single good thing.

Back in Olmsted, all four elevators are at the top floors, and because they take forever to get back down, I opt to trudge up the nine flights of stairs instead. Maybe the exercise and the concrete and the god-knows-what growing in the crevices will fire up my brain and set that neuron soup to boil. Give me some indication of what to do next.

Because it feels like we're doomed to repeat this day over and over and over until *something* of some magnitude happens, something that definitely hasn't happened yet. And I have no clue what it could be.

I'm between flights three and four when I hear an odd sound. I go up another flight, and my hunch is confirmed: someone's crying. It freezes me in place for a moment before I start back up again. I huff and puff up the next two flights until I spot the source of the sound, a small red-haired girl slumped against the wall, phone clutched to her chest.

"Lucie?"

Her shoulders go rigid when she sees me, and she swipes a hand across her face. At first I'm convinced she's been on the phone with someone in resident services and she's just learned she's stuck with me. Except these are not *my roommate is chaos personified* tears.

"Hey," she says in this voice I've never heard from her before, and I have had a *lot* of Lucie Lamont voices directed at me. The tentative voice when we started becoming friends on the middle school paper. The smooth, confident voice when we collaborated on stories. And the dismissive voice when my tennis-team article went out, replaced by an authoritarian voice once she became editor in chief.

This one sounds . . . *broken.*

Lucie's gaze won't meet mine, ice-blue eyes fixed on the ground. I've never seen Lucie cry, either, not when my article was published, not when she and Blaine broke up shortly after. "Sorry, I was just—"

"No, no, you don't have to apologize." Now my voice is morphing too. A soft, careful kind of voice, one I'm not sure I knew I was capable of until right now. "Is everything . . . okay?"

"Yep. I'm getting out of this hellhole—why wouldn't it be?" With a final sniff, she pushes to her feet, shoulders back, confidence restored. "Have a good freshman year, Barrett."

Her suede ankle boots carry her the rest of the way to the ninth floor, and when a heavy door slams above me, an idea takes root in my mind.

DAY TWELVE

THL THL ||

Chapter 16

"THIS HAS TO BE A MISTAKE," LUCIE LAMONT SAYS, and I hide a grin against my pillow.

I told Miles I wanted to try things my way, and I meant it. And while I've already made some of my own attempts, what I think I've missed is that in movies, the way out of a time loop often ends up being personal. Whether it's true love, like I joked about with Miles, or repairing a relationship with your family, or righting the wrongs of your past, it has to mean something to whoever's trapped. Nothing I've done has held any kind of meaning for me, aside from my deep personal investment in not getting arrested for burning down Zeta Kappa.

True love is off the table. If I've had this much trouble making friends, I can't imagine trying to lock down a soul mate. That leaves Lucie.

Once I've showered and dressed, I take the stairs down to Miles's Disneyfied floor. His door is decorated with pictures of Buzz Lightyear and Woody, along with the names MILES and ANKIT.

"Hi," I say when a South Asian guy in a gray T-shirt answers the door, realizing I didn't know the name of Miles's roommate until now. "Ankit? I'm looking for Miles."

He steps back and there's Miles, in his usual rigid Miles stance, bent over a book at his desk. The room is a carbon copy of mine, except for the fact that it looks like two people who don't hate each other live here.

"Ankit, this is Barrett," Miles says, and we exchange polite hellos. "We have physics together. Barrett, this is my roommate."

"Are you ready?" I ask Miles. "To do some more . . . studying?" By complete accident, I manage to say it in the most suggestive way possible. I might as well have fluttered my lashes and shimmied in here wearing only a feather boa.

Ankit tries his best to muffle his laughter and fails. "Physics, huh?" He glances between us with a lift of his eyebrows. "Are you sure you don't mean chemistry?"

The tips of Miles's ears flash a brilliant red as he grabs his backpack, shoving his feet into his green Adidas. "Let's go."

"Oh—before you leave," Ankit says. "Have you seen my UW T-shirt? I did laundry yesterday but can't find it."

"The laundry ate one of my favorite socks, too," I say. "Olmsted should come with an insurance policy."

Miles shakes his head. "I'll keep an eye out."

"Have a good time!" Ankit gives him a pointed look that seems to fall somewhere between *Really? Her?* and *Nicely done.*

For a few moments, I savor this questionable ego boost, despite the fact that there is no universe in which Miles views me as a romantic prospect. And vice versa. There simply isn't room in my heart for anything but annoyance and a small amount of curiosity.

Miles follows me out into the hall, head tucked at a near ninety-degree angle, shoulders stiff. True to his word, he doesn't complain about the mission, but he still has plenty of questions.

"You two had a fight in high school?" he asks as we approach the bus stop in front of Olmsted. "You and your roommate?"

"I'm not sure I would call it a fight." I check my phone—eight minutes until the next bus. After eleven days, I should have had enough foresight to memorize the schedule. "I'm not exactly her favorite person."

"And you don't like her, either?"

I don't answer him right away—because, truthfully, I'm not sure. I've been so focused on how much she dislikes me that I haven't paused to consider my feelings toward her. Complicated—that's what they are.

I can't get the vision of her puffy eyes ~~yesterday~~ today out of my head. Crying in a stairwell doesn't match up with the image of Lucie Lamont that's lived in my mind and haunted my life for the past few years. The Lucie who watched *Veronica Mars* with my mom and me. The Lucie who called the printer herself when our November issue was delayed, sweet-talking them into giving the school a discount for the next six months. The Lucie Lamont I admired, even after she cut me out of her life.

"I used to," I say quietly. "But I'm not sure I really know her anymore."

When the bus arrives, we take it through campus and down Forty-Fifth Street to University Village, an outdoor shopping center just north of the school. We wander through the maze of upscale chains and local eateries before finding the bagel shop on one edge of the mall.

"You're going to win her back with bagels," Miles says, a hint of amusement in his tone.

"You clearly haven't had Mabel's Bagels."

Operation Make Lucie Love Me—the name is a work in progress—hinges on making Lucie happy. And few things can spark that kind of immediate happiness like a dose of carbs.

Bagels are a delicate matter among Jews. Everyone has a favorite bagel place in Seattle, though none of them agree on which place that is. Some shops are acceptable and some are downright offensive, but the one thing they *can* agree on is that whatever it is that makes New York bagels so perfect—we don't have it here.

This kosher shop is my mom's favorite, and the SHALOM welcome sign written in both English and Hebrew instantly makes me feel at home. Which, with a painful twinge, instantly reminds me of Jocelyn's proposal.

Something else hits me: if we don't get out of here, it's not just the proposal I'll miss. I won't be able to see them get married, either.

This has to work.

Miles watches while I fill a bag with a baker's dozen, jaw twitching, an unreadable expression on his face.

"You're demonstrating remarkable restraint, not tearing apart this idea," I tell him.

"I just don't see how—" The words seem to rush out before he has a chance to rein them back in. He holds up a hand, gives me an apologetic look. "Sorry. Sorry. We're doing it your way."

But just as we're about to leave, my stomach lets out an

embarrassing growl. "Oh—I, uh, didn't eat breakfast."

"Well. We happen to be in Seattle's finest bagel shop."

So I order my usual: an everything bagel with honey-almond schmear. As for Miles—

"Thirty options. Thirty options, Miles, and you picked plain and plain?" I ask once we're seated with our bagels in a corner of the shop.

"I like what I like," he says with a defiant jut of his chin. "Yours looks like someone may have already eaten it. For dinner last night. Don't tell me *that* is the epitome of flavor."

"Mmm. It *is*." I take a big, fluffy, cream-cheesy bite. "You and Ankit seemed close, by the way. Or at the very least, not at each other's throats." I wanted to mention it when we were on the bus, but then I worried I might need to address the weirdness of That Look his roommate gave him, and I didn't want to go within fifty feet of that topic. Now that we've had some distance from it, it feels like a safer conversation.

He shrugs. "He's easygoing. Extroverted, but not aggressively so. We both moved in early, on the same day, and we just clicked."

"What about your high school friends?"

"We kind of . . . scattered." He takes another bite of bagel, though I know deflection when I see it. Evidently, the guy doesn't love talking about himself. "So I'm helping you with your roommate and you're really not going to tell me why you don't get along?"

I consider this. It doesn't hurt to give him a sliver of information, especially if he might be able to help with the plan. It doesn't mean I have to tell him the whole truth. Especially not the section of it that's locked in a vault at the back of my mind.

"We were friends for a couple years," I start. "Not close—mostly school friends. We worked on our middle school newspaper together, and then our high school paper." I pluck sesame seeds from my bagel, needing something to distract from the way Miles is so intently focused on me. God forbid he be anything less than an active listener. "I, um, unearthed this cheating scandal. With the tennis team. That her boyfriend was on. They were disqualified from the championships, which led to him losing a scholarship and the two of them breaking up. So. She didn't have a lot of love for me after that."

Miles blinks a few times. Frowns. "You realize that's not your fault, right? That someone's scholarship was taken away?"

"I know." But it doesn't matter. It certainly didn't matter to Cole. "I'm sure I'll deal with much worse when I'm writing for the *New Yorker* or *Entertainment Weekly*. And," I continue, wanting to linger on this as little as possible, "I wasn't a gem to her afterward, either. We were always clashing in the newsroom."

"Really? I can't picture that." He says it with such a straight face, daintily dabbing his mouth with a napkin. "If she's the one who was such an asshole to you, then why should it be up to you to fix the relationship?"

"Because I need the universe to see that I'm the bigger person here."

"Ah. The almighty universe, with its record keeping and score-cards."

"Do you always need to be the smartest person in the room?" I ask.

"I usually am."

I ball up my napkin and fling it at his shoulder.

"Fine, I deserved that." Then: "You're a journalist," he continues, as though something is just occurring to him. "Your first day, you tried to get on the paper but couldn't."

Unfortunately, I've told him all about it. "I tried twice. The editor's never outright said no, but it's been pretty obvious."

"Maybe that's the key to this. I mean"—he's quick to backtrack—"if your method held any scientific weight, which it does not."

"Nailing the interview?"

"Maybe it's not necessarily about the interview. Maybe it's about proving yourself. Coming to them with the right story."

"I'm not sure what I'd write about," I admit, but even as I say it, I realize it's not true. The days after I moved in, before school started, I kept noticing things around campus that might make for interesting features. The man at the parking booth who plays his saxophone at eight o'clock every night. Kendall from Save the Gophers. Even Paige, she of Milwaukee and celery allergy, must have a story to tell.

But an article about your awkward RA doesn't seem quite as important when your timeline is stuck on repeat.

"You're annoyed I came up with a good idea," Miles says, eyes glinting in a thoroughly smug way.

Even more annoying: that he has me pegged already. "'How My Roommate Poisoned My Face Wash and I Lived to Tell the Tale.'"

"'How the Star of the Physics Department Was the First Freshman to Be Awarded a Fulbright.'"

I narrow my eyes at him. "'Before His Life Was Tragically Cut Short by a Deadly Paper Cut.'"

And finally, *finally*, his expression cracks, a muscle in his jaw rippling before he lets himself go, offering up the smallest of grins. It's nice to see on him, I decide. Different. His mouth is still pressed together just a little, but there's clear joy on his face that wasn't there a second ago. It makes me wonder why he's so intent on hiding it, though we're nowhere near close enough for me to ask. Even after three full days in the library, most of what I know about Miles barely skims the surface.

Then, as though he's decided that's enough merriment for one morning, he stands and picks up his empty basket, posture back at a perfect 180-degree angle. "Okay. Let's go prove to your roommate that you're not a monster."

ʊ ʊ ʊ

Before we head back to campus, we make a stop at University Village's stationery store. The selection doesn't compare to my mom's, but it'll have to do. I'm not sure how it would feel to see her, knowing that my trip home was erased and/or happened to a different version of her.

Even when Lucie and I attempted to go to the party together or had A Moment in our room beforehand, we didn't talk about our history. If I'm going to free myself from this loop, maybe I have to not just unearth the past but allow myself to feel uncomfortable about it.

Undo three years of animosity in twenty-four hours.

The bagels and anthropomorphic fruit card that says WE MAKE A GREAT PEAR may not be enough.

I'm not sure of Lucie's exact schedule, but from our short-lived friendship, I know that her favorite color is lavender. And it is a fact I milk in the balloon aisle of a party-supply store as much as I can. Miles leaves after he helps me set up the room, a quick "good luck" before he disappears, probably off to the library to declare his undying love for a bibliography.

By noon there's still no sign of her, and my antsiness has manifested as balloon art. The balloons say HI ROOMIE and WHAT'S POPPIN', and a couple I've shoved toward the back have unfortunate attempts at a doodle of her face. It's very hard to capture her essence with latex and a Sharpie.

I don't want to miss her reaction to my big helium olive branch, so I wait. And wait. And wait. I'm considering zipping downstairs for a late lunch when the key jingles in the lock at two forty-five. The door opens, and there she is in her black mock-neck and denim skirt, bag slung over one arm.

Her jaw drops, along with her keys. "Did someone break into our room?"

"They caught the Big Bad Balloon Burglar last week, actually. This must be a copycat."

At that she looks confused, stepping inside and examining what's written on the balloons. "Are these . . . did you do all of this?"

"Guilty." I poke a balloon, watching Lucie's distorted face bounce down and then back up. Suddenly all of this seems very, very childish.

Lucie bats aside another balloon on the way to her desk, where I've arranged what was supposed to be breakfast. "And the bagels?"

"They might be a little stale, but . . . yes."

"Oh. Wow." She grabs a cranberry bagel. "I'm not sure what to say. Thank you?"

"I know we didn't exactly start off on the right foot." I elbow away more balloons so I can make eye contact with her, clutching one that says HELIUM IS HEALING. "I thought this could be a fresh start. Sort of like how we were before . . . well, you know."

I wait for her to apologize, to wrap me in a hug, to tell me she's so relieved I brought this up because it's been weighing on her, too.

"It was high school," she says with all the ego of someone who's spent exactly eight hours as a college student. Shrugging it off, when my brain has obsessed over it for months. Years. "I'm over it."

I'm over it.

As though what I did to her was so terrible, it was something *she* needed to recover from. Never mind what she did to me, instantly dropping me as a friend and siding with the rest of the school. Her boyfriend was the one who decided to cheat on that exam. I didn't do anything except shine a light on it.

Lucie, standing in a corner with her friends, laughing about #debloomed, at the flowers spilling out of my locker.

"You're right," I say, my face growing warm. "College was supposed to be different, right? We're whole new people and all that." I snatch up a poppy-seed bagel and bite into it as angrily as I can, sending seeds everywhere, teeth sinking hard into bread that's several hours past fluffy.

"Is there any way you could clean this up?" Lucie asks, struggling to get her bag onto her chair. "This room is small enough already. I can barely sit down."

"Aren't you rushing a sorority anyway?"

"I was thinking about it. How did you—"

"Lucky guess," I say quickly. "I'll clean it up. Don't worry." And then, before I can think twice about it, I change tactics. Clearly, I'm not about to make things right with Lucie—maybe I'm not even supposed to. I might as well say what I want before the universe flips over my hourglass. There's a hitch in my throat as I charge forward. "You know—I get why you were upset with me after the article. But back in May . . . it had been so long, Lucie. You didn't have to egg them on."

She whirls around, her eyes flashing. "What?"

"After prom. With the flowers, and that—that stupid hashtag." The rage that's simmered just under the surface all summer, the hot, acidic thing I've hid from my mom and Jocelyn—it's climbing up my throat, burning everything in its path. I stalk closer, pushing a few balloons out of my way, grateful for the three inches I have on Lucie. "You laughed right along with everyone else, like it was the funniest shit you'd ever seen."

This is as much as I've ever said aloud about it. I hadn't intended to bring it up, and now all the worst parts are flashing through my mind. The first time I was tagged on Instagram. The way Lucie was huddled with her friends when I walked into homeroom, a single rose on my desk. The look on the principal's fucking face. *I know a lot of young ladies who'd love to be in your position.*

I can't tell off everyone at Island who made me a punching bag, but Lucie is right here.

I can show her rage. What I can't show her is everything that's underneath it.

"If you think I'd do something like that," Lucie says, squaring her shoulders, refusing to shrink back, "then maybe we never really knew each other at all."

She swipes up her laptop charger, leaving me alone with all the lavender and gluten and processed cheese product. As though overwhelmed by the harshness of her reaction, one of the balloons pops as the door slams shut, making me jump.

I won't let this break me either. Not yet.

I cling to the rage, heading for my desk and rummaging in my pencil pouch for a pair of scissors. Then I grab the nearest balloon and sink the shiny metal tips into lavender latex.

Pop.

It's more satisfying than I expect it to be. Breathing hard, I reach for another. And another, each burst of helium making me greedy for more.

Pop. Pop-pop-pop.

Whatever Lucie might have meant—it doesn't change anything. #debloomed still happened, and maybe she's over high school, but I'm apparently still stuck there.

I have fully lost my mind, I think as I slice my scissors through the air like a sword, popping with giddy abandon.

It's the closest thing to fun I've had in days.

DAY THIRTEEN

卌 卌 |||

Chapter 17

"MY MOM HAS LUNCH HERE EVERY DAY," MILES says as we enter the elevator in the life-sciences building, with a quick glance around the hall to make sure no one spots us. "But students aren't technically allowed."

"You're breaking a rule?" I let out an exaggerated gasp. "I'm impressed. Here I thought you were a run-of-the-mill boy genius. I didn't realize you were a rebellious one too. Move over, Richard Feynman."

Miles rolls his eyes. "I'd hardly call Feynman rebellious."

"That's not what I read in one of your books," I say, leaning against one wall of the elevator. "Apparently he did a lot of his research at topless bars, writing out equations on paper place mats and sketching some of the women. They probably don't teach that in 101. But he was also a raging misogynist, so."

"And here I was, thinking you were suffering through all those books."

"Only most of them."

He drags his gaze to the floor, fighting a smile. The devil works hard, but Miles's jaw muscles work harder.

The elevator lets us out on the top floor, where we take the stairs to the roof. When Miles said he wanted us to talk to his mom today, I had to suppress a fist pump, since he brushed it off when I initially suggested it.

Lucie, of course, had no memory of bagels or balloons this morning. If what she meant yesterday was that she didn't laugh along with her friends, it's odd that she wasn't more specific. Lucie loves to take credit, even when something isn't her idea. Like when I pitched a piece about the history of our mascot, Salvatore the Salamander, for our senior back-to-school issue and she decided to write it herself, assigning me an article about a sophomore's Pomeranian that won third place in a local dog show.

My plan was never going to work, though I'm grateful Miles isn't lording it over me.

He pauses at the door, so abruptly that I run into his back, my face landing right between his shoulder blades and jostling my glasses. I get a whiff of that woodsy scent from the night I pepper-sprayed him, and something about it soothes a bit of the anxiety in my brain. It must contain some herbs or chemicals with calming properties.

"If I take you here, I have to swear you to secrecy," he says.

I put another foot of space between us and readjust my glasses. "If I told anyone," I say to his heather-gray T-shirt, "they're not going to remember anyway. So really, you'd never know."

He sigh-grunts at this but nonetheless opens the door.

This rooftop garden is exclusively for faculty and staff, though they're allowed to bring a guest once per quarter, Miles told me. The first thing I notice is *green*. Leafy plants and vibrant flowers spiral out from the soil, in between hammocks and wicker chairs and wooden tables. There are plants with whole curtains of leaves and plants that look like they could devour a pocket gopher or three. And then there's the view, Mount Rainier rising in the distance like it isn't quite real.

"This is beautiful," I say quietly, so as not to disturb the peacefulness. I can't summon a single sarcastic thing to say. That's how lovely it is.

There are a handful of professors up here, some eating lunch and others chatting with friends, one of them watering plants and collecting data on a clipboard. Dr. Okamoto is toward one end of the roof in a wicker chair, a sandwich in one hand and an iPad in the other. Earlier in class, Miles and I sat right in the front row. And when Dr. Okamoto asked a question, Miles typed something on his computer screen and tapped it with a pen to get my attention. *Answer the question,* he'd written, and I tried not to roll my eyes. Still, I raised my hand.

"Physics is the study of matter and energy and how they relate to each other," I said, the words practically drilled into my memory at this point, and Dr. Okamoto said, "Yes. Exactly."

At the sound of the heavy metal door shutting, she glances up, grinning when she spots Miles.

"Miles! I wasn't expecting to see you here," she says, waving him over with her sandwich. "Good first day so far?"

"I'm not sold on my physics professor yet, but overall, not bad. I think I might be able to squeak by with an A."

"She's a real piece of work, I hear," Dr. Okamoto says.

Miles Kasher-Okamoto, joking with his mother. I have to bite back a smile—there's something so unexpected and maybe even endearing about that. It strikes me that this must be difficult for him, seeing her nearly every day.

"This is Barrett," he says, motioning to me. "I hope it's okay that I brought her. She's working on a story about the physics department for the *Washingtonian*."

I hold up my hand in an awkward wave, still half unsure of myself. He didn't tell me he was going to introduce me that way, and something about it feels like bad luck: saying I'm on the paper when I feel further from it than I did after my first botched interview.

One corner of Dr. Okamoto's mouth kicks upward, and I wonder if she rations smiles the way Miles does. "Oh? I read the paper every day. Well—every Monday and Wednesday. It's a shame it's not daily anymore."

Miles's hand finds my lower back, giving me a nudge forward. It's the gentlest push, the briefest moment of contact, and yet it gives me some of the confidence I need. As though that gesture is saying, *I know you can do this.*

"I remember you." Dr. Okamoto places her iPad on the leather bag next to her chair. "You were in my 101 class this morning, weren't you?"

"Guilty."

"What's the piece about?"

With a few lifts of my eyebrows, I try to communicate to Miles that I will punish him with a thousand irritating questions about time travel later for springing this on me. He pretends not to notice. When I'm a real journalist, I'll have to think on my feet like this all the time. And not just on my feet, but on bare feet walking over shards of glass, depending on who I'm interviewing. "It's, uh, for the back-to-school issue. We're interviewing students' favorite professors, giving them a glimpse into their lives both in and out of the classroom."

"'The MO of Dr. O,'" Miles puts in, as though trying to be helpful. "That's what it's called."

"I'm not calling it that," I hiss at him.

"But you could."

Dr. Okamoto doesn't seem to have heard us. Rather, she looks touched. "And you decided on me?"

The lie feels like acid on my tongue. "Based on a poll from last year, you were the favorite in the physics department."

"I'm honored," she says, sounding genuine. "As it turns out, I have about twenty minutes before I have to get back to my office. I don't mind answering a few questions."

We pull up chairs next to hers, Miles's gaze lingering on a particularly menacing monstera hanging above his head. Dr. Okamoto is different in this environment—more casual. Relaxed.

"Okay, then." I fold my hands in my lap as though I am a True Professional. "Let's, um, start with a little background information. How did you begin teaching at the University of Washington?"

"I did my undergrad and master's at the University of Texas." She pauses. "Don't you need something to take notes?"

Ah, yes. A True Professional who forgot the most basic step. Journalism 101.

Get yourself together, Barrett. This may be an interview under false pretenses, but it's still an interview. I know how to do this. And if I can slip in some very casual questions about time travel, all the better.

"Right, of course," I say, working some smoothness into my voice. "You don't mind if I use my phone to record, do you?"

She gestures at me to go ahead, and so I accept the notebook and pen Miles has so helpfully presented to me and start up my recording app.

Over the next few minutes, Dr. Okamoto gives me her life story. She was born in Dallas to first-generation Japanese parents and met Miles's dad in grad school. Surely, Miles has heard all of this a hundred times before, but he listens politely, hands folded in his lap, only occasionally fidgeting with the strap of his backpack.

"Not long after we graduated, we had a baby—"

"Miles," I interject, but she shakes her head.

"Max. Miles's brother. Miles didn't come along until a couple years later," she says. "I taught at UT until tenure-track positions in both physics and history opened up at UW within weeks of each other. We lucked out—it was an easy choice to move our family up here. That was about twelve years ago. Anyway, I'm sure the *Washingtonian* readers would rather hear about my teaching."

Miles hasn't mentioned a brother, but then again, I haven't mentioned plenty. I give Miles a raise of my eyebrows, but he remains fixated on the possibly carnivorous plant.

Dr. Okamoto lights up as she talks more about physics, though I don't understand half of what she's saying about her research.

"I'd love to get into some questions that might be a little out there," I say, now that she's sufficiently warmed up.

"I'll do my best."

I tap Miles's pen on the notebook, considering my words. "The average person might associate physics with time travel. Is that something that's ever come up in your research? Not actual time travel, but theories that might indicate whether it's possible?"

She barely seems fazed by it. "I get asked about time travel in my 101 class every year," she says with a laugh. "I don't know if students are looking for an equation, or if they're being facetious."

A nearby professor, who's been taking measurements of a trio of birds-of-paradise, turns his head. "Hope you don't mind if I inter-ject," he says. "You weren't here when Ella was still teaching, were you, Sumi?"

Dr. Okamoto furrows her brow in the same way Miles does when he's buried in a textbook. "Ella . . . ?"

"Devereux." The professor, a middle-aged man with tawny skin and a neat gray goatee, retracts his tape measure and steps closer. "That class she taught, the one everyone went gaga for. Time Travel for Beginners."

Something clicks, and Dr. Okamoto's face lights up with recog-nition. "Oh! I believe my first year was her last year. Outrageous class, I'm guessing?"

"That's putting it lightly," he says, then holds up a hand to Miles and me. "I'm Professor Rivera, by the way. Horticulture."

"Barrett. Nice to meet you," I say. "I'd love to hear more about the class."

"You and everyone else," he says with a laugh. "It was a four hundred level, absurdly popular. It was about the physics of time travel—all theoretical, of course. Dr. Devereux taught it once a year and always had a wait list a couple hundred students long."

Miles lets out a low whistle. "That's unbelievable."

"Impossible to get an A, too, from what I heard," Professor Rivera says. "In ten years, she probably only gave out a handful."

"Ella Devereux, you said?" I ask. "Did she retire? Or go teach at another school?"

"That, I'm not sure about," he says with a scratch at his goatee. "I didn't know her very well, and none of us heard from her after she left UW."

"Sorry, but I have to head back to class in about five minutes," Dr. Okamoto says with a glance at her watch, and I stumble through a few more questions before it's time to go, the mysterious Dr. Devereux tapping at the back of my mind.

ʊ ʊ ʊ

"Devereux, Devereux . . . ," Miles says across from me at our usual table in the physics library. He hits a few keys on his laptop. "I'm finding an HR manager, a TikTok influencer, and someone who died in 1940."

I pop out one of my earbuds. I've been in the process of transcribing the interview. "Did you put her name in quotes? Or try 'Ella Devereux, physics'?"

Miles levels me with a glare, as though I've just asked him if he knows all the steps of the scientific method. "Tried them both."

His phone rings on the table between us—3:26—and he rejects the call with a quick swipe of his index finger.

"Maybe we're not spelling her name right." I go through a few searches of my own, scribbling down some different spellings, trying the *Washingtonian* archives too. "Or maybe Ella was a nickname and she went by something else professionally?"

At the end of an hour, we've tried Ella, Ellen, Elena, Isabella, Eleanor, Elizabeth, and about a dozen more.

"I found something!" I say. After Gladys hustles over and we assure her we're okay, I flip around my laptop to show Miles. "Eloise Devereux. Graduated with her PhD from Oxford in 1986." It's a photo from her graduation day: a petite, curly-haired woman dressed in a hooded red-and-purple robe, shaking hands with the head of her department. "That's badass. I'd get a PhD just for the outfit."

"Are we even sure that's her?" Miles says, and I let out a groan, because, well, no. The name matches, but this doesn't necessarily tie her back to UW.

I get back to transcribing, hoping it'll give me some fresh insight, but there's nothing from the conversation that isn't already imprinted in my memory. It's eerie enough to send a shiver down my spine that isn't just the draftiness of the library. The whole internet, and this class that was apparently wildly popular, if Professor Rivera is to be believed . . . and one single hit that may not even be her.

Almost like she was never there in the first place.

Chapter 18

MILES KASHER-OKAMOTO, IT TURNS OUT, HAS some major pop-culture holes.

"You've never seen *Groundhog Day*?" I say from where I'm sitting on my dorm bed, scrolling through a list of movies. "And yet you are, by all definitions, a human being on planet Earth?"

Miles is in my desk chair, long legs stretched out in front of him. His presence makes the room instantly feel smaller. Maybe even a little warmer, given how poor the air circulation is in here. "Nope. And I don't want you to drag me for it."

I hold a hand to my heart. "I'm not making fun of you. I feel *sorry* for you, Miles. It's a tragedy that you haven't yet experienced the joy of beloved character actor Stephen Tobolowsky as Ned! Ryerson!" He lifts a single eyebrow at me. "You'd get it if you'd seen the movie!"

There's that smallest of smiles again, the one he tries so hard to contain. *Let it go. Loosen those muscles. I believe in you,* I want to tell him.

I think some part of him might be starting to *like* my teasing, which is entirely too bizarre. Maybe he never got enough of it from his older brother. The mysterious Max.

We decided to set Dr. Devereux aside for now, but the journalist in me remains unsettled. After Lucie left for Zeta Kappa, I didn't love the idea of spending the rest of the night alone, and while I realize that party is likely not the only one happening within a half-mile radius, I didn't trust myself. Then I remembered: the movie playing in the quad is *Groundhog Day*. And it gave me an idea I couldn't believe I hadn't had earlier.

"Is there a reason we're watching this in here instead of out there?" Miles asks, waving his arm in the vague direction of the quad. His roommate sexiled him—he's been with his girlfriend, a freshman at SPU, for three years—so that was how we wound up in Candy Land as opposed to Disney World.

I adjust the pillows I've propped against the wall behind my bed. "One, it's cold. Two, it's easier to eat in here." I hold up one of the boxes of Thai curry I ordered for us. "Three, we might find some inspiration, because we can't just learn from books. This is me broadening your horizons. And four . . . I guess I wanted to see your reactions up close. Since you haven't seen it."

For some reason, this sounds stranger out loud than it did inside my head. I'm not sure why I'd care about his reactions—assuming we make it out of this loop, it's not as if we're destined to become lifelong friends.

"You want to see if we laugh at the same parts?"

"I already know we won't. You rarely laugh."

As if to prove me wrong, he lets out a soft laugh, then triangles one leg on his knee while he reaches for a box of red curry. Even attempting to relax, Miles looks awkward, unsure where to put his limbs.

"It's not that I don't watch movies," he continues. "I actually—okay, you have to promise not to laugh."

"I will do no such thing."

He tosses a grain of rice at me. "You're so predictable sometimes."

I try to catch it in my mouth, but it hits my cheek instead. "Not true. Did you know I was going to do that?"

Miles snorts, then clears his throat. He places his container on my desk, swishes his fork around in it, then rakes a hand through his hair. A few strands stick up in the back, but he doesn't seem to notice. Not to be outdone by the upper half of his body, one of his legs starts bouncing up and down, like he can't quite decide which anxious tic to focus on.

Miles . . . is *nervous*. Despite his frequent fiddling, it's a look I haven't seen on him before. It humanizes him, reminds me he's still a teenager, not an actual working physicist, and this realization is accompanied by a foreign tug of my heart.

"Okay," he says on a whoosh of an exhale. "I . . . want to double major in film."

I just stare at him, waiting for something else, like *I want to double major in film, and my go-to karaoke song is "Spice Up Your Life,"* or *I want to double major in film, and I'm raising a litter of kittens abandoned by their mother in the seventh-floor lounge.*

"I haven't declared it yet," he continues. "But I'm going to. I've been to my film class a dozen times now, and it's just an intro class—a prerequisite for the major—but even the syllabus is exciting. That's ridiculous, right? Getting excited about a syllabus?"

It both is and it isn't, and if anyone were to derive joy from a syllabus, it's Miles.

"What kinds of movies do you like?" I ask. "Or, sorry, should I say *films*?"

"*Movies* is fine. I'm not one of those purists." A grin spreads across his face. It's the brightest one I've seen from him yet—I've barely seen his teeth up until this point. "I watch a lot of genres"— when I open my mouth to protest, he lifts his eyebrows—"*except* for the ones you've decided I missed out on, but that's mostly because my favorites . . . are period pieces."

"Why would I laugh at any of this? I fucking love period pieces. Men in tailcoats and cravats? Those sweeping shots of the English countryside? That's the good shit."

Miles's posture softens the tiniest bit. "I don't know. Well—no, that's not true. I do know. But it's kind of a long story."

I link my fingers and tuck them under my chin. "Tell me?" Miles, the secret film buff. I sort of love it.

"So my parents, the professors, they weren't the biggest fans of TV, but they made this deal with my brother and me growing up," he says. "We couldn't watch TV during the week, but if we finished all our homework by Friday afternoon, then we'd get to watch a movie that night. We turned it into this big thing for Shabbat— we're pretty secular, so we'd do dinner, but my parents were okay with us using electronics. And after dinner, we'd get to watch a movie. Since there was no TV during the week, we always wanted to make it count."

"Well, sure. You wouldn't want to waste your one weekly pick," I say. "Your brother—Max? How old is he?"

Something odd passes across his face, so slight I almost don't catch it. "Twenty-one." Then he barrels onward. Guess they aren't the closest of siblings. "I compiled all these lists in a spreadsheet"— now *that* sounds like Miles—"making sure I was picking objectively the *best* movies I possibly could. We went through the AFI list, IMDB, *Rolling Stone*. And I really latched on to period pieces. Anything with royalty or nobles, or based on an Austen novel. They're just the best kind of escapism. Plus, the way people insult each other is much better than the way we do it today. There's nothing more scathing than an insult from the 1800s—like . . . *flapdoodle*, or *blunderbuss*."

His whole face has changed, eyes lighting up and turning dreamy, and it's almost unsettling, the way this makes me warm to him. It must be the journalist in me, curious about the parts of Miles he doesn't show the rest of the world.

"All of that sounds completely and utterly delightful," I say, unable to help grinning along with him. "Where's the part where I laugh at you? I'm feeling a little ripped off here."

"I was very briefly part of a film club in high school that . . . wasn't the best," he says, jaw tightening again. "It was a bunch of guys who wanted to talk about how much they loved *American Psycho* and *Fight Club*. It was your typical story: person likes something that isn't considered 'cool'; others make fun of them for it."

"That's some bullshit. Typical or not."

"I agree. But thank you. For not laughing." He returns to his food for a moment while I try to reconcile this new Miles with the old.

"So, what, you want to make movies about science?" I ask. "Period pieces about nineteenth-century physicists?"

"I don't know yet," he says, giving the side of my bed a light kick. "It's only the five hundredth day of freshman year, Barrett. Right now I just want to study what I love. And god help me if I still love it on day one thousand."

"Then I have just one crucial question for you." I give him my most serious face. "What's your favorite *Pride and Prejudice*?"

Miles taps his fingers on his chin. "I have to go with the 1995 BBC miniseries."

I groan. "Colin Firth was such a boring Mr. Darcy. He's way too . . . Colin Firthy. Nothing excites me about Colin Firth. But then you have the beauty of the 2005 version! Keira Knightley! The *hand flex*, Miles, the hand flex! It's just *lovely* in every way," I say. "My mom would agree with you, though. It's the source of one of our biggest arguments to date."

"You and your mom are really close," he muses.

I nod. "It's just the two of us. She, uh, had me when she was pretty young. Nineteen." And then I brace myself for the judgment that always comes after I tell someone this. Because it's one thing when someone slut-shames you. It's completely another when they slut-shame your mom.

But he just says, "That must have been really tough for her."

"It was. She still graduated in five years, though, which is pretty badass. And then she moved to the suburbs with her darling daughter and opened a stationery shop. She's been solidly thriving for over a decade and counting. It's always felt dorky to say this, but she's like . . . my favorite person."

"Not dorky." He points to himself. "The collection of science books on my shelves at home that I had a nearly impossible time deciding which to leave behind, despite the fact that I was only moving half an hour away? Definitely dorky."

I wag an index finger at my shelf of magazines. "Relatable."

This self-aware, self-deprecating side of Miles is new. I wonder if this is what he's like at home, with Dr. Okamoto and Dr. Kasher and a brother he maybe doesn't get along with. I don't hate it, and I'm desperate to make it last as long as possible.

"My mom went here too," I continue. "I never thought I'd go anywhere else. There are pictures of me as a baby in a tiny purple onesie with a *W* on it, posing with Dubs and crying because I wanted to take him home with me. I guess I spent so much time building it up in my head that I thought it would, I don't know . . . change me, in some way." I fight a grimace as I say it, worried it sounds melodramatic.

"Well, is it?" Miles asks, surprising me not for the first or even second time tonight. "Changing you?"

"To be honest, it's been a bit of a letdown so far. This physics nerd–slash–film buff won't quit following me through space and time."

When he laughs, the sound is so unexpected that I nearly drop my takeout container. It's warm and rich and a little too loud, and maybe that's why it startles me: because everything else about him is so measured, so calculated. This laugh, where he almost forgets himself for a moment . . . it might be my new favorite thing about him.

"Anyway," I say, forging forward, unsure why I'm struck

with the urge to make him laugh again. Probably because my mom's the only one who's ever laughed at my jokes. "I have a lot of my mom's taste because I grew up with all her favorite things, and she was just the coolest person in the world to me. My first concert was the Backstreet Boys' twentieth-anniversary tour. Take me to any early-2000s trivia contest, I'll know every answer."

My dorm bookshelf is so low that Miles is able to stretch a hand upward and grasp one of my magazines without any effort at all. "So you're a bit old-fashioned," he says, paging through a *Vanity Fair*. "You know you can find all of this online, right?"

"That interview with Jennifer Aniston is really great," I say. "And sure, but I love the realness of a physical copy. I feel more connected to a story that way."

"This is what you want to do?" He finds the cover story, the one where Jen opens up about her divorce for the first time, not just getting emotional but also shutting down sexist comments lobbed at her over the years. The author turns a larger-than-life personality into a person. "Articles like this?"

"Well, not *exactly* that," I say. "It's not just wanting to write about famous people or getting celebrities to spill tea. And I'm not talking about the articles that are like, 'So-and-so gingerly pokes at her shaved fennel salad, contemplating the meaning of life,'" I say in a faux lofty voice. "I want to dig deep, get inside someone's head, hear the stories they don't always tell. And I guess I just . . . want to make people care about something they didn't know they could care about."

"No one's gingerly poking at salads in your stories," Miles says with a quarter smile, which would be undetectable on anyone else. "No, I get it. Very specific taste, and I respect it."

I gesture to my laptop screen, indicating the reason Miles came over in the first place. This conversation took an unexpected turn, and something about him holding my magazines while I tell him about my career aspirations feels almost . . . intimate. *Personal*— that's a better word for it.

"And that includes *Groundhog Day*. Not to be dramatic or anything, but I kind of feel like I was born for this?" I flex my fingers, aware of his gaze on me and how it feels different, maybe, from how he's looked at me before. Probably because he hasn't been annoyed at me in at least five minutes. If his eyes are lingering, it's only because I'm talking.

It is definitely time to start the movie and stop thinking.

I reach for my laptop, nearly bashing Miles's head with it in my eagerness to position it at the top of my bed. When I swerve at the last moment, the laptop crashes into a bottle of Coke and sends it right into his chest.

"Shit—I'm sorry!" I say as the liquid pours down his shirt.

"I'm fine, I'm fine," he says, scrambling to catch the bottle before it hits the floor.

I jump off the bed and grab the first napkin-looking thing I see, which turns out to be my gray cardigan.

"You sure you want to use that? It might stain."

"If we wake up on Thursday morning, you can buy me a new one." I kneel beside him, realizing too late that the liquid has spread to his groin, which I am currently eye level with. Where I am currently swiping at him with the wet cardigan.

"I—um—I think I've got it," he stammers, holding out his hand.

I drop the cardigan and spring away from him, smacking my elbow against my bed frame. Lock me up. Please. I am a menace to society.

"Do you want to go change?" I ask.

He dabs at his shirt and jeans while I contemplate whether a Jewish girl would be permitted to enter a nunnery. "Sexiled, remember? They go to a party afterward, but that's not for another hour."

"Oh. You can borrow one of my shirts," I say, because shirts are safe. Shirts are not pants, and even better, they are not Miles's soda-soaked pants I was moments away from groping him in.

My closet is full of old pajama T-shirts, some mine and some stolen from my mom. And, well, the fact of it is that I might be shorter than Miles, but I'm positive I weigh more than he does. If I give him a shirt he ends up drowning in, I may perish.

I toss him a NEPTUNE HIGH T-shirt that's a little tight on me. He accepts it, hooking a finger in the collar of the one he's wearing. "Do you mind, uh, turning around?"

"Right. Of course."

And I do. I swear I do. But it's not my fault that he lifts the hem of his shirt a split-second before I'm fully turned, and I catch a sliver of tan skin above the waist of his jeans. Apparently I'm not just learning more about Miles today—I'm seeing more of him, too. It's the briefest flash, but it's enough to bring heat to my cheeks. Which is frankly unacceptable. Clearly we've been trapped in this room, trapped in Wednesday, for too long.

"Between this and the pepper spray, I must be destined to cause you pain," I say once he's safely clothed.

When he gives me this look, his dark eyes impossible to read, I wonder if maybe that pain goes both ways.

DAY FOURTEEN

꒐꒐꒐ ꒐꒐꒐ ꒐꒐꒐꒐

Chapter 19

IF ELLA DEVEREUX TAUGHT AT UW, THERE HAS TO be a record on her, and on the next Miles day, he suggests we try to find it.

There's a long line of students waiting to talk to the bored-looking woman behind the counter in the physics department office. "If this is about switching classes, you'll have to fill out one of those forms," she says when I get to the front, pointing to a stack on the desk next to her.

"Oh—it's not," I say. "I'm a reporter on the *Washingtonian*, and I was hoping to get some information about a professor who used to work here?"

She sighs as though I've asked if I can change my major to mushroom foraging. "And this is something that needs to be done on the first day of the quarter? I have a long line of schedule changes to process."

Next to me, Miles squares his shoulders, readjusting the collar of his typical plaid flannel. "We'll be fast. Her name is Ella Devereux, possibly Eloise Devereux."

"One moment." When she disappears, the people behind us in line let out a collective groan.

"We've just made a dozen new enemies," I whisper to Miles, who seems unfazed.

"They'll forget us by tomorrow."

The woman returns with an older man wearing a frown beneath a salt-and-pepper mustache. "You're the ones looking for Devereux?" he says, arms crossed over a UW sweatshirt. "We don't have records for anyone with that name."

"You—what?" I say, taken aback. "Are you sure you spelled it—"

"If there's nothing else we can help you with," he interrupts, "I suggest you get back to your classes."

I blink at him, aware we're being brushed off but unable to comprehend why. "You don't have any records at all? We were talking to Professor Rivera, in the horticulture department? He said she taught this class about time travel that was really hard to get an A in, and that she stopped about ten years back?"

When the man just stares at me, I realize how ridiculous my words sound.

"My mother is a professor in this department," Miles says, backing me up. "She recalls working with Dr. Devereux for a year before she left."

"We see thousands of students come through here every year. Hundreds of professors. Perhaps they got the name wrong."

"Then could you at least look in the back there"—I crane my neck to see around the corner—"and let us know who taught Time Travel for Beginners?"

"Are you fucking kidding me," a guy behind me mutters.

"I'm not sure what kind of a joke this is," the man says with a derisive laugh, "but we are an esteemed institution. That class sounds like pure fiction." He gestures to the exasperated crowd filling the office. "Now. We have a line full of physics students with legitimate concerns to help. If you're not one of them, I suggest moving on." With that, he waves forward the next person.

Shoulders slouched, we venture back into the quad, through Red Square, passing the swing dancers and Save the Gophers Kendall and all these people completely unaware that what they're doing today may very well not matter.

"It's a dead end," Miles says as we grab a bench near a group of slackliners. "We can't find someone the internet and physics department are telling us never existed."

But my journalistic instincts refuse to be quiet. We could pry more information out of Professor Rivera. We could keep digging. Desperately, I glance around at the scene in front of us, as though a hint is hiding in the trees or grass or buildings from the early 1900s. There has to be something we haven't tried yet. A burst of inspiration and hope that I could really use right about now. Even *Groundhog Day* didn't give me any grand ideas.

"Barrett." Miles says my name softly, wrapped in a sigh, a mix of reassurance and resignation. As though he thinks I haven't heard him, when the truth is that I am so attuned to Miles's voice at this point, he could whisper from twenty feet away and I'd hear him. "I'm not sure we're getting anywhere."

"You're supposed to be the optimistic one," I say, tapping his ankle with my SHITSHOW-socked foot. Not matching socks, because it doesn't matter and my other one is still lost. Earlier this morning, he told me the sock was the most Barrett Bloom thing he'd ever seen, and the fact that I had only one of them even more so, and I chose to take it as a compliment. And promised to buy him a pair of his very own if we ever get out of this.

When we get out of this.

"I am?"

"Well, it can't be me! I'm too cynical!"

Miles from a couple of days ago might have laughed at this, but either he's too tired or he's grown weary of humoring me. It was bound to happen sometime. He turns, yawning into his shoulder, and when he adjusts on the bench, his knee bumps my hip. It's not the worst thing, jean-to-jean contact. It feels like some anchor to this strange earth. Even if it's accidental.

"Are you okay?" he asks after a few minutes of silence. "You're not usually this quiet. It's unsettling."

"I'm not sure." One of the slackliners makes it to the middle before losing her balance. My eyes follow the rope stretched between the two trees, a knot of anxiety tightening in my stomach. "God, what if it's never going to be fall?"

"It will be," Miles says. "In some timeline."

I groan, pulling my knees up onto the bench and resting my chin on them. "But I'm a basic autumn bitch, Miles. I'm at my most powerful in the fall. I need PSLs and boots and cable-knit sweaters to survive. I need to frolic in a pile of leaves."

"I'd hate to see you even more powerful. You frolic?"

"Oh, I *frolic*," I say, slathering it with as much emphasis as I can, and it's only when it leaves my mouth that I realize it sounds dirty. "And I assume I'll never be able to switch out of Physics 101, either. Hilarious. I love this journey for me." And yet the joking around doesn't loosen the tension in my chest the way it usually does, the way it did all summer when I pretended I wasn't reeling from prom. I try to ignore the quickening of my heart rate, but the panic is stronger. It clenches a fist around my throat, a force so powerful it steals my breath. All the things I wanted to do in college—they've never been farther out of reach. "I wanted to go to a Hillel service, meet other Jews, but I guess it might never even be Shabbat! And write for the paper. And study abroad. And about a hundred other things. And I just—"

All of a sudden, I'm hopping off the bench, gasping out an exhale. Every cell in me is restless. Claustrophobic. Not just from being trapped in time, but on this campus. There's every opportunity at our fingertips, and we're just sitting here. Literally.

"Barrett?" Miles gets to his feet, a note of worry in his voice.

And I take off running.

I race through the quad, past the slackliners and clubs and students searching for their next class. Past old buildings and new buildings and buildings I don't know the names of. I have no patience for crowds, and my footsteps on the concrete stairs echo with a satisfying thump. But it's not enough. I need *more*.

Two weeks. *Two weeks* I've been stuck here. Barely moving.

I dart out of the way of a bus, speeding down the hill that'll take me off campus, sucking in giant lungfuls of air, and that's not enough either. *More,* my restless brain demands. I'm starting to understand why people do this, why they push their bodies beyond their limits—to fucking *feel something*. Something bigger than themselves and the comfort zones they've grown so cozy in.

Every so often, I hear Miles behind me, shouting my name, but I don't stop running until I can see water. A shimmering Union Bay and a tiny park hugging the shore and Husky Stadium, that U-shaped building supposedly designed to keep the sun out of athletes' eyes.

Running has always felt like a punishment. Today it feels like an escape. My lungs are burning and my legs are protesting and I love all of it. I love every ounce of discomfort, every ache when I bend my legs or when the wind slashes my cheeks as I turn my face up to the sky.

There's music coming from the stadium, something bold and brassy, and the front entrance is wide open. I slow down, half because my thighs are starting to chafe and half because I'm curious. I follow the bright purple arrows tacked to the massive gray walls, follow the sound past concession stands into a seating section in the visitors' end zone.

The full UW marching band is at the opposite end of the field, dressed in purple, white, and gold, the sun glinting off their instruments.

I don't even bother biting back a grin as I hop the railing to get down on the field. They're playing a version of "Seven Nation Army" by the White Stripes, and the whole thing is some kind of first-day celebration, groups of students running around the football field, eating and playing games and attempting to kick field goals.

There's a rush of breath and a rustle of footsteps as Miles approaches, his cheeks flushed from exertion, dark hair a complete mess. Maybe the stadium can keep the sun out of football players' eyes, but it's not stopping the late morning light from catching the angles of Miles's face.

"Are we training for a marathon now?" he asks, panting, and something about the word *we* lodges itself in my mind, though this is far from the first time he's said it. "Wow. I had no idea all of this was here."

In spite of everything, or maybe because I've fully lost it, I start laughing at the absurdity of his suggestion when—*shit.* A cramp slices through my side, yanking me down into the turf in a heap of sweaty exhaustion, across from a booth selling popcorn and cotton candy.

The stadium applauds when the song ends with a flourish. "Thank you, thank you!" the band leader says into the mic, voice reverberating. "Any other requests?" Someone near her calls out something I can't hear. She clears her throat. "Any *appropriate* requests?"

"Lady Gaga!" a girl shouts, and the band launches into "Bad Romance."

"We've been playing it so *safe*," I say to Miles, still trying to catch my breath. "I've barely left campus. What if this whole thing is about living life to the fullest?"

I don't want to go to class, I don't want to interview for the paper, and I don't want to decide whether to go to a frat party with my roommate. I want that magical, once-in-a-lifetime experience people are supposed to have in college. The experience my mom and Jocelyn talk about with a gleam in their eyes. And if the universe isn't going to let me experience it the way I always thought I would, then I'm just going to have to make it for myself.

Miles pats the turf to see if it's wet before dropping to his knees next to me. When his body sways, I feel a surge of *something* I can't quite name. Poised and perfect Miles, unraveling because he chased after me. "You think the universe is upset with you because you didn't carpe diem? I feel like whatever's out there has bigger shit to deal with than whether Barrett Bloom is living it up."

"Evidently not! Whoever Ella Devereux is or was, no one seems to be able to tell us anything useful. We're *stuck*, and who knows for how long. And we're not even having fun."

"I'm having fun," he says, defensive, dragging a hand through his hair. Much like mine, it refuses to be tamed. "Gladys and I have become great friends. She just doesn't know it."

"That's the other thing. We're never going to be able to spend time with anyone else, at least not in a meaningful way," I say, thinking of my mom. Of Lucie. "Maybe you and Gladys find a new way to reorganize the physics library, and she's so grateful she writes you into her will, and you stand to inherit a hefty sum of money. Maybe you join a knitting club together. Or maybe we rip every page from every book in that library, and the next version of Gladys will have no idea. And she never will."

Miles makes an odd noise in the back of his throat. "Just to be clear," he says, "there is nothing going on between me and Gladys."

I can't help it—I burst out laughing. "I'm sorry," I say. "My mind went to a weird place."

"Is that not where your mind usually lives?"

"True," I admit. It's an unexpected moment of accord between us. It shouldn't make me feel as fuzzy as it does, and yet very few things make sense about the Barrett Bloom who ran a half mile without stopping.

This time when the band stops, I jog toward them to give the leader my request.

Miles lifts his eyebrows at me as the horns and drums start back up. "Did you ask them to play 'Toxic'?"

With a few flaps of my arms, I motion for him to stand. I'm not a great dancer, but that's never stopped me before. At least half the crowd is cheering, getting into it, singing along. "You can't just sit on the ground while a marching band is playing Britney's greatest song. Arguably one of the greatest songs of the 2000s."

"It *is* a good song," he concedes, getting to his feet. But that's where he pauses. He simply stands there, in the middle of a football field, surrounded by a few dozen college students dancing to vintage Britney Spears.

"You've got to give me more than that." I move my hips and lift my hands to the sky, surely looking ridiculous but not caring. "No one's going to remember your slick dance moves tomorrow." I give him a wink. "Except for me."

"That's what I'm worried about." With an exaggerated sigh-groan, Miles starts moving to the beat. And, well, I *think* what he's doing might be considered dancing. On some planets.

If he were anyone else, I might consider inching closer, draping an arm around his shoulders. Attempting to dance together, since I'd love nothing more than to erase the last guy I danced with.

But we stay in our own bubbles, every so often catching the other's eye with a small smile.

"We should be doing things like this," I say when the song ends. Breathless, I fling an arm out, gesturing to the scene around us. "Getting out. Exploring."

There's a pause, and I'm sure Miles is going to come up with a hundred reasons why we shouldn't do the one thing that makes a time loop *exciting*.

"Let's do it, then," he says after a few moments, sounding resolute. "Let's go out and explore."

I stare at him, letting a slow grin spread across my face.

"Oh no. That look is scary. I already have regrets."

"We've just discovered that time travel exists, and so far? It's *boring*, Miles!" Maybe that's a simplistic way of putting it, but that's what it boils down to, right? "Best-case scenario," I continue, "we fix whatever's going on. Worst-case scenario . . . we finally have some fucking *fun*."

"I'm not opposed to fun," he says. He could swap *fun* for *invasive dental surgery* and his tone wouldn't need to change at all.

"Think about it. There are zero consequences. We can do whatever the hell we want. Anything you wouldn't normally do—this is our chance to go wild. Like, let's go rob a bank just because we can!"

Miles looks horrified.

"Okay, not a bank," I say. "But we could travel! Win the lottery! Those people who were shitty to you in high school—we can tell them to go fuck themselves or key their cars or give them brownies baked with dog shit. Or maybe you have some eternal unrequited crush—you can go tell them how you feel. That's kind of freeing, isn't it?"

"No. It's terrifying," he says quietly, and I can tell there's some real fear there.

I want to tell him there's nothing to be afraid of, only I'm not certain I'm right. "What's something you've always wanted to do?" I ask, a thrill working its way up my spine. This is it. The loop has already taken so much from us, but it's also giving us an opportunity. I want to hold on tight, refuse to let go.

He considers this, tapping a finger on his chin. "Take a four hundred–level physics class," he says, and it wins the award for the most Miles thing I have ever heard. "Just to see how much of it I could keep up with."

I shake my head and flash him a grin. "Buckle up, buttercup. We're about to have the time of our fucking lives."

DAY FIFTEEN

𝍷𝍷 𝍷𝍷 𝍷𝍷

Chapter 20

"IS NOW A BAD TIME TO MENTION THAT I HAVE A slight fear of flying?" Miles asks from the first-class seat next to me.

I pause with my glass of guava juice halfway to my mouth. When I asked for champagne, the flight attendant raised her eyebrows and asked to see my ID. "Didn't you try to go to Geneva?"

"I was on edge the whole time, and I couldn't bear the thought of doing it again," he says, sheepish. "One time when we visited relatives in Japan, I cried so much on the plane that my parents bought everyone on the flight a drink."

Miles fidgets with the seat-belt buckle, and then with the collar of his shirt. "That's what you're wearing?" I asked when we met in the lobby earlier this morning. "I tell you we're going on a once-in-a-lifetime adventure, and you decided that meant khakis and a striped polo?"

"What's wrong with khakis?" He frowned down at his clothes. "They go with everything. And I like this shirt!"

The truth is, Miles doesn't look bad at all, even if he does look dressed for a round of golf. In first class, he fits in. He also didn't look bad when he was changing into my *Veronica Mars* shirt, but that's completely irrelevant to today's mission.

I stretch out my legs as a family of four bumps down the aisle, a howling baby in tow. "Wait. What about roller coasters?"

If living life to the fullest is our way out, then Disneyland was the fullest thing I could think of that we could realistically do in a single day. Yesterday, I told Miles he had to think bigger: somewhere in between Geneva and a 400-level class. It's not a bucket list, exactly. More of a doing-whatever-we-want-because-there-are-no-consequences list, though that doesn't have the same ring to it. A fuck-it list, if you will.

This is exactly what we needed: no school, no libraries, no physics. No thinking about the mysterious Dr. Devereux, who the world is set on convincing us doesn't exist. For today, I leave all of that in Seattle.

"Oddly, I'm okay with roller coasters," Miles says. "It's the whole giant-metal-box-in-the-sky thing that makes me anxious."

"This is the moment I give you all the science that keeps this plane aloft."

"I'm aware. And yet . . . sometimes our brains aren't entirely logical, are they?"

The thing is, I assume Miles's fear of flying isn't as intense as he's making it out to be, if only because it's so opposite from the person I'm starting to know—until the engines roar to life. He shudders in his seat as the plane taxis, eyes shut tight, jaw clenched, seeming to almost shrink in on himself.

This does something to my heart, because as frustrating as Miles can be, I don't want him to be miserable.

"Do you . . . want to hold my hand?" I ask, unsure what else to offer. It's meant as a joke. A way to distract him.

Completely straight-faced, Miles says, "I might."

And just as the plane leaves the ground, I place my hand, palm up, on the armrest between us. Slowly, slowly, he threads his fingers with mine, a shy, uncertain graze at first before the plane hits a pocket of air and he grips my hand tight. His hand is warm, his nails short and clean. If I look down, I can see the tension in his fingers, the way his skin pulls taut over his knuckles.

"It's okay," I say, trying to sound as soothing as possible as he cuts off my circulation. "We're okay. We're safe."

We are holding hands. We are holding hands, and maybe I was offering comfort and he accepted it, but that doesn't change the fact that I have never held hands with someone not related to me until this moment, even if that someone is dressed like a suburban dad who raided an Eddie Bauer during a Labor Day sale.

I've never given a tremendous amount of thought to the concept of holding hands, but it's nice, I decide, especially when his hand relaxes into mine as the plane climbs higher. His eyes are still closed, his chest rising and falling with the sharp rhythm of his breaths.

And somehow, when he lets go of my hand somewhere over Oregon with a soft "thank you," I'm the one who's breathless.

DAY SIXTEEN

〜〜〜 〜〜〜 〜〜〜 |

Chapter 21

"BARRETT?" MILES CALLS A FEW YARDS AWAY from me, his leashes twisted in a knot. It's 3:26 and his phone is ringing, and he's dropped it on the ground in an attempt to turn it off. "A little help here?"

One of his dogs has stretched to the end of its leash and is just staring at me, never breaking eye contact. Two of the puppies are wrestling, one is peeing, and one is sniffing that pee.

"You know, I would if I could," I shout back, steering my own pack away from a woman and her aloof French bulldog.

In retrospect, adopting as many dogs as the shelter would allow us to was perhaps not the wisest idea. At first they would only let us adopt one—two if they were a bonded pair. But eventually they let us go with a whopping fifteen: three Labs, two pit-bull mixes, four Chihuahua mixes, a giant, gorgeous Samoyed, and a handful of complete mysteries.

It's amazing what a massive amount of cash can accomplish. We'd recently come into an inheritance, we said. We wanted to give these dogs the best life we possibly could, a life of treats and snuggles and scratches behind the ears.

And for today, we will.

"Who's the best boy? And the best girl?" The dogs seem to love when Miles speaks directly to them, because they stop what they're doing and look right at him, some of their heads tilting. "That's right, all of you!"

I make it to Miles's phone before he does, kneeling down to pick it up. "Max," I say, reading off the caller ID for the first time. "Your brother's the one calling you every day?"

"It's nothing," he says. "He's just going to ask if he can get a ride somewhere."

"Oh." If that's the case, it's strange that Miles has been so distant about it, but I decide not to push it. They're not close—maybe it's as simple as that.

We make it to the off-leash area of the park, and it's majestic, really, seeing all these creatures run wild. My dogs seize the opportunity to surround Miles, lowering onto their front legs and begging him to play.

"How do you get them to do that?" I ask. It's not like I'm running straight at my pack of dogs, arms flung wide, yelling *Let me love youuuu!*

"I have no idea," he says, laughing that warm, slightly-too-loud laugh. A black Lab named Otis and a tiny ball of fluff named Falafel sit down and wag their tails, waiting for treats. They're entranced, under some spell apparently only Miles has cast. He digs into his bag, telling them to wait as he produces a treat for each of them.

"I refuse to believe you didn't bathe in peanut butter before we left." I hold out those same treats, trying to entice them over to me. It's no use.

He pinches the collar of his shirt, takes a whiff. "Or they just really like Irish Spring."

Ah. So that's what his scent is. Maybe now I'll stop obsessing. I'll get my own bottle of Irish Spring, and then I can inhale Miles whenever I want to without being creepy about it.

Although maybe the concept of inhaling him whenever I want to is the definition of being creepy about it.

I try whistling at the dogs, throwing a few tennis balls, even getting down in the mud to play, but nothing works. They are gone for Miles and Miles only.

"Well, this is some bullshit," I fake whine, which only makes Miles laugh harder.

The dogs love on him so much that he eventually loses his balance. Miles on his knees in a muddy patch of grass, Otis and Falafel and Bear and Neo licking his face while he tries to pet them all at once—that's a sight I never thought I'd see, and it's kind of glorious.

The glimpses I've gotten of this Miles aren't nearly enough, even when they're making my heart skip and stutter inside my chest.

I stretch a hand toward him, pretending I'm going to help him up before swiping a line of dirt across his cheek. His face is flushed, eyes flashing with vengeance.

"You want to play dirty?" he says, reaching for my legs and dragging me back into the mud.

DAY SEVENTEEN
𝍢𝍢𝍢 ‖
Chapter 22

ELEVEN O'CLOCK AT NIGHT, AND MILES AND I ARE the only ones inside the drama building. It's a well-known fact that this was once a women's physical-education building, complete with a locker room, gymnasium, and pool. Today that pool is undergoing repairs for a broken filter, which I learned during freshman orientation. And, most importantly: it's drained.

The meager lighting washes everything in sepia as we haul a dozen huge bags down the hall, passing cast photos and performance stills. It smells strange and mostly unpleasant, chlorine and sweat and decades of wannabe actors now-is-the-winter-of-our-discontent-ing.

"This is absurd," Miles keeps saying, letting out a laugh that echoes around the windowless room. It is. And that's what makes it fantastic. "I can't believe creating a giant ball pit is on your list."

"Not a ball pit by name, exactly. But getting up to some kind of after-hours mischief." I think back to Jocelyn's story about sorority ice-skating. "You should be grateful I haven't made any ball jokes. Because trust me, I've wanted to."

"That's not true. When I opened up the first bag, you said, 'I thought they'd be bigger.'"

"And then you said, 'This is what god gave me!'"

His mouth twists into a smirk as he shakes his head, but he can't deny that days-1-through-65 Miles wouldn't have humored me at all. I love that he's embracing the absurdity. We haven't been to the library in nearly a week, and if he's twitching to open up a textbook, he hasn't said anything.

By the time we've moved all the bags from a truck out back—we paid way too much to borrow them from an indoor playground—I'm a sweaty, exhausted mess, my T-shirt clinging to my back and my jeans buttons digging into my stomach. But it's worth it when we stake out spots on opposite sides of the pool and start pouring. Adrenaline rushes through my veins as the balls stream out in brightly colored waves, red and yellow and green and blue.

Once we've emptied all the bags, Miles inches to the edge of the pool and stretches, as though gearing up for a dive into a real water-and-chlorine-filled pool. I kick off my shoes, not entirely sure of proper ball-pit-jumping attire.

"You want to do this together?" he asks, holding out his hand.

I stare at it for a few moments before glancing back at his face. Somehow, the eerie lighting casts his features in a soft, golden glow. He shouldn't look this . . . well, *attractive*. No one should, under these conditions. His eyes spark, the static electricity making his hair a dark, spiky halo around his face. And it's kind of cute, I decide, the way his ears stick out.

A concerning observation, right up there with my split-second desire to huff a bottle of Irish Spring.

I force myself to be rational, something the fluttering of my stomach seems determined to ignore. Miles is the only other person trapped with me. The only person who gets what I'm going through. If I ever make it to my Thursday psych class, I'm sure I'll learn that these feelings are natural. Miles is someone to sympathize with, nothing more. It's sheer proximity, tricking me into thinking it's something else.

I nod and link my fingers with his, trying not to think about the fact that this is the second time we've held hands, because holding hands doesn't mean anything. This isn't romantic—it's *Miles*, the guy who could probably only fall in love with a textbook.

We're stuck in a fantasy, and that means this cannot be real.

I wish my breath wouldn't catch in my throat when his thumb strokes up my index finger—gently. Delicately. I have to wonder if he's doing it without thinking, because he's staring out at the pit, looking pensive. *I'm glad we did this,* that stroke of his finger seems to say, and so I counter with one of my own. *Me too,* I tell him with a rub of my middle finger along one of his knuckles.

"Barrett?" he says. It must be the adrenaline that breaks my name into three syllables. His eyes leap to mine again, jaw pulsing. I don't know what's on the other side of his question.

Standing on the edge of the pit feels like we're on the precipice of something, only I'm not sure what. Even if it's nothing grand and metaphorical, it certainly seems that way.

"Sink or swim," I say, and it's a blessing that I only have a second to linger on the way he squeezes my hand before our feet leave the ground.

Breaking the surface feels nothing like diving into a real pool.

It's not painful, but I can *feel it*, my feet legs hips chest punching into the pit, the plastic giving way and making room for us.

Either because neither of us is a graceful jumper or because one of us leaped a moment before the other, our bodies tangle, one of my arms thrown across Miles's back, my right leg twined with his left. If I'm too sweaty or too heavy, he doesn't say anything, just lets out a rush of breath followed by some disbelieving laughter. The heat of him combined with the cool plastic of the balls is enough to completely overwhelm my senses, my skin buzzing in a weird and wonderful way.

"This is the best thing that's ever happened to me," I say.

We're only submerged up to our necks, but it's still ridiculous, trying to move ourselves through the multicolored spheres. The full reality that we actually pulled this off hits me in waves, and then I can't stop grinning. I feel *light*, like nothing we did before tonight matters. Like if the universe really is keeping score, it starts right now.

Miles ducks when I lob a ball at him, then pops back up with his cheeks a warm pink, his hair an electric-charged chaos. Mine must look absolutely wild. He throws back his head, his face open and warm and like nothing I've seen before, as though he's lit from within. *Lovely*—it's the first word that comes to mind, and it's the only one that seems to fit. He's let go, finally allowing his body to relax and simply savor the pure joy of something.

And this—*this* is the real smile.

DAY EIGHTEEN

卌 卌 卌 |||

Chapter 23

ANNABEL COSTA, EDITOR IN CHIEF OF THE *Washingtonian*, passes my story back across her desk with a furrow between her brows.

Sure, it's a little unorthodox to come to an interview with an article already written, but I spent the morning hunched over my laptop while Miles went to his 400-level classes—just in case he was right that getting on the paper will fix my timeline.

"It's clearly very well researched," Annabel says, a hint of disappointment in her voice. "And you're a talented writer. But without any quotes from Dr. Okamoto herself, or from any of her colleagues . . . I'm afraid I can't do anything with it."

My shoulders droop. I can't quite explain to Annabel the complicated ethics of not being able to quote someone I technically didn't interview—in this timeline. I did the best I could, cobbling together information from other articles and feature stories, and it felt incredible to dust off my skills. My last piece for the *Nav*, a profile of a beloved, retiring English teacher, feels forever ago. But, ultimately, I know Annabel's right. The story doesn't work if it's only my voice.

The rest of the interview is lackluster, mainly because I can't summon the energy to be interesting. For the first time, I wonder what Annabel does on the days I don't show up. Writes me off completely? Savors the bonus free time?

It lasts longer than my first two attempts, mainly because of the time it took Annabel to read my article, and when she leads me out of her office, there's a commotion in the middle of the newsroom.

"System's down," says a guy at one of the computers. "I can't open anything on our server."

Annabel lets out the kind of sigh that indicates this must happen often. "Shit. Is Christina here?"

"On it," a girl calls from the doorway, rushing inside in a blur of leather jacket and blue hair, tossing her bag onto a chair before plunking herself down next to it. "Sorry. That three-hour coding class is no joke, and neither are the lines at the counseling center."

"Thank god," Annabel says. "I don't know how we'd keep this running without you."

As I leave the building, I wonder if it doesn't matter whether I get the job or not—I may never be able to see one of my pieces in print.

I'm deep in my feelings when a jingly tune stops me in the journalism building's parking lot. Miles is behind the wheel of a bright pink ice-cream truck with THE BIG FREEZE painted on the side. He hangs an arm out the window, waving me over.

In spite of everything, I start laughing as I approach the driver's side. "They let you drive this off the lot?"

"Got a great deal on it too." He frowns. "You seem less Barretty than usual. Everything okay?"

I pull in a deep breath, then let out a heavy sigh. "My article wasn't good enough. I knew it wouldn't be, and I guess I could try to redo it, but . . . I don't know. So now that feels like a dead end." I rake an anxious hand through my hair. And none of this is getting us closer to Devereux, whether she exists or not. Maybe she's a dead end too.

"Maybe it just wasn't the right story," Miles says.

"Maybe," I say, and then, because I don't want to linger on it: "I think some ice cream might cheer me up."

We park the truck in the quad and stick a sign on it that says FREE ICE CREAM. As a result, we become the most beloved people on campus. For the next couple of hours, we busy ourselves scooping. We're not the best at it—there's a steeper learning curve than I might have imagined—but people don't seem to care when the ice cream is free. The truck is small, and we keep bumping against each other, trading mumbled *sorry*s as we wait for the line to die down. Spoiler alert: it never does, and neither does the electricity along my skin whenever we reach inside a container at the same time. Because my body is both deeply confused and deeply traitorous.

Christ, this needs to stop. Miles being the only person I talk to on a regular basis is really fucking with my brain. In no timeline would Miles and I be a logical couple. It doesn't matter if certain elements of him are appealing in a certain way during certain hours of September 21. It doesn't matter how kind he's become, underneath all that seriousness.

It's not real, and once our timelines right themselves, I'm sure we'll go our separate ways.

A thought that shouldn't feel as lonely as it does.

"What can I get you?" I ask what must be our two hundredth customer of the day. We're already out of chocolate and running low on strawberry.

"This all free?"

I hear his voice before I see him, certain at first that my memory is wrong. That it can't be him. But then he steps forward, tapping our open window, and every nerve ending in my body short-circuits at once.

No.

I have to grip the counter with one hand, my other wrapped tight around a scoop, my fingers going numb.

Cole Walker is here.

Cole Walker is *here*, on the University of Washington campus, asking for ice cream.

"Oh," he says when his eyes land on me. "Hi."

His gaze pins me in place, and I have no choice but to look directly at him. He's classically handsome, if predictably so. Blond hair curling at the nape of his neck, skin summer-tanned. Skin I kissed in ways he seemed to enjoy, given how he patted my head and told me he liked how *enthusiastic* I was.

Now the memory makes me want to throw up.

"I—didn't know you were going here." I hate that I stammer. I hate that I'm wondering if he still finds me attractive.

If he ever did, or if that was part of the joke too.

"Decided to transfer last-minute." He twists a lanyard hanging from his neck. "They have a better prelaw program than SPU."

My stomach clenches. Of course they do. Of course he goes

here now, and I'll have to spend the rest of these four years avoiding him, assuming I ever make it to Thursday.

I'm still holding an ice-cream scoop, lemon gelato dripping onto the floor.

Miles must be able to tell that I'm not in a great space, because he comes up behind me and addresses Cole. "We have to keep the line moving," he says, and if I'm not mistaken, there's a touch of sternness in his voice. "Do you want ice cream or not?"

And when Cole asks for a cone of cookie dough, Miles serves it quicker than he's served anything all day.

I turn my back on the window, retreating to the edge of the truck where no one can see me. It's supposed to be freezing in here—it's the name of the goddamn truck. But I'm sweaty and dizzy and even with Cole gone, my breathing won't return to normal. *Fuck. Fuckfuckfuck.* I squeeze my eyes shut and press a hand to my heart, willing it to slow down. My throat is too tight and the truck is too hot and too small and—

"Barrett?" Miles says softly. An anchor.

"Fine," I rasp out. He places his hand on my shoulder, and I wish that didn't feel so nice. "Just someone from my high school. We didn't really get along, so . . ."

"Ah." If Miles senses there's more to the story, he doesn't push.

With everything I have, I fight for a deep breath until I finally get one. And then another. Slow and shaky, but there I am. I'm okay. I straighten my posture, shove damp curls off my forehead. *I'm okay.*

"Then again," I say, eager to brush this off, putting my armor back on, "who *did* I get along with in high school?" But Miles doesn't laugh. After the line of students slims down, I try again. "I didn't know Miles Kasher-Okamoto living his best life meant serving ice cream to strangers."

He shrugs. "Not everything has to be skydiving," he says. "I bet if you asked a hundred people what's on their bucket lists, you'd be surprised by how tame the answers are."

"Okay, then." I lean my elbows back against the counter, crossing one ankle over the other in the small space between us. *Normal.* I can make this normal again. "Things you want to do before you die . . . go."

"Geneva, obviously."

"Obviously."

Miles purses his lips, lost in thought. "I want to make a movie, even if it's the lowest budget, most derivative piece of garbage and only the friends I force to watch it ever see it. I just want to have accomplished it." Then a new expression comes over his face, something I'm not sure I've seen on him yet. A little shyness, a little curiosity. "And . . . I guess I'd like to make love to someone, at some point."

The air in the truck turns so humid, I'm shocked the remaining ice cream doesn't immediately liquefy.

I'm going to try my best not to comment on the fact that he said *make love to* instead of *have sex with* or *sleep with*. It's hardly a clinical or scientific term, and there's something about it that feels so anti-Miles. I'd expect him to say "copulate" or "engage in coitus" before "make love."

"You haven't?" I ask, and I hope it doesn't sound judgmental, because I'm not. Not when my own history with it is so fraught, or when I literally came face-to-face with that history ten minutes ago.

He shakes his head. "I haven't really dated, unless you count the girlfriend I had for a week in kindergarten, which meant we sat together during snack time and shared our applesauce. Or the lab partner I went out with for two weeks sophomore year, during which neither of us spoke to each other at school because we were too awkward."

Now that sounds more like Miles.

"You don't have to date someone to make love to them." What Cole and I did definitely wasn't making love. It was two bodies clumsily writhing against each other until one of them let out a long groan and the other was left feeling unsatisfied in more ways than one. "All the times you've repeated this day, you've never had the urge to just bang it out with someone?"

One day I will learn not to utter every thought that enters my brain. That day is not today.

"That would require. Um. Someone wanting to bang it out with me," Miles says, beginning to turn the color of strawberries and cream.

I squint at him. "You're not bad-looking."

"Line up, ladies," he says, cupping his hands around his mouth and pretending to shout toward the quad. "Completely average-looking guy here, ripe for the taking!"

"Fine, above average, if you're fishing for a compliment."

The deepening blush on his cheeks indicates that maybe he wasn't, and it surprises him just as much as it surprised me. "I'm pretty sure every person who teased me about my ears as a kid would beg to differ," he says. "They called me Dumbo. Zero points for creativity."

"Are you serious? That's shitty *and* lazy. I love your ears. I mean—" I backtrack, regretting my choice of words. "I have a completely normal amount of affection for your ears."

He reaches up to touch one of them, as though making sure those are the ears I'm talking about. "You don't have to say that. But thank you."

"Maybe we should take this opportunity to get back at all the assholes who made fun of you." I punctuate my words with a few air-swipes of the ice-cream scoop. "What do you think about a Barrett-and-Miles revenge tour?" I get another flash of Cole. Until now, revenge has never really crossed my mind, and yet—if I wanted to mess with him, this could be the perfect, consequence-free opportunity.

"No. No revenge," he says. "Besides, I figure bullies are usually overcompensating for their own insecurities."

"There you go with your logic. You can't just let it fester into an ugly, long-held grudge like everyone else."

"Oh, trust me, there's plenty of festering. It took a while to get here," he says. "Your turn. Things you want to do before you die."

"See the pyramids, witness a flash mob, maybe win a Pulitzer, if I have time." I rattle them off as quickly as I can.

"Witness a flash mob? Why not be part of a flash mob?"

"I'm not a good enough dancer," I say matter-of-factly, because this is something I feel strongly about. "And I don't want to have to commit to all the rehearsals. I want to be going about my day and then completely awed when a flash mob happens right in front

of me. Something about it just seems . . . I don't know, magical."
I've gone down more than a few YouTube rabbit holes, getting emotional almost every time. I don't know what it is about them—the surprise and synchronization just go straight to my heart. "Okay. Now back to the more interesting topic of getting you laid."

Even as I say it, the words are as thick as rocky road. Why I decide to linger on this is one of the universe's many mysteries.

He gives me this long-suffering look. "You're incorrigible. What would I do, just go up to someone and say, 'Hi, I'm a time traveler, want to sleep with me?'"

"As far as pickup lines go, it's not the worst. Probably one notch above"—I put on my cheesiest voice and lean closer—"'hey, baby, did it hurt when you fell from heaven?'"

It's just a joke, but I am too close to Miles, close enough to see the rise and fall of his chest, the tips of his eyelashes. I clear my throat and back up. Still, this minor discomfort is a thousand times better than thinking about Cole and the campus we now have to share.

I whip off my apron and open the back door of the truck. "Hold, please."

I glance around the quad, buoyed by adrenaline, and zero in on my target: *there*. A guy in a corduroy blazer with a serene half smile on his face.

"Hi!" I chirp, putting myself in his path. "I have a proposition for you." He pauses, gesturing to the earbuds I didn't see when I selected him. "Hi," I say when he takes them out, a little less chirpy this time. "I'm a time traveler. Do you want to sleep with me?"

He slips his earbuds back in. "I have to get to my sociology class."

When I head back to the truck, Miles is bent over laughing.

"I can't believe you're laughing," I say as I hoist myself inside. "My ego is bruised. No, worse than bruised. My ego has been maimed."

"Tell me again how easy it is to find someone to bang it out with?" Miles asks between laughs, clutching his stomach. "You just—what is it, you just go up to them and ask?"

"I was expecting a very different response!"

"And what if he'd said yes?"

"Then obviously I'd have dragged him back to my dorm and had my way with him." I make a face at that just as Miles stops laughing, because in no timeline does that sound like me. "No, I don't know. I'm not sure I'm quite at the 'sleep with a random stranger' stage of this time loop."

He nods sagely. "Me neither. Or if I ever will be. Maybe I'm romanticizing it too much, or it's the period-piece lover in me, but I've always hoped that if or when it happened, it would be . . . meaningful. That I'd be in love, and it would just feel *right*."

"I had . . . kind of the opposite experience." I pause, fiddling with one arm of my glasses, wondering how much of it I want to share. I settle on: not much. This friendship between us is still so new. Breakable. "I sort of wanted to get it over with, I guess? To know what all the fuss was about?"

Because the fuss couldn't have possibly been what actually happened. Not enough foreplay on too-white hotel sheets, dimming the lamps because I didn't want a spotlight on my stomach or my thighs. "First time?" he said with his mouth on my throat while he pawed at my breasts, and my body quivered as I told him yes. A rustling of fabric as he shoved off his suit pants and positioned himself on top of me. It wasn't bad, exactly, but it wasn't good, either. When he asked if I was finished, I just said, "Mm-hmm," because he'd already been so generous to me, and then he fell asleep. I didn't have feelings for him, not really, but I'd still expected to feel *more*. Part of me even hoped he'd wake up in the middle of the night and reach for me again, just so I could feel wanted for a little longer.

Sometimes I wish I could have a do-over. Erase that experience I was so desperate to have and replace it with something that mattered.

Miles's face reddens again, but he charges forward. "So. What was all the fuss about, then?"

"Wish I could tell you. I hate to disappoint, but it was nothing to write home about, if I'm being honest. And it was pretty brief."

"Oh."

"Look, another rush!" I say as more students head toward us, and I never thought I'd be so excited to plunge my hands into frozen tubs of dairy.

Chapter 24

AFTER I WASH OFF THE ICE CREAM, SWEAT, AND overanalysis of everything I've said today, Miles texts, asking if I want to meet back up for dinner. Somehow I'm not sick of him yet, and it's better than sitting in my room and dreaming up ways to avoid Cole.

I show up in front of his room, freshly showered, curls scrunched. JUST KEEP SWIMMING—AND LEARNING!, the *Finding Nemo* bulletin board tells me.

"I'm trying," I mutter.

When Miles opens the door, he's wearing a button-up and nice slacks. I have on a striped tee and my perfect-imperfect jeans, because one silver lining of being stuck in time is that I'm really getting my mileage out of them. He's just showered too, water droplets clinging to the collar of his shirt.

"Should I change?" I ask, worrying the hem of my shirt. "Are we going somewhere with a dress code?"

"No, no," he says, pulling the door wider so I can see inside. "We're staying right here."

He's rearranged the furniture, moving one of the desks away from the wall to serve as a dining table. In the middle are two plates, a serving bowl, and long twin candles, some takeout containers peeking out of the nearby recycling bin. The lights are dimmed, and what might be an instrumental Britney Spears mix is playing from a speaker on the other desk.

Suddenly I have to grip the wall to keep my knees from buckling, because they've turned just as melty as the leftover ice cream.

I'm certain Olmsted has never looked lovelier.

"I know it's not Friday, but you said you wanted to go to Hillel, and I thought, well, if we couldn't go . . . then maybe we could do Shabbat ourselves. Just for us. On a Wednesday, but . . ."

Just for us. It's a simple statement, but there's something so sweet in the way he says it.

"Miles." I can't remember the last time anyone not related to me did something this nice for me—quite possibly because it's never happened. My heart doesn't know how to process it. And on top of that, I mentioned this to Miles once? A while ago? And he remembered. "*Miles.* This is . . ."

"Is it too much? We can't risk lighting the candles without setting off the smoke alarm," he says. "But I, uh, made these. I thought maybe we could tape them on, or something?" He holds up a pair of flame cutouts, made from orange and gold construction paper. "I wanted to get fake candles, but couldn't find any nearby. I guess could have tried harder, or maybe I could have tried to disengage the smoke alarm. . . ." He's fidgeting now, flipping the flames over in his palm. "Or maybe—"

I cut him off with a hand on his arm, his skin warm beneath

the smooth poplin fabric. "It's perfect. Thank you. Thank you so much." There aren't enough words to describe how I feel about it, so I just have to hope he knows. "Shabbat shalom."

"Shabbat shalom," he echoes, visibly exhaling.

We make our way over to the table, where a green salad waits in the serving bowl, along with plates of the most exquisite pasta I've ever seen.

"Do you want to do the honors?" he asks, gesturing to the candles.

I hold the unlit candle up to the other one and begin the blessing. Miles's voice threads with mine as we recite the prayer I've known longer than I can remember. *Barukh ata Adonai Eloheinu, Melekh ha'olam, asher kid'shanu b'mitzvotav v'tzivanu l'hadlik ner shel Shabbat.*

He's warm next to me, and if I get much closer, his scent might render me useless the rest of the night. I realize Irish Spring is a very common soap. There is no earthly explanation for why Miles makes it so appealing.

Then, with two precut pieces of tape, we affix the flames to the candles. Part of me wonders whether what we're doing is blasphemy, but a stronger part feels certain it would be okay. Much of Judaism is about making do with what you have, and I've always loved that there are so many ways to observe.

This is ours.

"I assume this is exactly how you do it at home," I say, touching a hand to the fake flame.

"To the letter." He dips his fork into a salad that probably cost more than any salad should. The food is incredible, but I'd be just as touched if he'd served us burgers from the Olmsted dining hall.

"I miss it. I know I see my mom almost every day, but it's not exactly the same."

"What kinds of things did you do growing up?" I ask. "Did you do Christmas and Easter too?"

"We did," he says. "They've never had any religious significance for my mom, though. Christmas has really only been celebrated as a secular holiday in Japan for a few decades. New Year's Day, Shōgatsu, is our most important holiday. My mom will go all out—we'll do a deep clean of our house, put up decorations, and drink amazake, which is this sweet sake that's mostly alcohol-free. And if we're visiting my grandparents in Texas, which we usually are, my grandma will make her ozoni—that's a mochi soup, and it's one of my favorite things." He gets this dreamy look on his face. "I've always felt so connected to that, and to the Jewish holidays."

"I love that." I twirl some pasta around my plate, imagining Miles giddy over his grandmother's soup. "That you get to have both."

He nods. "I'm not half Japanese, half Jewish. I'm both— Japanese and Jewish." He takes a bite of pasta. "What about you?"

"We went to synagogue pretty regularly when I was younger, but after my bat mitzvah, we started going less and less. We still celebrate Hanukkah, which is usually our chance to get each other the most ridiculous gift we can find."

"Even without having met your mom, that sounds perfectly in character for you both," he says, which sparks this strange, shimmery feeling in my stomach.

"And we do Passover with my mom's family. That's always been my favorite. Nothing tastes better than a hard-boiled egg after you've waited forever to eat."

"Or a bitter herb," Miles adds. "I would *die* for maror by the middle of the seder."

"God, too true. And your dad—he teaches Jewish history?"

A nod. "Growing up, there was a lot of emphasis on the origins of the holidays," he says. "He'd quiz us—me and my brother—on history and specific traditions. It was always important to him that we knew *why* we were eating unleavened bread or reclining at the seder table." Then he lets out this small, disbelieving laugh. "This might be the first time I've had this kind of conversation outside of my family."

"Me too," I say, and it's nice, connecting with him like this. "Were there many Jews at your school?"

"Hardly. I think there were eight of us? And I was the only Asian Jew, which always made people do a double take when they learned I was Jewish. I'm guessing it was the same at your school?"

"Yep. I'd been hoping to meet some here."

Beneath the table, he taps his foot against mine. "I guess we both did."

Miles Kasher-Okamoto: not an awful person, I've realized. A week ago, this kind of dinner would have been stilted, awkward. Uncomfortable. But now, despite everything that happened earlier, it might be one of the best Wednesdays I've ever had.

"Making lifelong friends is another thing on my list." I flutter my lashes at him. "Miles, I don't want to get too ahead of ourselves, but I think we're *bonding*."

He rolls his eyes, but I don't miss the way his jaw softens to hint at a smile. It's not a full-on ball-pit smile, but it's more than I usually get, and you know what, I'm going to celebrate that.

Once we've finished eating, he refuses to let me help clean up because, well, it doesn't matter. Another silver lining.

"Thank you," I say as Miles undoes the top button of his collar. "For all of this. Not just tonight." *For helping me feel less alone, even if neither of us has any clue what we're doing.*

"I have to admit that you were right—it's been a lot more fun than I imagined it would be."

"And we haven't even robbed a bank yet."

When he works to smooth out a wrinkle in his collar, I have to fight the urge to reach across the table and do it for him. There's the tiniest sliver of tan skin beneath it, and I wonder if he'd be smooth or rough if I touched him there. Hypothetically.

"I'd be remiss if I didn't thank you, too." He turns serious, and he might even be inching closer. I wrench my gaze away from his collar and up to his eyes—but that might be worse. His eyes are fixed on me, sweetness and gratitude and something I can't name. "It's possible I've been . . . a bit stuck in my ways."

I hold out my thumb and index finger. "Just a little."

But what he said—I've noticed the shift in him. He's less stiff, and he doesn't fiddle as much. He's still attached to his shell, but occasionally he forgets that he's lugging its weight around with him. Like maybe he's needed all of this as much as I have. Maybe more.

His shoe finds mine again, this innocent warmth that I like a little too much. For all I know, he thinks my shoe is the table leg. For some ridiculous reason, I think back to what he said this afternoon. About wanting to make love to someone. My first instinct was to tease him for calling it that, but there's an undeniable tenderness to it.

Because here is something I'd never admit to him: I might want to make love to someone someday too.

When he half smiles at me, there's a different weight to it. Now the way he's looking at me feels heavy, laced with anticipation. My heart is in my throat, thumping an unfamiliar rhythm, and I'm afraid to know how I'm looking at him back.

"I should go," I say quickly, three words that don't make sense unless you consider the complicated Miles feelings swirling through my mind.

"Oh—okay." A furrow of his brows, but he doesn't question it. He just waits for me to collect my keys and my bag, then follows me to the door like a good host.

"Tired," I say by way of explanation. It's a terrible one. "All that scooping took a lot out of me."

"It should be an Olympic sport."

"And Ankit will probably be here soon," I say, because what I really needed was to give Miles another excuse.

"Right."

I fight a momentary pang of regret as I open the door and glance down the hallway, abuzz with post-dinner activity as people get ready for parties and other college adventures. I'm suddenly unsure what to do with my hands. What do people do with their hands? Just let them hang there? That seems wrong, so I brush an imaginary crumb from my striped sleeve, then reach for the top of the door, even though I'm too short and end up awkwardly grabbing air instead. *Jesus, get it together.*

I don't want him to think I'm eager to escape, but he must know me well enough at this point to know my idiosyncrasies, too. Oddball, unpredictable Barrett!

If I stayed, I'd have to unpack what that look might mean, and that's something better left unpacked, stowed in an overhead compartment, and sent on a red-eye to Switzerland.

"Well—good night," I say.

"Good night, Barrett," he says, the words as soft as starlight.

And for the first time, I find myself wishing today didn't have to end.

DAY NINETEEN

||| ||| ||| ||||

Chapter 25

EVERYONE CALLS DRUMHELLER FOUNTAIN IN THE center of campus Frosh Pond because of a decades-ago prank that sparked a tradition of sophomores dunking freshmen in the water. My mom claims she saw it happen one night when she was walking home from a concert, but I've never believed her.

I wait across from the fountain, outside the computer-science building. With her flash of blue hair, Christina is easy to spot. Naturally, her gaze sweeps right by me.

"Are you Christina?" I ask, leaping off my bench and hustling to fall in step with her. Bless her for mentioning her three-hour coding class yesterday today, which took five seconds to find online. She nods, dyed-blue eyebrows furrowed. "You're good with computers, right?" I fight a grimace—this makes me sound like my grandma Ruth asking me to help install Skype on her ancient desktop.

But Christina doesn't flinch, just stops walking and narrows her eyes. "Who told you that?"

"I, um, heard it around campus," I say. "I need some help. With a computer issue. An internet-search issue, to be specific."

Finally she softens, looking pleased that word of her genius has spread. "What are you trying to find? I don't do anything, like, super illegal."

Briefly, I wonder where the line is between illegal and super illegal. "Can you find out if something's been scrubbed from a website?"

"Might be able to," she says. "I was on my way to the counseling center, but I could be persuaded." Right—she'd mentioned something about waiting in line. Given it's two thirty now and I saw her at the *Washingtonian* at four thirty, it must be one hell of a line.

"For a hundred dollars?"

She grins. "Why don't you step into my office . . ."

"Barrett," I say. "Thank you."

I follow her to Odegaard, which has the distinction of being the ugliest library on campus. She grabs an alcove on the second floor with such familiarity that I have to imagine this is a regular spot for her.

I pull over an aging wooden chair while Christina unpacks not just one but two laptops, and reaches under the table to plug in a charger.

"What are you looking for?" she asks. "Or—who?"

"Who." This was our only lead, and I don't want to leave a single stone unturned. "A professor who used to teach here in the physics department, Ella or Eloise Devereux." I think back to the grad announcement Miles and I found. "She might be in her sixties?"

As she logs in, I get a look at her username, and my world tilts on its axis.

Christina Dearborn from Lincoln, Nebraska. The girl who was supposed to be my roommate.

"Something wrong?" she says, and I wonder if she can sense my heart tripping over itself.

"No, I—" I shake my head, laughing at the cosmic coincidence of it all. "I think we were supposed to be roommates?"

Her face completely changes. "Oh my god. *Barrett.* Yes! I thought your name was familiar, and I guess there probably aren't too many Barretts on campus. They made a mistake—I'm a sophomore, and Olmsted is a freshman dorm. So they moved me to Cleary last-minute," she says by way of explanation. "Hopefully your new roommate is half as delightful as I am?"

"She's a real treat."

"Good," she says. "I guess we were destined to meet regardless. Funny how the universe works." Then she returns her attention to her computer. "Okay. Eloise Devereux, you said? We'll try a few options for spelling." She hits a few keys, lets out a low whistle. "You weren't kidding. She's not easy to find."

We fall into silence for a few minutes, except for the sound of Christina punching at keys, muttering "hmmm" under her breath.

"I was able to pull up this cached page," she says, spinning her laptop around so I can get a better look at the screen. "This your Devereux?"

Professor Ella Devereux receives annual Luminary Award from Elsewhere Foundation, the top of the page reads.

The article is on Elsewhere. Lucie's parents' site.

In the photo is a petite woman with graying brown hair shaking hands with the Lamonts. A tiny Lucie in formalwear is at the edge of the photo, staring straight into the camera as though annoyed she's not the center of attention.

Oh my god.

My breath catches in my throat. I knew there was more to this story. People don't just disappear in this day and age. Not without an explanation.

"You are *magic*, thank you," I say after Christina prints it out, passing her a handful of twenty-dollar bills I got from the campus ATM earlier this morning. Christina Dearborn, the girl who was supposed to be my roommate, saving my life. Possibly literally.

"Of course, roomie," she says with a wink. "Feel free to mention my services to anyone else. I could always use the extra cash."

I promise her I will, and if we ever get out of here, I intend to make good on that promise. For now I message Miles, who's just asked if I have any non-revenge, non-bank-robbery ideas for today. Following a lead today. Talk later.

And I can't deny that after yesterday, a little space from Miles might be a good thing. Because just his name on my screen takes me back to last night, and that weighted moment before I fled the room.

It's three fifteen when I get back to Olmsted 908, psyching myself up to grovel.

"Hope you still like iced hazelnut lattes," I say when I enter the room, presenting Lucie with a cup.

She's at her desk, fighting with an extension cord. "Thank you?"

I close the door behind me and place the coffee on her desk. I haven't exactly been a saint to her over the past few days of fuck-it-listing with Miles, but I also haven't gone out of my way to push her. "Lucie. I know you're less than thrilled to be rooming with me. But I need to ask you something."

Maybe the gravity of my voice convinces her this is important, or maybe it's mere curiosity, because she shuts her laptop and turns to face me.

"Do you remember this?" I unfold the article from my bag. "Specifically, that woman in the photo?"

She pulls it closer, examining it. "My parents used to do a bunch of these things before passing them off to their lackeys. I was always bored out of my mind."

"So you don't have any idea who she is?"

"Nope," she says, and my heart sinks. "But my dad would. He never forgets a name."

"This is going to sound ridiculous, but I really need to talk to your dad. And I can't explain why." It's a long shot, but there's no way I can get to him without her help.

She barks out a laugh and opens her laptop back up. "Why, so you can join the hordes of people dying for an Elsewhere internship?"

"God, no." I say it with too much distaste. Insulting her parents' company isn't the way to get into her good graces. "I mean—I read it, and there's plenty I like. But I'm not looking for an internship."

At this, Lucie softens.

"If you help me, I'll—I'll do your laundry for a week." An empty promise, but she doesn't need to know that.

"I can do my own laundry, thanks."

I pause, taking a long breath. There's something else. Something I've assumed I'd never use. "Do you remember the last article we worked on together?" I ask.

It wasn't that long ago—early senior year, a retrospective for our school's fiftieth anniversary that a few of us collaborated on. Lucie fumbled some alum's quote, and he called the school to complain.

Please, Barrett, she said, and if I looked at her hard enough, I could see a hint of the old Lucie in there. *I won't hear the end of it if my parents think I screwed up.*

So I took the blame, the disappointed look from our advisor. *I owe you one,* Lucie said. I waved it off, only barely thought about it afterward.

Now it's time for her to pay up, and from the recognition dawning on her face, I can tell she knows.

"I guess I'm done with classes for the day. . . ." She trails off. "I'd have to go with you, though."

I give her my most angelic grin. "I'm free now."

☾ ☾ ☾

"You're really not going to tell me why this professor is so important to you?" Lucie asks when the Uber drops off us in front of Elsewhere, a downtown Bellevue skyscraper. At the very top is the company logo, the SEWHERE perched on the horizontal line in the L.

"It's for an article. For the *Washingtonian.*" The lie is easier now. This seems to satisfy her, at least. "Did you interview for the paper?"

"Oh—no. Not exactly. I'm not actually sure I'll write for it this quarter."

"Wait, what?" That doesn't compute. "You were the editor in chief of the *Nav,* and you're not going to write for your college paper?"

Lucie's quiet for a moment, toying with the end of her auburn ponytail. "Journalism . . . was always more of my parents' thing than mine," she says finally.

"I guess I assumed you were going to major in it too." I think about her crying in the stairwell, realizing how little I know about her.

"Guess we both have secrets," she says before hitting the buzzer at the building's entrance.

Elsewhere is a high-octane mix of clickbait and hard-hitting journalism. They have offices in Seattle and New York, and the Lamonts fly between the two. I wasn't lying when I told Lucie I didn't want an internship here. When I picture myself as a professional journalist, I imagine the kind of office that doesn't have its own cereal buffet or racquetball court. I'd meet my subjects wherever they were most comfortable, and then I'd take my work to a coffee shop, typing away until the baristas asked me to leave. And I'd be so immersed, I wouldn't even notice they were about to close.

"My dad's up on the twelfth floor," Lucie says, leading me forward into the chaos: bright colors and brighter lights, people running between each other's desks, one of them even riding a scooter. "My mom flew back to New York from St. Croix." None of the hullabaloo seems to impact her, even though a couple of people stop what they're doing and go quiet, as though Lucie Lamont herself has some control over their jobs. She walks with an indifferent kind of confidence.

The elevator is all glass, modern, and one entire wall of the twelfth floor is a window with a view of Lake Washington. Her dad's office is at the end of the corridor.

"Luce?" Her dad gets out of his chair when she knocks on his open door. "I was just about to call you! This is certainly a surprise."

Because it's four o'clock. This is who she's talking to every day.

This is who makes her cry in a stairwell: Pete Lamont, twenty-first-century media mogul, millionaire, consistently on lists of most influential people in journalism. Even though I've seen him in passing at school functions, I never went to Lucie's house during our short-lived friendship, so this is the first time I'm seeing him up close. He has a mustache and the same ice-blue eyes behind thick-framed glasses, and he's dressed more casually than I thought a media mogul would be, in jeans and a button-up over a T-shirt that says ELSEWHERE COMPANY PICNIC 2007.

"A good one, I hope?" she says, and when he grins, I can see how he's charmed hundreds of investors and other important people over the years. His teeth practically shimmer.

"What brings you in? You change your mind about that internship?"

"Not exactly."

Her dad makes a clucking sound. "You realize how many people would kill for an in like that?"

"Maybe I'm not feeling especially murderous," she says quietly, her cheeks pink. I can tell it's not the kind of conversation you want to have with your parent while your former friend/current nemesis is in the room. She clears her throat, straightens her spine. "Dad. This is Barrett Bloom, from Island? She was also on the paper."

Not sure what her dad has heard about me over the years, but he's purely professional as he holds out his hand. "What can I do for you, Barrett Bloom from Island? Please, sit."

Lucie and I take the two chairs in front of his desk.

"I'm researching a piece about important professors in UW's history," I say, unfolding the article from my bag. "I found this online, and I haven't been able to find any other information about her. Which is especially bizarre in . . . you know, the age of the internet." Once again, I manage to sound like a senior citizen using a computer for the first time. I should not be allowed to talk about technology.

He takes the article, eyes lighting up with recognition. "I remember this. Dr. Devereux—she was a real firecracker. Made a lot of waves."

"That's what everyone seems to say. At least, the couple people who've been open to talking to me about her."

"She did make quite a few enemies in her department, if I recall. Her class stirred up some controversy. And you couldn't find anything else about her online?" He turns to his laptop, I imagine running a quick search. A wrinkle appears between his brows. "Huh. I know for a fact we had a number of pieces on her—we do for all our Luminaries. They're prominent people in the arts and sciences we choose to honor each year."

"Do you know what might have happened to her?"

His cheery demeanor falters. "Afraid not, Barrett Bloom. Wish I did." I wonder if repeating the first and last name is a trick to remember people's names when he talks to them. "We haven't been in contact since . . . well, it probably wasn't too long after this article ran. Our foundation makes it a point to check in with all our Luminaries every few years, though, so I can ask around for you. And I ought to check with our tech team about those articles."

My heart sinks. It's unlikely he'll be able to get back to me by the end of the day, and he won't remember this conversation tomorrow. "That would be great," I say, trying to sound upbeat. "Thank you."

Mr. Lamont turns to Lucie. "Classes going well so far?"

"They seem okay," she says. Then, speaking to her hands tangled in the hem of her sweater, she adds: "But . . . I have an audition tomorrow for that troupe I told you about."

At that, her dad's brow furrows. "The dance troupe? I thought we discussed this. No non-academic extracurriculars your first year. Nothing that detracts from your studies. Maybe we can reopen the conversation once you declare a major."

"In journalism," she says flatly.

He fixes her with a tight grin. "What else would it be?"

"Plenty of people major in dance," she says. "And go on to have successful careers in a variety of fields."

I get a flash of memory: two years ago, Lucie performing at Island's annual arts assembly with a dance she choreographed herself. I'd even been impressed, though we were no longer speaking at that point. And I recall her mentioning dance class when we were friends back in middle school, but for the longest time, I've associated her solely with journalism.

I'm not actually sure I'll write for it this quarter.

Journalism was always more of my parents' thing.

Mr. Lamont snaps those sharp blue eyes to me. "What are you majoring in, Barrett Bloom?" he asks, and it kills me to say "journalism." My teeth are gritted, and I can only look at Lucie out of the corner of my eye. I should have lied.

"I know I could manage it with the rest of my classes."

Lucie's smaller now, shoulders hunched into her chair.

"Lucie. The answer is no." Then he puts the CEO mask back on. "Good to meet you, Barrett Bloom. Best of luck with the article."

ʊ ʊ ʊ

"I'm sorry about that," I tell Lucie on the drive home. "With your dad. I hope—"

"It's fine." Lucie stares down at her fingernails, picking at her black nail polish.

"It doesn't have to be. I know we're not—I don't know what we are. But I swear, the last thing I want to do is judge you."

She seems to consider this, but she doesn't glance up from her hands. "It's just—I had my audition piece all prepped. You probably don't remember the dance I did sophomore year—"

"I do," I say, surprising even myself when I say it out loud.

"Oh." She clearly wasn't expecting that response. "Well—it's been updated, and it's more complex, and I've added onto it. But that's what I built it from. Maybe it's silly, that I've been working on that one dance for so long, but it's tough to know when you're *done* with something, you know?"

"I've felt that way with articles before."

"I'm not sure if it's ever been that way for me. Not with writing, at least," she says, giving me a wry not-quite-smile. "I know what you're going to say. Poor little rich girl, right?"

I shake my head, still trying to process this. Not just the reality of Lucie being sad, but Lucie sharing it with *me*. "You don't like writing? Or editing?"

"It's not that I don't like it," she says. "But there's a difference between liking something and wanting to do it the rest of your life. Between liking something and turning that something into a career. And I know dance would be really fucking hard. That I'd have to work for it in a way I wouldn't have to with what my parents would give me if I, you know, do what they want. But I *want* to work for it." Her expression turns sunnier, a new warmth in her eyes. "This modern dance troupe, they're *amazing* and avant-garde, and they always have these kind of disturbing costumes that I'm really into? Like—here." She pulls out her phone, swiping around on a browser before finding the image she wants. The dancers are dressed in dark green with long dragon tails, their hair twisted up in elaborate styles. "They started at UW just last year. Even if my parents won't let me major in dance, I thought this could be a way to keep myself sharp. I'd get a part-time job, and I'd try to make enough to cover my own tuition. And then maybe . . . maybe I could study whatever I wanted to."

I try to match this up with everything I know about Lucie. The times she tapped her feet to music playing in the newsroom, or put in AirPods and drummed her fingers along her desk as she edited a story. Lucie Lamont, modern dancer.

"That would have to be a hell of a well-paying part-time job," I say, and she winces.

"I'm interviewing with food services tomorrow."

"Oh. Good." I try to imagine Lucie serving me all-you-can-eat pasta, telling me I'm not supposed to leave the dining hall with any of their bowls. I try to imagine her going through today nineteen times, devastated again and again and again, completely unaware she's been through this before. Nineteen times, and I never knew.

"They've always just assumed I'll follow in their footsteps and take over Elsewhere someday." She glances out the window as we take the exit for UW. "I really thought college would be different. I'm grateful for what they do, and their hard work. But they still want me to be their perfect clone, and sometimes it feels . . . suffocating."

"What about your friends?"

A scoff of a laugh. "My friends? The ones who went to WSU and forgot about me, or the ones who asked if I could hook them up with an internship at Elsewhere, and when I told them no, they promptly stopped texting me back?"

In high school, Lucie was always surrounded by people. Always seemed happy. Meanwhile, the closest thing I had to friendship was the time I interviewed a girl about robotics club and asked to hang out and she said, "For the story?" And I lied and said yes.

Maybe Lucie and I have more in common than I ever thought.

"I don't even know why I'm telling you all this," she says.

"Because I'm a great listener who never judges or makes inappropriate jokes?"

To her credit, she ignores this, barreling onward. "I thought I'd double major at first, and they'd be fine with it. But that turned into minoring, which turned into this *one extracurricular*, and they won't even let me have that. No matter how many times I assure them I can do both, that I can handle it, they don't want me to do anything else that would distract from what *they* want."

"That's really rough of your parents," I say, meaning it. "I'm sorry."

She nods, and then falls quiet for a while. "Barrett. I tried to stop them, you know. Last year."

My whole body goes rigid. "You . . . what?"

"After prom," she clarifies, and that dark, icy feeling uncoils in my belly. "Cole and the rest of those assholes. I told him to knock it the fuck off."

"I—" I just sit there, mouth half-open, unable to believe what I'm hearing. Half my body is here, but the other half is back at Island, flowers on my desk and acid in my throat. "Why?" is the only thing that comes out.

"I know I wasn't amazing to you after the tennis article. And Blaine wound up being . . . well, a bit of an asshole. Cole wasn't much better. I hated going to their house because he'd always ogle me, and Blaine would just tell me I was reading too much into it."

"I'm sorry," I say automatically, my stomach turning, because regardless of how I feel about her, she didn't deserve that.

"I could have done more, though," she says. "I'm sorry too. I'm sorry that happened to you. It really, really shouldn't have."

"We weren't our best selves in high school," I say finally.

Her eyes meet mine with a soft flicker of understanding. "No. We weren't."

At the start of today, Lucie was a means to an end. But now that I'm trying to piece her together, I'm realizing everything I thought I knew about her was surface-level. Those bagels and balloons I thought would fix our relationship—meaningless.

Still, I'm not sure how to heal the wounds both of us have, the hurt high school inflicted on us and we inflicted on each other. It's not something we can solve in a single conversation. It takes time.

The only thing we don't have.

"I've got to pick up a textbook at the bookstore," Lucie says as the Uber pulls up to Olmsted. "But I'm going to a frat party tonight. Maybe you want to come with?"

"I have plans," I say, and only feel a little guilty about it. Years ago, I'd have killed for an invitation like this.

"See you around, then."

"I know where you live." I mean it to sound like a joke, but because I am me, it sounds like the prelude to chopping her body into tiny pieces and making a feast for the campus squirrels. "But not in a creepy way."

The worst part is, as terrible as Lucie's been to me in the past, part of me does believe we could be friends one day. I'm not sure when, and I don't know what that friendship might look like, but if there's one thing I recognize in another person, it's loneliness.

And I'm heartbroken that no matter what progress we've made, it'll all be erased by tomorrow.

DAY TWENTY-ONE

TtH TtH TtH TtH I

Chapter 26

"THIS WOULD BE CUTE ON YOU," I SAY, FLIPPING A page and pointing to a photo of a guy with an onion tattooed on his armpit. We're sitting on a shabby leather sectional in a Capitol Hill tattoo shop. "Or a massive . . . Art Garfunkel? Right in the middle of your chest?" Not Simon & Garfunkel. *Just* Garfunkel. There's a real chaotic energy there, and frankly, I respect it. "You think you could rock that?"

Miles gives me his patented *you exhaust me* sigh. "What I think is that I'm having many, many regrets."

Over the past week, we've had, to the best of our abilities, the time of our lives—at least, with the limited resources available to us as eighteen-year-old college freshmen. Yesterday, in an effort to pack the ultimate college experience into a single twenty-four-hour period, we rounded up as many people in the quad as we could and attempted to break a Guinness World Record for most Frisbee catches, just falling short. I toppled headfirst into a tree when I tried to learn how to slackline. We went downtown and rode the

Great Wheel for hours and tried every sample in Pike Place Market. We bought a Porsche from a very skeptical car salesman and Miles taught me how to drive stick, and neither of us murdered the other.

Three weeks I've been stuck, and many more for Miles, and I have to admit, all the excitement is starting to feel exhausting. No matter what we do, I always wake up to Lucie's voice. I always get a text from my mom at seven thirty, and that skateboarder always crashes into the swing dancers at ten to four. Over and over and over.

"I think we've made a decision," I say after about twenty minutes, bringing the book up to the counter. Lately, I've started to feel like we're only going through the motions of living life to the fullest, and I'm not going to lie: part of me hopes we'll wake up tomorrow with properly regrettable tattoos and a profound sense of relief.

"I can take you both right now," the artist says. "Couple's tattoos?"

I make what I hope are heart eyes at her, even as my stomach does something odd and unfamiliar. Something fluttery, like maybe the Olmsted Eggstravaganza was a bad choice this morning. "Yes. And we trust each other so much, we wanted to let the other person pick them out."

"Isn't that romantic," she says in a flat voice, as though I've just told her we plan to feed each other food we've scraped off the side of the street for lunch.

Miles points to a page in the book I can't see. "This one for her," he says, then flips forward a few pages. "With this on it."

"And I did my own design for him. If that's okay." I hand over a piece of paper. I am not an artist. I cannot wait.

The artist, a woman with a lavender bob and ink spiraling up her arms, introduces herself as Gemini and leads us back to a private room. I volunteer to go first, since Miles is looking a little pale.

"You're getting yours on your forearm," Miles says from a seat a few feet away from the tattooing chair. "Because that's supposed to hurt the least, and I'm a *nice person*."

"And you're getting yours in a very secret, very special place." Though I'm relieved he didn't pick somewhere that would require exposing my back rolls or the roundness of my belly. But that relief quickly turns to worry that he picked my forearm because he'd rather not have to look at other parts of my body.

Gemini preps the area, cleaning it with rubbing alcohol and then swiping a razor across it.

"Don't look," Miles calls. There's more glee on his face now, his eyes light. All at once, the strange swirly feelings from the night in his room come rushing back, turning my cheeks warm. It was accidental, the way his foot touched mine. And it didn't mean anything when his gaze lingered—or when mine did.

Thankfully, as soon as the machine starts up, all those feelings are banished to the back of my mind. The pain isn't as sharp as I expected it to be, though I still grimace as Gemini works.

"All done," she says about an hour later, and I glance down at my forearm and burst out laughing.

It's an anthropomorphized mozzarella stick, which is only made clear by the small dish of marinara sauce next to it. The stick has arms and legs and dots for eyes, and it's wearing a cape.

But the thing is, even with the sauce, it does not look like a mozzarella stick at all.

It looks like a crime-fighting penis.

"Big fan of mozzarella sticks?" Gemini asks.

"The biggest," I say, shaking my head at Miles, who looks thrilled.

"It looks perfect on you," he says, which is not the same as *you look perfect* or *I would look perfect on you*, and yet. And *yet*.

While she cleans up, I can't stop staring at the fresh ink. Even though it'll be gone tomorrow, even though it's the last thing I'd have picked for myself, there's something poetic about it. It's designed to be permanent, and yet we're getting them for the sole reason that they're temporary.

"So where are we putting this?" Gemini asks when she's ready for Miles.

I twist, tapping my lower back, just above my belt.

Miles groans. "I should have known," he says with a half grumble, but to my surprise, he doesn't protest as he makes his way to the chair.

"You just wanted to get me shirtless again," he deadpans as he tugs off his shirt and drapes it on the chair next to me. It's such an un-Miles-like thing to say that I have to muffle a cackle.

I try not to look at his chest. And I succeed—but then Gemini adjusts the chair for him and he positions himself facedown, giving me a full view of his back. Broad shoulders he hides beneath flannel shirts, the long length of his spine that curves slightly upward before disappearing into his jeans. A smooth landscape of muscles and tan skin. And . . . what the hell? This shouldn't be *worse* than his chest.

It's just his back. His *lower* back. It's a completely non-sensual, non-sexual part of the body . . .

. . . except when I remember what Miles said about *making love* to someone, which I absolutely need to stop thinking about, along with how he might be in this kind of position during it.

I need to get my hormones under control.

Gemini starts working on the transfer while I contemplate tattooing CALM THE FUCK DOWN on my forehead, and when she holds up a mirror so he can take a look at it—because I'm too giddy to wait until she's done—his mouth falls open.

"You put 'property of Barrett Bloom' on my ass?"

"If we want to get technical, it's on your lower back," I say. "But yes. Yes, I did. Do you love it? The font is *beautiful*, and the petals of the rose are just . . ." I kiss my fingers.

"If we wake up on Thursday," he says, "I hope you're ready to pay for tattoo-removal appointments, along with all the therapy I'm going to need to recover from this traumatic experience."

Gemini turns on the machine, blessedly oblivious to our conversation. Every so often, Miles lets out a staccato breath, the muscles in his upper back tightening. I'm relieved when his phone rings from the pocket of his jacket, which is draped across the back of my chair.

"It's your brother. Again," I say as I dig it out, even though of course he already knows. "You're really going to keep ignoring him?"

"I've already answered about a dozen times," Miles says through gritted teeth as Gemini works the pen along his back.

"And yet you've given me hardly any details about why he's calling." The phone continues to vibrate in my hands. "What if it's the key to—"

Miles brings his head up, eyes sharp. "You really want to know why he's calling?" It's not anger in his voice, but there's a sternness I'm not used to. He beckons me over, and I accept the call and hold the phone up to his ear. "Hey," he says into it, and I can't hear his brother over the buzzing of Gemini's machine. "I—I know. No, I didn't forget . . . yeah. Okay. I can be there in about an hour."

I take the phone back as Miles turns his head to talk to Gemini. "I'm sorry about this, but we have to take off."

"You sure?" she asks. "Because right now, I just have half a flower and PROPERTY OF BAR."

If Miles didn't look so distracted right now, I'd laugh.

"Where are we going?" I ask.

He grimaces as Gemini applies a bandage to his lower back. "We're going to pick up my brother from rehab."

Chapter 27

MAX KASHER-OKAMOTO IS NOT AT ALL WHAT I expected, but given that Miles has barely mentioned him, maybe I should have been prepared for anything.

Max is at least six feet tall and wears his height with confidence bordering on ego. No slouching or leaning—only towering. His ears are pierced and there's a tattoo behind one of them, a whorl of dark ink I can't quite make out. In black jeans, a distressed denim jacket, and vintage Chucks, Max looks like he could be the fifth Ramone. If Miles is marginally attractive on certain days, at certain angles, Max is a certified thirst trap.

Max and Miles. It would be adorable if this situation weren't so serious.

"A Thousand Miles," Max says, opening his arms, and okay, there is definitely something adorable about that nickname. "Good of you to decide to make an appearance."

Miles hugs him. "Sorry. We were . . . indisposed."

"I'm just screwing with you. Means a lot that you're here.

Really." Max pulls back and assesses me with a lift of one eyebrow. "And you, enticing stranger."

I'm not sure who's blushing more, me or Miles.

"This is Barrett," he says. "Barrett, Max. She's a friend from school."

On the drive here, Miles explained in a calm, collected voice that today his brother is finishing his program. I didn't want to pry, didn't know what questions to ask. *Rehab* could mean a hundred different things.

But here we are, in front of the addiction recovery center of a Ballard hospital.

"Barrett. Good to meet you." Max drags a hand through his hair, which is nearly to his shoulders. "I'm starving. I've been having dreams about Zippy's burgers—that's how badly I miss them. Can we grab some on the way home?"

Home.

"Of course."

Max prods his brother with an elbow. "And your girlfriend can come too."

The tips of Miles's ears redden. "We—we're not—" he stammers, just as Max starts cackling.

"Couldn't resist," he says with a rough laugh, leaving me to wonder whether it's because I'm not a viable girlfriend, or because Max knows the extent of Miles's inexperience.

I let Max take the passenger seat next to his brother, and he scrunches his face at the station playing the biggest hits of the eighties, nineties, and today. "This is what you've been listening to?"

"It's a rental," Miles says, his eyes firmly on the road. All of a sudden he's morphed back to the stiff, serious Miles he was when I met him.

Max drums his hands on the dashboard, playing around with the stereo when he realizes there's no hookup for his phone. I can't help cataloging the differences between the two of them. They're both fidgety, but Max's posture is less harsh. Max seems immediately comfortable, whereas Miles almost never is. In the span of ten minutes, Max's face has gone through about a hundred more expressions than Miles's does on a daily basis.

"I've never been to Zippy's," I offer, trying to lighten the mood.

Max twists in the seat to face me. "You're gonna love it. They have this special sauce that's the best thing I've ever tasted. They used to sell it by the jar, but they couldn't keep it in stock."

Zippy's is an old-timey burger joint with red-checked tablecloths and a jukebox in one corner. Once we order and grab a booth, Miles starts to soften, his shoulders no longer touching his ears. And yet the whole time we're here, I'm wondering why their parents aren't.

"Remember when we tried to build a replica of the Space Needle out of fries?" Max says, gesturing with his chocolate shake. "That was right here. In this booth."

Across from me, Miles allows a grin, a welcome crack in his exterior. "We kept saying we needed to go to the bathroom and then came back with another cup of sauce to glue them together. Mom and Dad were so pissed."

"I thought they would never let us eat fries ever again."

I slurp some of my strawberry shake. "I can't imagine Miles doing something like that."

"This kid? Miles Per Hour was a regular rebel back in the day."
Max gives his shoulder a nudge, and Miles almost glows under his
attention.

And it's there, in that moment, that I see a fragment of what
their relationship might have looked like once upon a time. A boy
who idolized his brother.

Our food arrives, and Max is 100 percent right about the special
sauce, which is a perfect mix of sweet and savory, so delicious I
could swim in it. But Max isn't eating yet, instead eyeing me with
a half frown.

"What?" I ask, worried I have special sauce on my face.

"Nothing." His mouth quirks into a grin. "I'm just trying to figure out how this happened." He flicks an index finger between the
two of us, and now he is every bit the embarrassing older brother.

Miles has turned so red, his gaze could probably incinerate his
burger. "Like I said, we're not—"

"Whoa, whoa, whoa, no need to jump to conclusions. I was refer-
ring to *this friendship*," Max says, throwing an exaggerated wink at me.

"We have physics together, and we're in the same dorm," I say.

"Mom's class?"

Miles nods. At that, a look of genuine worry passes over Max's
face. "Do you think . . . It's going to be okay with them at home,
right?"

"I hope so." Miles takes a delicate bite of his burger. "They're
going to be glad you're back. Really."

"So glad they couldn't be bothered to pick me up."

"It's hard for them. You know that."

Max is quiet for a moment, absently toying with a straw wrapper. "I know."

Miles reaches across the table and lays a hand on his brother's arm. "I'm really happy you're here. I'm—I'm proud of you."

My heart swells to the point where I'm no longer sure what's keeping it inside my chest.

"That means a lot. It hasn't been easy, and that just . . . thank you." Then Max clears his throat, aiming a mischievous grin at me. "Who wants more fries?"

When we finish eating, Miles drives us to their house, a deep blue Tudor on a quaint residential street in West Seattle.

Gingerly, I follow Miles inside. The house is about twice the size of mine and even roomier on the inside, with polished hardwood floors and large windows that let in natural light. It beautifully reflects both sides of his family, with a gorgeous Japanese silk painting on one wall and next to it, a silver plaque reading TIKKUN OLAM in Hebrew and engraved with a tree of life.

Miles stares straight ahead at a framed family photo that must have been taken about five years ago. It's one of those photos I've always thought were kind of corny, with everyone wearing the same thing—in this case, jeans and buttoned white shirts. They're posed on Alki Beach, and Dr. Okamoto's hair is longer, past her shoulders, the wind lifting it off her neck. She's holding hands with Miles's dad. An awkward preteen Miles with ears that are too big for the rest of him is gazing up adoringly at his brother, who's looking out into Puget Sound. Somehow, it doesn't seem corny at all.

Max is in the kitchen, opening up the fridge and taking out a can of Sprite. When he holds one up to me, I shake my head.

"How long were you—" I break off, unsure how to talk about it.

"In rehab? It's okay to say it." He opens up the Sprite and leans against the marble island. "Ninety days. Missed all of Seattle's summer weather," he adds. "And damn if I didn't miss Mom's terrible physics puns and Dad's cooking." And then, as Miles joins us: "And Miles's outdated taste in movies, but I guess his roommate will have to deal with that now."

"I'm sure you're devastated," Miles deadpans.

Max clutches his heart. "Deeply."

Miles glances around the kitchen, stretching his arms. There's a slight waver in his voice as he says, "So . . . this is it."

I can tell he's anxious about leaving Max alone, and I can't imagine what it feels like to need to decide whether to do this again tomorrow.

The decision he's been making every day for nearly three months.

"Dad's on his way," Max says. "He just texted me. I'm about ready to crash, so you can head out if you need to. You don't have to babysit me."

"You sure?"

Max waves this off. "And we're all doing dinner together this weekend, right?"

"Right." Miles is back to fiddling with the collar of his plaid flannel. It's a wonder his clothes aren't all helplessly wrinkled. "I can't wait."

Max slings an arm around Miles's neck, and this clear brotherly affection does that thing to my heart again. "Hey. Miles to Go Before I Sleep. It's going to be okay."

At that, Miles chuffs out a laugh. "I don't think that one works as well. Doesn't quite roll off the tongue."

"It doesn't, does it? I was trying something new. Really got into poetry while I was away."

"Keep working on it, Maximum Capacity."

Max turns on his brightest grin so far. The nicknames are absolutely killing me.

"You two have fun. Don't do anything I wouldn't do." Max looks over at me. "I've been wondering this whole time—is that a dick tattooed on your arm?"

"Yes," I say at the same time Miles says, "No."

"Cool." Then, before he shuts the door: "Oh, and in case I don't see you tomorrow—happy birthday."

ひ ひ ひ

We barely make it five silent minutes in the rental car before Miles pulls over.

"Sorry, I just—need a moment," he says, leading us onto a side street and cutting the engine in front of a sprawling rhododendron. It's clear that ever since we arrived at the hospital, he's been holding back his emotions.

I'm not sure what it'll look like when—*if*—he lets the dam burst.

"I'm sorry," I say, in part to fill the quiet but also because I was the one who pushed him to answer the phone.

"You have nothing to be sorry about," he says to the steering wheel, shoulders as stiff as ever. If I reached over and touched him, he'd be as solid as brick.

"Is Max . . . an addict?"

Slowly, Miles nods, fingertip moving back and forth along a loose thread on the wheel's stitching. I'm about to tell him that we don't have to talk about it, not if he doesn't want to, but then he swallows hard before opening his mouth again. "We were so close as kids. I was obsessed with him, wanted to wear the same clothes, do the same things. And he always let me tag along with his friends—I was never the annoying little brother. Max was the life of the party, the literal embodiment of 'the more the merrier.' There could never be too many people around, and they were all usually half in love with him."

"I can see that," I say.

Miles taps the side of his face, just underneath his left eye. The crescent-moon-shaped scar. "I got this when we went sledding down that big hill over there as kids. Smacked right into a tree, got scraped up by some branches. Max felt so terrible about it, he brought me breakfast in bed for three weeks afterward. He also—he didn't have the best grades, but when he set his mind to something, he just *did it*. When he was thirteen, he decided he wanted to teach himself Japanese before we visited some of my mom's family for the summer. For six months before the trip, he immersed himself in it, and when he talked to our grandparents and aunts and uncles, they all remarked on how amazing his Japanese was.

"When he started using, I was in seventh grade." Miles lets out a long, shaky breath, as though the memory is causing him physical pain. It might very well be. "It was maybe a year before our parents caught him. I didn't understand it at first. We'd had all the antidrug programs at school, and I couldn't even conceive of how someone could *get* drugs. It just felt so outside my world." He glances at me for the first time since he started talking, and there is so much ache behind his eyes that I can't believe he hasn't overflowed until now.

Can't fathom carrying this every day. "This was his third time in rehab. He's relapsed each time, and I want this to be his last time so fucking badly, it feels—it feels like a physical piece of me. I volunteered to pick him up because my parents were working, and it happened to be the first day of school, and I just . . . wanted to make things easier for everyone, I guess."

Everyone except himself.

He's back to picking at the steering wheel.

"Miles. I'm so sorry." *Sorry* feels too light in this situation. My throat is dry and there's a painful squeeze in my chest and I wish I could give him more than *sorry*. I think back to that family photo on the beach. Had this already started happening then, or was it about to?

"I've picked up the phone at least a dozen times today, but this was the first time in maybe a month. I love him. I do. And I want more than anything for him to get better. Whenever I don't go pick him up, I hate myself a little. I wonder who he calls, and if it's one of his old friends, and if he falls into those old habits."

"Don't," I say, gently but firmly. "You can't be expected to do this seventy-odd times."

Miles being Miles, he can't help correcting me. "Seventy-nine, at this point." Any hint of superiority vanishes as he continues, "And it breaks my heart, every time I go. Every time I don't go. Every time my phone rings. Every time I ignore it. Every time I answer it. Every single time—another little piece of it breaks off." His voice cracks, and when he speaks again, it's in a whisper. "I'm surprised there's any of it left."

Jesus. I want to wrap this boy in cellophane and then wrap that in a blanket so he never has to get his heart broken ever again.

It breaks my heart. Four words I never imagined Miles Kasher-Okamoto saying. It's wild, really, that you can spend ~~a single day~~ weeks with someone and still barely know them.

"There is," I say, turning in my seat so I can fully face him. I need him to know that it matters to me, that he's telling me this. That I'll keep it safe. "If there weren't, you wouldn't be here. Or you would have kicked me to the curb a long time ago."

Miles allows a smile at that, one of his slight ones, but still, it has to be a good sign. "No," he says. "I—I'm glad you're here. Sometimes I think . . . if I never leave the loop, then I never have to know if he relapses. He'll always be getting better."

"I'm not going to pretend to know what this feels like, because I don't," I say. "But I want you to know I am really, truly sorry. And if it's something you want to talk more about, or less about, or anything at all . . . I can listen."

"Thank you." A pause, and I think he'll tell me he's done talking. That we should leave. But instead he says, "I want to be normal with him. I don't want to be weird and stiff or act like he's something delicate. It maybe wasn't my best showing, when we were with him today. I didn't want you to see me that way." He averts his eyes when he says this, the bashfulness in his voice sounding somehow both foreign and familiar.

"I'm not judging you," I say softly.

His hand is right there. Just right there on the console between us, and I can't help myself. Maybe it's all the years of wishing someone would comfort me, but whatever it is, it compels me to reach out and stroke his fingers.

There's a slight tilt of his head as he glances down at our hands, as though confirming what's happening is actually happening: my hand cupped around his, thumb dragging up and down his index finger.

This isn't like when we held hands on the flight to Disneyland, or when we jumped into the ball pit. This is something different, something new and delicate and terrifying.

"You put so much pressure on yourself," I say as I run my fingers along his, from the bumps of his knuckles to the joints and then back. My hand should know his at this point, but the touch sends a jolt down my spine nonetheless. "That doesn't come from your parents, does it?"

Slowly, slowly, he turns his hand, fingers clumsy as they slide against mine.

"If it does, they don't talk about it." He's not looking at our hands anymore, probably because he's barely thinking about what they're doing. "But after everything with Max . . . I didn't want them to have to worry. I know not everyone starts college sure of what they'll major in, but I've always loved physics. My mom didn't push me to study it—our parents wanted us happy and healthy, more than anything—but I knew she loved that I loved it. So I didn't do anything in high school that might jeopardize my future. I didn't spend much time with friends and I didn't go to parties. I didn't join any clubs, except for the one month I tried out film club. I took the SAT four times, and that last one was just for fun. My parents didn't even give me a curfew—because I never needed one. I just . . . studied. A lot. I always wanted to go to UW—because it would make my parents happy, and I wouldn't be too far from Max. And when I got in, it felt like the biggest sigh of relief."

Now my heart is the one that's breaking. The version of Miles from only months ago, who shut himself inside and shut himself off—he was aching in ways I couldn't have imagined.

"I know that I'm awkward around people," he continues. "That I probably come off as a condescending asshole at first. And I think it might be because I've been on my own for so long that I'm not used to thinking about anyone else."

"I definitely never thought either of those things about you," I say, as straight-faced as possible. I think back to Miles suggesting that we go out and explore, to him showing up with that ice-cream truck, to our makeshift Shabbat. "And it's not true, that you don't think about anyone else. You're—you're a good friend, Miles."

The way it tugs at a corner of his mouth, I can tell he likes hearing this. "You're kind of the first person I've hung out with for an extended period of time in a while," he says.

"And you almost had the tattoo to prove it."

He gives my hand the gentlest squeeze before pulling away, and I'm left feeling strangely light-headed.

"My mom's the same," I say, trying not to miss the warmth of his fingers linked with mine. "She always told me, 'I don't care if you study something impractical, as long as you don't get pregnant.' I think she's happy with the way her life has turned out, though, even if things were rocky for a while." I shake my head, wondering how I let all of this spill out. "Sorry, this isn't about me."

"No, I appreciate it." His eyes are back on mine, deep and vivid and full of more courage than I ever could have imagined. "I . . . want to know about you, too."

Those words feel like he's wrapped a hand around my heart.

Before I register what's happening, he's stretching his right hand toward me, and I am honestly not certain if I can handle holding hands with him again. Not this soon. But he doesn't linger. He just grazes his fingertips along my wrist, drawing an arc between two freckles, before dropping his hand again. A gesture of understanding, I'm sure that's what it's meant to be, but it sparks all my nerve endings. Makes my stomach swoop low, low.

"Journalism and early-2000s pop culture and rarely thinking before I speak. That's pretty much it." Any other response to *I want to know about you* has turned to dust in my throat. I'm not ready to give him my complete history, and only in part because no one's asked for it before. Despite his reassurance, I don't want to take anything away from what he's processing with his brother. The fear of going through this all over again. The hope that this time will be different.

"I do need to ask," I continue, because it's about all I can come up with right now. "Why have you never told me that tomorrow is your birthday?"

At that, Miles actually laughs. And then he can't stop. "My birthday—it's tomorrow," he manages, trying and failing to muffle his laughter with his shoulder. "September twenty-second."

"I can't believe you didn't say anything!"

"To be perfectly honest, I forgot."

And then I'm laughing too, because if that isn't the greatest cosmic joke.

DAY TWENTY-TWO

卌 卌 卌 卌 ||

Chapter 28

THE NEXT MORNING, IT'S NOT LUCIE'S VOICE THAT pulls me from sleep, but a tight, hot sensation along my forearm. I jolt awake, remembering the buzz of the tattoo needle and the soreness and swelling Gemini warned I'd be feeling for the next few days.

When I open my eyes, there's no Lucie. No Paige.

Holy shit holy shit holy *shit*. This can only mean one thing.

It happened.

Relief sings through my veins, bright and shimmering and absolutely unreal. I've never been so delighted to be in pain. I grin into my pillow, nearly sobbing with joy. We made it to Thursday. Maybe we got terribly ill-advised tattoos, but *we did it*.

I will wear this ink like a badge of honor, a reminder that I went through hell and came out of it stronger than ever. I'll laugh at the jokes people make about it—hell, I'll make plenty of them myself. I will grow to love this ridiculous tattoo because I traveled through fucking *time*, and now I'm on the other side.

I'll race down the hall to Miles's room and we'll go out and celebrate his birthday. Or, you know, we'll go to class, because that's how Miles would want to spend his birthday. My Thursday psych class—I'll finally get to go. Sure, I ditched yesterday's classes, but it was just the first day, and even if Dr. Okamoto and Hot Grant aren't thrilled with me, I have them memorized at this point. Catching up won't be a problem.

I roll over and bring my forearm up to my face and—

There's nothing there.

A knot of panic works its way through me as I skim my fingers along my forearm. The skin is warm, but it's just skin. Inkless. No mozzarella stick that looks like a piece of anatomy, no cape. No redness. I even hold my arm to the window to catch the shards of natural light, and all the hair Gemini shaved is back.

And yet the pain is still there, pulsing beneath the surface, a reminder of something I did yesterday.

A day that does not exist.

There's a knock on the door, and then the sound of a key in the lock, and then there's Lucie, and Paige, staring straight at me.

"This has to be a mistake," Lucie says, and now I may start crying for an entirely different reason.

I don't have the energy to make nice with her, not again, even though I know now that it can be done, so I let her stomp around and complain about my pasta bowls before pretending to go back to sleep. The devastation shouldn't feel as heavy as it does right now, but it's a ten-ton anchor, keeping me chained to this room. It's a relief when a text shows up from Miles an hour later, when I'm still moping in bed.

Yesterday was . . . a lot. I need a little space, if that's okay? Not sure I'm in a zero fucks kind of mood.

Of course it's okay, I write back, pushing away a flash of concern. Take all the time you need.

I want to ask him about whether the site of PROPERTY OF BAR is sore and whether he's feeling any of what I'm feeling. If he woke up at the same time, and if he has any theories. But that can wait.

More than that—something changed between us yesterday. Yes, we held hands in a rented 2013 Toyota Prius, a moment my brain helpfully replayed for me over and over before I fell asleep last night. But he also let me in, allowed me to see this piece of his private life, a history he hasn't shared with many other people. And I might actually be starting to understand him. We've both been lonely, trapping ourselves in these prisons of our own making. I never would have guessed we had something like this in common, but I think the two of us have been yearning for human connection more than either of us would readily admit. For the first time, it really does feel like we're partners.

In a strange way, though . . . well, I don't *miss* him, because that doesn't make sense. We've been nearly inseparable for the past two weeks. It's probably just that I miss having someone to spar with. Someone who indulges that combative side of my personality, the side I have always feared is my entire personality.

Mom: How do I love thee? Joss and I are wishing you SO MUCH LUCK today!

The text doesn't frustrate me the way it has for the past few days. Instead, it invigorates me. This is longer than we've ever gone without seeing each other—well, longer than *I've* ever gone, since she is ostensibly living her timeline the way she's meant to.

I throw back a couple of Tylenol for the pain in my arm and order an Uber. By the time I get to Ink & Paper, the pain has faded to the point where I can almost forget it didn't happen.

And there she is in jeans and her Seattle skyline graphic tee, her hug rose-scented.

"Don't tell me you're already homesick," my mom says, and the déjà vu makes my head spin.

"Deeply. The doctors say I don't have long."

"Barrett. My darling of darlings. Treasure of treasures. It's only been a few days. Not even you can be this attached to your dear old mom."

"Nineteen days," I say.

She rummages behind the counter, not paying attention. "What? Anyway, now that you're here . . . look what showed up yesterday." She holds up that package of greeting cards, the ones from the new Seattle letterpress.

"Nineteen days, Mom," I repeat, my voice level.

"Is this a reference to something?" Her mouth pulls into a frown, a crease appearing between her brows as she tries to think. "You're going to have to give me a hint."

"It's not a reference to anything. I haven't seen you in nineteen days." On trembling legs, I take a seat behind the counter. Maybe I'm testing another theory, or maybe I'm eager for some non-Miles camaraderie, since my heart and brain are thoroughly mixed up by his presence. Whatever it is, I'm going to try telling her the truth again. "What if I told you that I've been stuck in a time loop. And I've repeated this day twenty-two times."

My mom stares, and then she cracks a smile. "Is this for your psych class? Some experiment?"

"I'm being serious. This is real."

"Well, then. If you really are a time traveler, should we go buy a lottery ticket?"

"We could, but it won't matter tomorrow." I nod toward the door. "Close the shop."

She sputters out a laugh. "What?"

"What have you always wanted to do but never had the time for? Something we could realistically do today. Quick, the first thing that comes to mind."

"This is absurd, Barrett, I—"

"Mom. Please. Just tell me."

Her eyes are squinted, her mouth scrunched to one side. Her thinking face. I can tell she's just playing along, that she doesn't entirely believe me, and to be fair, neither would I. She's probably assuming this is another one of our games.

"This might sound silly, but I've always wanted to go up the Space Needle. Even though it's touristy, it feels like something we should do, right?"

Maybe it doesn't matter that she doesn't believe me, or that she's bad at pretending. Maybe it just matters that she's here.

"Then let's do it," I say as she grabs her keys. "Let's be tourists."

ʊ ʊ ʊ

We gaze down at a tiny Seattle from the Space Needle's glass floor, the buildings and cars and trees looking like toys.

"I can't believe it took us so long to do this," my mom says. All around us, early-fall visitors point and gape at the city below, taking advantage of the mild weather before the winter gloom sets in. "It was a badge of honor, almost. You know how much Jocelyn loves teasing us about it."

"She really does have a little too much fun." At the mention of Jocelyn, my heart twists. If I can't get us to tomorrow, at the very least, I can give my mom today.

My mom gets to her feet, and we head toward the outer observation deck. "So, if you're stuck in a time loop," she says, "there must be something you're supposed to fix in order to get out, right?"

"I've tried that. What would you do?"

"Hmm. Acts of kindness? Attempting to right wrongs?" She gives me a hopeful look, and I shake my head.

"Tried them all."

"What about unfinished business?"

I pause where I've been dragging my hand along the glass. Of course, the only thing that comes to mind is the one I've been trying my hardest not to think about.

All these months later, I'm still not sure how to tell her about prom. About everything that came before it. Today should feel low-stakes, since she'll forget it all by tomorrow, but it's not so much about telling her as it is putting what happened into words. *Hey, Mom, I was casually bullied most of high school and it culminated in a sexual nightmare I still can't think about without breaking out in a cold sweat.*

If prom really is my unfinished business, I have no idea how to finish it.

"Nothing I can think of," I finally say.

She throws an arm around my shoulders. "Maybe you just needed to spend some time with your beloved mother."

"That seems to solve just about everything."

I can't ruin this moment, however bittersweet it is. Because if I tell her, even if—*when*—we all wake up on Wednesday again and she forgets it, *I* won't. I'll have said it out loud, given a name to everything that's broken me. I'll have acknowledged the thing that has always terrified me the most—that no one has ever truly wanted me—and I won't be able to take that back.

"What do you think—should we do Smith Tower next?" she asks, and I force a smile and tell her yes.

DAY TWENTY-THREE

 TH̶L T̶H̶L T̶H̶L T̶H̶L III

Chapter 29

"THINK OF IT AS A BELATED BIRTHDAY GIFT," I TELL Miles when I pull up in front of Olmsted in another rental car the next day. A stick shift, just because I can. There's a folded T-shirt on the passenger seat that says BIRTHDAY BOY. "Or technically an early birthday gift, I guess?"

"Please don't tell me I have to wear that." Gently, he pushes the shirt off to the side before he slides in.

"Um, you do if you want to be cool like me." I turn in my seat to face him, showing off the almost-matching shirt I fancied up with some glitter and quick-dry paint. CHERISHED FRIEND OF BIRTHDAY BOY, it says, and Miles rolls his eyes. Three weeks ago he'd probably have groaned, so I'm calling it progress. "And look, I'm driving stick!"

"Well done."

"I feel like you're about right here"—I hold my hand out at waist level—"and I need you to be at least here." I move my hand above my head.

Miles lets out a long-suffering sigh and tugs on the shirt over his long-sleeved thermal, and I spike the volume on my early-2000s mix before speeding out of the parking lot and off campus.

Truthfully, I think we just need to get out of Seattle. West Seattle wasn't far enough, and maybe this won't be either, but the change of scenery has to do *something*, even if it's just to give our brains a break. I've needed a mission.

I don't care what I sound like when I sing out loud, and while Miles sings much, much quieter than I do, I kind of love this version of him. The window down, a slight breeze, his elbow resting on the door . . . there's something carefree about him I've never noticed before. Maybe because it's something he's never allowed himself to be.

"You're probably not going to tell me where we're going, are you?" Miles asks. "Although I'm guessing Canada, since you asked me to bring my passport."

It is indeed Canada, and I struggle a little navigating the roads as the signs switch from miles to kilometers, while Miles goes off on a mini lecture about why we should all be using the metric system.

"What is this?" he asks when we hit Vancouver and I stop in front of a museum, rolling down my window to grab a ticket for the parking lot. Then he draws in a sharp breath as he spots the ad covering half the building. "You brought me to an exhibit of period costumes?"

"They have the original gloves Jane Bennet wore in the 2005 *Pride & Prejudice*," I say, pulling into the parking structure. "I know, I know, it's not your favorite, but they have a bunch of costumes from the original *Little Women*, and some dishes from *Downton Abbey*. . . ."

I trail off, partially because I can't remember what else they have and because the expression on Miles's face has made me forget anything I was about to say. His eyes are fixed on the museum, and when he turns them back to me, I can see his jaw working to keep his smile at bay. For what might be the first time, he seems speechless.

"Barrett," he says after a few long moments, and then he releases that weapon of a smile. It makes the car seat go melty beneath me. *Jesus*, that's powerful. No wonder he keeps it locked away—the United Nations might need to intervene. "This is incredible. Thank you. Thank you so much."

ʊ ʊ ʊ

Miles in the museum is like a kid in a candy shop. No—like a kid with their own credit card and no spending limit in a candy shop that also sells puppies and video games and Baby Yoda merch.

Most of the time, I'm content to just observe him observing everything else. Because this is something I've noticed about Miles: all his passions, science and period pieces and even mozzarella sticks, he throws himself into wholeheartedly. He told me how his brother did this, and I'm not sure he realizes that he has that trait too.

It's impossible not to admire, and it makes me feel wildly lucky that right now I'm the one who gets to see what lights him up.

After we finish marveling at dresses and top hats and aprons and boots and parasols, we spend the rest of the day exploring the city. We eat too many delicious things at a public market and then wander through the Vancouver Aquarium. I feel out of time, out of place, for the first time since all of this started. Up here, I can breathe.

"There's something I wanted to talk to you about," I tell him hours later. We're on a picnic blanket in Stanley Park, awash in greenery with the bay spread out in front of us. It's nearing seven o'clock, and the park is full of families and couples, joggers and cyclists. I roll up my sleeve, running a hand along the place my tattoo was. The tattoo I had for less than a day, the pain that's lasted longer. "The tattoos we got. Obviously mine's gone, but yesterday, I didn't wake up the way I usually do. The pain in my arm woke me up, but there was nothing there."

"Does it still hurt?" He brings his hand up, until it's hovering above my arm, and then lifts his eyebrows at me as though asking if it's okay to touch me there. As though maybe touching my forearm is more personal than the way we held hands in the car. I shift my arm closer, giving him permission.

"Only a little. It's a shame," I say. "It was such a beautiful tattoo. Some of Gemini's finest work."

He draws his fingertips along it, featherlight, and I'm no longer interested in joking about it. I feel myself take a sharp breath I did not wholly anticipate, but if Miles notices, he doesn't give any indication. It almost tickles, the way he's touching me—I have to fight the urge to squeeze my eyes shut. That light touch is jamming my senses, a tiny but significant earthquake.

"A phantom pain, maybe?" he says. "That's the only way I've been able to rationalize it."

"It's happening to you, too?"

A nod. "It didn't used to, but maybe now that we've been here for a while, our minds are messing with us. My memory was already starting to blur when you got stuck." His fingers might be retracing Gemini's design, or maybe they're drawing something completely new. Whatever he's doing, I don't want him to stop. "It happens sometime with fatigue, too. If I stay up late the previous day, I'm more tired in the morning. It's difficult to measure, and sometimes I don't trust my own brain, but sometimes I swear that's what's happening."

"Do you think it's anything to . . . I don't know, worry about?" I laugh off the absurdity of this question, as though our entire situation isn't enough to worry about on its own.

"I don't know," he says softly, and when he drops his fingers from my forearm, my skin still hums. It's criminal, how badly I wanted him to keep going. Or for him to ask me to trace the spot where his half tattoo was. "It's not that I'm losing hope. I have to believe that something we try will work. Time isn't supposed to stop like this. It's not natural. The universe should *want* to right itself."

"If I recall, a very wise man once told me not to personify the universe."

"Even very wise men are known to make mistakes sometimes."

"This just won't do," I say, nudging his foot with mine. I kicked off my shoes on the grass next to us, and now my mismatched SHITSHOW and plain blue sock are on display. "You're supposed to have all the answers."

We fall into a silence again, but not an uncomfortable one. It's sunset, and if I were a different person, this is the kind of date I'd want to have with someone. Casual and relaxed, enjoying the scenery and each other's company, wrapped up in our own world in the middle of the grander one that surrounds us.

"Can you tell me more about you and Max?" I ask. "Something from when you were kids?"

The side of his mouth quirks upward. Glitter from his BIRTHDAY BOY shirt has started spreading onto his jeans. "You like those embarrassing stories, huh? Is this practice for all the profiles you'll write one day?"

"Maybe," I say, and perhaps that's true, but I also just really want to know.

Miles adjusts on the blanket, stretching out his legs. He's still Miles, of course, so his posture is excellent, but he's more relaxed than I've seen him in days. "One year for Hanukkah, my parents got me a crystal-growing kit. After I set it all up, Max waited until I was asleep to swap the tiny crystals for these enormous ones he bought, and I was so convinced for about five minutes that I was the most brilliant scientist who'd ever lived." A laugh, a shake of his head. "Devastating to find out that I wasn't."

"Please tell me you have pictures."

"Of course I do," he says, swiping through his phone to find them.

There's a commotion across the grass about a dozen yards away, and that's when I notice something strange.

Almost everyone sitting in this park with us is wearing a red T-shirt.

All of a sudden, music starts streaming from a massive speaker propped on a park bench, and all the people wearing red, at least two dozen of them, leap into formation.

"Oh my god," I say as they start to dance, unable to believe this is happening. "It's a flash mob."

I recognize the song right away: "Run Away with Me" by Carly Rae Jepsen. The dancers start out in a few staggered lines, all controlled movements. Arms, legs, hips in slow rotations. Then they break apart, allowing their dancing to get bigger, louder, skipping along the grass and bouncing off one another and throwing their hands high.

It's a million times better than any video I've watched.

"Did you know about this?" I ask Miles, heart in my throat as a trio of dancers body-roll in front of our picnic blanket.

"You're the one who brought me here," he says. "How could I have known?" He eyes me carefully, and I do my best to hide my face from him. "Are you . . . are you crying?"

I swipe away a tear. "It's really amazing how in sync they are!"

I think he might be laughing, but when he presses his shoulder against mine, it's clear it's an appreciative kind of laugh. A *you're weird but I'm into it* laugh.

At the end, the flash-mobbers whip off their shirts, and the tank tops they're wearing underneath spell out the name of the song. The crowd bursts into applause.

"I think that might be the best thing that's ever happened to me," I say, still clapping.

"Was it as magical as you thought it would be?"

"Even better. You really didn't plan this?" I ask, though of course he couldn't have. He didn't know we were coming here.

Miles shakes his head, a breeze catching some of his dark hair. "Just a perfect coincidence." Then he shifts on the blanket, digging his hand into the fabric. Loose threads everywhere must fear him. "I—uh. Wanted to give you something." He reaches into his backpack. Anxiously, like he's been working up the nerve to do this, but as soon as I see what it is, my heart starts racing and my lungs tighten and—and I can't breathe.

Miles is holding a single yellow rose.

My whole world goes sideways, and suddenly I am back in high school. Opening up my locker and sitting in homeroom and feeling like a fucking idiot, throwing all those flowers away, those flowers that were only meant to make me feel awful about myself. Wishing so desperately for school to end.

I hold a hand to my chest, as though if I press hard enough, I can keep all of it inside.

No. Not here. Not now. *Please.*

"I wanted to thank you for today," Miles continues. "I looked through the museum gift shop, but most things seemed silly, because you wouldn't be able to take any of them with you the next day. But then there were so many flowers at the market, and I realized there's a metaphor there, since those don't last either, and in my mind it was almost poetic. So I got it while you were waiting in line for empanadas. . . ." He stops his rambling when he sees my face, his eyes going wide. "And . . . *oh*. Oh no. Do you not like roses? I shouldn't have assumed. This was a terrible idea, I'll just—"

"No no no," I say quickly, dragging a hand across my face so he can't see whatever emotion is no longer hiding there. "You didn't—you didn't do anything wrong."

"Okay." The rose drops to the blanket, its petals slightly mashed from its time in Miles's backpack. Then he glances back at me. "Holy shit. You're really not okay, are you?"

I press my lips together tightly, terrified of what might happen if I don't. And yet that might be worse, because I can't get a proper inhale and my lungs are screaming and the more I will my body to calm down, the more it protests.

Don't.

Can't.

Please.

I gasp out a breath, squeezing my eyes shut. As though maybe if Miles can't see me, I'll disappear.

"I don't—I don't want you to see me like this," I manage, eyes still closed. *Fuuuuuck.* "People are—they're probably staring."

I can hear Miles moving closer, feel his hand landing on my back. "They're not," he says softly. "No one's staring."

My breathing races away from me, hard and fast. My chest is on fucking fire and my throat might be closing up, but maybe—maybe that would be okay. Then I wouldn't have to tell him why.

The world slides away from me again, and I'm no longer in a quaint park on a picnic blanket with Miles stroking my back. I'm in the hotel room, asking Cole to turn the lights off. I'm in a bed that's too big for us, a thousand new things happening all at once. I'm opening my locker at school on Monday.

"You're going to get through this," Miles says from somewhere. "Do you want to try breathing with me?"

I nod, forcing myself back to the present, listening to Miles's steady breaths. I do my best to match mine to his, but they're too loud, too shaky.

"You can do this," he says, and I want so badly to prove to him—to myself—that I can.

Inhale. Exhale. He goes slowly, waiting for me to catch up.

"That's it. You're doing great."

A strangled laugh slips out, because I never thought breathing was something I could be good at until I suddenly couldn't do it at all.

Inhale.

Exhale.

I'm not sure how much time has passed when my breathing returns to normal and I can finally open my eyes. At some point, I grabbed his sleeve. I hope I wasn't holding on too tight.

"Thank you," I rasp out as I release my grip. My eyes are wet, but I am *here*, in Stanley Park. I am here with Miles. "How—how did you know what to do?"

He turns a little sheepish. "I, um, looked it up. That day in the ice-cream truck. It seemed like maybe you were about to have a panic attack, so after I got back to my room, I did some research. I wanted to make sure I'd know what to do in case it happened again."

He did some research.

Of course he did, and in this moment I'm immensely grateful.

"You don't have to tell me what's going on," he says. Gentle. How is he always so gentle in these moments I feel made of glass? "Unless you want to."

I press a hand to my forehead, brushing away sweat-damp hair. "I—I don't know. It's stupid. Really."

"Somehow, I get the feeling that it isn't." His hand is on my back again, hypnotic, easing some of the lingering tension. "Whatever you're going through, whether it's loop-related, or about something else entirely . . . I'm a good listener, or at least I like to think so."

I let this sit between us for a moment. He's not pushing me to talk if I don't want to. And I can't deny that I've wondered if this is something I need to do in order to move on from it. To become someone different from that girl I was in high school, and maybe even to become the person I thought I'd be in college. Or at the very least, someone in between.

I want to know about you, too, he said the other day, and I might want to tell him.

Because maybe I don't need a push. Maybe all I need is a gentle tap. A featherlight touch. A good listener.

I take a few shuddery breaths. It feels impossible to tell him when I haven't told my own mother, and yet, despite all the reasons they shouldn't, the words start spilling out.

"I told you about the tennis scandal, and how it kind of turned the school against me. Not just Lucie—everyone, or at least what felt like everyone. I guess I've always been an odd duck, but it got worse after that." I stare down at the blanket's strawberry pattern, debating how much I want to share. Then again, he hasn't exactly left anything unturned for me. With another exhale, I keep going. "The only thing I could do was pretend it didn't bother me. Develop an even thicker skin. So that's what I did for the next three years."

I chance a look at Miles. He tenses, as though he wants to say something. But he can sense I'm not done.

"By senior year, things started to feel okay. I kept to myself, but no one was whispering about me or going out of their way to avoid me. Most people had graduated and moved on by that point, but I was used to shutting everyone out, so I just kept doing it. But then . . . I got asked to prom."

I expect the words to dry up in my throat at this point, but they don't. I make a fist in the blanket, anchoring myself to the present, as I keep going. "Do you remember that guy who showed up when we had the ice-cream truck? The one I told you was from school? That was who asked me," I say, and a muscle in Miles's jaw leaps. I try to turn the mood lighthearted. "It's like the scene in every teen movie where the cool guy invites the tragic girl with glasses to prom, and suddenly she takes off her glasses and she's gorgeous."

"I like your glasses. They suit you," he says, and my face warms at the compliment. Though it's not exactly a compliment—it's not as though he's saying he likes my eyes or my hair or my mouth.

"Remember when I said my first time was, um, brief?"

Miles blushes at this too, no longer making eye contact. "It was on prom night?"

I nod, gripping the blanket tighter. "It was my first everything, all at once. And I wanted it to happen. He was cute, and he was nice, and he sure as hell paid me more attention that night than anyone had in years. Part of me thought . . . well, I thought that if I didn't do it, if I didn't get it over with with him, then maybe I never would. Maybe no one would want to." I say that last part quietly, and even though it hurts, I charge forward, suddenly wanting to get all of this out of my brain and into the space between us. *Needing* to.

Four months, it's been trapped there, and I don't think I can carry the weight of it alone anymore.

"The next week at school, my locker was stuffed with flowers. Cole . . . was the brother of someone who'd been on that tennis team, someone who'd lost a scholarship, and I'd had no idea. It was this hilarious thing, that he'd 'deflowered' Barrett Bloom. He and his friends even created a hashtag: debloomed. I still don't know their exact motive—maybe Cole wanted to ruin my life because he blamed me for what happened to his brother. Or maybe they just wanted to turn me into one more joke, and they did." My breath is coming in sharp bursts again, and I can't look at Miles anymore. "They left a rose on my desk every morning in home-room, and everyone who knew what was going on would laugh or shake their heads, like they pitied me but couldn't be bothered to say anything about it. And the people who didn't know probably thought I had some secret admirer. They just . . . couldn't let me leave high school without reminding me who I was."

I relax my grip on the blanket and bring my gaze up to Miles. His jaw is set, his dark eyes flashing with something I've never seen before.

"That," he says, more venom in his voice than the most poisonous flower, "is fucking *appalling*. Barrett . . . I am so, so sorry."

"I haven't talked to anyone about it." My words are high-pitched. Unfamiliar. I am a fucking mess in the middle of Stanley Park on a day that doesn't exist. "I just—I've been scared of what it means about me if I finally acknowledge it out loud."

Miles blinks at me a few times, as though he doesn't understand what I'm saying. "Why the hell would this mean anything about *you?* You did absolutely nothing wrong. It shows that you went to school with some pathetic lowlifes." There's empathy in his gaze now, alongside the rage. I didn't expect Miles's anger to feel so validating. "That is one of the most horrendous things I've ever heard," he continues. "I can't—I can't believe they did that to you. This thing that's supposed to be special, that—"

"I didn't want it to be special," I say, interrupting him, because I never thought Cole was going to rock my world in that specific way. "That wasn't what I was looking for. I just wanted it to happen, I guess, to know what it was like."

And to feel wanted for a few moments. The press of his hands and mouth, the weight of him on top of me . . . sometimes it's impossible to separate the act from the aftermath, but for a short time, I did feel wanted.

It just wasn't enough.

"And all you did was bring me a flower. It was a sweet thing to do. How fucked up is that, that I can't be given a flower?"

"It's not fucked up. I get it," he says. "I'm so sorry. If I'd known, I wouldn't have—"

I cut him off with a sharp shake of my head. "I don't want to not be able to receive flowers from anyone. I mean, I like flowers, or I did before. And I like my last name." It doesn't feel as terrible as I thought it might, telling him all of this. It feels—lighter. I can't believe I didn't know him three weeks ago, and now he has all these pieces of me I've never given anyone before. "So there it is. My whole traumatic history," I say. "Maybe I should have waited. Maybe I should have done what you're doing."

"It's not your fault," he says emphatically. "None of it. They should have acted like fucking decent human beings."

His words are sharper than I've ever heard them. Miles being so upset on my behalf . . . it's almost *sexy*.

I try to shove away that revelation but it only intensifies, speeding up my pulse and settling low in my belly. A spark of desire.

"I've never told anyone," I say. "Not even my mom."

"Thank you." His eyes are heavy on mine, and I have an overwhelming urge to ask him if he'll hug me, which I valiantly beat back with my waning willpower. "Thank you for telling me."

"We don't have to keep talking about it," I say.

"If that's what you want."

I nod, unsure how to explain that this should have been too much, but it isn't, and that's something I'm not ready to unpack either.

"There should be a buzzer that goes off, or a light that flashes to let you know you're with the right person," I say, trying to lighten the mood.

"Someone who comes out and waves a flag."

"Yes! Is that really too much to ask?"

Miles laughs. "Can I tell you something?" he says.

"That sounds ominous."

"It's not. I swear." He takes a moment to collect himself, and then: "When my days started repeating, before you got stuck too, we interacted. A bunch, as you know. And . . . well, I started saying things to see how you'd react. I'd make a comment about your T-shirt, or about physics, or I'd ask you about your classes. Mostly surface stuff, but still—because when I said something different, *you'd* say something different, and it made me feel less alone." He gives me this sheepish half smile. "You were the most interesting person on campus."

"I was the one with the raging temper, you mean."

"No," he says. "You seemed like someone I ought to be paying attention to."

I can barely formulate a response to that.

So he keeps going, each word chipping away at the steel in my heart. "I'm not sure I've ever laughed as much as I have in the past few weeks. Even if I tried my absolute best not to humor you at first." He taps each side of his mouth, leaving behind a constellation of glitter. "I'm going to develop early wrinkles here, and it's all going to be your fault."

Without thinking, I raise a hand to his face, placing my fingers next to his mouth as he drops his hands. Tracing the imaginary lines there. He's kind of beautiful, and it's a shame I've been this slow to notice how lovely he is to look at. Or, at the very least, slow to let myself acknowledge it.

"Aww, you'd look cute with some mouth wrinkles," I say. "Distinguished."

His breath catches, and that concerning thought I had a few moments ago—it's no longer an *almost*. That catch of his breath sends an electric shock to the parts of my body that aren't already on high alert. "What about gray hair?" he says.

I move my hands up into his hair, wind my fingers through the dark strands. It's nice, thick hair, somewhere in between soft and coarse. A few dots of glitter are spread throughout, and I imagine I'm covered in it too. His eyes close, and I wonder if it's involuntary. "You could pull it off."

Miles's hand drops to my knee, and it's then that I notice how much of the space between our bodies has disappeared. Maybe we've been moving closer this whole time, his heat and his scent muddling my brain.

"Barrett," he says on an exhale, just as my thumb brushes the shell of his ear. He says my name like it's something delicate. A slip of silk. Dandelion fluff. "I wanted to tell you—you know you don't have to turn everything into a joke. And maybe that sounds strange, given what I just said about how funny I find you. But it doesn't have to happen every time. It's okay to also just . . . live in those bad feelings a bit more."

Our lips are a breath apart, and I'm no longer in denial. I'm wearing a shirt that says CHERISHED FRIEND OF BIRTHDAY BOY and he's that birthday boy, and we are stuck in time but not in our ways, and there is only one thing I want before today ends.

"I've done enough of that," I say, shifting closer on the blanket, my thigh pressed right up against his. "I want to feel something good."

A dark, determined flicker crosses his face, and I want to etch it in stone. He wants me the way I want him—I'm certain of it. This boy I thought was so rigid, who's shown me again and again that he's capable of change. He is sweet and unique and so fucking cute, and I'm not even sure he's aware of it.

I'm leaning forward, ready to take that final leap between something safe and something terrifying, when it happens.

A flash behind my eyes.

Miles and me, in the room of a house I only half recognize. It's too loud, too packed. Dark. Fuzzy. His mouth on top of mine, my hands in his hair.

275

"Barrett," says the Miles in front of me again, but there's none of that tenderness in his voice anymore. Now he's drawing away from me, backing up. "Wait."

We've done this before.

Chapter 30

THAT FLASH—IT'S NOT QUITE A MEMORY, AND IT comes with a headache so fierce I have to bend over, pressing a hand to my temple and jostling my glasses, cursing under my breath.

"Barrett? What's going on? Are you okay?"

"Fine," I manage. I get to my feet too quickly and stumble backward, knocking over a bottle of wine belonging to the family next to us. "Sorry. Sorry!"

Miles and me. Miles and me *kissing*, somewhere I don't remember. I try to cling to the not-memory, searching it for details, for a way to make sense of all this, but it's a slippery thing, unwilling to be pinned down.

My heart thrashes inside my chest. Whatever I just saw didn't happen to this version of me. That much I'm certain of, the way I'm certain that somewhere out there, in a timeline parallel to this one or in some shape my puny human mind can't possibly fathom, Barrett Bloom kissed Miles Kasher-Okamoto.

"We've kissed before, haven't we?" I say. "In one of your

timelines, before I got stuck with you. We—we *kissed*."

Miles's features are painted with shock, mouth slightly open. "How did you—"

"I don't know. I don't know what the hell is going on, only that I *saw* it happening in my head, even though I don't remember it at all." The pounding in my skull intensifies. "So if you could just tell me whether or not we've kissed, that would be really fucking helpful."

Now he looks like a small animal that's been caught in a trap. "Yes," he says quietly. His hands are limp in his lap. "We did. I'm sorry. I'm so sorry, Barrett. I should have told you. I should have—"

I clutch my head as another flash of pain tears through it.

"Tell me." I sit back down as the nearby family glares daggers at me, cleaning the spilled wine and shifting their picnic blanket away from the wet spot. I try my best not to make any sudden movements, since that seems to anger the headache even more. "Tell me exactly what happened."

Miles takes a few moments to respond, as though picking his words carefully. "It was one of the nights you didn't pepper-spray me," he says. If it's an attempt at levity, I'm not laughing. "We were both at Zeta Kappa. There was . . . some flirting. And dancing."

"I danced with you?"

"You danced with a lot of people."

I groan. "Great. Did I kiss all of them too? Was I drunk?"

"Not that I saw," he says seriously. "You were having fun, but I don't think you were drinking. I never would have guessed you had . . . the history that you do. From high school. Because you were talking to everyone, making them all laugh."

Figures. The one time I'm the life of the party, it's in a parallel universe. Who among us hasn't been there?

"We started talking," he continues. "You—you told me you liked my khakis. In retrospect, I can see that was probably sarcasm."

I want to tell him that it wasn't, but how the hell do I know? I don't know who that person was, who danced and laughed and kissed a near stranger.

"Was it, like . . ." I mash my hands together in an attempt to illustrate what I'm trying to say. "Just a peck? Or a full-on make-out?"

Miles's face is pained. "Somewhere between the two."

Okay. I can handle this, I think. Maybe.

"And it was just the one time? That one iteration of the party?" When he nods, I fire off more questions. "When was it? When in your timeline?"

"Maybe a month in."

I do some quick mental calculations. That means it happened about a month and a half ago for him. He and I have been stuck together for three weeks, and he's kept it hidden this whole time.

The person I thought was worth my worst secret, keeping one of his own.

"What has all of this been, then?" I ask. "You buttering me up so you could hook up with me?"

He looks horrified. "*No,*" he says firmly. "Not because you're not—I mean—you're—" Fumbling for the right words, he crushes a hand into his eyes. "*Fuck.*"

I know enough about him to know that's not something he would do, and yet I can't stop myself. "Well, it worked. I'm properly buttered, Miles. We were just about to kiss, so you obviously did something right. Well done."

"Barrett . . ." Miles scrapes a hand through his hair. The hair I just touched. His mouth, the one I wanted to kiss, is twisted to one side, like he's trying to let only the right words out. He clears his throat, charging forward. "Just a moment ago, we were talking about wanting it to be special. Being with someone. And this wasn't—it wasn't *that*, it wasn't anything more than kissing, but it also wasn't—" As though realizing he's dug himself into a hole in the most roundabout of ways, he breaks off.

"It wasn't *special*? Should that make me feel better?" I snatch up my bag and get to my feet, unable to sit politely in this park a moment longer. "You should coach elementary school soccer because you are just an endless well of positive reinforcement."

With that, I turn and weave my way through families and couples and flash-mob members toasting how great their routine was. And it was. If I weren't a jumbled, furious mess, I'd stop to tell them how much I loved it.

"I meant—I thought it was special at the time," Miles says, jogging to keep up with me, backpack over one shoulder, blanket trailing on the ground. "Romantic, even. You seemed so cool, and you felt . . . I don't know. Unattainable, maybe. But I didn't know you then. Now that I do . . . well, things are different."

Unattainable. Surely, no one has ever used that word to describe me. I try to see myself through his eyes, but I don't get any more flashes. Whoever I was that night feels utterly, hopelessly lost.

It's the strangest betrayal, because it's not just that I'm angry with him. I'm angry that he felt something for this person during an event that, by all logic, did not happen to me. There might even be a flicker of jealousy, even if somewhere deep in my neural network, I am connected to that other Barrett.

"If this is your way of asking for a redo, you're doing a really shitty job," I say as we reach a gravel path, dodging a bicyclist. "So you were going to kiss me again and pretend that first time never happened?"

"I wasn't going to." He's breathing hard, his cheeks flushed. "I wouldn't have let myself do that without telling you first. I wanted to tell you, but things were moving too fast."

Moving too fast. We haven't been moving for weeks. Months.

"But you waited so long, Miles! You pulled away at the literal last second. We're not just two people randomly stuck in a time loop together anymore. We're *friends*, and—" *I thought we were becoming more? I wanted to press my mouth against yours and shove you down onto the strawberry-patterned picnic blanket?* I decide not to finish the sentence. "Why are you only telling me now?"

"I didn't want to make you uncomfortable. Which I realize now was a bad call. I thought you wouldn't trust me. Or worse, that you'd think I was making it up to try to get you to do something you didn't want to do. To get closer to you, especially when we didn't instantly click." He shoves out a breath. I'm not used to seeing him flustered like this, so clearly aware of his mistake. "I'm so sorry. I should have told you. I fucked up."

When I don't say anything, he keeps going. "It hurt, at first. That you didn't remember anything, since it didn't happen to this version of you. I had to be the one with those memories, but you . . . you didn't have to carry it with you. You didn't have that moment with someone you were certain was too good for you, a moment that turned out to be—yep, too good to be true."

Someone you were certain was too good for you. I can't linger on that, and yet it breaks the small part of my heart that isn't already wrecked by Miles's confession.

"You want me to feel sorry for you?" I say. "You kept this from me for weeks, and you want me to feel sympathy because you had this great moment with some other me?"

Miles bunches the blanket more tightly beneath his arm. "This is coming out all wrong. I swear, Barrett. There's nothing nefarious here. I just—I just want to make things right."

"Fine. It didn't happen to me, so I shouldn't be upset about it." I hang a left at the sign arrowing toward the parking lot. "Let's just go home."

He doesn't even argue. Originally, we figured there wouldn't be a point in driving back, since we'd wake up in Olmsted ~~today~~ tomorrow anyway. We were going to stay out all night in another city, another country. This perfect day, now completely shattered.

Part of me might have wanted to kiss him to make myself feel better. Feel *wanted*. But it's a good thing we didn't do it. I shouldn't have trusted him with my secrets, and now I know I can't trust him with my heart.

Miles offers to drive, maybe as some small slice of penance, and I'm too tired to fight him. It's a slow, silent drive. We stop at a gas station in Bellingham, where I go inside and snatch every bottle of 5-Hour Energy off the shelves.

I'm not letting myself go to sleep tonight even if it kills me.

"It's past midnight," Miles says when I get back in the car, slamming the door behind me.

"Thank you, Father Time."

He gestures to the bottles in my hands. "I've tried that. It's not going to work, if that's what you're thinking."

The seat belt is too tight around my stomach, but I can't bring myself to care, or to readjust it. And there's glitter on my hands that isn't coming off, no matter how hard I scrape at it.

"Well, you do seem to be an expert on what I'm thinking." Half a bottle goes down my throat, slick and overly sweet. "And I have too. Hopefully the universe will know how determined I am this time."

A pause. "I never know what you're thinking," he says quietly as he puts the car in gear. "All these Wednesdays, and you're still a mystery to me. And maybe this makes me an idiot, but all I want to do is keep trying to figure you out."

And I have no idea what to say to that.

Even now, I'm thinking the same thing. I've genuinely enjoyed getting to know him, and in some ways he's exactly the person I thought he was. But in even more, he's something completely different. I liked that completely different Miles so much, and that's why this is so crushing. I wanted him to be the person who kept those shattered pieces of my history safe, but maybe the truth is that no one can. They can't be unshattered.

We pull onto the highway, a darkened stretch of I-5 that winds through mountains cloaked in fog.

"There has to be a way I can make it up to you," Miles says, easing the car through a tight turn. "You want me to wear one of these shirts every day? Done. Lead my own Save the Gophers march? I'll do it."

"This fucking cap," I mutter, twisting at the next bottle.

"Here, I'll—" He takes one hand off the wheel, reaching out to help me.

But I push his arm back with more force than I intend. "I don't need any—"

In our scuffle, the cap flies off the bottle, the energy drink spraying us both.

"Shit," I say under my breath, just as Miles grabs the wheel again.

Twin bright lights cut through my vision, temporarily blinding me.

"What the—" Miles says, leaning into his shoulder to swipe energy drink off his face.

Up ahead, a semitruck has drifted from its lane, and now it's speeding right. Toward. *Us.*

"Holy fuck holy fuck holy fuck!" I shout, the energy drink forgotten, gripping the seat with more force than I thought I was capable of.

Miles slams the horn.

On our left is a steep hill covered with evergreens.

On our right, a rough edge and a rushing stream.

I have never had my life flash before my eyes. I always thought it would be an organized, chronological kind of thing—I'd recall my childhood, my teen years, all with fondness and peaceful reflection.

Now that it's happening, there's not enough time for any of it, only a brief ache for my mom. And then all I can focus on is that the last thing I did on planet Earth was argue with someone over a bottle of 5-Hour Energy.

"Hold on!" Miles yanks the steering wheel to the left, but he's too late.

The truck careens toward us, stark white against the near-black road. *We're going to die,* I think, the fear a hot and sticky thing in my throat.

I'm not ready.

Horns wail and tires screech, and I can only squeeze my eyes shut and hope this isn't the end.

The last thing I register as metal smashes into metal and glass rains down on us is Miles's hand finding mine and holding on tight.

DAYS TWENTY-FOUR AND TWENTY-FIVE

####### ||||| ||||| ||||| ||||| |||||

Chapter 31

". . . HAS TO BE . . . MISTAKE . . ."

The words are far away. Or maybe underwater. It's hard to tell because I am on a cloud.

A strange, sort of bouncy cloud, and it's funny, really, because it's not quite as fluffy as I thought a cloud might be. But maybe that's what I get for living a mediocre life: a sad little cloud somewhere in a lonely part of the sky.

I drift.

Somewhere in my fog of consciousness, I remember that Jews don't believe in the afterlife. Whatever this is, wherever I am . . . maybe there aren't even words for it yet.

More muffled sounds, but it doesn't matter. Nothing matters up here in Cloud World.

I roll to my side, trying to find a more comfortable position on this cloud of mine. When I reposition my body, a sharp pain shoots up my left side, from my shoulder to my wrist and then from my knee to my ankle.

With my other hand, I pat the ~~cloud~~ mattress beneath me, and slowly, slowly, the reality drips in.

". . . talk out in the hall," someone says, and the sound of the door shutting and something dropping to the floor is enough to rattle my brain inside my skull.

I am not dead.

No, I'm back in Hellmouth Hall, and my body is *fucked*.

I push up onto my arms as gingerly as I can, careful not to do anything that might cause more pain. ~~Tonight~~ Last night comes back to me in fragments that start with Miles and me arguing at Stanley Park and end with a truck splitting the windshield of our rental car.

We *died*.

And yet we didn't.

This is the tattoo pain from I've-lost-track days ago multiplied by a thousand. This is my entire body having been fed through a wood chipper and then feasted on by a pack of wolves. I squeeze my eyes shut, scared to look down, and when I do, there's a long bruise vaguely the shape of California sweeping from knee to hip. I didn't think it was possible to look worse than I feel . . . but there it is.

An arctic, bone-deep chill runs through me. The relief should be stronger, but I'm stuck in the terror from those moments before the truck crashed into us. In some other timeline, did the authorities dig me out of the rubble and call my mom to identify my body? What would they have told her, and would she have believed them? Would she have known, deep down, that there was a reason her daughter was on the freeway between Vancouver and Seattle late on a Wednesday night?

Our timeline resets sometime before six a.m., and yet the car accident happened around midnight. And afterward, it was just . . . nothingness.

Waking up back here when I could have just as easily never woken up at all.

I swallow hard, aching for that version of my daughterless mom, a thought too horrible to linger on. I get my bearings again— patting the bed beneath me, wiggling my fingers and toes, holding a hand to my heart.

Thump-*thump*. Thump-*thump*. Thump-*thump*.

Alive.

In a sleepy panic, I reach not for my phone but for the Tylenol in the top drawer of my desk, downing a couple and praying they kick in fast. This didn't used to happen, yesterday bleeding into today in a hazy, nightmarish blur. A million theories race through my mind. We've overstayed our welcome. We've pushed the limits of space-time too far. We've made a mistake, and the universe wants us to pay.

Don't personify the universe, someone says in my head, and I don't even have the energy to ask fake Miles to shut up.

Miles.

This time, I grab my phone. As if I've summoned it, a message is waiting for me.

I'm sorry for yesterday. Again. I'll apologize every day we're stuck, if it helps at all. And if it doesn't, well, I'll do it anyway, at least until you tell me I'm being annoying.

Please, Barrett. Tell me I'm annoying.

God, why are those words messing with my heart?

Every text I compose to him sounds thoroughly absurd.

Did we die last night?

Are we in hell?

Is this some kind of twisted afterlife, and we're both doomed to repeat this day until some higher power gets bored of us? Is that our eternal torture?

The urge to remain silent is too strong, but finally I just write, **Okay. You're annoying.** Then I shut off my phone, collapsing back into bed and staring up at the ceiling, tracing the coastline of my California bruise with a single fingertip.

Miles's betrayal hurts just as much today as it did ~~today~~ yesterday. Our feelings weren't quite out in the open at the park, but our desires were. We were about to kiss, and the knowledge that we did it in the past (present?) has tangled up all my wiring. I'm not sure I can trust him. All these weeks we've forged a connection, all those times I let him in—and yesterday, when I took him down my darkest corridors—and he's never been honest with me.

I didn't want to make you uncomfortable.

I should have told you.

Too good to be true.

As though a compliment would make it all less painful. To that I say, bullshit.

Whatever we are moving forward, I won't make the mistake I almost made last night. The mistake a different Barrett made all those weeks ago.

When the door opens again, Lucie steps inside, and I expect her to launch into a speech about how I've ruined her life. Instead, she freezes when she sees me.

"Barrett?" she says, something like empathy in her voice. "Are you okay?"

"I didn't realize I was that bad at hiding my agony," I say, trying to make a joke, but she's not having it. "I was, uh, in a car accident yesterday." Not entirely a lie. *And I might have died. And none of this might be real.*

"Should you go to the hospital?" Her eyes widen when she sees the bruise on my leg, and I hurry to cover it up with the sheets. "I can go with you, if you need—"

"No!" I say quickly. "I mean—I went yesterday. They checked me out, said I seemed okay and that I should just take some painkillers."

Lucie's expression is still suspicious, but at least she drops it. "So," she says, waving a hand around the room. "You and me, huh?"

"Someone in resident services has a twisted sense of humor."

"Seriously." With some effort, she hops onto her brick of a bed, smoothing a flyaway back into her ponytail. "This room is barely bigger than the journalism supply closet back at Island."

This is new. She's not in a rush to *let me speak to your manager* about it. She's sitting there like she's completely okay with the fact that we're roommates. Not resigned to it—accepting it.

I remember the Lucie who cried in the stairwell. The Lucie who popped one of my lavender balloons when she slammed the door. The Lucie who took me to Elsewhere and spoke dreamily about UW's modern dance troupe.

I'm not sure where this version of Lucie falls.

"Were you going to room with someone else?" I ask, trying my best to be friendly. I prop myself up on my elbows, fighting a grimace as my left arm snaps with pain.

She shakes her head. "I signed up for a single. Most of my friends went to WSU." She doesn't make eye contact as she says this. The friends who forgot about her, she said the other day. The friends who tried to use her for an internship. "What about you?"

"My email said I was with a girl named Christina Dearborn." I shrug, not hating the serendipity of Christina having found the article that led me to a place where Lucie and I started to understand each other. "Evidently, fate intervened."

Lucie unzips her designer duffel. "And I'll make new friends, I know," she says to her clothes and her electronics and her high-end hair products, as though trying to convince herself. "It's just . . . overwhelming, I guess."

"Don't I know it," I say under my breath. "Hey. I know you just got here, but I have to eat breakfast, or else I become even more unbearable than I usually am. What if we go downstairs and get some food?"

"You don't have class?"

"Not until the afternoon," I lie.

Lucie considers this for a few moments, toying with the end of her ponytail in this way I've noticed she does when she's anxious. "Maybe that wouldn't be terrible," she agrees.

ʊ ʊ ʊ

Lucie pokes at her plate with a compostable fork. "So what exactly *is* the Olmsted Eggstravaganza? Is it an omelet, or a burrito?"

"That's the beauty of the Eggstravaganza," I say. "It's both and neither at the same time."

"Sketchy, but okay." Lucie chews thoughtfully. "Is that rosemary? Or maybe thyme? Whatever it is, it's magical."

It usually is. And yet I'm not hungry.

The reality of Lucie Lamont and me eating the Olmsted Eggstravaganza together is too strange for words. We ask about each other's summer, and I learn that Lucie spent it interning (unpaid) for her parents. I tell her I mostly helped my mom in her shop, leaving out all the times I stared at my ceiling and replayed what happened at prom and afterward. Occasionally, my heart sinks, knowing the phone call that awaits her later.

I could tell her. Warn her.

But what would that even sound like—*hey, your dad's going to call later and make you cry*? Yeah, no. Not when what we have is already so tenuous.

"You should really eat something," she says. Before we left our room, she changed into her first-day outfit—black mock-neck sweater and denim skirt—but left her hair in the ponytail. "It'll help you feel better."

I stare down at my food, knowing she's right but certain my stomach will revolt if I do anything but create an abstract egg-based art project on this plate. Whenever I shift in my seat, the bruise rewards me with a flare of pain. My body is wrecked. My mind is wrecked. My relationship with Miles—most likely wrecked, though I'm not sure to what degree.

It's almost funny—without even planning on it, I'm living in my bad feelings, just like Miles suggested.

And that's when I get an idea.

Miles and I have never used our knowledge of September 21 for evil. We've stuck to positive things, puppies and ice cream and Disneyland. But what if the thing that would fix this, the only thing I haven't tried, is what I joked about to him all those days ago?

Revenge.

The sudden darkness of it fills me with more hope than I've had all day. A sharp and spiteful kind of hope. Maybe that's why I'm stuck here—to get back at the people who made my life hell. What if this has been my unfinished business all along? My means to escape?

"You know what would really make me feel better?" I say, letting it swirl up inside me like possibility. "Screwing with Cole Walker."

Lucie freezes with her fork halfway to her mouth, icy blue eyes lit with confusion. "What?"

Shit. Too late, I realize we haven't had the conversation about prom yet. She doesn't know that I know that she tried to intervene on my behalf. Once again, my brain is three steps behind my mouth.

"For, uh, what happened last year," I say. "You don't like him very much either, do you?"

For a few moments, Lucie just blinks at me. And then I watch her shut down, eyebrows pulling together, returning her gaze to the plate in front of her. "The Walkers can fuck all the way off," she says with a stab at her eggs. "But they're not worth wasting any energy on."

And then she rushes to finish her breakfast.

ᴗ ᴗ ᴗ

After Lucie disappears to class, I do a little recon.

Cole's social media is private, but on ice-cream day he was wearing his student ID on an orange lanyard around his neck. I know that lanyard—Paige gave them out during move-in, explaining that each dorm had a different color. I immediately stashed my yellow one somewhere in my suitcase because lanyard doesn't match my aesthetic, but a quick search reveals that orange is the color for Brimmer Hall, on UW's southern edge.

I camp out in the Brimmer lobby for a couple of hours, pretending to read an oral history of *Clueless* my mom gave me for my birthday last year, ignoring the way my whole left side screams at me when I sit in the same position for too long—until he emerges from the elevator, tanned and damp-haired, lanyard around his neck. And then I follow him.

All day.

The next morning, I gain Lucie's sympathy again, oddly grateful my bruises haven't disappeared. Again we go to the dining hall for Eggstravaganzas, and this time when I bring up Cole, I ease into it.

"There's something I've wanted to talk to you about," I say between the few bites of breakfast I can manage today. "All summer, actually."

Lucie lifts her eyebrows at me, interest piqued. "Okay . . ."

"I know what you did at the end of the year. Telling Cole Walker and his friends to quit it." His name will never not taste sour on my tongue, but I power through. "And—I wanted to say thank you."

"I didn't do it because I wanted credit for doing the right thing or whatever," she says, almost sounding defensive. "I did it because that was fucked up."

"It—it means a lot to me. Really."

Slowly, she nods, seeming to soften, and I hope she can tell I'm being genuine. "Are you . . . okay? About what happened?"

"Are you asking if I have any lasting psychological damage? Only time will tell." When her mouth drops open, I try to laugh this off. "I'm . . . working through it."

And maybe I am. Telling Miles helped, at least for a few minutes, which is an infuriating realization to have when he's the last person I want to think about right now. He texted again this morning, a desperate **can we please talk?** that I left on read. He had hundreds of chances to talk, and every single time, he told me only half-truths. All those days we spent discussing our previous loops, and not once did he consider the fact that I deserved to know about that kiss.

Still, the fact remains that I let him in, and it didn't kill me.

Well, it did, but the two things are, I assume, unrelated.

It's okay to live in those bad feelings a bit more. I hate that he was right. I've painted over the past with jokes and faux confidence. I convinced myself I was fine, that I was okay on my own. All those years I thought my armor was impenetrable, when inside I'm as soft and gooey as the inside of a mozzarella stick fresh from the fryer. The past few years have been all about making sure no one scratches up that armor, no one sees inside.

And it's fucking exhausting.

"I'm sorry," Lucie says, fidgeting with the end of her ponytail.

"For the way I acted toward you. I was a piece of shit to you in high school."

"I didn't exactly make it easy for you to be anything else."

"You're not *wrong*," she says. "But everything with Blaine feels like it happened a hundred years ago. And he was . . . well, a bit of a jackass, to be honest. But at the time, he was my first love, my first everything, and I blamed you for the relationship ending. Which isn't right, because you weren't in that relationship. You can't have been at fault."

Hearing that eases some of the pressure in my chest. "Thank you. For saying that."

A slight nod. "Besides, I'm pretty sure Blaine was only with me because of my family." Now that she's started to open up, it seems to get easier. Like there's a lot she's been waiting to tell someone. "He'd always ask if my parents were going to be home when we hung out, and it seemed like he *wanted* them to be, which was the opposite of how I thought that would go. And every so often he'd 'forget' his wallet. I was happy to cover the bill, but then it started happening only on our most expensive dates."

"Jesus." I knew the Walkers were trash, but not quite to this extent. "I had no idea."

"The most ridiculous thing"—Lucie breaks off, letting out this half laugh as a light blush appears on her cheeks—"is that I'm not even sure I'm attracted to men. I loved being an underclassman dating a senior, but everything we did together . . . we were safe, and nothing bad happened, but I didn't exactly enjoy it, either." She shifts her gaze to her Eggstravaganza again, giving it a few jabs with her fork while I process this. "I don't know. I can't believe I'm telling you this. I kind of thought maybe it was something I could figure out and explore in college."

"You can," I say firmly, hoping there is a Lucie out there who's doing all the exploring she wants. "Thank you—for trusting me with that."

She nods before going quiet for a while, and I wonder if she's thinking about dance, too, and all the ways she hopes college will change her. Over the past few weeks, I've been given all these pieces of a girl I thought had everything, and here she is, feeling just as raw as I do. Looking at her now, I can see she might be on the verge of shattering, but every Wednesday, she manages to hold it together, except for those few minutes in the stairwell.

Lucie isn't the hardened, uptight person I thought she was. There's a gentle bravery in her, a vulnerability, and she needs to be comfortable to reveal it.

I should know—it's possible I've been the same way.

"This doesn't have to be how it was in high school," I say. "We can be . . . different."

"How?"

I push my empty plate to the side of the table and lean in, dipping my head conspiratorially. "For one," I say, "we don't have to let people like Cole and Blaine get away with what they did to us."

By the time I've explained the plan, she's on board. Nothing dangerous, I assure her. Just a little fun.

Cole's first class, I learned yesterday, is an eleven o'clock history course: Nineteenth- and Twentieth-Century Europe. That gives us plenty of time to sneak inside and tape a friendly little note to the projector.

SOMEONE'S WATCHING YOU, COLE WALKER.

We wait outside the classroom in Smith Hall, one of the stunning brick buildings that anchor the quad, adrenaline racing through my veins. *Yes. This is it. This feels right.*

"How did you know he's in this class?" Lucie whispers.

I was prepared for this, and I practiced my response in the mirror yesterday until it sounded real. "He's rooming with my cousin." I gesture between the two of us. "Resident services has an interesting sense of humor."

Lucie still looks a little skeptical, but she doesn't question it.

The professor turns on the projector to a rush of gasps and awkward laughter from the class, students glancing around, searching for Cole Walker and who, precisely, is watching him.

"Cole Walker?" the professor says.

From the second to last row, he raises his hand, looking . . . smug? "Right here, sir."

"Any idea what this is about?" the professor asks, and Cole shakes his head. "Hmm. Must be some kind of first-day prank. Still, you might want to check in with campus security later."

Cole waves this off and refocuses on his laptop.

I shrink back from the open door, trying to calm my anxious heart. Seeing him two days in a row turns my stomach, yanks me back in time. Because now I'm picturing his hands on me, the way he laughed that Monday afterward, morphing what we did into something cheap. Something tawdry, even.

Lucie, though, is cackling into her sweater sleeve, as though we've gotten away with something much worse than a vague projector-based threat.

"That was *wild*," she says. "I can't believe we just did that!"

"Yeah," I say flatly. "Me neither."

She readjusts her shoulder bag. "I think that was enough espionage for me today. But I'll see you back at Olmsted later?"

Lucie might be done, but I'm just getting started. When she heads to her freshman seminar, I beat Cole to the Dawg House, where I've taped another note to the paper wrapper of the burger he orders.

Bruises aching, head swimming from the Tylenol that wasn't strong enough, I wait a few booths away from the one he's sharing with some friends.

ENJOY YOUR LUNCH, CW.

His brow furrows as he reads it, and then he huffs out a laugh. "Some lunatic is fucking stalking me or something," he says, tossing the note into the center of the table.

"Ex-girlfriend?" one of his friends asks.

"Probably."

Another guy, someone I vaguely recognize from high school, says, "You gotta stop breaking hearts, man." And they all laugh.

Apparently, I can't even do revenge right.

I spend the rest of the afternoon plotting my grand finale, and once Lucie goes to Zeta Kappa, I make my way to the quad for *Groundhog Day*. A movie that Cole really loves, which I learned yesterday while he and his friends talked too loudly on a UW logo-printed blanket.

What the person operating the projector turns out to really love: cold hard cash.

I'm watching from behind a cherry tree when the words COLE

WALKER: 0/10 STARS IN BED, WOULD NOT RECOMMEND appear on-screen, stark white against a black background, the whole crowd erupting into laughter. He can't possibly ignore this one.

On a picnic blanket a few yards away, his friends nudge him, howling. "You really pissed someone off," one of them says, and Cole pretends to hide his face before laughing right along with them.

My message disappears, replaced by the movie's opening credits. A too-peppy song.

I grip the tree so tightly, I'm shocked I don't snap a branch in half. The fury simmers inside me, filling me up until it boils over. Like hell this is happening.

I march over to where he's sitting, plant my feet on the fleece blanket. "Cole."

He swivels his head toward me, a blond curl hanging over one eyebrow. I watch as his face registers the shock. ". . . Barrett? What are you—"

"I need to talk to you."

"I'm kind of in the middle of something," he says as Bill Murray reports the weather.

"This is important," I say, and there must be something in the timbre of my voice that convinces him to get up. I keep a good half-dozen feet between us as he follows me to the other side of the quad, toward Red Square, not loving the idea of sharing so much physical space with him.

I hug my sweater, his eyes growing wide as they track my hands. "Holy shit. Are you preg—"

"No." Deep breaths. *No consequences.* I can't meet his gaze, not when the way he hovered over me is playing over and over and over inside my head. So instead I focus on the tip of his left ear. "I need to talk to you. About what happened. After—after prom."

"You're still hung up about that?" When he folds his arms over his chest, I don't understand how it makes him seem bigger. I'm doing the same thing, and yet in this moment I feel microscopic.

It's almost funny, the way Cole and a weeks-ago Lucie have been so dismissive about high school being *so long ago*. I thought I was eager to leave it all behind too, and yet it's so etched in my memory that it's impossible to move on.

The lingering pain from the car accident mixes with the static electricity in my brain, and the force of it is so intense, I feel myself start to sway. Hands clenching at my sides, breath uneven. This might be my only chance. The only time I have the courage to confront him, when everything in me is screaming to run.

"You were clearly still hung up on that article," I fire back. "You made me feel like shit."

"That was kind of the point, after what you did to my brother." Still not looking him in the eye. The sharp jut of his chin. A trio of freckles on his right cheek. The entitlement and calculation of him asking me to prom, being kind to me all evening, whisking me into a hotel room. A confidence that I've never known. "Are you the one who's been fucking with me all day?"

I nod, unable to articulate my precise frustration at his total non-reaction. He's almost smirking, now that he's identified me as the culprit. Realized I'm not a real threat.

On-screen, the clock radio hits six o'clock. Sonny and Cher.

Okay, campers, rise and shine, and don't forget your booties 'cause it's cold *out there today!*

"You were so nice to me at first." It comes out in a whisper. *No one had been that nice to me in so long.* I press those feelings back down, urge myself to put the armor back on. I will not cry in front of him. "Did you plan it out with your friends beforehand? Brainstorm different seduction tactics? Or did you figure I was so pathetic, I'd jump into bed with you just because you deigned to speak to me?"

His expression hardens. "I wouldn't call it brainstorming, exactly. . . ." But the way his voice trails off does plenty to answer the question, making me feel even more ill.

Still, I make myself keep going. "I hope that hashtag and all those flowers gave your brother his scholarship back. I hope they fixed his self-esteem, or whatever it is you think I stole from him."

"Look," Cole says, craning his neck to see the screen, "I don't want to be a dick, but my friends are waiting for me, and I really like this movie."

It occurs to me that I could stand up in front of all these people, yell that I am, in fact, pregnant, and that the baby is his. I could ruin his Wednesday in a thousand different ways, worse ways, and it wouldn't change what happened in May.

Everything I want to say jams in my throat. *You fucking pathetic made me feel worthless made me feel insignificant how could you think in what universe was that did you ever feel sorry did you ever regret it I thought you were kind nice decent asshole asshole asshole* <u>asshole</u>.

Instead the only thing that comes out is "Okay."

"You know—" He breaks off, as though weighing what he wants

to say next. "You weren't bad, if that's what you're worried about. You were . . . eager. *Fun*." His lips curl upward at that. "Hardly a zero out of ten."

Of course, my sexual performance was what kept me awake at night. "I'm glad ruining my life wasn't such a chore for you."

He might actually roll his eyes. "No one ruined your life. School was almost over, and you're here in college, aren't you?" As though there's only one way to ruin someone's life. "If anything, consider it a favor. Now you won't have to stumble through it with the next dude, whoever that lucky guy ends up being."

But just as he turns his back, I get another burst of adrenaline. I can't let it go. Can't let him just walk away, perfectly content with the kind of person he is.

Courage. Come the fuck on.

"You—you really made me hate myself," I say, and when he faces me again, I finally drag my eyes to his, letting the blankness in his expression fuel me even more. I press my feet firmly into the ground, as though it might be tugged out from under me at any second. "All the flowers. Turning my last name into a joke. It was my first time, as you know, because I told you, and you went on to make that clever hashtag." I told Miles I didn't have any sentimentality attached to it, that I hadn't cared if my first time was special. But I was wrong, wrong, wrong. It was never up to me—it was always up to the guy standing right here. I was never in control. "You can move on, have all the fun you wanted to in college. I'll be a footnote, something hilarious that happened in high school that you can laugh about with your buddies when you're in your forties and wondering why you can't form lasting romantic relationships with anyone. Meanwhile, I'm going to have to remember this for the rest of my life. The rest of my fucking *life*, because *you took that away from me.*"

I'm breathing hard, choking on a gasp, my chest tight and hot and vision blurring at the edges. It's a physical pain, letting all of this out—and yet while it's exactly what I wanted to say, I don't instantly feel better.

So I keep going.

"And," I say, and this was really the least important part of it all, in hindsight, and he probably didn't care, but I might as well bash his ego while I'm at it, "I didn't come."

He examines me, head to toe, one arm lazily triangled behind his head. For a moment I think he might apologize. He'll fucking *grovel*, drop to his feet and smack his knees on the cement and beg my forgiveness.

Instead, he turns around and says absolutely nothing.

DAY TWENTY-SIX

卌 卌 卌 卌 卌 |

Chapter 32

LUCIE LAMONT STARES ME DOWN IN OUR DORM room, certain the school has made a mistake.

Again.

Of course she's still annoyed with me. Of course she doesn't remember what happened yesterday.

Once she leaves, I yell a stream of colorful curses into my pillow, banging my fist against it until it's a flat blue pancake. My left side is still sore and Jocelyn will never propose to my mom and I won't make it onto the *Washingtonian*. Lucie and I might briefly reconcile, if I can bring myself to put in the effort again, but we'll never be *friends*.

And prom.

If Cole was the major loose end in my life, then the thread is only longer and more tangled than it was before I confronted him. If he really was my unfinished business, like my mom suggested, then today should be September 22. I said exactly what I wanted, but I'm not free and I don't feel any better. If anything, I feel worse.

What did I think, that Cole would suddenly question his morals just because I wrote a silly little note? That he'd devote himself to becoming a good person? More likely, I expected a lifting of the pressure that's been tightening my chest since May.

And the one person I thought I could rely on through all of this, the one person I'm desperate to talk to in spite of everything, is only two floors beneath me but seems farther away than ever.

We tried to do good deeds and we're still here.

We tried to right our wrongs and we're still here.

We lived life to the fullest and I faced my demons and we fucking *died*, and we're *still here*.

I might need to scream again.

My phone lights up. How do I love thee? Joss and I are wishing you SO MUCH LUCK today!

Even my mom's text does absolutely nothing for me. I am deeply, utterly lost, with no idea where to go from here. All I know for certain is that nothing I do makes any kind of impact.

And if none of it matters . . .

Then I might as well throw two middle fingers up to the universe.

☾☾☾

I show up in the middle of physics, everyone's heads whipping toward the front as I sashay inside, my makeshift cape trailing behind me. Today felt like the kind of day for a cape, which I fashioned out of a half-dozen T-shirts knotted together.

"Sorry, did I interrupt anything?" I say, and as the room dissolves into nervous laughter, I feel a pang of guilt toward Dr. Okamoto, who doesn't deserve this. Who's never done anything wrong except possess a timeline moving at a slower pace, something even a brilliant physicist like herself isn't aware of.

Miles is in an aisle seat a few rows up, dressed in that red plaid shirt again. It's the first time I've seen him since we almost kissed, and he has the gall to look . . . well, I'm not sure. Of all the Miles looks I've classified and reclassified over the past few weeks, this one is maybe the hardest to analyze. His face is almost blank, but not quite—there's something in his eyes, something vast and dark and perplexing. He's either embarrassed by me, or . . .

He pities me.

That's it.

I simply won't look at him, then, because if I don't, then my heart won't do that stuttering thing inside my chest.

Dr. Okamoto stalks toward me, arms crossed over her tangerine blazer. "If you're in this class," she says, "I won't tolerate any disruptions. If you have a legitimate reason for not being on time, please enter as quietly as possible."

I sit down, making a big show of fluffing out my cape. As disruptively as I can, I unzip my backpack, taking out the giant pencil I bought at a dollar store on the Ave, which was the reason I was half an hour late. Just as Dr. Okamoto is about to pass out the syllabus, I raise my hand.

"Yes?"

I hold my pencil high in the air, waving it back and forth: "Does anyone have a pencil sharpener?"

More laughter.

"Maybe I wasn't clear enough earlier," Dr. Okamoto says. "It's crucial that students come to my class *prepared* as well."

"Is this not prepared?" I say. "One might even make the case that this is *overly* prepared."

She blinks at me, clearly unable to comprehend a student doing this on the first day of school. "Please don't waste any more of our time." Her exasperated tone turns me silent for the rest of class.

Afterward, Miles catches me outside the lecture hall. "What are you doing?" he hisses, brows pulled together. Two days ago, three days ago, who cares how many days ago, I wanted to press myself against him. I'm not immune to his scent or his gaze or the adorable way his ears stick out, but I pretend that I am.

"Haven't you heard? Nothing matters!" I say it in a singsong, tapping his head with my giant pencil. "We could rob a bank or set the whole school on fire or commit fucking *murder* and no one would have a clue!" As students stream by, I speak louder. "You hear that? Do whatever you want today, no consequences!"

A few people raise their eyebrows at me, shaking their heads. I pose dramatically with my cape as one snaps a photo.

Miles rakes his hand through the hair I've just mussed with my pencil. "You're going to feel really ridiculous if tomorrow is Thursday."

I lean in, giving him a pat on the shoulder. I don't let my hand linger. I cannot linger on anything remotely Miles-adjacent—I don't trust myself. "Miles, Miles, Miles. Don't you understand? It's never going to *be* tomorrow. *This* is our tomorrow. And the next day. And the next day. And . . . well, you're smart, you get it." I do a flourish with my cape as he just stares, wide-eyed and slack-jawed. "Now, if you don't mind," I say, "I have more mischief to attend to.

ꝰ ꝰ ꝰ

For the next few hours, I am a tornado. I whirl through campus, tipping over trash cans and bursting into classrooms with bizarre proclamations. "Building's on fire, better run!" I shout to a chemistry class before pulling the fire alarm. "The school just declared bankruptcy—all classes are canceled!" I declare to English 211 before disappearing outside with a cape swish.

I'm not just living in my bad feelings—I've become them.

In the afternoon, I'm forced to go back to Olmsted because I've torn my cape. I'm on my bed reknotting it when Lucie enters with puffy eyes, swiping at her face. Four o'clock.

"I just heard there was someone running around campus dressed in a cape and—what the fuck?" Lucie gapes at me. "That was you?"

"Guilty." I tie a vintage No Doubt concert tee to my Neptune High shirt.

"You really love alienating people, huh," she says, and if I don't think about what happened between us yesterday, then it doesn't need to hurt. "Wild. Okay. Well, I'm sure as hell getting out of here as soon as I can."

"Good luck!" I say brightly. "Pretty sure we're stuck here forever."

She looks at me like I'm scaring her, and maybe I am. Maybe I'm scaring myself a little too.

I wreak as much havoc as I can before changing into all black for a late-night mission, leaving my cape behind. It's ten o'clock, dark enough for me to creep into the journalism building undetected. Everyone else is immersed in their first-night activities, as though they're still important after all these weeks.

Sparse lights cast the hallways in an eerie greenish glow. I'm lucky the paper is only put out on Mondays and Wednesdays, or the newsroom would probably be full of people staying late. But that's where my luck ends, because the door is locked.

I let out a growl of frustration as I wiggle the doorknob back and forth, then try heaving all my weight against the door—nothing. I stare down the glass and take a deep breath, psyching myself up.

Before I can talk myself out of it, I smash my elbow into the glass with every ounce of force in my body.

"Shit shit shit!" I gasp out, glass shattering around me. I wait for a few moments, my breathing rough and shaky, just in case I've triggered an alarm. When nothing happens, I slowly extricate my arm and—*oh god*. There's blood. Not a tremendous amount, but enough trickling along my elbow and down my forearm to make me sway for a second.

I'll be fine tomorrow, if a little sore, but it still fucking hurts and there's so much glass and and and—

Doesn't matter, doesn't matter. I am an invincible nightmare of a girl.

I stick my arm back through the hole I've created, trying to avoid the sharpest shards of glass, fingers grasping for the lock.

Once I'm inside, I shove out a breath and collapse against the door, clutching my injured arm to my chest. Letting the blood disappear into my black T-shirt. Jesus fucking *Christ*, this is batshit, and I must be delirious because I suddenly start laughing. Nothing is funny. Everything is funny.

I'm definitely losing my mind.

Slowly, slowly, I come back to my senses. When I can breathe normally again, I let the newsroom fill me with a much-needed sense of calm. Everyone says newspapers are dying, and they have been for years, small papers folding all over the country. And yet I remain nostalgic. At home we get the *Seattle Times* every day, and I always look forward to it, especially the Sunday editions with their thick arts-and-culture sections. My online subscriptions are great, but nothing compares to the feeling of newsprint in your hands, graying up your fingertips, or the thrill of a magazine showing up in your mailbox every month.

I run my hands along the walls, the Sharpie quotes that don't make sense but were surely hilarious when first uttered. I'll never have a chance to work here? Fuck it. I'll make my own mark.

I swipe a pen from a nearby desk and uncap it, finding a spot on the wall just above where somewhere scrawled, *I don't want to put that in my mouth, but I'll do it for you* in tiny letters. And . . . irony of ironies, I can't come up with anything to write. Maybe *Barrett Bloom was here,* but that just reminds me of PROPERTY OF BARRETT BLOOM, Miles's half-finished, long-gone tattoo. And thinking about Miles is a bad idea, no matter how much I wish we could go back to how we were before.

It's a realization that startles me so much, I'm not quite sure what to do with it.

I shake this off, stalking through the newsroom, past Annabel's office, into a dark little alcove. ARCHIVE is printed on the plaque on a door. And this one is unlocked.

"Oh my god," I breathe out as I switch on the single light bulb overhead.

Every issue of the *Washingtonian* is in here, from decades ago and just last week, stowed away in labeled filing cabinets stacked floor to ceiling.

That article Christina Dearborn found on Elsewhere was from 2005. I open up a drawer, starting with January of that year. An article about a new dorm being built, a review of *Hitch*. Nothing in February or March, either. But in April, right there on the front page—

SPRING QUARTER RUSH: REGISTRATION SITE CRASHES WHEN TOO MANY SIGN UP FOR TIME-TRAVEL CLASS

I clutch the paper tightly, the words swimming on the page. *She exists.* And she doesn't just exist—she was *beloved*.

I find her again in 2007, in an article about people wanting to shut down her class because they thought she wasn't teaching real science. Angry parents calling her a quack, a fraud. A manipulator. "She's clearly not all 'there,' if you know what I mean," one of the parents is quoted as saying.

Jumping ahead a few years, I learn she was placed on administrative leave, and just as I'm slipping a November paper out of its slot, a neon-yellow sticky note glares back at me.

Removed from online W archives
per E. Devereux's request.
For further information:

E. Devereux
17 Grand Ave
Astoria, OR

ʊ ʊ ʊ

I take the stairs up to the seventh floor because I am #evolved and unafraid of exercise. Mostly. There's a frenetic energy in my veins as I tear down the hall, past JUST KEEP SWIMMING—AND LEARNING! It stops me in my tracks momentarily, only because I could have sworn it said STUDYING instead of LEARNING. Or was it always LEARNING, and my mind warped it because the alliteration would have looked better? Then again, I only closely examined it the night I pepper-sprayed Miles, which might as well have happened in 1998. My memory is playing tricks on me, the same way Miles's was when I first got stuck.

The need to see him in person is overwhelming. Which is utterly bizarre, because I've been spending time with only him for the past day few weeks. And yet there it is: a pulsing need in the center of my heart.

Please don't let him be asleep, I think as I knock on his door. His roommate, if I recall correctly, should have headed to a party with his long-term girlfriend after hooking up in their room earlier this evening. *Please don't let him be out at a party or finding his one true love and finally getting out of this godforsaken mess.*

It takes an eon and a half, but finally, finally, he opens the door a crack. The sight of his face is an instant relief, his messy hair and tired eyes a balm for all the anarchy of the past three days. I hate how nice it is to see him, how badly I want to collapse right into his room as long as he'll hold me up. I can almost forget about the kiss I don't remember.

"Barrett?" He runs a hand through his hair, pushing the door wider. "What are you doing here?"

He's not wearing a shirt.

Miles Kasher-Okamoto is standing in front of me, not wearing a shirt, and suddenly it's like I've never seen a human man before.

"You're not wearing a shirt," I blurt out, ever the observant journalist.

He glances down, as though just realizing it. "Oh—just give me a second." The door closes, and there's some shuffling around, and a few moments later, he opens it again. "Sorry. I was about to go to sleep. Is everything okay?"

I wave the newspaper in front of his face. "I found these articles about Dr. Devereux in the *Washingtonian* archives. Miles, she's *real*. And she lives in Oregon. We could go find her."

But Miles doesn't seem to be processing any of the words I'm saying. "Holy shit." A hand flies to his mouth, and then he gestures to me. "Your arm. You're—you're bleeding."

His voice has turned completely soft. However angry he was about what I did in his mom's class—there's none of that now.

I blink down at the broken mess of skin. "It doesn't matter," I say. "What's one more injury on top of getting hit by a truck? I'll be as good as new tomorrow."

"Just in case, we should disinfect it." *Just in case.* The past few weeks have been a deluge of *just in case.* Today is the one day I am certain I don't want to repeat. He motions for me to sit down in his desk chair, and I am too tired to do anything else, so I hold out my arm. Dr. Devereux can wait until tomorrow, because there is always a tomorrow. And I've already memorized the address. "My parents made me get a mini first aid kit for the dorm. I thought it was overkill, but now I'm glad they did."

He picks it up from his closet as I sink into the chair, then holds up a packet of disinfecting wipes, as though asking permission. I give him a nod, using my other arm to brush messy curls out of my face. I'm a little afraid of what I look like right now, but nothing about me has ever made Miles flinch.

Miles stands next to me, steadying my arm with one hand, a light press of his thumb, while he lowers the wipe with his other. It trembles in his grip, right before it meets my skin, and I wince at the sting.

"Sorry," he says, pulling back.

"It's okay. Just keep going."

He bends over, so gentle as he dabs back and forth, deeply focused, like not even a hurricane could break his concentration. I can't explain it, but that gentleness makes me feel a little like crying. That storm of a person I was in the newsroom, around campus—she's foreign to me now. Everything all day, all of yesterday, was too loud, my brain buzzing, buzzing, buzzing. But here . . . it's quiet. Peaceful. An oasis in the middle of the chaos my life has become.

I thought I was exhausted. Hopeless. But here in Miles's room, I suddenly feel wide-awake.

Miles is constant, and not just because he's stuck here with me. His mere presence has tugged me back into orbit. Even after everything that's happened . . . I do trust him. Not just to bandage my arm, but with my secrets. My fears.

That's the scariest thing of all: that deep down, I understand why he kept the kiss from me. And I know I can forgive him.

With nimble fingers, he tucks the wipe back into its packet before dropping it into the wastebasket, then unwraps a bandage and pats it across my arm. Smooths it down at the edges. I watch his hand, seeing how careful he is with me. This close to him, I can feel the heat from his body, hear the consistent rhythm of his breaths. I can count each of his raven-black eyelashes. All of it makes me a little light-headed.

"Good?" he asks, eyes flicking up to mine, and, dazed, I manage to nod.

So good, I want to tell him. "Thank you. You didn't have to do that."

"I would have felt terrible if you woke up with an infection tomorrow." He leans against his bed, this casual pose that shouldn't be as appealing as it is. "Are we . . . okay?"

I swallow hard. *Are* we? I want to be. "I think so."

"Good."

"Good," I echo, and I wonder how many times a single word can be uttered during the course of one conversation.

He fiddles with the edge of his navy striped comforter. "I've been worried about you. Since we, uh—died." This last word, he says so quietly, as though he can erase it from our shared memory by only barely acknowledging it.

"I was pretty out of it in the morning. I thought we'd escaped."

"I did too, for a moment. But then . . ."

"Reality."

"It can be a real piece of shit, huh."

"I'm glad you're not dead," I say.

A tease of a smile in the corner of his mouth. "That might be the nicest thing you've ever said to me."

I nudge him with my unbandaged arm, and then, once I'm

close, it only takes another few centimeters—I'll mentally use the metric system just for Miles—for me to get to my feet and hug him, a gesture that seems to surprise us both. He falters for a split second, the bed frame keeping him from falling backward. Then he steadies himself. Steadies us. *God*, he's warm and perfect and solid, his hands locking at the base of my spine in a way that makes me feel impossibly *safe*. I have to fight the urge to clutch at his hair, settling for a gentle grab of his collar.

Even so, something happens in his throat when I do this, the softest, purest rumble. In the most depraved part of my mind, I wonder what other sounds I could drag out of him.

I inhale his clean woodsy scent. A hint of sweat. My face against his neck, his heart pounding right on top of mine.

I missed him.

"I'm sorry," he says, voice slightly muffled by my hair. "For not telling you. For waiting until the last possible second. As you might have surmised by me being your sole company most of the past few weeks, I'm not the best at friendships."

I draw back, meeting his gaze. Slowly, we move apart, this awkward repositioning of limbs and readjustment of clothing, his eyes fixed on the ceiling, mine on the floor. It feels intimate, being in his room this late, even if he's barely had a chance to leave a mark on this space.

I remember his hand, reaching for mine in the car as glass rained down on us. Squeezing tight.

Like if we were going to go, he wanted us to go together.

"I forgive you," I say. "Thank you. For saying all of that."

After everything, Miles is still so kind. Stoic and reserved at first, but beneath all that, he's calm and caring. Funny, too, often unintentionally. He barely has to do anything to dig me out of this bad mood. I've been so set on skulking, and yet he is unskulkable.

"You sure?" he asks, but that smile is back, not quite the one I love the most, but close. "Because I was going to bring you this."

He reaches into a small paper bag on his desk and holds up a salted chocolate-chip cookie as big as his face. I am grinning like an absolute loon.

"Obscene. Those cookies are obscene." And then, because I'm learning not to brush things off, because I want to be genuine too, the thing I'm learning it won't kill me to be: "Yes," I say, not wanting to leave any doubt. "I can see you were in an unusual, uncomfortable situation, and I still don't love the way you handled it, but I can understand why you did it. And—I guess I haven't hated getting to know you. I want us to be . . . friends."

Friends. The word is a small, fearful thing. It isn't that Miles and I aren't friends; we're well past those declarations. You don't turn a swimming pool into a ball pit with someone who isn't your friend, even if the two of you happen to be the only people trapped in a time loop.

It's just that I'm not sure if *friends* is the only thing I want to be with Miles. It shouldn't be romantic that he wanted to hold my hand when he thought we were about to die. And yet it's suddenly the only thing I can think about, and it's so goddamn beautiful that now I really think I might cry.

Miles brightens slowly, like he's trying to fight it, sunshine inching across his face. "I'm honored to be your friend, Barrett Bloom," he says as he tears the cookie monstrosity in half, and it sends something sweetly electric up my spine.

I don't know what to do from here, so I try to ignore the complex swirl of feelings and opt for a joke, the way I always have. "I told you about the membership fee, right?" I say.

"I've got ten thousand dollars in my bank account. You can have all of it, but only if you promise not to buy dogs or ice cream."

Then we're both laughing, and things are back to normal, but it's a charged kind of normal, a normal that could light a fire and burn down Zeta Kappa. Worst of all, now I'm imagining what it would be like if we really had kissed, the way we did in Miles's timeline but not mine. The moment we had at Stanley Park, before the flash—I want another chance, but for all my bravado, I'm inexperienced. I don't know how to put us in that situation again.

Still, it doesn't stop me from wondering how he'd kiss me. Because I know exactly how I'd kiss him: hard enough to make a mess of his hair and find out what would deepen that rumble in his throat. Slowly, just to see if it would torture him. I'd kiss him up against a wall and horizontal on a dorm-room bed and—

"What have you done the past couple days?" I ask, desperate to focus on anything but the images in my head.

Miles hops up onto his bed while I take the chair again, propping my feet against the bed frame. "There was some wallowing, I won't lie. And then some librarying." He gives me a sheepish half smile. "Somehow, it didn't feel right without you there."

"Who could make fun of scientists' dirty names the way I can?"

"Julian Schwinger is not a dirty—okay, I hear it."

When he asks me the same question, I tell him about bonding with Lucie. "And I, um, confronted him. The guy from the ice-cream truck. The one who—who did those things after prom."

Miles's jaw tightens. "How . . . did that go?"

"Terribly. It made me feel worse," I say, trying to forget about the way Cole just turned and walked away. "I know I have to let it all go. But it's going to take time."

"You don't *have to* do anything," he says, softer. "You feel however you feel about it, for however long you need to."

"I—you're right. Thank you." I stare down at the bandage he applied so delicately. "I'm sorry about what I did in your mom's class," I say, wanting a completely clean slate. "That was shitty."

"And are we going to talk about that cape?"

"I was going through something, okay?" I say. "When we went to Vancouver—it was a good birthday, though, right? Before everything happened?"

"My best almost nineteenth birthday."

"Good." The newspaper on the other side of his desk catches my eye. The reason I'm here. But I have plenty of time to tell him about Dr. Devereux. For now, I want to pretend none of that exists. "Miles?" I say, cursing the way my voice sounds. High-pitched and uncertain, completely unlike the cool, collected kind of voice I want to have. The words in my head might as well be physics equations. $\Delta B/\Delta M$ = ???[2] "How would you feel about watching a little *Pride and Prejudice*?"

He grins. "Firth or Macfadyen?"

"Dealer's choice," I say, and I shouldn't feel a rush of satisfaction when he picks the 2005 version, elevating his laptop with a few textbooks and tilting it toward us. We settle on his bed together, exchanging half smiles as we stretch our legs, and when his knee settles against mine, I know I won't be able to focus on the movie.

The force of all the want thrumming inside my body is too heady, too much. It's an awful thing, wanting to be wanted, and it's led me down plenty of questionable paths. And yet I never stop *wanting*.

I don't want to feel lonely tonight, even if it only lasts for a couple more hours, so I settle for a desire I know I can satisfy: being next to someone who's made it okay for me to slip out of my armor.

For better or for worse, Miles has become that person.

DAY TWENTY-SEVEN

‖‖ ‖‖ ‖‖ ‖‖ ‖‖ ‖‖ ‖

Chapter 33

THE TINY COASTAL TOWN OF ASTORIA, OREGON (population: just under ten thousand), looks like it was pulled from a fairy tale, a place where the Pacific Ocean spreads salt into the air and quaint, colorful homes dot the hillsides. It took us four and a half hours to get here even though it should have taken three, mainly because we got coffee before we left, which I drank too fast and as a result needed to pee at two rest stops in varying states of cleanliness.

My brain has started doing Bad Things involving Miles. While he sipped his coffee at a slower, more reasonable pace, I imagined kissing away the foam on his upper lip instead of saying *You've got something right there.* I imagined leaning over and whispering in his ear to take the next exit, where we'd park in a secluded forest. I'd climb over the console into his lap, rake my hands through his hair again, drop my mouth to the space where his neck meets his shoulder, and breathe him in.

I imagined how he'd react to all of this, the shy scientist wanting to repeat everything to make sure the results matched the first time.

Because the problem is, now that we've reconciled, every inch of him has become impossibly attractive to me. Knuckles. Elbows. The hollow of his throat. It's extremely inconvenient and altogether alarming, especially because I have no idea whether he still has feelings for me after all we've been through.

So when we pull up to the squat yellow house and Miles yanks the parking brake, it sparks something not entirely unpleasant in my belly. I am really truly gone if the sight of Miles engaging the parking brake is hot.

The house only looks a little out of place on this block of Victorian-style homes. There are solar panels on the roof, and the fence is swirled with neon paint to look like a galaxy. The lawn is overgrown but not untidy, filled with plants and flowers that remind me of UW's rooftop garden. Clay gnomes are nestled throughout, and as we get closer, I can see that a couple of them are holding test tubes, others magnifying glasses, and one has a teeny telescope pointed at the sky.

An older white woman is sitting on the front porch in worn jeans and a lavender tunic, a newspaper in her lap.

Miles and I approach cautiously. Aside from a handful of questions we lobbed back and forth during the drive, we haven't exactly scripted this out.

"Dr. Devereux?" Miles asks. We're at the edge of her property, where a pebbled driveway meets the sidewalk. Careful not to intrude.

"Yes?" She doesn't glance up from her copy of the *Astoria Bee*. A slight breeze catches her hair, piled on top of her head in a haphazard gray bun.

"My name is Miles, and this is my friend Barrett. We're students from the University of Washington."

At that, she glances up at us with sharp blue eyes. "Did Amy send you?" she asks, and now I can hear her British accent. "Because you can tell her I'm not teaching that class anymore. I'm not going back to that school."

A chill runs along the back of my neck, and I hug my cardigan tighter around ~~today's~~ yesterday's bruise and broken skin. I assumed that someone had gone to great pains to remove her from UW. In my wildest daydreams, I wondered if she'd time-traveled her way out of here.

Until I saw that sticky note in the *Washingtonian* archives, it never occurred to me that maybe Dr. Devereux is the one who doesn't want to be found.

"No, no." I chance a few steps forward. Gold and silver, bronze and pewter rings adorn her fingers, at least a dozen of them. "We found some articles about you, and we came here on our own. We're freshmen. It's the first day of the quarter."

"Well—kind of," Miles adds, and we share a look that intensifies that chill, sends it skittering down my spine.

One of Dr. Devereux's pale eyebrows climbs higher. This has clearly caught her attention. "Kind of?"

"For most people, it's their first day," I say, with a healthy amount of trepidation. "But we've been here a little longer than that."

She's silent for a while, folding her newspaper and placing it in her lap, thumbing a large opal ring. I'm convinced she's going to yell at us to get off her property and never come back.

Instead she says, "I'm about to make some tea. Would you like to join me?"

U U U

Inside, the house looks like the love child of an antique shop and a junkyard, and I mean that in the kindest way possible. There's barely any walking space; the hallway and living room are covered with artwork in ornate frames, metallic gadgets I couldn't begin to name, and at least a dozen old clocks *tick-tick-tick*ing away. Half-upholstered chairs and towering armoires and a fainting couch in the most gorgeous shade of plum. It becomes clear right away that the house can't quite accommodate the amount of furniture in it, most of which is being used to hold tchotchkes on top of tchotch-kes. Two cats, one completely black and one completely white, weave their way through the clutter like they could do it with their eyes closed. Hell, they probably can.

"Neighbors file a complaint with the city every few months or so," Dr. Devereux says, dropping her newspaper on top of a table scattered with vintage mugs. "I have to bite my tongue to keep from saying, 'You think the outside is bad? Wait until you see the inside.'"

"I love it." I'm not buttering her up—this house is genuinely fucking incredible.

On our way inside, Miles balanced a hand on my lower back, and that was genuinely fucking incredible too.

Dr. Devereux warms noticeably at the compliment. "I've become a bit of a collector over the years, I suppose. It's been an amusing way to occupy my time."

When the teakettle whistles on the stove, she pours water into three mismatched mugs. Everywhere looks both too lived-in and too delicate to sit, so I'm grateful when she waves a hand at two velvet armchairs across from a Victorian couch heaped with old books, which she nudges out of the way to make room for herself.

"That's Ada Lovelace and that's Schrödinger," she says, gesturing to the cats. The black one, Schrödinger, leaps onto the chair next to me. "You'll have to excuse them. They're the rare kind of cat that loves people, and they don't get visitors very often."

Miles, animal whisperer that he is, pets Ada Lovelace under the chin as she purrs her appreciation. It's as though he's discovered exactly what turns me to goo and he's determined to do it as much as possible.

"So." Dr. Devereux crosses one leg over the other, fiddles with one of her rings. "You two are physics students?"

"I am," Miles says. Our chairs are diagonally pointed at each other, and when the ankle of his jeans brushes mine, he doesn't move it away. "I haven't declared it yet, but I plan to."

"And I'm journalism. Or I will be."

"Fine work, journalists do," Devereux says. "Most of them, anyway." She stirs her tea with a spoon shaped like a tiny hand, and then her eyes meet mine, bright blue and inquisitive. "I have to admit, I'm surprised that you found me."

"You wouldn't believe how hard we've looked," I say. "I thought that maybe you'd actually traveled through time." A quarter smile tugs at her mouth as she taps her spoon against her cup. I can barely process the fact that we're here with her in the flesh, this elusive person who seemed to have vanished. "We heard about your class, and we just thought—we thought you might be able to help us. With our . . . predicament."

"Ah. And can you be a little more specific about what that predicament might be?"

My heart trips inside my chest. This is what we came here for. It's too uncanny, the fact that she taught a time-travel class at UW and we've been trapped in our first day there. And she knows what it's like to be called a phony, a liar. If anyone could help us—or at the very least, listen without judgment—it would be her. I'm certain of it.

"We've been stuck living this day for weeks," I say quietly, allowing the warmth of Miles's ankle against mine to give me courage. "Well—a few weeks for me. Much longer for him. No matter what we do the day before, we wake up in the same place, on the same day. September twenty-first."

"We've tried to jump-start the timeline in numerous ways." Miles sips his tea. "Retracing our steps, doing good deeds, living life to the fullest. And that was after spending hours upon hours conducting research, none of which turned up anything."

"Basically, we're desperate," I say with an awkward laugh.

All the clocks strike three p.m. at once, startling me so much, I spill scalding tea all over my hands. Or—not quite at once. Some of them lag behind, creating a cacophony of chimes. There's even a cuckoo clock that struggles its way out, the bird emitting a sad little cough.

"My apologies," says Dr. Devereux, who's been quiet this whole time. "A few of them need to be wound." With trembling hands and clanking rings, she sets down her tea on the table in front of her, Schrödinger sniffing it once before turning up his nose. When she brings her hands back to her lap, they're still shaking. "And you swear this isn't some kind of prank?" she asks.

"Absolutely not," Miles says.

After several more moments of silence, Dr. Devereux lets out a long breath mixed with a laugh. "I can't believe it. That isn't to say I don't believe you—I do," she's quick to add.

"But you researched this," I say. "You had a whole class devoted to it."

"Yes, but that was all about the theoretical."

Miles straightens his posture, and it's only then that I realize he's been sitting much less stiffly than usual. Like he's no longer fighting with his body. "What are your theories, then? What would you have taught in your class?"

Dr. Devereux presses her lips together, as though deciding what she wants to share with us. Then she gets up, muttering to herself as she wades through her museum until she pauses in front of a rolltop desk. I flash Miles a concerned look, and he gives me his most hopeful one in return.

"I have two major ones," Dr. Devereux says, rummaging in the desk. "The second one, I nearly got laughed out of grad school for writing a paper on it." Finally she plucks a thick sheaf of paper from the drawer, holds it up with a victorious thrust of her arm. "But we'll start here. Have you heard of the many-worlds interpretation of quantum mechanics?"

I shake my head, while Miles nods. Three weeks ago, I'd have teased him about it. Now it only endears him to me even more, my heart swelling with something like pride, because of course Miles knows. And if he didn't, I have zero doubt he'd be taking notes.

"Essentially," she continues, "it means that there are many worlds that exist in the same time and space as ours. In parallel. I've always been fascinated by it. It would keep me awake at night, my brain going wild with the infinite possibilities. Somewhere out there might be a version of me who wore a red blouse instead of blue thirty years ago, and it changed the trajectory of her life. A version who decided to learn piano instead of violin as a child. A version who prefers coffee to tea."

I glance down at the liquid swirling in my mug. It's eerily similar to what Miles was talking about all those days ago with the mozzarella sticks.

"The MWI is what sparked my interest in time travel, which is impossible to consider without parallel universes. The MWI lets you examine time travel without the intrusion of the time-travel paradox."

"The whole *Back to the Future* thing," I say.

"Without getting too into the weeds, yes. You can't disturb a timeline, because there are an infinite number of parallel universes, and therefore any changes made as a result of time travel would simply create a new universe. Now, a *loop*, though," Dr. Devereux says. "That's exceptionally fascinating. Although, at its core, if the MWI is to be believed, you're creating a new universe each time you wake up.

"My theory," she continues, "was that there were connection points between parallel universes, places where information could be transmitted from universe to universe. If you imagine a universe as a sphere, those connection points are spaces where the universes, and by extension, our parallel lives, come closest to touching without actually doing it. But in rare instances, because much of the universe is unpredictable—they *do* touch. And that's when transmitting information might be possible."

"Information like . . . people?" I ask, struggling to visualize it. In my head, it looks like two cans tied together by a piece of string, a pair of kids using them to relay messages back and forth to each other. Somehow, I doubt that's what Dr. Devereux pictures.

She laughs at this. "Not quite. I was trying to expand on the work of another scientist, and we focused on a single ion." *Oh.* "But if we could send information, then there's no reason—theoretically, of course—that we couldn't eventually develop the equipment to transmit more than that."

Miles's brow furrows as he puzzles all of this out. "Those connection points," he says. "Is that how we could get home?"

Home. The word sounds too deliciously distant. I wonder if he can sense me shivering with my ankle next to his.

"Again, I need to emphasize that this is all theoretical. No one has been able to test it. I can tell you that yes, it sounds the most logical that finding some way to cross over at a connection point would lead you out of this universe. But where would it take you? Would you arrive in the 'right' universe, the one you were meant to continue in before you got stuck? Would you meet yourselves and risk a great disruption to the space-time continuum . . . ?" She trails off, giving us a sad smile. "That, I can't answer. I'm also afraid I would have no reasonable idea where those points are located."

I groan, dropping my head into my hands. "So it's basically hopeless."

"I didn't say that." Dr. Devereux returns to the couch, her cats snuggling up next to her. "It's merely . . . complicated."

Despite knowing that the rules of the universe are unlike what I've always expected them to be, all of this has made my mind spin. All the other Barretts out there who'll never know that Miles loves period pieces. All the Mileses who'll never hold hands with Barrett Bloom.

It's kind of heartbreaking.

"Do you have any idea why we might be repeating a single day?" Miles asks. "Why wouldn't we just keep moving forward through time in this parallel life?"

"My best hypothesis is that something is malfunctioning. The universe is not infallible. There's something causing you to remain stuck in this day, repeating it, instead of moving forward. Almost like—like a cat with its paw on a keyboard, accidentally hitting zero over and over and over."

I try to picture it, some celestial feline sitting at a space computer, 00000000000 and screwing up our lives.

"Why us, though?" I say.

"That actually segues perfectly into my next theory," Dr. Devereux says. "We didn't place as much emphasis on this one in class, for the simple reason that it's a bit more . . . magical. And that would be that maybe you strayed onto the wrong path somehow, and time intervened to shift you onto the path you're supposed to be on."

I raise my eyebrows at Miles. "And you told me not to personify the universe."

This earns me a smirk. And maybe I'm imagining it, but his shoe seems to press more firmly against mine, which shouldn't make me nearly as dizzy at it does.

"Time is a strange, slippery thing," Dr. Devereux continues. "Even when it's acting normally, or whatever our concept of 'normal' is. How often do you do something you love and swear only a minute has passed, when it's been several hours? Or the opposite when something is a slog? It can play with our memories, too, and possibly even more so when it's not acting the way it should. Call it fate, call it an accident, but whatever it is, you've been looped in." She cracks a smile. "Forgive my choice of words."

"It can play with our memories," I echo. That could explain the flash, and the pain that sometimes lingers. I touch the place where Miles bandaged my arm yesterday. "We've noticed that."

Miles nods. "In the beginning, whatever happened the previous day wouldn't affect us at all. But now, if I so much as get a paper cut, then I feel it the next day."

Knowing Miles has been in pain for much longer than I have makes me want to wrap him in the biggest fleece blanket I can find.

"Let's say one of your theories is right. The more scientific one," I say, with a sideways glance at Miles, who gives me this small quirk of his mouth that is ridiculously adorable. The fact that I can keep my hormones in check enough to ask the professor somewhat articulate questions is a feat of tremendous strength. "And let's say we found that connection point. What would you do then?"

She taps a few fingers on her chin, her rings catching the light. "Gravity," she says finally. "If I knew the connection point, I'd go where the gravitational pull is strongest."

"Closest to the center of the earth," Miles explains, but not in a condescending way.

"You always reset at the same time, correct? To the best of your knowledge?" We nod, and she continues, "Then I might try to be at that connection point at the time of the reset."

My mind works to process this. "But that connection point could be anywhere."

"Presumably somewhere you've both been, but yes. At the bottom of the Grand Canyon or in the closet of a child's bedroom, that place they're certain there's a monster behind," she says. "Or a million spaces in between."

The weight of it settles over us. Miles tries to get a sip of his tea with the two cats now in his lap. We're closer than we've ever been to figuring this out, and yet I only feel farther away. For all her knowledge, Dr. Devereux has never tested any of these theories. Finding a connection point, if that's even the solution, sounds about as easy as finding a dandelion seed in a snowstorm.

Dr. Devereux gets up to pour more tea.

There's something else I've been wondering, and this might be my only chance to ask. "Could I ask why you left UW?" I say, knowing full well that any decent journalist would start with softballs. But we must be beyond that.

She pauses halfway to the kitchen. If I hadn't been studying her for the past half hour, I might not have noticed the new droop to her shoulders. "My class wasn't very . . . respected," she says, fumbling for the right word. "Parents thought it was a waste of money, and I can understand that—university tuition is a crime these days. They certainly made it no secret that they wanted me gone."

"So you had yourself completely erased from the internet," I say, my heart breaking.

"I was done with people telling me I was a fraud. That I'd lost my mind. I couldn't focus on my research with all those voices in my head," she says. It's clear this is a painful topic, one that isn't easy to talk about. "But it's been a long time, and I miss teaching. When I left, I always assumed I could never go back, and now that it's been just over a decade . . . well, I wonder sometimes. Part of me worries they wouldn't want me anymore, but . . . I don't know."

"I'm so sorry," I say, meaning it. "I'm sorry that happened to you."

When she looks at me, her eyes soften, and now she sounds wistful. "I've had a lot of time to process it, but thank you."

"I would have been bribing my way off the wait list to get into that class," Miles says, and god, I love that he says it—not just because it's classic Miles, but because it makes her eyes glow even brighter.

Ada Lovelace jumps onto the couch next to her, and Dr. Devereux runs a hand along her back. "I wish I could do more," she says. "But I'm afraid I have a town-council meeting to attend tonight. Time to defend this 'eyesore' for the hundredth time." She waves her hand around to indicate the house. "It certainly *feels* like a time loop sometimes." We join in when she laughs, but it's muted. "You're welcome to come, but I'm not sure how thrilling it'll be."

"You've already given us so much." I get to my feet. "Thank you. Truly."

"Please, don't hesitate to reach out to me anytime." She scribbles ten digits on a piece of paper. "Memorize this if you need to call me. Although I suppose it may very well be a different version of me. *Extraordinary,*" she says, and the word follows us out the door.

Chapter 34

WE'RE QUIET AS WE GET BACK INTO THE CAR. IT'S my turn to drive, but I spend as much time studying Miles's face as I do the road in front of me, his eyebrows pinched together while he fiddles, always fiddling, with a loose thread on the seat of the rental car.

I want to know exactly what's going through his head, for him to let me in the way he's done before. And yet he says nothing, and so do I.

He can't be losing hope. Yes, he's been stuck much longer than I have, and if anyone's earned the right to feel hopeless, it's him. But if he doesn't think there's a way out of this, then . . . well, then I'm not sure how to feel either.

Because it isn't just that I want to kiss him senseless. It's that I want to truly *know* him, to be the person he talks to when he isn't sure he can talk to anyone else.

We're crossing the border into Washington State when I spot a familiar sign.

"We should go to the beach," I say abruptly, pointing to the sign. LONG BEACH: 15 MILES.

Rain splatters the windshield. "In this weather?"

"My mom and I used to come here when I was a kid. Maybe it would be good for us to clear our heads. Get some fresh air."

Miles might be demoralized, but I refuse to believe we're doomed. We can't both be pessimists, and we don't have plans the rest of the day. All we have is a whole lot of nothing, stretched ahead of us like an opportunity or a curse.

"Okay," Miles says, and before he can change his mind, I take the exit.

With the grayest sky pressing down on us, we pass tourist shop after seaside tourist shop, until I pull into the parking lot of an inn, hoping this will give us a chance to unwind. I summon all my journalistic confidence when I ask the front desk to give us their best room.

A welcome laugh bursts from my chest when we unlock the room on the eleventh floor. The whole thing is covered with rose petals—the floor, the dresser, the hall leading to the bathroom. Probably the bathtub, too. And then there's the petal-draped bed, the single, solitary bed in this room I assumed would have two, with its wrought-iron headboard and its come-hither scarlet sheets.

"Looks like their best room was the honeymoon suite," I say, trying to lighten the mood, snip some of that tension from the room.

Turns out, I'm only carrying a pair of kids' safety scissors. And they're broken.

Miles drops his backpack, surveying the sex suite. "Should we ask for a different room?"

"Nah. It's not like we'll be sleeping much anyway."

A blush attacks his cheeks with such fervor that you'd have thought I just suggested he jump into bed with me.

Oh. I kind of did.

"I mean," I say, feeling my own face grow warm, "we're not going to be hanging out in here. This is just in case we get tired later and don't want to drive back. Though I guess there's no point in driving back, huh. . . ."

I wish he'd cut me off, keep me from rambling, but he doesn't. And he remains distant well into early evening, as we explore the boardwalk and buy saltwater taffy and eat fried food. No matter how many jokes I make, he's lost somewhere in his head.

After dinner, we go for a walk along the darkened beach. The rain has let up, and there's a haunting serenity to this clear, windy night. The only sounds are the sky and the waves, a few other people daring one another to step into the water. The wind whips our hair around our faces, and my light coat probably won't be warm enough.

It's cruel how beautiful Miles looks pinned against the dusk, hair wild, eyes matching the sky. It's the kind of image that makes me wish I were an artist, if only for tonight. That's what I should have spent all these loops doing—it's so clear now. Learning to paint, so I could capture this moment.

It's easier, thinking about the past than about our future.

"Well this is flat-out wrong," I say, gesturing to the sign that says WORLD'S LONGEST BEACH. "I remember googling it the first time I was here, just to make sure, and being extremely disappointed. And yet."

Miles only offers up a slight smile. If there's any way I can help him through this the way he's helped me, I have to try. We're not alone, and whether that's by design or simply by accident, there's a connection here. A point where two things weren't supposed to touch, but did anyway.

"Okay, enough pity smiles," I say gently. I stop walking, clutching my thin rain jacket tighter around me. "Tell me what's going through that impressive brain of yours."

"Everything," he finally says, and allows himself a self-deprecating laugh.

"Oh, is that it?" I grimace. "Sorry. Less joking. I'm thinking about everything, too." I throw my arms wide toward the ocean. "Maybe we'll get lucky and find a connection point right here. Or the universe will decide we've learned something and that we're ready to move on." Somehow, saying these things out loud makes them sound equally improbable.

"Or any number of other possibilities," Miles says. "But Dr. Devereux isn't actually what's been weighing on me the most."

"I'm a good listener too," I say, remembering how he helped me open up. "When I'm not being combative."

Miles scuffs the sand with one of his dark green Adidas, hands jammed in his puffer coat pockets. He's dressed more appropriately for this weather than I am, but I don't mind the cold. I'd mind it a lot less if I could press up next to him, tuck my head against his shoulder, but I digress.

"I feel like I'm being torn between two extremes," he starts, speaking more to the sand than to me. "Sometimes I can't think about anything but what happens if we never get out. And other times . . . I feel so fucking lucky."

This stuns me, both the profanity, because he doesn't swear as often as I do, and the word choice. *Lucky.* Not a word I'd have ever used to describe our situation.

Before I can say anything, he continues, "For the longest time, I've felt like I didn't really know how to have fun. I realize that must sound ridiculous. I'm eighteen, living in a major city in a world with every conceivable comfort. And yet . . . I was so scared, I think, of going down Max's path, so set on being the perfect son, that I just closed myself off to any of it. I made myself be *so* careful, so safe, and I probably missed out on all these 'regular' teen experiences as a result." His gaze meets mine, honest and searching, and it draws out the ache in my chest. "I tried to prove I'd be his opposite by being only this one thing: the studious person, the person who turned down any chance at *life* because there was a risk that came with it, and I couldn't afford to risk anything. These extra days . . . sometimes they felt like the universe telling me to lighten the hell up."

Personifying the universe, I want to say, but I don't. "You did," I say quietly, reaching out to graze his coat sleeve. The briefest touch, and then I'm back to hugging my jacket again. "You have."

Miles acknowledges this with a slight nod, as though unable to accept the degree to which he's lightened the hell up. Then he glances down at the spot I just touched. Brushes it with a fingertip. "The idea of letting go of control, of not knowing what's going to happen—that's daunting. It's part of why I love science. Everything needs to be reproduced about a thousand times before arriving at an answer." He takes a few steps closer to the ocean. "I had all these hopes of college being different. But even with the freedom we have, sometimes I've felt more isolated than ever before. You said you couldn't believe I'd spent two months in a library. And until you got stuck too, I didn't realize how badly I wanted to get out. Not just out of the loop—out of this self-imposed prison I've been in." Now he pauses and faces me again, his lovely features in full focus. "When we were talking about living life to the fullest? I couldn't even come up with anything."

"Our definitions of fullest don't have to be the same."

"But that's exactly it. I'm not sure I even had a definition. Truthfully, I didn't know if I was capable of the kind of fun we've had. Adopting fifteen dogs? Creating an illegal ball pit? Getting half a tattoo? That doesn't sound like something any version of myself would do."

"It was," I say. "And I was jealous of how much those dogs loved you."

That earns me a tiny smile, a slight softening of his jaw. I never want to stop being able to make him do that. Even when it's slight. "In a strange way, all of this has changed my perception of myself. It's made me realize I don't have to be that reserved, cautious person I used to be. That it's okay to take risks, because they might yield something really great. And maybe you'll tell me that's corny, but go on. I can take it."

He pats his chest and lifts his eyebrows at me in this way that makes my knees wobble. A challenge.

I shake my head. "It's not corny." My voice is so small, the ocean could easily swallow it up. "I've felt the same way."

"Yeah?" He inches forward, only a couple feet of space between us. All the hope he folds into that single word lets me know it is okay to be vulnerable with him. That he'll be delicate with whatever I have to tell him.

"I built up college in my head as this thing that would change my life," I say, watching as a gust of wind blows a hat off someone's head a dozen yards away. "And even before I got stuck, everything was going so wrong that I was worried this place wouldn't change me at all, and that I'd emerge the same person I've always been. The person who uses sarcasm and nonchalance as armor."

Because if I pretend I don't care, if I don't let anyone in, then I don't have to get hurt. I don't have to show them the scars I already have.

Or admit that underneath it all, there's a soft center that cares *so much*.

"Logically, I know that was only one day, and I'd been on campus less than a week," I say. "But now we're literally stuck, and it's getting harder and harder to see how anyone comes out of this a brand-new person. I feel like the same exact person I've always been, and I am so fucking sick of her sometimes."

There's an odd look on Miles's face as he takes this in. "Barrett," he says, "you *are* different. You're not that person who informed me she was switching out of physics and that was the last time our paths would ever cross. You're . . . I'm not even sure I have the right words for what you are, and I . . ." He trails off, words disappearing into the night.

I'm not sure how to tell him how deeply reassuring this is.

"You terrified me at first," he says, and I laugh, even though it warms my heart in this weird sort of way. "I know we met for the first time on two different days, technically, but that first time I met you in class, I was an absolute saint. You have to believe me. It took time to develop that dickishness you saw."

"I don't think you've ever told me what I was like that first day."

He rakes a hand through his mess of hair before returning it to his pocket, mouth curling upward. "You stormed into class like a tornado," he says. "Like you'd just climbed a mountain to get there."

"That's certainly one way of saying I was sweaty AF."

He laughs, pushing against my shoulder, sending enough electricity down my arm to power a small village. If I wondered whether he still has feelings for me, something in that push confirms it. His arm stays connected with mine for a beat too long, and even with all these layers between us, I feel it in my toes. "I meant it metaphorically. Mostly. You surveyed the room like you didn't want to make the wrong choice about where to sit, even though there were easily a hundred empty seats. You had these cute glasses and this wild hair that I couldn't stop looking at. You were wearing a Britney Spears T-shirt, but in what seemed to be an unironic way, which I respected. And I thought maybe I could tell you I liked Britney Spears unironically too, and that would be the beginning of a friendship. But I was too shy."

All of this is an even deadlier electric shock.

"Then you asked for the Wi-Fi password," he continues. Now the look on his face is pure joy, and it might be the sweetest fucking thing I've ever seen. "And I swear, I really did give it to you that first time. I was glad you said something to me first, because I had no idea how to talk to you. But *god*, the moment you sat down, I wanted to." A blush tinges his cheeks. "It was ridiculous, how proud I felt, telling you the password. Even though it was up on the board. You just seemed like—if I had a league, you would be so far out of it."

"I don't buy that." It's easier than believing him, even as my heart speeds up and I bite back a grin. Day 1 Barrett would absolutely perish. Day 27 Barrett might be well on her way.

"I'm serious," he says. His words in Stanley Park come back to me with stunning clarity. *You were the most interesting person on campus.* More than anything, I wish I could remember those first times we met. "My whole life, I've never let anyone get close. And it turns out, I still don't know how to navigate a—a relationship." His blush deepens, and he turns his face to the water. "Not that this is a relationship, at least, in that sense. Just . . . a connection. Between two people. Jesus Christ, see?" He groans, dragging a hand through his hair again. "I'm a complete disaster."

"From one disaster to another, I'd say you're doing pretty all right."

It's started to rain again, a light drizzle that sends most of the other beachgoers running back to the boardwalk. Sand climbs up my ankles, dotting the hem of my jeans, but there's nothing I care about less right now.

"For me, the worst part has been knowing something's supposed to happen later this week and not getting to see it," I say. "My mom's girlfriend is going to propose tomorrow. And because it's never tomorrow . . ."

"Barrett. I'm so sorry," Miles says, laying a hand on my sleeve, and I know he means it.

I give him a long-suffering shrug. "Such is life in an infinite loop."

"What if you could talk her into proposing today?" he says. "Well, not *today* today, but tomorrow today. I could—I could help you, if you want."

"Of course I want." Such a simple sentence, and yet there might be more to it than the literal. *Of course I want.* "You know . . . that might be worth a try, and I'm almost mad I didn't come up with it myself. Thank you."

We walk in comfortable silence a bit more, pausing every so often to admire the white-pink shells embedded in the sand. The rain picks up and Miles even offers me his coat, but I shake my head. The cold is refreshing, my mind the clearest it's been in ages. And that lets me admit something scary to myself: exactly how much I like Miles Kasher-Okamoto, whether we're arguing or joking or quietly searching for shells on the not-longest beach in the world.

This loop has become an exercise in being afraid and doing it anyway, that quote my mom has on some of her greeting cards. Having the courage to hope when it all feels hopeless. And Miles— Miles doesn't make me feel hopeless. In fact, he makes me feel like my whole self in a way no one ever has. Whatever this is between us, I want to leap into it, clutching the fear tightly to my chest so I don't forget how it started while allowing something bigger to open up my heart.

With Miles, I think we can be scared together, and there's something really lovely about that.

Whatever the reason the universe singled us out, Miles and I found each other in this strange echo of a world. And that means something.

"Maybe it wasn't that college was supposed to change us." I inspect what I think is a perfect sand dollar, only to turn it over and find a chip. "Maybe it was never supposed to."

"That's sort of a dark way of looking at it."

I shake my head, because it's not coming out right. "Maybe people weren't wrong when they said college was going to be this amazing, life-changing experience," I say. "Because I've gone through nearly thirty first days at this point, and every time it's felt amazing, I've been with you."

It takes about a metric ton of courage to say this, so I'm shocked when Miles scoffs.

"What!" I say. The rain turns even heavier, splashing my cheeks and blurring my glasses, but neither of us moves. "I'm trying to give you a compliment over here. And maybe be a little profound. Let me have this."

"You can't really believe that. That I—that I'd be the reason anything is amazing." He trips over that last word, not meeting my eyes.

"Miles, do we need to have a talk about self-esteem?" I stop walking, hoping it'll make him turn his head. When he does, the uncertainty on his face breaks my heart. He really doesn't believe me. It makes me want to start my own newspaper only to fill it with things I like about him, photos of him caught off guard. Especially photos that show off his ears, and his eyes, and the curve of his jaw. "You're right that when we met, you were a bit rigid. But we all have our cushy comfort zones, and some of them are cushier than others. Harder to leave. You have your passions, and your ways of doing things, but you're also so—so *open*. You want to soak up every bit of newness you can, categorize it, analyze it, make a plan to do it again. And most of all, I think you *want* to enjoy it. That's why it feels amazing. Because I get to see everything through your eyes, too."

And *this*. This is the reaction I was hoping for, but the reality of seeing it spread across Miles's face is even better than I imagined. He clings to the smile at first, holding himself back, as always, but it's too powerful even for his practiced jaw muscles. It grows and grows, his eyes glimmering, until it could light up this entire beach.

I'm no longer filling up a newspaper. I'm starting a whole media conglomerate just to declare the unabashed brilliance and quiet charm of Miles Kasher-Okamoto. We'll interview the world's top scientists and run ads for every upcoming period piece. We'll have an entire website dedicated to his smile.

That's what makes *me* feel lucky, like Miles said earlier: the fact that I get to learn all these hidden parts of him.

"Thank you," he says in this earnest, perfectly Miles way. I'm not sure anyone has meant a thank-you more than he does in this moment. "For a while at the beginning, you were so intimidating. Even though I'd met you dozens of times before, I still couldn't figure out the right things to say around you." He inches closer. "And nothing could prepare me for actually getting to know you."

"I can't possibly still intimidate you."

He shakes his head, bringing up his sleeve to swipe raindrops off my glasses. "Not in a bad way. In a thrilling way, because I never know what you're going to do or say next. You're challenging and frustrating and fascinating all at once, and hilarious in this unique way that always keeps me on my toes. Making you laugh feels like winning the lottery. When you laugh at something I've said—even if you're laughing *at* me—there's no feeling quite like it."

Fascinating. It's my new favorite word. For years I've pretended I was the farthest thing from insecure. That I wasn't lonely.

All this time, I've been fascinating, too.

"You're funny," I insist, because somehow I get the feeling it's not an adjective Miles has ever associated with himself.

When his arm bumps mine, it stays there. His fingers wrap around my cold ones as my heart thumps wildly inside my chest, and I want to give him another adjective: *brave*. He is so brave, and he makes me want to be brave, too. With my thumb, I draw circles on his knuckles, on his palm. He closes his eyes for a moment, hand trembling but never leaving mine.

"When you talk about what happened in high school," he says, "I just . . . feel so bad for all the people who could never appreciate this side of you. It's a fucking shame."

"Miles, stop." I need more than our fingers threaded together. I throw my arms around him and hold him close, inhaling his Irish Spring soap and something that's purely *him*, this intrinsically Miles scent that I cannot get enough of. He's solid heat as he hugs me back, so tightly that I think I'd float away if he let go. Now I let myself touch the hair at the base of his neck, gently slide my fingers through it. It's probably for the best that we're not making eye contact, because it would only stop my heart. "I'm going to cry."

He laughs, and I feel the rumble against my throat. "I mean it. I could wake up on the same day a thousand times, and every single one would be different because of you. Every single one would be life-changing. Because of you."

He says this with his mouth a whisper away from my skin, and when I exhale, the icy tip of his nose finds my pulse point. Pauses there. And then, ever so slowly, he traces a searing line along my neck.

Oh.

Up, up, up, until I'm positive I'm seconds away from passing out. And it's the nicest thing I've ever felt. I'm stuck on an inhale, worried that if I move even a fraction of a centimeter, he'll stop.

But he doesn't.

His mouth moves across my jaw, warm and wanting. But instead of finding my lips, he diverges, arcing toward my right ear instead. A hot, urgent breath, either his or mine or both, and then I feel his tongue sweep away a raindrop. And another. *Jesus.*

I shudder against the wind, against the sensation of Miles this close to me, mouth tucked right beneath my ear.

"Still going to cry?" he asks, voice rough.

All it takes is for me to start to shake my head, a shift that brings my mouth right up against his.

Yes.

The kiss is desperate, needy, and I'm not sure who moved in first—only that nothing has ever felt this *right*. There are weeks and weeks of memories poured into that kiss, long nights and early mornings and road trips that never led us back to where we started. Arguments and truces and theories. I lose my hands in his hair while he holds me tight against him, arms around my waist. Anchoring me.

I part my lips and swirl my tongue with his. He is heat and sweetness and hope, and I love the way he sighs against my mouth, this low hum that makes my limbs go weak.

I drag my hands along his shoulders, down his back. "Why is your coat so fucking puffy," I mutter, and he laughs, unzipping it as quickly as he can. And—there he is, chest waist hips pressing against me. Wanting me. I loop my thumbs through his belt buckles. Learn he's ticklish when my fingers brush his waist.

He brings his hands to my face and then into my wet, matted hair. *"Barrett,"* he says on an exhale, and wherever that sentence was supposed to go gets lost in the stunning groan he lets out when I use my mouth to map the contour of his jaw, all the muscles that used to prevent him from smiling. His neck. The hollow of his throat. He grips me tighter, one hand drifting to my lower back, under my jacket, as I taste the rain-salt of his skin. Miles, apparently, likes being kissed just about everywhere.

There's too much of him I want to get my hands on. To see. But for now, in the dark, I can be content with just touching. *Feeling.*

"Better than the first time?" I ask when we break apart, breathing in time with each other. Quick. Slow. Quick, quick, slow. His hair is a mess, his eyes half-closed.

"There's no comparison." He tugs me closer, as though he can shield me from the wind and rain, and then gets a better idea— bringing me up against his chest, and then attempting to zip his coat around us both. I'm about to tell him I'm certain I'm too big for this to work and it's probably going to end up being awkward for both of us—but miraculously, it does. It might be the warmest I've ever been, zipped up in his coat like this.

I run my hands along his chest, his shoulders. As though I need to keep making sure he's real. Against my cheek, I can feel his heart racing. "God. I like you so much," I say. "Everything and nothing about this moment feels real."

Even in the dark, I can see his full-wattage smile. "I hope it is.

Because I'm kind of head over heels for you, if that wasn't already clear. I've had the most helpless crush on you for weeks, and I've probably done an abysmal job showing it, and—"

I pull his mouth down to mine again.

I'm not sure how long we stay out there, bundled inside his coat, the stars and ocean making the night feel endless.

Two lonely people with the entire world at our fingertips.

Chapter 35

ONCE THE RAIN BECOMES A DOWNPOUR, WE can't get back to the inn fast enough. Anxious, eager hands fumble with key cards until finally we get the door open and he pins me against it in a kiss that tastes like the ocean.

"Oh my god, the rose petals," I say. "I swear this wasn't some long con to get you into the honeymoon suite."

"I don't think I'd mind even if it were."

I throw off his coat, and when we kiss again, it's even more frantic, tongues and teeth and greedy hands. We struggle with our sweaters and our shoes, every moment my lips aren't fused to his feeling like a wasted one. It's only when the backs of my legs bump against the bed that it hits me: we are alone in a hotel room with no one to answer to and no curfew, and it's a heady, intoxicating feeling.

"God, you're beautiful," he says, eyes fixed to mine, hands lost in my hair. "Can I say that? Because I kind of can't believe this is happening."

"Yes," I say with a laugh, even though hearing it makes me dizzy.

I drag him down onto the bed with me, on top of me, skimming my hands up his back beneath his T-shirt and then ridding him of the T-shirt entirely. A few moments later, mine joins his on the floor. Warm skin and sharp inhales and—*god*, there is just no part of him I don't like. He gently takes off my glasses and places them on the table beside us. His mouth travels down my neck, scorching the same path he did on the beach, only backward this time. On the beach it was anticipation. Now it's agony.

"I think your ears are excellent," I whisper. He lets out a low, rough sound as I kiss one and then the other, gently sucking on his earlobe and discovering this is something he really, really enjoys. "Just felt like you needed to know that."

Then I press my lips to the crescent scar beneath his left eye, and along my ribs he traces the bruise that shouldn't exist. "Does this hurt?" he asks.

"Not anymore." I find a similar patch of reddish skin on his abdomen, a fading reminder of that night that almost broke us. It makes me kiss him harder.

When I push my hips against his and he pushes back, I see stars. I can't remember ever wanting anything the way I want him right now, and I absolutely love it. I rock against him, finding a rhythm, and he groans into my ear before he bites down on it. I love that, too.

"I know we're in a hotel room, but we don't—we don't have to do anything you don't want to do," he says, breathless, his words crashing into one another. "Or—what *do* you want?"

I consider this. It's not that I want to erase my past, the way I might have before. It's that I want him, completely and definitively, in any way I can have him. And even if this day is stuck on infinite repeat, tonight feels tinged with an electric, precious urgency.

I don't want to hold anything back.

"You. Everything."

A pause. A persistent thudding of his heartbeat. Then a rush of breath as he exhales, "Me too."

"You want to make love to me," I say, a teasing lilt to my voice, remembering the way he said it back in our ice-cream truck. I try not to fixate on the word *love*, and yet it slides past my lips without stumbling.

He blushes. "Yes. I do."

We readjust so he can unbutton his jeans, and I pray mine will come off without too much tugging. When they do and I reposition myself on top of him, the reality sinks in: I am nearly naked with a boy who is much thinner than I am.

So I pull back on my heels, staring down at my breasts that are a little too big for this bra, my stomach that spills over the elastic band of my underwear. My thighs that are probably equivalent to one and a half of his. I don't know what he sees when he looks at me, and in this moment, the not knowing is frightening.

"I . . . ," I start, unsure where to go from there. "I don't know if I'm what you expected. I know—I know I'm big. I just don't want that to be the only thing you're thinking about when this is happening. I mean—I'm making it worse. Now of course you're going to be thinking about it."

He just looks at me, eyes filling with an emotion I can't name but that bears a shocking resemblance to whatever's blooming in my heart. "You are *perfect*," he says, running his hands up my arms, over my shoulders, cupping my jaw. "So gorgeous, Barrett—every part of you. I've held myself back from saying it on at least a dozen different days. You are a thousand times better than anything I expected."

It's criminal, the way he's able to undo me like that. I kiss him again and again, harder and faster until I'm certain he knows how much his words mean to me.

With Miles, I want the lights on.

Then his mouth is between my breasts while he struggles with the clasp of my bra until I reach back and help him. He treats every part of my body with both curiosity and care. Soft kisses and light touches until I indicate something feels good, and then he lingers. I'm much less anxious to shed my underwear, especially with his hand fluttering between my legs.

"Oh," he says when he touches me. Somehow, the lightest sweep of a fingertip turns my whole world hazy. I close my eyes just as my heart leaps into my throat. "How does that feel?"

"Good—really good." Then I grow more daring, moving his finger a bit higher. "But . . . this is even better."

A shaky breath. A new rhythm. "Here? Like this?"

"Yes."

His mouth joins his finger after asking if it's okay, and I simply exit this earthly plane. I probably pant his name a hundred times, paint the ceiling with it as I grasp at his hair. *Miles. Oh my god. Don't stop.* Deep inside me, something bright and shimmering builds and sparks and burns—until all at once, it bursts.

I return to earth with Miles kissing along my thighs, pausing to let out a surprised laugh. "I can't believe . . . ," he says, voice trailing off.

"That I was that horny for you?"

This only makes him laugh more, but now I can tell he's pleased with himself too. I'm overcome with the need to touch him, readjusting so I can splay a hand over his boxer briefs.

"Jesus," he bites out, head falling back against the pillow. I grip him through his underwear and move my hand faster. Harder. It feels like a privilege to watch Miles unravel this way, to see him abandon all logic and just *feel*. Eyes shut. Breaths unsteady. And *god*, that groan. "*Barrett*. As incredible as this is, if you don't stop, it's going to be over in about five seconds."

I withdraw my hand, grinning like he's given me the very best compliment.

"This is deeply embarrassing," he says, "but my parents gave me a giant box of condoms when I graduated high school. Just in case."

"I don't know if we need a giant box quite yet."

A smirk. "There's one in my wallet." He hops up to retrieve it, kissing me long and deep when he returns to the bed.

The first time, I was so focused on feeling wanted. I was filling up some emptiness inside me, seeking validation. This time, it matters that he's the one over me, under me. It matters, the way he kisses my neck and whispers my name and runs a reverent thumb along my cheekbone.

I don't just feel wanted.

I feel adored.

☾☾☾

It's two in the morning, and we only have a few more hours before we're whisked back to Seattle.

We're sitting up in bed now, sheets pooled around our waists. I'm in just a T-shirt and Miles isn't wearing one at all, which I've got to say is an excellent look for him. If the physics department ever puts out one of those firefighter-type calendars, he should be Mr. September.

"What are you going to do on Thursday?" I ask with my head against his shoulder. My hair is dry now, still messy, and even though I'm sure it's tickling him, he doesn't budge from this position.

"Go to my freshman seminar, I suppose. And my math class meets every day. You?"

"I'm going to pay so much attention in my psych class. Like, an unsettling amount of attention. I want the professor to be *terrified* of how good of a student I'll be."

He smiles at this. "I think they'll be terrified of you regardless."

"You know, you very rarely show one of your real smiles. I think it took more than two full weeks for me to see one. The day we made the ball pit—that was the first time."

"You mean like this?" He bares his teeth at me in a growl.

"That's the one!" And I lean forward and kiss him again.

Only occasionally does the possibility hit me that we may never leave this place. That we'll live an entire life of Wednesdays. Would we age? Lose our memories? Get sick of each other but never be able to escape?

Every outcome scares me.

His fingers play against the back of my neck, winding around a strand of hair. Unearthing a rose petal. "If we ever get out," he says, "I want to go on a proper date with you. A non–September twenty-first date. A winter date, or a summer date."

"What would we do?"

"Something tragically normal. Like a baseball game. Or dinner and a movie."

It's absurd how lovely that sounds. "Dinner and a movie," I repeat, the image tugging at my heart. "I can't wait."

I love you, I almost say a half-dozen times, but every time it hovers on the tip of my tongue, I swallow it back.

"I didn't think I could like someone this much," I say instead. "Or maybe it's that I didn't know someone could like *me* this much. If you—you know. Like me."

He grins my favorite full-wattage grin. "Barrett. I am a thousand kilometers past like. Worlds. Galaxies."

"I don't know if affection can be measured in kilometers," I say, and he valiantly attempts to show me how.

ʊ ʊ ʊ

"I changed my mind," I say later, when the sky outside is darkest black and Miles can barely keep his eyes open. "I want to wake up next to you. That's what I want on Thursday."

"Then let's just not go to sleep."

"It won't work." I don't mean it to, but my voice breaks. It's fucking unfair, that's what it is. Unfair that I can have the things I want only within these specific parameters.

He brushes curls away from my face, settles his head beneath my chin. "Maybe not," he says. "But it's nice to dream."

DAY TWENTY-EIGHT

|||| |||| |||| |||| |||| |||

Chapter 36

I CAN STILL SMELL THE OCEAN AIR, THE ROSE petals, Miles's Irish Spring soap, as though it's been dragged along my skin. I can still hear his earnest whispers and taste his shy, sweet exhales. My name, bitten off at the edge. The heat of his body next to mine, and our promise of a real date.

I am utterly, perfectly gone for him, and it's this realization that warms the cold hard truth of another September 21.

It shouldn't break my heart when I wake up back in Olmsted Hall, and yet it does. I had all these jokes prepared for a potential Thursday. I was going to say that maybe I was onto something with orgasms trapping us in time, and we had to have them together in order to jump-start our timelines again. And Miles would groan but secretly love it.

It should be scary, letting someone have this much of a heart I thought was made of steel, but now the only thing about Miles that seems scary is not getting to experience a weekend with him. An October. A winter.

Lucie has come and gone, and I can barely remember when we messed with Cole, or when we bonded after she took me to Elsewhere. Five days ago or ten? Two or twenty? My brain is jumbled, a blurred calendar that begins and ends on a single page.

The only thing it seems capable of doing is playing last night over and over, and I don't mind that one bit.

A knock on my door startles me into a sitting position, my head swimming.

"I'm indecent," I yell out, assuming it's Lucie or Paige. When it doesn't open, I throw my knitted sweater over my UW T-shirt and open the door a crack.

It's worth the light-headedness for the way Miles's face lights up, eyes brightening, a touch of a blush spreading across his cheeks.

The way his face lights up for *me*.

"Good morning," he says in this rough, sleepy voice that's warm enough to melt me back into bed.

In response, I fist a handful of his shirt and yank him inside, smacking my calf into Lucie's suitcase in my rush to get my mouth on his. I try to pour all my feelings about Long Beach into that kiss.

His hands are in my wild morning hair and mine are reaching under his shirt. And though his breath is minty fresh and mine is decidedly not, he clearly doesn't care, given the way he groans into my ear, snapping us around so he can bracket me against the door. This new confidence in him—I'm a little obsessed with it.

"As much as I'd love to keep doing this," he says, letting out a low hum against my neck, "we have a proposal to make happen."

"Right. We should get going."

Neither of us moves.

"Or," I continue, "hear me out."

"Hmm?"

"I just think," I say, running my fingers up and down his spine, making him shiver against me, "that if and when we get out of here, we'd be disappointed in ourselves if we didn't spend an entire imaginary day . . . doing this."

"You do raise some excellent points." A kiss to my collarbone. "Ironclad argument. No objections."

So that's exactly what we do.

DAY TWENTY-NINE

卌 卌 卌 卌 卌 IIII

Chapter 37

CONVINCING JOCELYN TO PROPOSE TODAY IS shockingly easy.

Less easy: assembling a map of three-dimensional landmarks out of greeting cards.

"This didn't look quite as complicated in my head," Jocelyn says as we kneel on the floor in my living room, glue and tape and scissors scattered around us. We assess the lopsided Eiffel Tower made of thank-you cards, the wobbly Golden Gate Bridge made of mazel-tovs.

"I think it's almost there." Miles squints, turning his head. If he turns too far to the left, he'll expose the heart-shaped mark I left on his throat yesterday. The one that was still there this morning. "If we add a few more cards on this side, we should be able to maintain the Eiffel Tower's structural integrity."

I swear to god, only Miles could make the words *structural integrity* sound hot.

When we showed up at Jocelyn's Bellevue law firm with a

fabricated story about the two of us meeting at freshman orientation and immediately clicking, there must have been something in
the urgency of my voice that made her agree to do this today.

"Being spontaneous is romantic," I said in her office, feeling a
little like I was pleading my own case, of sorts. "And there's just
something about today. September twenty-first."

Jocelyn sat back in her ergonomic chair, tapping her red nails
along her chin. "Like the Earth, Wind & Fire song! I do love that
song, and so does Mollie . . . and I could probably use some help
for what I have in mind."

And on the drive back to my house, when we passed Island
High School and I turned in the passenger seat to point it out to
Miles, he reached for my hand and held it tight.

Jocelyn has been secretive about her proposal, but she's been
collecting supplies for weeks. The plan is to re-create their favorite
trips in greeting-card form, including a small rendering of Ink &
Paper made out of—well, ink and paper.

"I wanted you to be part of this at first," Jocelyn says once we
fix the Eiffel Tower, moving on to what I think is supposed to be
Powell's Books in Portland. "But with school . . ."

"Light schedule on the first day," I say. "Mostly just listening to
professors read the syllabus. Being told not to plagiarize."

"And prove you did the assigned reading," Miles says, mouth
quirking to one side.

Miles and I keep trading these glances that bring heat to my
cheeks, and every other time, Jocelyn raises her eyebrows at me. I
pretend I can't see her, knowing my face is turning red but not caring.

It's nearing the end of the workday when we finally finish,

our hands sticky with glue and crisscrossed with paper cuts, Jocelyn having thanked us both about a hundred times. The living room has been transformed, a miniature museum of my mom and Jocelyn's relationship. She deserves this, after all her late nights and single-momming and trying her best to give us a life that for years she could only dream about.

At first Jocelyn wants to light candles around the living room, but we realize that might be a fire hazard, given all the paper. So we improvise, creating some mood lighting with scarves strategically draped over lamps.

"Thank you for letting me be part of this," Miles says as we position ourselves on the staircase, where my mom won't be able to see us.

"I'm glad you're here." I bat my lashes at him. "As a token of your gratitude, could you say *structural integrity* a few more times?"

"Where was this when I was talking about relativity?" he says, pretending to my bite my shoulder while I try not to laugh.

When my mom gets home, I'm ready with my phone camera for a video that will disappear by tomorrow but I know she'll want to replay at least twenty times tonight.

"Hello?" she calls, and my heart starts speeding up. "Joss?" Then her eyes land on the scene in the living room, and she freezes in place, her purse hitting the floor with a muted thump. "Oh—oh my god."

Jocelyn appears from the kitchen, looking radiant in a shimmery gold jumpsuit. "Mollie." Her voice shakes in this way I've never heard before, and it makes my own knees go weak.

Miles's arm fits around my waist, anchoring me to the earth like he's been doing it for much longer than a day. And maybe he has.

My mom's hand flies to her throat, as though she knows what's about to happen but doesn't quite believe what she's seeing. *"Oh,"* she says again, soft and full of awe.

"These past two years have been unreal," Jocelyn says. "As you can see, I tried to capture some of the highlights. Although I couldn't figure out a way to re-create that time you accidentally summoned a flock of New York City pigeons because you fed *one* of them a pizza crust."

"You have to admit, some of them were cute. The ones that didn't look demonic."

Jocelyn laughs. "But being with you isn't just about trips we've taken, or wild stories we tell our friends. Sometimes my favorite thing to do is just sit on the couch watching a movie, or cook breakfast together. Because when we're together, every day feels like we're on an adventure."

"I feel the same." My mom's voice a notch above a whisper.

Miles clutches me tighter, and I drop my cheek to his shoulder. *This is it.* The moment I thought the universe had stolen.

Jocelyn drops to a knee, removing a small velvet box from her jumpsuit pocket.

And my mom lets out an audible gasp before getting down on her knees too. "Yes," she says emphatically, which makes Jocelyn's eyes go wide.

"I haven't even asked yet!" she says. "You totally just stole my thunder."

My mom attempts to compose herself. "Sorry. Sorry. What was that? I'll make a big show of considering my answer."

"Mollie Rose Bloom. Will you marry me?"

I didn't know those words would make me feel like crying, but now that she's said them, of course my eyes are about to spill over. Miles's hand is warm on my shoulder, and everything about this is too good. I couldn't have missed it—I know that now.

Suddenly it feels like a great kindness from the universe, the fact that I'm able to experience this today. I can't picture it happening on September twenty-second. I can't picture anything but *this*, my mom and her fiancée embracing in our living room as a dozen greeting-card monuments collapse around them.

And then I can't stay hidden anymore.

"Barrett!" My mom gets to her feet, pulling me in for a hug. The ring glitters on her hand. "You were here this whole time?"

"I had some help," Jocelyn says. "They were amazing."

My mom nods toward Miles. "And we have a special guest, too?"

"Miles," he says, extending a hand in this formal, very Miles way. "I'm Barrett's . . ."

But when his voice trails off, it isn't awkward. *I'm Barrett's ellipsis*—somehow, it fits.

As they shake hands, my mom lifts her eyebrows at me. I just shrug, but I can't contain my smile. I have a feeling I won't be able to for the rest of the night.

Jocelyn suggests going out, but I don't want to share these people with anyone. Not today. Everyone I need is here in this room. So we order way too much takeout and argue over board games and then my mom and Miles bond over movies. There's something so domestically normal about it, the two of them discussing late-nineties cinema, of all things. Eventually we're full and happy and draped across the couches in the living room, and it all feels so *right* that I can't bear to leave it in the past.

When Jocelyn nods off around midnight, my mom taps my arm and beckons me into the kitchen.

"That was really something," she says, dropping a few plates into the sink. "I think I'm speechless."

I wrap my arms around her from behind, resting my chin on her shoulder and inhaling her comforting floral scent. "You're the best. I love this for you, and I love Jocelyn," I say. "But if you don't let me pick my own maid-of-honor dress, I'll make a slideshow of that summer you thought you could pull off pigtail buns and play it during my toast."

"Oh, you're that confident you'll be my maid of honor?" she quips before turning around, and I try not to think about when—or if—that wedding will happen. Slowly, she raises one eyebrow. "I didn't know what to think when Miles appeared. But the way you two keep looking at each other . . ."

"I thought we were being sneaky."

"Nope. Not even in the slightest."

I glance out toward the living room, where Miles is tidying discarded napkins and takeout containers, careful not to wake Jocelyn. "He's . . ." Now it's my turn to be speechless, because I'm not sure it's possible to sum up Miles in a single word. "Incredibly sweet. Unexpected. Fascinating."

"Good," she says. "Those are wonderful things to be." Then she pushes some of my hair away from my face. "Barrett. My darling of darlings. Treasure of treasures. You know I love you more than anything, right?"

"Yes. And it's embarrassing."

A hesitation before she speaks again, her brows creasing together. "I don't want to get too heavy on a night like this, but things are probably going to change. Not just because of Jocelyn, and not dramatically—but a little."

"I know," I say quietly.

"We'll still have weekends—any weekends you want. Holidays. And Judy Greer Is Doing the Most Night."

"Unless Hollywood sees the error of their ways and finally casts Judy Greer in a leading role," I say.

But there's something solemn in my mom's tone, and as perfect as this night is, I'm suddenly reminded of what I'm keeping from her. The things I haven't told her, the things I'm still finding the courage to admit to myself.

The things I cannot possibly tell her tonight.

There's a sound of shuffling from the living room, and then: "Let's order more cake!" Jocelyn calls. "I swear I'm still awake. I'm not old. I can still party."

My mom fails to hide a smile. "We're being summoned."

"Better not upset your fiancée."

And the way she glows at that is worth a thousand tomorrows.

ひ ひ ひ

The sky is liquid black when Miles and I get back to campus, drowsy and loopy and unable to stop smiling.

"Good night," he says in the elevator between slow, lazy kisses.

"Good morning," I say back, before he gets out on the seventh floor and I go up to the ninth. It didn't feel right to deprive my mom of this first night with her fiancée. Even if they won't remember it, something that's hitting me harder now that we're back in Olmsted.

When I unlock the door, I'm shocked to find Lucie in the room, taking off her makeup in front of the closet mirror. It's three a.m.—I guess I've never been here awake at this time. And that means I've never seen Lucie come home.

"Good party?" I ask as we do a complicated choreography for me to scoot by her. This morning with Lucie landed somewhere in the middle of the friend-enemy spectrum, so she shouldn't be overly hostile.

"It was okay. Some guy spilled a PBR on me. Just threw a few things in the laundry." She swipes a cotton ball over her eyes. "For some reason, I couldn't get any of the machines on the ninth floor to work. It was the strangest thing, though . . ." With a tilt of her chin, she gestures toward something on my bed. "I found that in the laundry room. On the eighth floor. I could have sworn you had a pair just like them, and for some reason, I thought . . ." She shakes her head, eyebrows pinching together. "It's probably silly, but I just had this memory of you and your mom in these matching socks at your house back at the beginning of high school. Although obviously more than one person can own this ridiculous pair of socks. And there's only one, so . . ."

Lucie might keep rambling—I'm not sure. All I'm focused on is the bright blue single sock on my bed.

RINGMASTER OF THE SHITSHOW.

Holy shit. Show.

With trembling hands, I pick it up and run my thumb along the familiar worn patch on the heel. The frayed stitching on the tiny circus tent beneath the lettering. I open the closet, where its mate is waiting in the drawer I placed it in after doing laundry all those yesterdays ago.

"Oh," Lucie says. "I guess it was yours after all. Weird."

All this time it's been missing, and it wound up in a dryer on a different floor.

Suddenly, everything starts to click, disparate puzzle pieces finally falling into place.

This missing sock. Ankit's missing laundry.

The changing sign on Miles's floor.

The lingering pain when we wake up.

"Oh my god," I say quietly, tightening a fist around the pair of socks.

Lucie pauses patting moisturizer onto her face. "Jesus, Barrett. They're just socks."

The reason we're trapped, the reason we always wake up back here. That place where, if Dr. Devereux is to be believed, parallel universes shouldn't meet but do. The connection point.

It's Olmsted.

DAY THIRTY

Chapter 38

"THIS HAS TO BE A MISTAKE," LUCIE SAYS IN ALL her September 21 indignation.

"No," I say calmly. "I don't think it is. Excuse me." I throw back the sheets and slip out of bed, grabbing a few things before shutting the door behind me, leaving Lucie and Paige staring.

In the eighth-floor laundry room, I open up every dryer until I find it: my missing sock, an innocent swatch of blue. As though it's been waiting for me.

I get dressed right there in the laundry room, pulling up the socks like they're battle armor, zipping up my favorite jeans, and smoothing a wrinkle in my Britney tee. I tie my hair back, preparing to wage war against the dorm that's been out to get me since the very beginning.

We're going home. We have to. Miles and I can't have a real relationship in this vacuum—we need to move forward. And I can't handle being the only one to remember the proposal, even if in some other dimension, some other Barrett is still celebrating with her mom and Jocelyn, throwing around ideas for their wedding. I want to give them a happily ever after in every timeline possible.

As always, my mom's text arrives at half past seven. Right on time today, despite Olmsted's terrible reception.

How do I love thee? Joss and I are wishing you SO MUCH LUCK today!

Thank you, I type. I'm going to need it.

ʊ ʊ ʊ

"This is extraordinary," Dr. Devereux says on the screen. Behind her, Ada Lovelace hops up onto an antique chest of drawers, her white tail flicking back and forth out of frame. "You visited me, and I gave you advice?"

We've just finished explaining our predicament to her—again. It's ten to eight, and we were the first people in the physics library. Miles hooks a casual hand on the back of my chair. Casual—that's what our touches have become. *I want to be closer to you,* this one says.

"Seventeen Grand Avenue," I say.

Dr. Devereux's eyes widen, and she leans in toward the screen, as though examining us more closely will jog her memory. "I haven't had visitors in years."

"You had this theory about connection points," Miles says. "Places where parallel universes could send information to each other, where they just barely touch, even though they're not supposed to."

She nods, mouth half-open, tucking a strand of gray hair into that haphazard bun. If she didn't believe us before, she definitely does now. "That's right."

"We thought," Miles continues, "even though it seemed like a long shot, that if we found one of those connection points, we might be able to get home."

"And we think we might know where it is." I can't believe we're having this conversation. That we might really be this close. "Or at least the general area. So I guess what we're wondering . . . is what we'd specifically have to do to get out of the loop."

Dr. Devereux blinks at us. "You found one? You realize the odds of that must be one in a trillion, right? Less, even." Ada Lovelace meows, clearly enjoying the sound of her voice, and Dr. Devereux beckons her to jump into her lap. "You have to understand, this is all theoretical. I could tell you something truly wild—you need to stand in a certain spot and speak a certain phrase directly into a northeastern-facing wind three times on the night of a full moon. But I wouldn't know what's going to happen if you do. It may very well be nothing."

"We've dealt with plenty of that over the past few months," Miles says. "You said something about getting to a place where the gravitational pull is strongest."

"That does sound like something I'd say." She tents her finger-tips, considering all of this. "If it were me, yes, I might try getting as close to the center of the earth as possible—at the time of the reset. If you really have found a connection point, the gravitational force might be substantial enough to knock you back into your proper orbit."

"Like . . . a basement?" I ask.

"Possibly," she says. "There's also the chance this is something else entirely, which I probably told you as well. You may have made a mistake, and the universe could be trying to set you two on the right path. In that case, it wouldn't matter if you said the phrase only two times into a southern-facing wind on a moonless night. If the universe thinks you're ready, then . . ."

"Then we'd go home." Miles's voice is strangely flat.

"Just to be clear," I say, "there is no magic phrase, right?"

She laughs. "I wish there were."

Her words race through my veins like hope, warm and electric. I can barely sit still, one of my legs bouncing up and down while my heart thrashes against my rib cage. Even if this is all theoretical, it's closer than we've ever gotten. It feels *right*, more than anything has so far.

Miles's hand drops from my chair, and he just nods, staring out into the library. Since earlier this morning, when I banged down his door with my Olmsted theory, he's seemed different. Off. Sure, he smiled and hugged me close, kissed the top of my head in this way I could easily become obsessed with, but I thought he'd be beside himself with joy, whatever that happens to look like for him. This feels more like the Miles from weeks ago, the one who lived life to the fullest at this exact table. The old Miles.

I nudge his shoulder. "You still with us?"

He blinks, seeming to come back to himself. "Yeah. Yeah, sorry. Just tired, I guess."

"I hear Thursdays are especially good nights for sleep," I say, and when he smiles, it doesn't touch his eyes.

Dr. Devereux's black cat leaps into the frame, batting Ada

Lovelace's tail and drawing her into a play fight.

"Schrödinger, how'd you get over here? I thought you were in the bedroom!" Dr. Devereux makes a clucking sound. "I have to go take care of them. Sometimes they don't know their limits. But if you make it—you'll let me know, all right? Even if you have to explain all of this again?"

"Of course," I assure her. "Thank you. For everything."

Her back turns, and we hear "Good luck—oh, Ada, not the curtains!" before the screen goes dark.

Miles and I are quiet for a few moments. I'm convinced I hear a clock ticking somewhere in the library, until it grows louder and louder and I realize it's my own heart.

"If she's right," I say slowly, "we should go through today one last time. Make sure we're setting ourselves up for tomorrow."

"You want to do this tonight?"

"No time like the present," I say, echoing what he said when we first started doing research right here at this table. If he remembers, with that giant brain of his, he doesn't give any indication. A ribbon of worry settles low in my stomach, but I push it away. He's tired, he said. That's all it is.

"We can still make it to physics," I say after checking the time on my laptop.

He gives me a lazy smirk. "Did you do the assigned reading?"

I groan, clapping a hand over my mouth. "You can fill me in on the way there. Or we could finally get those lottery tickets."

At that, he allows a soft *ha*. "We should try to do things as 'right' as possible. Be the best versions of ourselves, and all that."

And for the rest of the day, that's exactly what we do. We go to physics and English (me) and math and film (him), and I raise my hand once in each class. I play nice with Lucie and Miles picks up his brother from the hospital, sending me a photo of the two of them at the diner, milkshakes in hand. I even return my pasta bowls to the dining hall, giving the woman working the dishwasher my guiltiest look and about a dozen *sorrys* before handing them over. At four o'clock, I stare down the journalism building before making a split-second decision.

I've never nailed this interview, and I don't want to risk screwing anything up by floundering again. I'm not sure I know how to be the best version of myself in there. It wouldn't be the worst thing, I decide, if I don't get on the *Washingtonian* until sophomore year, and maybe I'll be so overcome with the joy of making it to Thursday that it won't feel like something is missing. So instead I camp out in the Dawg House with some mozzarella sticks and watch the clock, waiting waiting waiting.

"Ready?" I ask Miles at six thirty in the morning. We've been sitting on the couch in the ninth-floor common room, cozy underneath a fleece blanket from Miles's room. At first we tried to watch a movie, but we were a little too jittery to pay attention.

"Should be," he says around a yawn. "Sorry, I swear I'm awake."

"Hey. I get it." I bury my face in his shoulder, and his hand comes up to pull me close. Tightly. He presses a kiss to the top of my head, and I savor that moment of reassurance. Once we get home, everything will be back to normal. "I'm anxious too."

Except for the sound of Miles's steady breaths and the slight squeak when his shoes hit the floor, the walk downstairs is silent. Starting from the lobby, the first floor, felt more right. I link my fingers through his, squeezing his hand to remind him that he isn't alone.

The lobby isn't as empty as I expected it to be, students heading out to early classes. The first elevator comes and goes, with neither of us making a move to step inside.

"We'll get the next one," I say, the nerves climbing up my spine and turning my voice shaky.

But we don't take that one either.

We stand there for ten minutes before we finally inch forward, and the doors shut us in with a resounding clank.

We're really doing this.

Beneath the numbered buttons are three letters I've never paid much attention to. Come to think of it, I haven't spent much time in general assessing the inner workings of an elevator, but here we are. Metal sides and a wraparound railing and fifteen floors of dorm rooms. And then three letters denoting lobby, parking, basement.

With a dramatic lift of my eyebrows at Miles, I hit the last button.

I expect the ride down to be slow, rickety. Cinematic, maybe.

The reality is that it feels like just about every other elevator ride I've taken in this building.

Miles stands close to me, his hand on my back. Somehow, he still smells like the ocean. His mouth drops to the side of my neck for just a moment, the sensation a startling shot of warmth in this cold metal box. When he lifts his head, though, he doesn't meet my eyes.

This is big for him, I realize. A scientist testing a theory, one with cosmic repercussions. Maybe, finally, arriving at a conclusion. It makes sense he'd be more than a little on edge.

At least, I hope that's all it is.

Down, down, down. It feels like it takes an hour. In reality, it's probably less than ten seconds.

Deep breaths. Whatever's on the other side of these doors—red-hot lava, a swirling vortex of doom, absolutely nothing at all—I'm ready for it. We can handle it.

I've already done so much I never thought I'd be able to.

I squeeze my eyes shut. When I open them, my heart sinks.

It's . . . a basement.

No fiery pit, no time machine. Only storage and pipes and pieces of machinery I can't begin to guess the names of. It's gray and dark and deathly quiet, with an unmistakable chill in the air, though it should be warm with all that machinery. A sudden disappointment claws up my throat.

Until Miles lets out a half laugh. "There's a subbasement," he says, pointing a few yards away, because of course there is. "We have to take another elevator."

The door opens instantly, which somehow feels wrong. It feels like something we should have to wait for. This elevator is smaller. Older. Probably only used by maintenance workers and kids trying to get out of time loops.

Inside, there are only two buttons: B and SB.

"Part two," I say, leaning forward and pushing SB. No hesitation this time.

As soon as the elevator starts its descent, Miles lets out a sharp breath. His face has gone ghostly pale; when I graze his wrist with my fingertips, his skin is cold. "Miles? Are you okay?"

"I—I don't know."

"Talk to me," I say gently, not wanting him to feel this way.

Miles, the uncertain scientist. The one who pulled me out of my routines while I pulled him out of his. "We're in this together."

He nods, as though summoning the courage for what he says next. "Barrett . . . I don't want to leave." Another hard swallow, his Adam's apple leaping in his throat. "I think I want to stay."

And with that, he reaches out and yanks the emergency brake.

Chapter 39

THE ELEVATOR LURCHES WITH A GRATING metallic sound, the floor quivering beneath my feet before we come to a stop. I have no idea where we are, only that we're somewhere in the darkened depths of Olmsted Hall, the elevator's sole light flickering above us.

I watch that light cut across Miles's face, trying to process what just happened.

"I can't do it." He backs up against the wall, his shoulders drooping into the deepest slouch I've seen from him so far, as his breaths grow quicker. Then he runs a hand over his face, avoiding eye contact. "I'm sorry. I'm so sorry. I don't want to disappoint you, I just . . ."

The words ping off the metal walls, echoing in the tiny space between us. *I can't. I'm sorry . . . sorry . . . sorry.* I'm hearing them, but nothing makes sense.

"You can't be serious," I say, biting down hard on the inside of my cheek to keep my voice from turning harsh. I want to understand him, want to be gentle with him, but *fuck*—I might be *angry*. "All this time, and you don't want to get out? You don't want to go *home?*"

Because that's what it is. Even though we live here, even though we are Barrett Bloom and Miles Kasher-Okamoto, this isn't our home. Our shard of the universe has wobbled and warped, and we have to get back on the right path. We don't belong here anymore—maybe that's what Olmsted has been trying to tell us.

"I—I don't know what I want. But I sure as hell don't want you to get hurt again." He grazes the spot on my arm where I punched in the *Washingtonian*'s glass window. Where he bandaged me up and nearly made me cry. Miles sinks to the floor, but the elevator is so small that he can't fully spread his legs. "I do want to go home. I'm just not sure how to explain any of this."

"Can you try?" I get down on the floor with him, tugging up the socks that I somehow thought would make today easier. I drape a hand over his knee, waiting for his breathing to stabilize.

"Or maybe we don't have to do this right away," he says. "Maybe we could wait."

"We've done enough waiting." I tap on the wall with a few knuckles. "We don't even know what's going to happen when we hit the subbasement. Like Dr. Devereux said, it might—it might be nothing."

Only when the words leave my mouth do I realize how devastating *nothing* would be.

"It's not just that." He rakes a hand through his hair until it's properly mussed. The fiddling is out in full force now. "We don't know what happens tomorrow, *period*. It's one big question mark."

"We know some things. I'll go to my psych class, and you'll go to your freshman seminar and report back to me what, exactly, a freshman seminar is, and we'll see what Olmsted serves for lunch on a Thursday."

"Those can be easily predicted," he says. "But Max . . . it's still so early. "

His fear, even unspoken, hangs heavy in the space between us. He said it back when we picked up his brother: if he never leaves the loop, then there's no risk of Max relapsing.

"Miles," I say, my heart breaking, "I'm sorry. I didn't think about that."

He offers up a sad smile. "I know it's beyond my control, and it's possible there are a thousand Maxes out there doing a thousand different things. But—it's not just Max." A shaky breath. A pause. "I'm worried about *us*."

The sentence lands right in the middle of my heart.

Now that he's found the words, he barrels onward, a determined set to his jaw. "We're good in this loop, Barrett. You and me. I don't want that to change," he says. "Will everything we did together be erased from our memories? Will we have to start over?" He glances up at the elevator ceiling, at that flickering light bulb. "I'm not just worried. I'm fucking *terrified*."

In an instant, any of my residual anger fades. Miles is *scared*. And here he is sharing it with me, trusting me to be gentle with him. Barrett Bloom, the girl who has always had the sharpest thorns.

"We're not going to start over," I say, soft but firm, trying my best to reassure him. Because the thing is, I *do* believe it. I don't know if it's science or fate that I trust, but I'm so full of hope that

I might burst. I've never been more sure of anything, and I can't explain why. Whatever happens when we hit that button again, my feelings for Miles are as constant as a coastal tide. "We've been through too much."

"But there's no guarantee. Even with all my posturing, there's a hell of a lot I don't know." Miles from a couple of weeks ago would have paired this with a sly grin, a smirk, but there's none of that now. "What's so bizarre," he says, "is that as maddening as this has been, it's also been the best few months of my life."

His eyes meet mine, fearful and hopeful at the same time. *Mine too,* my eyes tell his.

"If none of this had ever happened, we wouldn't have become anything but two people who sat near each other in a lecture hall once," he says. "You'd switch out, and maybe we'd see each other in the dining hall or pass each other in the quad and have a brief moment of recognition, but that's it."

"But that's not what happened," I say. "We were stuck together. And maybe it was coincidence at first, but it turned into something else."

He shakes his head. "If we hadn't had that extra time . . ." This seems like something he's been holding on to for a while, maybe even longer than the past few days. "Once everything's back to normal, we won't be going on constant adventures. We won't be flying off to Disneyland or turning swimming pools into ball pits." He stretches a shy finger toward where my hand rests on my knee. "You're hilarious, and gorgeous, and sexy, and I'm still half convinced you're only humoring me here. If you want, you'll be able to have your pick of guys. I won't be your only option anymore."

If I thought *structural integrity* was hot, it's nothing compared to what the word *sexy* in Miles's voice does to me.

"We're not together because you were the only option." My heart hurts, hearing that he doesn't have the same confidence in himself that I do. I run my thumb over the hills and valleys of his knuckles. "I don't need to have my pick. I've already chosen."

He clamps his thumb over mine. "See," he says, gesturing to where I'm touching him, his shoulders relaxing the smallest smidge. "This between us. It's *good*. It wouldn't be the worst life, if we stayed here. We have no idea what's going to happen tomorrow, but we know what's going to happen today. And we have each other. If . . . if you still want me, after all of this."

Miles has always been so calm and collected, so logical. I never thought I'd be the one consoling him. Convincing him to be part of an experiment with me.

"Of course I want you," I say. "I've wanted you for weeks. But I don't just want you in September. It's not enough. I want you in winter, too. I want you in spring and in summer. I want you the whole fucking year, and then I want you in September all over again."

I try to imagine it, the two of us with long scarves and mugs of hot chocolate, in a field of sunflowers, or on a beach while the sun beams down on us.

His eyes flutter shut, and I can tell he's imagining it too. I hope it looks as lovely to him as it does to me.

"You thinking about me in a swimsuit?" I ask, nudging his shoulder.

One side of his mouth curves into a smile as he places a hand on my ankle, right where it says RINGMASTER. "Now I am."

The light bulb above us flashes off for a second longer than usual before falling back into its pattern.

"Even living life to the fullest gets old after a while," I continue. I'm getting through to him. I have to be. "Sometimes you don't want every opportunity at your fingertips. Sometimes you just want to be bored, and that's okay. Sometimes you just want dinner and a movie.

"We know what to expect when we're here, that's true. The unknown is scarier. I think—I think you've just gotten too comfortable. And I know you've changed, and I have too, but it's easy to fall back on what we know best."

His head snaps up at that, and I worry for a moment that I was too harsh. But then he recovers, his features softening. "You may have a point there."

"Neither of us has to be who we were in high school, though," I say. "Maybe that's it. Maybe that's the whole point. And sure, I'm personifying the fuck out of the universe, but you know what?" I turn my head to the ceiling, that ominously flashing light bulb. "Whatever's out there or not out there—I'm not afraid of it. I've been through worse. We both have."

Back before the loop, I was so focused on being someone new in college. Having the chance to reinvent myself. And then getting stuck convinced me that would never happen.

It's not that college was supposed to change me. I had to be the one to change, even if I literally haven't been able to move forward. I've let people in, allowed them to see the softness in me that I've spent years pretending didn't exist. I've realized that it's okay not just to need people, but to *want* people. I've allowed myself to want things unashamedly, to put that out in the world and let the world respond. A risk I'm learning is okay to take.

Miles told me I was different, and I'm starting to see he was right. College *has* changed me, in a way I never could have predicted. Maybe I'll never make it onto the *Washingtonian* or join Hillel or study abroad. Maybe I'll never say something worth immortalizing in Sharpie. But right now I have this person next to me, and the knowledge that I mean something to him, the way he means something to me.

And that's all the certainty I need.

"Miles." I bring my hand to his jaw, his cheek, skimming a thumb along his cheekbone. Another deep breath, and then I become brave. "I love you," I say, and it instantly feels right. "And I promise I'm going to love you tomorrow, too."

His face goes slack, eyes filling with a new kind of affection. "I—I love you too, Barrett." He clutches me to his chest, and I can feel his heart pounding against mine. The night we embraced on the beach feels so very long ago. I can't remember ever not hugging him like this. "*God*, I love you."

I kiss him, right there on the grimy elevator floor, that damn light bulb swaying above us and casting half the space in shadow. I kiss him like it's the first time, the last time, all the times in between. I kiss him to make up for all the days I didn't kiss him but wanted to, and the way he kisses back with a tender desperation, I wonder if he's doing the same thing.

His hands are in my hair, pulling my body to his, and a tiny groan slips past my lips—that single day we spent in bed wasn't enough.

When we draw back, I hold out my hand. "Do you trust me?"

He's taken so many chances with me. I just need him to take one more.

"Yes." He says it without hesitation, around a deep exhale that sounds like *relief*. His shoulders straighten, and there he is, the boy I love. We get to our feet, shaky but sure. "I trust you. Whatever happens . . . we'll figure it out."

"Together," I add.

"Together."

Miles threads his fingers with mine, and I bring our joined hands up to the elevator button. With our fingers tangled, I'm not sure who hits it first.

There's a split-second pause, as though the button needs a moment to process what we've asked of it.

And then the light above us blinks out as the elevator plunges into darkness.

Chapter 40

SOMEWHERE, AN ALARM CHIMES.

It's instantly familiar, though I haven't heard it since June. I shut it off all summer, until a few days before I moved in, then spent too long playing each alarm tone before settling on the one I've used the entire time I've had this phone. Insistent, but not too intrusive. Repetitive, but not annoying. The kind of alarm I'd find myself humming sometimes and convince myself it was a real song.

And . . . it's still chiming.

I roll over, fumbling around on the nightstand for my phone. Except—it's not my nightstand at home in Mercer Island, the wooden one my mom and I found in a resale shop and fell in love with, with its curved legs and scalloped edges. The surface is smoother. Colder.

Olmsted, I realize, and in a moment, it all comes rushing back. My sluggish fingers finally hit snooze. With my heart hammering in my chest, I crack one eye, blink a few times, and spy the date on my phone screen.

Thursday.

Thursday.

September 22, 7:15. 7:16 now, since it took me so long to find the snooze button.

I jolt awake, head swimming as I sit up too quickly, not ready to celebrate quite yet. My memory of yesterday is fuzzy. The light went out, and the elevator started dropping . . . and then nothing. A blank.

I need more proof. Because any good scientist needs to test their hypothesis, I swipe through my news apps, my social media, my calendars.

Thursday.

Thursday.

A brilliant, gorgeous, magical fucking *Thursday*.

My alarm chimes again, and god, that's a glorious sound. They should score movies with this sound. Write entire symphonies.

I turn it off for real this time, clutching it to my chest, unable to keep from grinning as the sweetest relief courses through my veins. For several long moments, I just *breathe*. Savoring. Luxuriating.

It *worked*.

This whole time we've been here, and the answer was quite literally underneath us.

After I grasp for my glasses on the desk, I can see that the other bed is occupied, Lucie's red hair spilling over her pillow. If she weren't here, I'd blast music, dance out of bed, throw the window open to take in the crisp Thursday air.

It's almost seven thirty now, and my Thursday class starts at—it's been so long that I have to check my schedule—ten o'clock, but I can't bear to stay in bed any longer. I hold in a laugh as I think about today finally being Miles's birthday and wonder if I have enough time to find some balloons for him before his first class. I throw off the sheets and head for the closet, reaching for my perfect-imperfect jeans on instinct.

And just as I'm tugging them up my legs and over my thighs, the top button pops off.

I can't help it—the laugh bursts out. After everything they've been through, they've clearly had enough.

So I reach for a vintage wrap dress instead, one I haven't worn yet because it exaggerates the roundness of my stomach. But today is a celebration, and when I put it on and take a look in the sliver of a mirror hanging from our closet, I love how it looks. I love how *I* look.

I let out a breath of either satisfaction or relief or some mix of the two, and it must be too loud, because Lucie stirs.

"Sorry," I whisper, still smiling because holy shit do I love Thursdays. "Did I wake you?"

"No, no," she says, and I'm not sure yet who this version of Lucie is. "I was already half awake."

She props herself on one side, reaching for her phone, while I silently panic about whether I completely alienated her by my strangeness yesterday morning. I tried my best to make up for it the rest of the day, but at best, she's neutral toward me.

"Lucie," I start, but I'm unsure where to go from there. This version of Lucie hasn't helped me with Dr. Devereux or messed with Cole Walker. We haven't opened up to each other.

But we did it once before. I know we can do it again.

"I know rooming with me probably wasn't what you were expecting," I say. "And I know you're going to rush, but . . ."

She puts down her phone. Yawns into her elbow. "Oh—I thought about it, but I'm not sure yet. I went to a frat party last night, and it wasn't really my scene. The Greek system might not be for me."

Carefully, I nod.

"I'm not sure why," she says, regarding me with a wrinkle of her nose, "but I have the worst case of déjà vu."

"Oh?" I try my best to sound only mildly interested. I don't understand the rules of the universe any more than I did a month ago, but I suppose it's possible all our interactions had some echo of an impact, even if she doesn't know it. "I have a little of that too."

Lucie gives me a weak smile. She's still not sold on this, me as her roommate. I can tell. Here I am again in Olmsted 908, trying to convince Lucie that I'm not her enemy.

Except this time, I know I can.

"So . . . do you think you might join any clubs?" I ask.

"Don't know yet." She's back to scrolling through her phone.

I try to sound casual. "I saw that there's a modern-dance troupe on campus. It made me think of you."

Her blue eyes flick up to mine, brow furrowed. "Really?"

"When you performed at that assembly sophomore year? I don't know if you still dance, but . . ."

"I do," she says, sitting up in bed now, sifting a hand through pin-straight hair. "My parents don't love it, but I do. I . . . can't believe you remember that."

With a shrug, I attempt to play this off. "You were good," I say simply, because it's the truth.

I wish I could give her more than that. And I will, because we have more time, not to rekindle the relationship we used to have, but to become something different. Even if it takes some time.

Because somehow, I feel like Lucie Lamont and I could be really good friends.

Before I head to the bathroom, I text Miles. Meet me at the library in twenty minutes? Then I relish the simple joy of saving his number in my phone.

I take a long, indulgent shower, reveling in the grout and grime and mysterious puddles. This is my home, for better or for worse. And I might be starting to love it.

Until I see Miles's response.

Who is this?

I stare down at my phone, unsure how to reply. Is he making some kind of joke? Because it's extremely not funny.

My steps back to the dorm are quicker, more anxious.

"Everything okay?" Lucie asks as she looks for a shirt on her side of the closet.

"Fine." I stuff my feet into sneakers and race for the seventh floor, the birthday balloons forgotten. "Hi, sorry," I say when Ankit opens the familiar Woody-and-Buzz door. "I'm looking for Miles?"

"You just missed him," he says, and I thank him and head for the quad.

Outside, the campus feels at once different and exactly the same. The temperature's dropped at least five degrees, so there are more sweatshirts and jackets and even scarves. Kendall is still out there, saving the gophers, and the screen they played *Groundhog Day* on last night hasn't been taken down yet. I might even spot Christina the hacker, striding confidently through the quad with her blue hair tucked into a beanie. I want to take my time to breathe in all these details, but everything is underscored with a layer of panic.

Then I spot him across the quad, a flash of red flannel I recognize from my first day.

"Miles!" I hurry after him, not caring who sees me sprinting across the quad in a dress that's working very hard to contain my breasts. It takes a few seconds for me to catch him, probably because the quad is packed and he doesn't hear me. That has to be the reason. "Happy birthday! I was going to get some balloons, but then I saw your text, and it kind of freaked me out, so . . ." I trail off with an awkward laugh.

Except that when he turns around—his hair still damp from a shower, that Irish Spring scent hitting me like a sensory scrapbook of all my favorite memories—his brows are furrowed in confusion. He's still attractive, because he always is, with his dark eyes and ears that stick out and the confident jut of his chin. He's just . . . different. Distant, somehow, even while he's standing right in front of me.

He takes me in while I wait for a glint of recognition to cross his face.

It never does.

"Do we know each other?" He hitches his backpack higher on his shoulders. "How do you know it's my birthday?"

"Miles." This has to be a joke, and once we're past it, I can forgive him for messing with me. For sending my heart into overdrive. "It's *me*. Barrett Bloom."

"I'm sorry," he says. "Is this some kind of freshman mentor program?"

I shake my head. *No. No no no no no.* This can't be happening. "Miles," I say again, like saying his name enough times will remind him of all the different ways I've said it over the past month: out of frustration, out of fear, out of love. "Miles Kasher-Okamoto. We've known each other for weeks—well, months for you, weeks for me. We—we're friends." The word isn't right, but then again, none of this is.

"Oh! Are you in the drama department?" His eyebrows draw together even more, as though he's giving it everything he has to try and place me.

"No," I say, my voice rough. "I'm not."

It was too cold to leave the dorm in just a dress, but I can't bring myself to care that I'm shivering. We're supposed to banter and laugh and make plans for dinner and a movie. We're supposed to argue about whether it was science or magic that brought us here, and he's supposed to tell me what he remembers from yesterday after we pushed the button.

He's supposed to remember the girl he's in love with.

"I should get to class," he says, and with an awkward half wave, he's gone.

ひ ひ ひ

I don't want it to seem like I went running home to my mom when Miles broke my heart.

But here I am. Standing in front of Ink & Paper. Because I really, really need to talk to someone.

I wish I'd had a chance to enjoy my psych class, but my mind was racing the whole time, trying to piece together what's going on with Miles. My most ridiculous theory, which maybe isn't more ridiculous than anything that's happened to us so far, was that skipping my *Washingtonian* interview made some kind of impact, but Miles doesn't have any connection to the paper. I could talk to Dr. Devereux, see if she has any theories. And yet everything we experienced together feels so personal that I can't imagine asking for more help right now.

I need to feel like I'm still in control.

"Barrett. My darling of darlings. Treasure of treasures," my mom says yet again. Only today she's on the opposite end of the shop, standing on a chair and messing with a light fixture. She's still in her unofficial work uniform, jeans and a graphic tee—this one featuring Luke's Diner's yellow coffee-cup logo—and something about that is deeply comforting. "You had a break from school?"

"The joy of only fifteen credits," I say, and then let out a steadying breath. "I . . . have to talk to you about something. Do you have a moment?"

She nudges the light back into place and steps down from the chair. "Of course. I can take a long lunch."

"Maybe we could walk?" I suggest, because I have a feeling I'll need more space for this than what's inside these four walls. My mom agrees without hesitation, flipping the shop sign from OPEN to BE BACK SOON.

Downtown Mercer Island is a mix of condos and chains and cute shops like my mom's, large enough to have everything you need and small enough to keep from feeling overwhelming. We find a bench in a parklet the city created over the summer, in between a bookstore and a yarn shop. With kids in school, Thursday morning here is quiet.

"Is everything okay with your classes?" my mom asks, worry creasing her brow, and I assure her that my classes are fine. Great, even.

"It's about high school, actually." I fidget with the hem of my dress, summon the bravery I now know I have. I've talked about this with Miles. With Lucie. I can tell my mother. "You remember that article I did—the one about the tennis team scandal? The way the school reacted to it . . . wasn't the best."

"People were upset with you," she says, which was the extent of what she knew about it. "Because the team was disqualified, right?"

"Yes. But it wasn't just that. And it wasn't just for a short period of time, either. It went on for a while. Other kids, teachers—they weren't always kind." I have to let go of my dress hem, because the fiddling reminds me of Miles, and I can only focus on one heartbreak at a time. So I tangle my hands in my lap instead. "High school was not good for me. And I'm still coming to terms with it."

My mom looks uncomfortable as she digests all of this, and I can't blame her. The daughter she sometimes treats more like a friend has been keeping a massive secret. "Barrett," she says softly, placing a hand on my knee. "I'm so, so sorry. I had no idea."

"Because I tried really hard to keep it that way," I say to my hands, my voice breaking. I was so convinced that telling her would change the balance of our relationship, but now I see that it might have done something else, too.

It might have helped me feel less alone.

"We could have talked to your teachers, or to the principal. . . ."

I know a lot of young ladies who'd love to be in your position.

"Maybe." I don't want to unwrap that particular package of awful. "But I didn't want to tell anyone. Because aside from you and Jocelyn . . . there hasn't been anyone to tell."

"Is this why Lucie stopped coming over?"

I nod. She and Jocelyn knew she was a dictator editor, but not the reason why. "But—and this is wild—Lucie is actually my roommate? And it might be a good thing?"

"That is certainly a plot twist," she says, allowing herself a small laugh, and for a moment, I join in.

Then a hard swallow as I prepare for the worst of it. "There's more," I say, and she stiffens. "I told you I slept with someone after prom." I have to force the words out, but it's not because I don't want to tell her. Maybe one day, they won't feel like sawdust in my throat. Maybe one day, I won't think about high school at all. "The guy I went with turned out to be the brother of someone on that tennis team. And he sort of turned it into a joke?" My voice goes up at the end, turns high-pitched. "I'm okay now, but the last few weeks of senior year were absolute hell. Or at least—I think I'm mostly okay. Maybe . . . maybe I'm not."

I don't go into all the details. Each sentence feels more impossible than the previous one, and I'm not sure I can give her much more than this. Not now. Not today.

"Jesus fucking Christ." Her fist tightens in her lap. "You kept this from me so I wouldn't go to jail for castrating a toxic little shit, right? Because if I ever see him, Barrett, I swear to god, I won't fucking hesitate."

"As much as I'd pay to witness that . . ."

"Sorry. I'm just . . . trying to process all of it. I don't want to make this about me, but I have to know. Was there anything I did that made you feel like you couldn't tell me? Because we've always—we've always talked about everything, haven't we?" Now her voice is cracking, her dark eyes watering.

"Mom, *no*," I say emphatically. "You didn't do anything wrong. I just needed you to know. Because it's been terrible, keeping this from you."

I examine her, my beautiful mother who has always seemed fearless. I know I didn't need to tell her any of this, that plenty of people hide things from their parents forever. But it hasn't felt right for her not to know this huge piece of my history.

"I'm sorry," she says again, pulling me close, gentle hands stroking my hair. "I'm so sorry."

It's strange—I thought telling the person I love most in the world would somehow free me of this burden, and yet that doesn't happen. I don't feel the magical weight of it being lifted. I'm *glad* I've told her, but I still hate that it happened. I still hate thinking of that night, and that Monday at school, and all the weeks that followed. I hate that UW is a campus of forty thousand people and he is one of them. Because eventually I'm going to run into him. If I accept that, maybe it'll make me less afraid. And maybe he'll pretend not to see me or maybe he'll give me an awkward wave, but I won't react. That pathetic asshole—because that is what he is—isn't worth the effort. Even when my timeline wasn't moving, he wasn't worth it.

The loop changed me—that's what I told Miles, and it's true. Maybe Dr. Devereux was right: the universe intervened to give me time to become who I needed to be. The kind of person with the courage to have this conversation.

"Are you okay?" My mom releases me from the hug, but she keeps a hand on my arm. "Do you want to talk to someone, or talk to me more, or . . . ?"

"I—I'm not okay." Once I finally say it out loud, it feels like I can breathe easier. This whole time, I haven't been okay, and what I'm learning is that it's okay not to be. "And I might want to do something like that."

My mom must be able to sense that I'm done with it for now, because she asks if I want to grab sandwiches before she goes back to the shop. We talk about my classes, about her work, about Jocelyn—who she says is coming over to the house this afternoon to cook something special, but wouldn't tell her what it is. I try my best to act nonchalant.

Sometime soon, I'll see her get married. Our tiny family expanding.

"Going back to campus soon?" my mom asks as we finish eating, switching her sign back to OPEN.

"I should, yeah. Can't let freshman year happen without me." Except that going back means contending with Miles.

Miles, who has no earthly idea who I am, even after I told him I loved him only hours ago.

"Before you go, then—I have something to show you. I was going to wait, but . . . this seems like the right time."

"I like presents," I say, hoping it's enough to distract from what's waiting for me on campus.

She disappears into the shop's storage room and returns with a single cream greeting card. "I've been working on it for a while with a designer," she says, suddenly sounding nervous.

How do I love thee? Let me count the ways . . . is written on the front in a swooping brush script. And right above it is a bouquet.

"It's for you," she says, pointing to the words and then to the flowers. "Barrett. Bloom."

My heart swells, and for a moment I'm speechless. Even though she couldn't have known, it feels like a subtle reclaiming of my name. A victory.

"I love it." I run my fingers over the bouquet, roses and lilies and dahlias. "Can I take one? For my dorm?" The place could use a little sprucing up.

"Please, take ten." She grabs a compostable paper bag and starts packing them up for me. "I know this makes me a sap," she says. "And you don't have to come back every week, or even every other week, but every once in a while, okay?"

"Of course." The words are scratchy, thick with emotion. "You know I won't be able to stay away."

During the bus ride back to Seattle, I consider how I've spent my whole life thinking it was my mom and me against the world. What I'm realizing is that she can't protect me from everything. As much as she's a part of me, she isn't all of me. It's possible I've relied too much on her at times, locking myself in our own world when there was so much *more* out there. I didn't think I needed other people, and I was so, so wrong.

Maybe the truth is that we're each fighting our own battles, and even if she's on my side, she can't always be with me on the front lines.

I have to learn to do battle on my own.

And right now, that battle starts with me at my desk in Olmsted 908, opening up a blank Word document.

LOST IN TIME:
THE FORGOTTEN PROFESSOR

by Barrett Bloom

If you ask Dr. Eloise Devereux if time travel is possible, she'll fix you with a lingering stare, one eyebrow quirked.

"For years, I told hundreds of students that yes, theoretically, it is," she says from her home in Astoria, Oregon, a place bursting with memories and color and objects collected from numerous antique shows over the years. "And that was exactly what led me to retire early from teaching."

Dr. Devereux grew up just outside of Bristol, England, later graduating with her PhD in physics from Oxford. She taught at the University of Washington for nearly two decades, and her course, Time Travel for Beginners, boasted a wait list longer than any other class in UW's history. She was even granted one of Elsewhere's prestigious Luminary Awards, given to experts charting exciting new territory in their fields.

And then, eleven years ago, she just . . . vanished.

"She was one of a kind," says a colleague of hers, Dr. Armando Rivera. "An absolute dynamite instructor. We were all stunned when she left."

Dr. Devereux hired a data-cleaning company to scrub as many mentions of her online as they could. It was a tremendous undertaking, but she says the anonymity was worth it. At the time.

"Too many people called me a fraud and even petitioned for the university to fire me," she says. Her black cat, a troublemaker named Schrödinger, hops onto her lap. "Your heart can only take so much of that criticism before you start questioning it yourself."

The time and space away from UW have given her perspective, she says. Now she might be ready to return to the public eye, and maybe even to teaching.

"We'll see what the future holds," she says, "but for the first time in quite a while, I'm feeling optimistic."

Chapter 41

THURSDAY LASTS FOR ONLY TWENTY-FOUR hours, exactly as it's meant to, before giving way to Friday. No fanfare, no confetti cannons, no revelations about the ever-shifting nature of the universe.

I've spent so much time focused on Thursday that Friday seems like a foreign concept. I wake up to photos from yesterday's proposal, the greeting cards looking like a tornado rolled through our living room. Maybe the sculptures don't have the structural integrity of what Jocelyn, Miles, and I built together, but with my mom and her fiancée embracing in front of them, they look perfect.

And then I'm back in Physics 101, Monday-Wednesday-Friday, taking Miles's seat from my first first day.

I even bought the textbook and did the assigned reading.

Miles, creature of habit that he ~~was~~ is, heads up the stairs, a frown tugging his brows into a crease when he spies me in his seat. Still, he sits down next to me, each lovely detail of him setting off alarms in my brain. His hair, artfully mussed the way it always is in the mornings, especially if I've just run my hands through it. His shoulders, and how I fit against his chest when he wraps his arms around me. His throat, and the spot I kissed until I left a mark.

How can he remember none of that?

"Do you know the Wi-Fi password?" I ask, right as he's taking out his laptop.

The frown deepens. "You. You stopped me in the quad yesterday." He punches a few keys on his laptop. "It's on the board."

But, miraculously, he doesn't change seats.

He's wearing another button-up over a T-shirt, a blue one this time. I have to fight the urge to climb into his lap and nibble on one of his ears. It's cruel of the universe that he doesn't remember the day we spent entirely in our rooms, switching whenever we knew our roommates were on their way, learning what we liked and what we *really* liked, telling secrets and unraveling histories. Talking about our hopes for the future. A future we weren't sure we'd get to have and one I'm not sure I can bear alone.

He was the one worried we might not remember each other, and he's the one who's forgotten me. Those memories of the past month are precious, and even if something went wrong and this is an entirely different version of Miles, I can't accept that they're not in there somewhere. The flash I experienced when we almost kissed is proof of that.

I'll just have to jog his memory. I dig into my bag, piling a salted chocolate-chip cookie, a bagel from Mabel's, and a batch of freshly fried mozzarella sticks on the desk next to me. One could argue it's too early for mozzarella sticks, and to that I say, clearly you've never experienced the culinary delight that is deep-fried cheese from the Dawg House.

"Did you bring a whole refrigerator to class with you?" Miles says. Good. I've gotten his attention.

"You haven't tried these yet?" I open a compostable cup of marinara and swirl a mozzarella stick through it, trying to recall exactly what he said about them all those days ago. "They're perfectly crisp but not burnt, and the cheese melts in your mouth. I've had them every day since I moved in."

Miles's frown flattens for a moment.

"What is it?" I ask, taking another bite.

"I'm just . . . having some déjà vu." He drops his gaze back to his computer. "But enjoy your mozzarella sticks, I guess."

When class starts, I take the opportunity to raise my hand at the first question Dr. Okamoto asks.

"Physics is the study of matter and energy and how they relate to each other. We use it to understand how the universe acts and predict how it might behave in the future," I declare.

She gives me an odd look. "That's correct," she says, "but the question was about Newton's third law."

Someone in the second row raises their hand, and Dr. Okamoto calls on them.

"What are you doing?" Miles hisses, and I just smile sweetly and offer him a mozzarella stick. Sadly, he refuses.

Come on, I urge him. *You know me. Those memories have to be in there somewhere.*

The person I fell in love with can't just be gone—because what if he doesn't fall in love with me this time?

By the end of class, I'm shocked Miles hasn't made a mad dash to the other side of the auditorium. I've made a messy show of eating mozzarella sticks, which unfortunately lost their crispiness on the walk from the Dawg House to physics, answered as many of Dr. Okamoto's questions as possible, and even pulled up r/BreadStapledToTrees. Nothing.

As he's packing up, sliding his PHYSICS MATTERS laptop into his bag, I turn to him again.

"Hey. So you might have noticed I've been acting a little weird—"

Miles chokes out a laugh. "Oh *really*? Have you?"

I can't hold the annoyance in his tone against him. I'm sure I'd be doing the same thing—and out there in another universe, maybe I am.

"I promise, I'll explain everything. Can you meet me in the physics library later? Around one?"

"I'm free now."

"I have to do something first." I try to stay positive. He has every reason to be wary of me.

Unless—

Unless he never remembers.

And what if he was right, that we can't get back what we had in the loop?

I can't dwell on that.

"Okay," he says, but his gaze doesn't leave my face. Something flickers across his eyes, a spark of recognition or a flash of frustration—hard to say.

Whatever it is, it vanishes in an instant.

ᔕ ᔕ ᔕ

"You missed your interview on Wednesday," Annabel says when I get to the *Washingtonian* newsroom. The glass window, of course, bears no sign of my ill-advised but unexpectedly triumphant B&E.

"I know. I'm so sorry. I had something come up." I pass her my fresh-from-the-printer story. "I realize it's a little unusual to show up with an article already written, but I really thought this would make a good piece for the paper."

Annabel slides on her tortoiseshell glasses. "'The Forgotten Professor,'" she reads. "I'll get to this after . . ." But then her eyes keep flicking over the words, and she settles back in her chair. "Actually, I can read it now, if you don't mind."

"Please," I say, biting back a smile. "Go ahead."

I contacted Dr. Devereux yesterday afternoon and we talked for hours. She remembered the video call from the day before, and after I explained what had happened with Miles, I asked if she had any theories.

"Give him time," she said as her cats pounced on a treat in the background. "The brain is just as complicated as the universe. Perhaps even more so. Your systems have been through quite a lot."

And then when I asked if she might want to tell her story, she said yes.

I stayed up nearly the whole night writing, but today the fatigue is welcome. It feels *earned*. This will be my last attempt, I've decided. If it doesn't work, then I'll lick my emotional wounds and wait until next year.

"This is fascinating," Annabel says when she finishes, placing the sheets of paper on one edge of her desk. "I think my aunt took this class. Even though she graduated with a degree in something else, she said it was the best class she took at UW. And the way you leave the reader wondering whether time travel is really possible . . . I got chills. It's a lovely profile."

"Thank you. That's my favorite thing to write—profiles."

"Maybe you could even do a whole series." She leans back in her chair. "People on campus that we don't usually get to hear about."

"I'd love that," I say, hoping I don't sound overeager when this is exactly the kind of journalism I've been dying to do.

And the fact that I was able to write about Dr. Devereux made it all the more perfect—the person who wanted to be forgotten, giving me a chance to reintroduce her.

It's not unlike what I wanted college to be for myself, I realize. A chance to reset. Redo.

And I have four more years to keep doing it.

"I'm getting ahead of myself," Annabel says. "I'll have to see if we have the space first. But I admire this kind of grit. I want people on staff who want to be here. There are always a handful of freshmen who end up turning out to be complete flakes." She pauses for a moment, tenting her fingers together. "Tell you what. I still don't love that you ghosted your interview, but I have a story about the student-government budget that needs to be written. It was my old beat, so I might be a harsh judge. You nail it, and the job is yours."

"Thank you. I swear I'll do my best." For a moment, the excitement overpowers my fear about Miles. I make to take the article from her, but she hangs on to it with her thumb and forefinger.

"And—we might want to print this too. If that's all right with you."

I can't hide my grin. "Absolutely."

∪∪∪

"I haven't been in here yet." Miles gazes around the physics library in all its dusty-shelved, dimly lit glory. Maybe this is the strangest thing so far: how uncomfortable Miles looks in the library that's been a second home to him over his past few months.

"None of this is familiar?" I ask, weaving through the aisles and plucking out books I remember. When I toss *Black Holes and Baby Universes* to him, he just barely catches it.

I'm still riding the high of my *Washingtonian* meeting. Annabel asked for a few edits to my profile, and as long as I can get them to her by the end of the weekend, they can fit it into next Wednesday's issue.

Barrett Bloom, *Washingtonian* reporter. That might finally be real.

I had some extra time before meeting Miles here, so I stopped at the campus health center and made an appointment with a counselor for next week. I don't know what to expect, but that feels right, too.

All of it has given me the courage I need to see if the Miles I fell in love with is still in there somewhere.

"Are we working on a project?" Miles leans against our usual table, fiddling with his pen in that cute way he does. "I don't recall my m—Dr. Okamoto assigning one."

"Relax. I know she's your mom."

I finish stacking books on our table and go to the chalkboard, trying to summon his loops from memory. *Library. PHYS 101. LHC attempt.*

"Look, I don't know why you brought me here or what you're doing, but I'm starting to get a little anxious. First you approach me by wishing me happy birthday, and then you show up with mozzarella sticks in an eight thirty class, like—" His face goes slack.

"What?" I pause in the middle of scribbling *learned how to drive stick.* "Feeling a particular way about all that fried cheese?"

"Nothing," he says, scraping a frustrated hand through his hair.

I tap the chalk against the board. "What did you do on Wednesday?"

"What does that have to do with anything?"

"Just answer the question." I flutter my lashes at him, hoping he can remember he finds me irresistible. "Please."

He lets out a heavy sigh. If memory serves, that's his *your mere presence exhausts me* sigh. The way this is riling him reminds me of our first time in the library, and despite how contentious that meeting was, there's some nostalgia there, some affection for the Miles who was still wearing his own armor.

We can do this.

We've gotten through much worse.

"Wednesday. The day before yesterday. I—" And then he breaks off.

"What is it?"

"I—I can't remember." His shoulders hunch in a very un-Miles way, and he grips the edge of the chair, as though this whole situation is starting to freak him out.

"Would you believe me if I told you we've been trapped in a time loop for months?" I drop the chalk, inching closer to him. "And that you were alone at first, but then I got stuck too, and we didn't completely hate each other, but we definitely didn't get along, and then we gradually became . . . friends? And when we got back yesterday, you didn't remember any of it?"

He shrinks back against the table, jaw tightening. Four days ago, in the middle of our sweaty, indulgent afternoon, I told him I wanted to kiss away all the tension there. All the tension everywhere. And he laughed as I proceeded to do exactly that, dragging my lips along his cheeks and his neck and his shoulders and his chest, until I moved lower and lower and then he stopped laughing altogether.

"No, I wouldn't." Now his eyes are fixed on the dingy brown carpet. "Because that's impossible."

I fling an arm out, gesturing to the campus above us. "Then how would I know that your dad also teaches here, in the history department? Or that vanilla is your favorite ice cream flavor?"

"It's a very popular flavor," he insists. "And you could have easily looked up my dad."

"What about how you and your brother hit a tree while sledding, and that's how you got that scar." I touch that spot beneath my own eye.

"I don't—"

"Or that you love period pieces and want to double major in film," I continue, and when he looks back up at me, I keep my gaze locked to his. "Or that you get scared on airplanes, but holding my hand made you feel better. Or that—that before you kissed me for the first time, you asked me if I was going to cry?" My voice breaks.

I'm no longer moving closer, but Miles keeps backing up, seeming to forget the table behind him. He shoves against it too hard, and the ancient piece of furniture scoots backward, banging into a bookshelf.

It seems to happen in slow motion, my haphazard stack of books crashing to the table and then to the floor. Together we watch, Miles tripping over his feet in an attempt to catch the falling books, managing to save only one from landing in a mess of pages and well-worn spines. *A Short History of Nearly Everything.*

Miles places it gently on the table before turning to face me, stricken. Pale face, shaking hands. I don't dare say anything, waiting for him to speak.

"Barrett." There's none of that confusion in his tone anymore. Only a familiar warmth wrapped around my name. "Did it—did it work?"

I let out what feels like my first full breath since I saw him in the quad yesterday. "Yes," I say, and then he squeezes his eyes shut and collapses against the table.

Chapter 42

"I NEED TO SIT DOWN." A WOBBLY MILES ATTEMPTS to maneuver himself into a chair, and I rush forward and help pour him into one. "I'm . . . feeling a little light-headed."

"Hey. It's okay. I'm here," I say, my sudden rush of relief now threaded with panic. *He's back.* Kind of. "Whatever you need—I'm here."

He nods, folding his arms together and pressing his head against them, taking deep breaths while I contemplate how to best help him. I dig into my backpack for a water bottle, place it on the table between us, and then give him my hand, just so it's there in case he needs it.

My heart settles into a calm, constant rhythm as he weaves his fingers with mine and holds on tight.

"It's a good kind of light-headed," he assures me. "Almost like . . . like I'm experiencing all of it for the first time."

Oh. Holy shit. I'm shocked he's still conscious—it must be what I was experiencing after my flash multiplied by a thousand.

Of course, the two of us arguing was what snapped him back.

I slide into the chair next to him and inch it closer, as though I can relive everything playing behind his eyelids.

"I'm right here," I tell him again.

He lifts his head, dark eyes shimmering. "Is it happening to you, too?" he whispers.

"It already did."

And I just sit with him while the memories flood back, listening to his even breaths, the way he cringes or smiles or brings another hand to the table to steady himself. It must be emotional for him, getting all of this at once. I'm not sure how long it takes—ten minutes, two hours. I can't see what's rushing through his head and lighting up his memories, but just being here, somehow I can feel it. The way our ball pit opened up for us. The overly sweet scent of the ice-cream truck, and the makeshift Shabbat that made me scared of how much I was starting to care for him. Our trips to Canada and Oregon and everything in between, the trips that required only two flights of stairs between his floor and mine yet felt sometimes like two entire galaxies.

Now his face is flushed.

"Long Beach?" I ask, and he nods, bending to touch his forehead to mine.

"And—and the day after." A sly smile. A squeeze of my hand.

Finally, it all seems to stop. His eyes flutter open, and he spies my water bottle and takes a long sip.

"Oh my god," he says with a horrified-sounding groan, and there's something about it that makes me certain *this* is the Miles I know and love. "This morning, and yesterday—I'm sorry I was such an asshole to you."

"Fortunately, I was used to it."

A slight smirk as he nudges me. "Still. I'm sorry."

"You're forgiven," I say. "But only because you're so cute."

We're still holding hands. He makes a move to bring mine closer toward him, as though asking if it's okay to hug me. "Can I . . . ?" he says quietly, and because I can't shout *I might die if you don't* inside a library, I simply nod.

He pulls me to his chest, my cheek against his heartbeat, and I inhale the scent that's uniquely him. Over and over, I breathe him in. He's never felt more fantastic than he does in this moment, and I feel my entire body relax against his as he slides a hand into my hair. His fingertips are gentle, working their way through my tangles, his chin resting on top of my head. Jesus Christ, this boy. How a hug from him can turn me to putty every time, I'll never know.

"This is ridiculous," he says, shaking his head.

"In a good way?"

"The best," he says, and then I tilt my head up to kiss him.

I intend for it to be a chaste little library peck, but Miles's mouth opens against mine, eager and wanting—and fuck it, I'm powerless. I wouldn't want to be anything else. I fist my hands in his hair while he gets to his feet, pushing me against the table, his hands on either side of my hips. I kiss him harder, tug him closer, until he's laughing because "I never thought I could be this turned on in a library," he says.

"Clearly, you're not reading the right books."

He slides hair away from my ear, mouth against my skin. "Thank you. For all of this, and—for not giving up on me."

"I missed you too much," I say, shivering as he lingers in the spot beneath my ear, because at some point on day 27 or 28, Miles developed *moves*. "Oh—and I really missed *that*."

But of course he's still Miles, still sweet and a little bit awkward. And I love it all. "I don't know what just happened or why it did, but I'm very, very happy to be back."

I'm about to yank him closer when a voice freezes us both.

"Ahem."

Gladys the librarian is standing on the opposite side of our table.

I'm nearly on top of the table at this point, Miles half bent over me.

"Sorry, Gladys," I whisper sheepishly, smoothing my shirt as Miles backs away.

"Just nice to see you two doing something other than argue, for a change." And with that she turns on her heel and walks away.

Oh my god.

"Did she just—" I say, staring unblinkingly at Miles.

Miles laughs. "I think she did."

"You think—the whole time?"

"It's very possible," he says, leaning forward once more to muffle his laughter against my shoulder.

Once we've regained control over our amusement and our libidos, we try our best to puzzle out why the hell this happened.

"I was uncertain about leaving," he says when we sit back down, his hand linked with mine again. As though now that he remembers me, he can't bear to stop touching me. Every so often, he grazes his forehead with his other hand, the pain of remembering so many months all at once gradually fading. "That could have been why it took me longer to remember?"

"Are you admitting it may not have been wholly scientific?"

"Maybe science is a little magical. Everything that's now been proven scientifically—thousands of years before, it was considered magic." There's not resignation in the soft curve of his mouth, but a compromise. "Do you remember what happened when the elevator opened?"

"I don't know," I say, tightening my grip on his fingers. "We could go back and check?"

But neither of us makes a move to get up.

"I'm not sure if I want to risk it," he says. "I think I'm okay with it—with not knowing."

We spend some time catching each other up on the past day and a half. I tell him about my mom and the counseling appointment I made, and he tells me that in his freshman seminar, he learned how to maximize the use of UW's libraries, which makes us start laughing again.

"And you're coming to the birthday dinner with Max and my parents this weekend," he says, the statement imbued with a kind of confidence I'm not sure I've heard from him before.

"I am?"

At my question, that confidence falters for a moment. "I think they'd want to meet my girlfriend?"

I can't stop grinning. God, I love the way that sounds. "Your girlfriend can't wait."

Then we're quiet for a long, long time. A good kind of quiet. The world is so loud sometimes, and I've missed slowing down, listening to breaths and heartbeats.

It's just before sundown when we finally leave the library, our grumbling stomachs steering us toward dinner. As we step outside, it strikes me that neither of us is the person we were the first time we met here. Somehow, we were able to move forward when we were standing still.

Summer seems to have turned to autumn overnight, leaves glowing orange in the last rays of sunlight. Incredible what a difference ~~thirty~~ two days can make. There aren't as many students tabling, but the swing dancers are out again. There's a sign for a student art exhibit I haven't seen before, and someone dressed as a husky handing out free doughnuts. And I realize I don't actually know the names of every building in the quad.

There is a whole world here, and we've barely scratched the surface.

"Do you think you'll stay in physics?" Miles asks as we walk through Red Square. "I know it was never your first choice. . . ."

"You know, I think there are probably a few things I haven't learned yet. So I might," I say. "And I kind of have a crush on this guy in my class."

Suddenly, Miles stops. "What you said in the elevator. After I pulled the brake." Now he looks nervous again, an expression I recognize all too well. "I have to know. You meant all of that?"

It comes back with the brightest clarity. *I love you. And I promise I'm going to love you tomorrow, too.*

I wrap my arms around him, tugging lightly on the collar of his shirt. "I love you, Miles," I say. "But I thought it might be too much if I told you that right away."

"I don't know," he says. "If I wasn't too busy freaking out, I'd have been wondering what I did to get this strange, gorgeous girl to like me so much."

"Forced me to read books about physics. Introduced me to Dawg House mozzarella sticks. Made me get a tattoo that looked like a penis wearing a cape."

His hands settle around my lower back, a thumb brushing along my spine. "I really, really love you. Please never stop being weird."

For a moment, I think that if I could stop time right here, I would.

But it keeps moving. And maybe that's even better.

The sun sets, washing the sky in citrus hues while the next four years stretch out in front of us.

"I just have something to ask you," I say as we start walking again. "Will you go out with me? On a date?"

"What did you have in mind?"

I tap my phone, bringing up the event page I found earlier today. "There's a showing of *Pride & Prejudice* tonight at an art house theater downtown. I know we saw it only a few days ago, but if I'm being honest, I was too focused on your leg next to mine to pay much attention."

"I might have felt some of that too," he says.

"Unless that's too normal. We could see if there's an abandoned building on campus to break into? A litter of puppies to adopt?"

"A movie sounds perfect."

And it does. After all this time, I crave the normal of sliding my hand into his in a darkened theater. Arguing over adaptations. Telling him I'll see him tomorrow—and being right.

"It starts in forty-five minutes," I say. "If we want to grab dinner first, we might not make it."

He gives me this look that's become my very favorite thing,

jaw twitching, one side of his mouth upturned as he tries to hold back how he feels. I know he's going to give in at any moment, and because he's a scientist, he'll need to repeat the experiment again and again and again.

"Barrett," he says, just as he surrenders to a brilliant smile, "we have all the time in the world."

Acknowledgments

THIS BOOK WOULD BE A PILE OF NONSENSE IF not for my earliest readers and friends: Carlyn Greenwald, Kelsey Rodkey, Maya Prasad, Sonia Hartl, and Marisa Kanter. I couldn't have finished it without you.

Thank you to Jennifer Ung for the early enthusiasm and to Nicole Ellul for guiding this book the rest of the way to publication. At Simon & Schuster Books for Young Readers, I'm so grateful to Cassie Malmo, Morgan York, Sara Berko, and Chava Wolin. Laura Eckes, thank you for another adorable cover! Copyeditors Karen Sherman and Marinda Valenti helped untangle my timelines in a massive, massive way. (I'm sorry for all the chaotic strikeouts!) And my agent, Laura Bradford, is always working magic behind the scenes.

To anyone who's picked up my books, shared them with a friend, posted about them on social media . . . there aren't enough words for my gratitude. You've given me the best job in the entire world, and I don't take any of it for granted. Thank you, thank you, thank you.

And to Ivan, for keeping me fed and loving both time travel and literal travel—I'm so unbelievably happy to be on this adventure with you. Where to next?